The

Chri… Kisses

Three exciting, heart-warming romances from three favourite Mills & Boon authors!

Christmas Kisses

MAGGIE COX

ALISON ROBERTS

FIONA HARPER

First published in Great Britain 2011
by Mills & Boon, an imprint of Harlequin (UK) Limited,
Eton House, 18-24 Paradise Road, Richmond, Surrey TW9 1SR

The Spanish Billionaire's Christmas Bride, Christmas Bride-To-Be and *Christmas Wishes, Mistletoe Kisses* were first published in Great Britain by Harlequin (UK) Limited in separate, single volumes.

ISBN: 978 0 263 88450 0

05-1211

Printed and bound in Spain
by Blackprint CPI, Barcelona

THE SPANISH BILLIONAIRE'S CHRISTMAS BRIDE

BY

MAGGIE COX

The day **Maggie Cox** saw the film version of *Wuthering Heights*, with a beautiful Merle Oberon and a very handsome Laurence Olivier, was the day she became hooked on romance. From that day onwards she spent a lot of time dreaming up her own romances, secretly hoping that one day she might become published and get paid for doing what she loved most! Now that her dream is being realised, she wakes up every morning and counts her blessings. She is married to a gorgeous man and is the mother of two wonderful sons. Her two other great passions in life—besides her family and reading/writing—are music and films.

To Suzy, for your boundless enthusiasm
and encouragement.

CHAPTER ONE

DOMINIQUE couldn't believe what she was hearing. It was as if her worst nightmare had come to life. Still in shock from the news her mother had called to deliver, she was having trouble taking in the rest of the tirade.

'Let me get this straight,' she said to her mother. 'You told Cristiano Cordova where I lived so that he could come and see the baby and… What was it you said? See for himself the dreadful conditions in which I'm living?'

She stared at the telephone receiver in her hand as though it were an unexploded bomb, mute outrage gripping her throat while fear and dread cascaded through her bloodstream like a swollen river bursting its banks.

'Why? Why would you do such a thing?'

'Why do you think? I told him because the Cordovas obviously aren't short of a penny or two, and they *owe* you! Since that good-for-nothing Ramón is dead, and you've been saddled with his child to try and raise on your own instead of finishing your degree, they ought to take some sort of responsibility for what's happened, wouldn't you say?'

'Is that what you told him? That he was responsible for Matilde?'

'Yes!' There was stubborn defiance in the other woman's voice. 'And he agreed!'

'Listen…they owe me nothing! It was my own decision to go ahead with the pregnancy and have the baby, and it's nothing to do with anyone else! If Ramón himself wasn't interested in his daughter why do you think for one moment that I would be remotely interested in making contact with the rest of his family? Much less have one of them come visit me!'

'Well, someone should pay for the mess that man got you into—and why shouldn't his family cough up? He ruined your life, Dominique! You were on course for a wonderful career and now look at you!'

For a moment Dominique couldn't speak over the raw pain inside her throat. Her mother made it sound as if she was the biggest failure that ever lived! Was there nothing she could ever do to please her? Already knowing the answer, she fought off the wave of shame and despondency that washed over her and dispiritedly murmured a strained goodbye.

* * *

A week on and still she greeted each minute in dread of Cristiano Cordova showing up at her door, possibly wanting to assume some sort of control over her baby's future. The already broken nights she endured, waking to feed Matilde, had been disrupted further by anxiety and fear. The freedom to lead her own life that she'd so desperately sought when she'd finally left her mother's house to care for her baby on her own had been horribly threatened and spoiled.

She had already been feeling strangely disconnected from the rest of the world—the only light in her life being derived from her beautiful baby girl—while other people were looking forward to the holiday season, busy flitting in and out of the shops that were bursting with glittering arrays of Christmas paraphernalia, and counting down the days for the big event itself. The restaurant where Dominique worked as a waitress was already inundated with orders for lunch on Christmas Day, and she could have increased her hours in a heartbeat if she didn't fiercely guard the maximum time she could afford to spend with her baby. But other people's anticipation of Christmas only served to heighten her sense of isolation.

And now her mother had betrayed her. She had colluded with Cristiano Cordova—Ramón's rich and influential cousin—behind her back, and encouraged the idea that Dominique's baby was now *his* responsibility, since there was now no hope of Ramón himself ever fulfilling that role. The revelation still had the power to stun her senseless. She was still reeling from the news that Ramón was dead...killed in a car accident on some remote mountain pass in Spain. The catalogue of heartbreak since Dominique had met him was surely now complete?

Cristiano declined the offer of more coffee from the smiling air stewardess and, making a steeple of his fingers, stared out at the dazzling vista of pale clouds that resembled sun-struck snow-covered mountain peaks in the sky. For a poignant moment he imagined his young cousin's restless and unhappy spirit, roaming free amongst those selfsame clouds—no longer bound by the constraints of the physical existence that had seemed to cause him so much turmoil and difficulty while he lived... Emotion welled up inside him and painfully cramped his throat. *If only he had been able to get through to Ramón as he'd longed to...get him to see that the family would have forgiven him every transgression if he had only met them halfway...*

But it was too late for recriminations. The situation was *beyond* rescue now. Cristiano had never voiced out loud his terrible fear that perhaps Ramón had *deliberately* sought to end his own life by driving his car over a clifftop that dreadful night—but he could not help thinking it just the same, and the thought gave him nightmares.

When a letter had been discovered amongst Ramón's things after the funeral—from a girl none of the family had ever even *heard* of before—Cristiano and the family had honestly been stunned by its contents. The girl…*Dominique*…wrote to tell him news of the birth of her baby—*Ramón's* baby—and had even included a photograph of the infant. Although things were well and truly over between them, she wrote, she thought he should at least know that he was the father of a healthy and beautiful little girl.

The letter had been dated six months earlier, and though he knew he would have to go to the UK and investigate for himself the legitimacy of the girl's claims, Cristiano had also realised it must fall to him to convey the news that Ramón was dead—and that could not wait. But he had not had the opportunity to speak to Dominique herself. Instead, when he had called the telephone number she'd included in her letter, the girl's mother had answered. Upon his revealing to her who he was and why he was calling the woman had not held back.

His 'heartless, good-for-nothing cousin' had wrecked her daughter's life, Cristiano had been told in no uncertain terms, and his family had better do something about it. Dominique had only had a year to go before she finished her degree, and had had a bright future to look forward to. Now, instead, she was weighed down with the responsibilities of a baby!

When Jean Sanderson had calmed down sufficiently for him to get a word in edgeways Cristiano had soothingly but authoritatively told her that if it were true that her daughter's baby was Ramón's then he would of course take steps to ensure their future prospects were comfortable and to her liking. Certainly Dominique would not be denied the opportunity to finish her education. The Cordova family took their responsibilities seriously and would not turn their backs on one of their own. Slightly placated, Mrs Sanderson had then volunteered Dominique's new address—she had apparently moved out since her letter to Ramón—and was living in a 'grubby little bedsit' in one of London's least attractive boroughs.

The accusations had come hard and fast. Dominique's mother's anger and resentment were glaringly evident. *Even in death it seemed that Ramón's reckless and thoughtless behaviour was still having massive repercussions on people's lives...*

Yet again it had been left to Cristiano to smooth the troubled waters his cousin had left in his wake.

Releasing a troubled sigh, he pulled his gaze

away from the spectacular view offered by the small window beside him and concerned himself instead with thoughts of his family. A family whose sorrow at losing a beloved son had been unexpectedly eased by the revelation that he'd fathered a child…a child they hoped and prayed Cristiano would be bringing back with him on his return—*back where they were convinced she belonged…*

There was a knock at the door, and in the same instant the milk she'd been heating on the stove for hot chocolate boiled over. Cursing softly, Dominique turned off the gas, surveyed the burnt sticky mess clinging to the side of the saucepan, and unhappily mourned the diminishing ability of her once sharp brain to concentrate for even two seconds flat. The trouble was Matilde was teething, and they had both had a horrendously sleepless night. Now fed, and finally asleep, the baby lay cosily wrapped up against the cold in her cot, and Dominique had been looking forward to the comfort of a hot drink for herself.

No doubt the person knocking on the door at that inopportune moment was Katie—the ballet student who lived in the bedsit opposite. Frequently out of milk, sugar, tea, coffee…*food*—anything you cared to name—she often walked across the landing to see if Dominique could help out. Leaving the cramped space that laughingly masqueraded as a kitchen and padding across the thin, worn carpet in her stockinged feet, Dominique opened the door with a resigned smile already in place—and a swift, silent prayer of thanks that she had done her shopping yesterday, before Matilde's teething problem had kept them both awake for half the night…

'Dominique Sanderson?'

She stared up at the imposing male on the other side of the door with her heart racing a mile a minute. He was obviously foreign—even if his accent hadn't alerted her to the fact, his dark and striking looks strongly confirmed it—and Dominique half closed the door again, feeling sick with dread. 'Who wants to know?' she answered, the smile she had automatically summoned for Katie firmly banished.

'I am Cristiano Cordova…Ramón Cordova's cousin. May I come in and speak with you?' he enquired formally.

'No, you can't!' In a panic, Dominique glanced over at the tattered Chinese screen behind which her infant daughter's cot was positioned—grateful that at this angle it was completely hidden from view. 'It was very wrong of my mother to give you my address, and I told her so! I'm sorry, but you're just going to have to turn around and go back to wherever you came from. Because although you want to speak to me, I do *not* want to speak to you!'

She went to shut the door, but he was too quick for her and grabbed the edge with a grip like steel. Dominique gasped.

'If you shut the door in my face I promise you I will wait outside all night if I have to!' the man warned. 'And I do not make idle promises. So, if you want to avoid the embarrassment of explaining the reason for my presence to your neighbours, I suggest you simply let me come in and talk quietly to you in private.'

Seeing by his steely-eyed, hard-jawed expression that he was more than capable of carrying out an all-night vigil if she went back inside and closed the door, Dominique reluctantly moved away to allow him entrance. Her legs had gone to jelly, and she wondered how she even managed that small feat.

As the tall Spaniard came in through the door she couldn't help glaring at him. From the moment her mother had announced she'd given him her address—and implied that he and his family were now responsible for her predicament—Dominique had been quite prepared to dislike him and all he stood for intensely. After all, hadn't she already had a bitter example of how his family could behave in Ramón? Why should this man be any less heartless?

Even though her first view of him was through a red mist of anger, she saw nothing in the striking bronzed face with its sleek, taut lines to change her mind in any way. All she saw was another unwanted authority figure who believed it was his God-given right to try and take control of her and her baby's life, and she wanted to physically push him out the door and yell at him never to come back.

'What do you want to talk to me about?' she demanded, folding her arms to try and still the tremors that had seized her.

'The baby, of course…and the fact that her father was my cousin, who is now dead. There are things to discuss relating to both these matters.'

'Well, I don't want you here. Can't you see that? Ramón and I broke up several months ago, and he couldn't have cared less when I told him I was pregnant! I'm really sorry if you've had a wasted journey, but I didn't ask you to come in the first place!'

'No…you did not ask me to come,' Cristiano Cordova replied, his voice smooth but with a rich undertone that made Dominique's senses snap to attention. 'But I would very much be failing in my duty to Ramón if I had elected to stay in Spain and ignore his baby's existence. I found your letter, and I am aware of all that has happened. Now I am here to help alleviate some of the considerable stress and worry you must undoubtedly be under in such a difficult situation.'

'You're not going to take Matilde away from me, so don't even *think* it!'

Stepping boldly in front of the six feet plus frame that exuded a bearing nothing less than regal—even here, in her deplorably shabby little bedsit with its threadbare floor covering and faded ancient wallpaper—Dominique was enraged at even the mere thought of such a possibility. She might only be twenty-one, but she still had rights—even if nobody else seemed to think so!

'I think you need to calm yourself, Dominique. How can we discuss anything if you are in such a state of agitation? Perhaps we should start over again?' The Spaniard considered her gravely for a moment, before extending his hand and letting his previously solemn mouth curve briefly into a smile. 'It is unfortunate that our paths should only cross after such a tragic turn of events, but even so…I am very pleased to meet you, Dominique.'

Dominique warned herself not to be won over by the appearance of warmth and charm. Ramón had once told her that his rich and powerful cousin could be described as 'dynamite in a silk glove', and that people would do well not to be deceived by his amenable exterior and underestimate him. She remembered Ramón had sounded impressed when he'd revealed this—as though he *envied* his cousin's gravitas and power. Apparently he was a man with a formidable reputation—and not just professionally. Cristiano commanded great respect and admiration from all those who knew him, and in the hallowed circle of the influential and respected his word and opinion was *law*.

A tiny shiver scudded down her spine as his large hand with its sprinkling of fine dark hair across the knuckles enfolded hers. His eyes were black as impenetrable caves, fringed with luxuriant sable lashes, and for a suspended moment Dominique was magnetised by them.

'Well…' She pulled her hand free as quickly as possible, to dispel the sense of deep disquiet that rippled through her, and took a step back. 'All I want is to be left alone to raise my child in peace. Ramón's family are under no obligation to help me in any way. It was my decision to have her, and I'm certainly not looking for hand-outs from his relatives!'

Her imposing visitor held up his hand as if to restore calm, the gesture conveying all the authority and command of Moses overseeing the parting of the Red Sea. His dark gaze was pensive as he focused it on Dominique. 'Your bid for independence is admirable… but I have to tell you that there are certain things about our family that you *must* understand, and one of them is that we have a code of honour that must be upheld in all circumstances. Part of that code is that we take care of our own.'

Clearly Ramón had missed that memo, Dominique thought wryly. As much as she had judged Ramón for his lack of responsibility, now she could not help resenting his cousin's presence with a vengeance. But the formidably broad shoulders encased by the superbly tailored jacket he wore over a black cashmere sweater seemed to signify an indomitable fortress that she had no hope of breaching, and she suddenly knew without a shadow of a doubt that this proud, handsome Spaniard had no intention of going quietly away and leaving her to manage Matilde on her own.

Her heart slammed up against her ribcage in alarm. 'I told you—I don't want anyone's help! Least of all help from the family of a man who proved anything *but* honourable!'

She had sandy brown hair fashioned into one long silky plait that fell over a slender shoulder, eyes the colour and appearance of a placid blue lake on a summer's day, and features that might easily have been the inspiration for any of the Grand Masters if she had but been born in another century.

The realisation of how *young* she was hit Cristiano like an iron fist. Ramón himself had only been twenty-five, but even so...Dominique Sanderson barely looked out of the schoolroom! What had his thoughtless irresponsible cousin been thinking of when he took up with such an innocent and why hadn't he protected her from possible consequences when he had decided to seduce her?

He fielded the strong sense of outrage that unexpectedly burned inside him and mentally stored it for contemplation at a more appropriate time. Despite that, a muscle at the side of his temple continued to throb with tension. The girl presented a challenge. He knew now she was not going to be easily won over and persuaded to accept the aid that was due to her and, confessing silent surprise at that, Cristiano sensed he had a battle on his hands.

There were two well-worn tapestry-covered armchairs, one either side of a fireplace that housed an inadequate electric bar heater rather than a comforting glowing fire, and he gestured towards them. 'Let us sit down, shall we? Now, tell me…where did you get the astonishing idea that I came to try and take the child away from you?'

'Didn't you?'

'Of course not! A child belongs with her mother—unless that mother is unfit, of course—and that is where she should stay.'

'I am a *good* mother!' She sat forward in her chair suddenly, and Cristiano could tell by the way the muscles in her face were working that she was having trouble keeping back her emotions. 'We may not live in the lap of luxury, but I work hard and do my best, and I would die rather than let my baby come to harm in any way!'

Cristiano frowned. 'Please…do not distress

yourself. Your ability as a mother is not in question. Regarding why I am here: I told your mother that as the head of the Cordova family I see it as my duty to oversee the care and protection of my cousin's child, since he has so sadly died, and I naturally extend that care and protection to include you too, Dominique.'

'I don't need anybody's care and protection! I can manage quite well on my own, thank you!'

Her huge blue eyes were suddenly bathed in tears, but Cristiano quickly realised that the reaction was born out of fury and frustration rather than self-pity.

'My mother only wants rid of the baby…can't you tell? She wants me to go back to university and complete my degree as if nothing has changed! She sees Matilde as an inconvenience that needs to be dealt with, and that's why she jumped at the chance to invite you over here! I think she was really hoping that you would take Matilde away!'

'I am very sorry to hear that. But if that is true, then it only confirms my opinion that you and your daughter would be better off returning with me to Spain than remaining here in England. If Ramón were still alive, I am certain he would come to that conclusion too, given time.' *He was not certain about that at all, but Cristiano would say anything he had to if it would help him achieve the outcome he desired.*

'I want you to know that I told him I would never make any claims on him regarding the baby. It was clear he didn't want her right from the start, so why would I humiliate myself by pursuing some sort of recompense? Besides...having Matilde was my decision and my decision alone. Becoming a father and being responsible for another human being—even his own child—held no appeal for Ramón whatsoever.'

'I do not doubt it!' Cristiano returned acidly. 'But it is a shame he did not think of that before he impregnated you!'

She blushed, and the sight of that subtle spread of pink fanning across her smooth pale cheeks, and the way her innocent unadorned mouth parted softly in surprise, caused an acute charge of electricity to explode in the pit of his stomach. It so disturbed him that for a moment Cristiano lost his train of thought.

'It wasn't all his fault. I was equally as foolish... as reckless—though I don't regret having my baby for a second!'

Frankly incredulous at her immediate defence of his wayward cousin—especially when he had to all intents and purposes abandoned her—Cristiano flattened his hands over his knees as he released an impatient irritated sigh. 'I am appalled that he did not make proper provision for you and his daughter whether he wanted to be in your lives or not! How did he expect you to support the baby when you were still a student and living at home with your mother?'

A tiny furrow appeared just above the bridge of her nose, and her slim hands moved restlessly in her lap. 'He probably didn't think about it much, if the truth were known. But I want you to know that I *am* supporting my baby quite adequately without him! Just before I left home I got myself a job. I waitress five nights a week at a local restaurant, and my friend Marie minds Matilde for me while I'm working.'

So that was how she earned her living and paid for this inhospitable room.

Instantly any fear Cristiano might have played in his mind that Dominique could turn out to be some opportunist gold-digger, seeking a chance to be financially supported for life once she knew Ramón's family was wealthy, was completely rendered null and void. She simply did not seem capable of such subterfuge. And someone looking to benefit from the Cordova estate would hardly try and slam the door in his face when he turned up on the doorstep, would they? She was *not* the kind of girl he'd been expecting to meet at all. She was the polar opposite of the other immature females Ramón had played fast and loose with in his short and disreputable life! Instead of sulky demands she radiated a quiet dignity and resolve that was impressive in one so young.

Cristiano felt the renewed throb of painful

tension pulsating in his temple like a relentless drumbeat as he glanced round once more at the poor state of the room he was in. It looked clean enough, but its aging furniture and fittings and inadequate heating made his stomach clench in dismay. Considering the child, he guessed she must be with this friend of Dominique's right now, because there was no sign of her. A shame. He had very much been looking forward to seeing her.

'Faced with the reality of how you live—' he frowned '—I would dispute your assertion that you are managing even adequately. These are clearly not the kind of circumstances conducive to raising a child and giving her the sense of security and comfort that she deserves! Especially when her father came from a privileged and wealthy background with a family who would have moved heaven and earth to help him if he had only come to us and revealed the truth of his impending fatherhood!'

'I got the feeling Ramón didn't like the idea of being under any sort of obligation to his family.'

'Under an obligation?' Cristiano hardly knew how he stayed sitting in his seat. His expression was formidably grim. *This* from a man whose proclivity for taking what he wanted—no matter who it hurt—had been second nature? A man who had been busy squandering his inheritance on fast living and reckless and sometimes dangerous pursuits without a care for anyone but himself right up until the day he died!

'Anyway...whatever people think of him...he's dead now, isn't he? He's not here to defend himself against what anybody says any more.' Her faultless blue eyes momentarily dazzled Cristiano with the flare of pain he saw reflected there.

'Yes, he is dead.' Feeling as though someone had taken a sledgehammer to his middle with this distressing reminder, he momentarily rubbed at the tension that had now extended to the front of his brow. 'Which is even more reason why this completely unacceptable situation cannot continue. Having met you, and acquainted myself with your situation, I have no doubt in my mind that you and the child must return with me to Spain,' he announced commandingly, rising to his feet.

CHAPTER TWO

'Now, wait a minute!' It was Dominique's turn to jump to her feet. 'Before you get too carried away, don't you think you ought to listen to what *I* want? This is my life we're talking about here…mine and my daughter's!'

'I am well aware of that, and I am only suggesting this solution because I have your best interests at heart! And because, as far as I am concerned, your child is a Cordova and should be where she belongs—enjoying the advantages of her birthright in Spain, with a family who will love and cherish her!'

'*I* love and cherish her!'

'And what about the rest of your family?'

'There's only my mother.'

'And clearly from what I have heard so far your mother does *not* love and cherish your daughter, and that is *not* an acceptable state of affairs!'

The beautiful face in front of Cristiano drained

of colour, but he felt no remorse for simply stating the truth. He saw his solution to this predicament as imperative, and had to admit that his family had been absolutely right when they had declared that Ramón's child belonged with them.

'But Spain…?'

'It is hardly a million miles away.' He allowed himself an ironic little smile. 'In these days when you can catch a plane to anywhere almost at the drop of a hat the world grows ever smaller, no?'

'It's just that—'

'You are concerned about not finishing your education, perhaps? Your mother indicated that was a big regret for you. Let me allay your worries on that score. I will be quite happy to pay for the rest of your education, Dominique, and there will be no shortage of offers to help take care of Matilde so that you can study, I assure you! We have some wonderful universities in Spain, and I see no reason why you cannot complete your degree there.'

'Well, my mother misled you, *Señor* Cordova. Not completing my degree was *her* big regret—not mine! I'm a mother now, and that's my first priority. And even if I did want to go back to university I certainly wouldn't be happy to have you foot the bill for it!'

Again Cristiano was struck by how fiercely independent and proud she was, and his unexpected feeling of admiration was genuinely disturbing. It was far from the way he had expected to be feeling at this meeting—in fact, he had prepared himself for the worst.

'In that case I cannot see that there are any obstacles whatsoever to prevent you from coming to reside in Spain.'

'Can't you? Well, you're not me, are you? And I have lots of doubts about the whole idea—despite what you say!'

'Listen to me!' Calmness suddenly gave way to the frustration and impatience Cristiano had hardly realised he was harbouring. 'You are not the only one to think about in this distressing situation! Ramón's mother is desperate to see the baby. She has lost her only son and is destroyed! Learning that he fathered a child has helped give her solace in the midst of her terrible grief. Would you deny her that solace, Dominique?'

She looked stricken. Then she made an agitated movement with her hand, before lifting it anxiously to her throat. 'I know so little about how he was killed…will you tell me more?'

Even though he'd known this was coming, Cristiano was still ill prepared to relive the disturbing events of that night, and his mouth flattened grimly. *He silently resolved to keep the explanation as brief as possible.*

'He was driving too fast on a hazardous

mountain road in the early hours of the morning,' he intoned, his tongue feeling thick in his mouth. 'The light was poor, and the investigation concluded that he probably lost control of the car on a sharp bend that no doubt took him by surprise. It would have happened very quickly and he was probably killed outright. His car was found at the bottom of a cliff the next morning by a couple walking on the beach. The coroner recorded a verdict of accidental death. I cannot tell you any more than that.'

Cannot or *will* not? Inside Dominique despair set in. Ramón might have died in considerable pain. She might have stopped loving him a long time ago, but he'd still been the father of her baby. She wrapped her arms around her chest to hold in her grief.

Needing to divert her unhappiness, she grasped at what Cristiano had said previously. 'I understand how much his mother must want to see Matilde, and I am truly sorry for her suffering…the poor woman must be demented at losing her only son! But Christmas is just a couple of weeks away, and it's the busiest time of year at the restaurant I work at. You must understand that I have responsibilities too, and if I were to go to Spain I couldn't possibly go until the New Year.'

His black eyes stared at her in disbelief. 'You would put this unimportant job you have in a restaurant before letting a grieving woman see her only grandchild?'

His lip curled contemptuously, and Dominique flinched at the scorn in his voice.

'Unimportant? It's the means of earning my living so that I can provide for Matilde and me! You might not be aware, but job opportunities aren't exactly overflowing for women in my situation, so don't you *dare* look at me as if I'm deliberately creating problems where there aren't any!'

'You talk about opportunity...can you not see that is exactly what I am offering you by suggesting you move to Spain? There we can provide opportunities that will improve your lives a hundredfold.'

Moving onto her opposite hip, Dominique scraped her hand wearily through her hair. 'Even if I agreed to go with you and meet Ramón's mother and his family you must understand it could only be for a short visit. You can hardly expect me to just leave everything behind and decamp to another country as though I was just moving round the corner! And to go and live with a bunch of strangers too!'

'They would not be strangers for very long. They are warm, loving people, and they would embrace you as though you were one of their own—which, of course, by virtue of being the mother of Ramón's child, you are. It is a shame your own mother could not be as forthcoming! I have heard myself her obvious antagonism towards you for taking a path she did not want by bearing the child of a man she clearly despised. The sooner you and the baby are far away from such a woman the better, as far as I am concerned!'

Cristiano's words hit their mark. The relationship between Dominique and her mother had deteriorated to an all-time low from the moment Dominique had confessed her pregnancy, and even Matilde's arrival had not softened the other woman's heart in any way. She refused to even *hold* the baby, let alone mind her for any length of time! Her lack of affection had blighted Dominique's own childhood, and it was heartbreaking that she was now treating her grandchild in the same cruel way. Yet even so…it would be a hell of a gamble to go and live with the family of a man Dominique knew had never loved her, who had callously turned his back on her when he'd found out she was pregnant.

'I'm sorry… But, like I said, I can't go *anywhere* until after the New Year—and then only for a visit.'

'So you say.'

'I've explained my reasons. Why won't you—?'

'Where is the baby tonight? With this friend of yours?' Cristiano interrupted. 'I was very much hoping to see her.'

The annoyance in his voice was clear, and Dominique felt her body tighten even more in response. 'She's not with my friend.'

'Then where is she?'

'She's right here…asleep in her cot behind that screen. It helps shut out the light a little, so it won't disturb her.'

She was already moving towards the other side of the room, and Cristiano followed her with a stunned look on his face. Dominique knew she could have deceived him by agreeing that the baby *was* with her friend, but whilst she was afraid to let him see Matilde for fear of future demands, in all conscience she knew she could not refuse his request. As overwhelming as the thought was, Cristiano Cordova was part of her daughter's family.

'Here she is. She's teething at the moment—that's why her cheeks look so pink.' She heard the love and pride in her own voice as she stood to the side to allow Cristiano a better view.

The sleeping infant looked blissfully peaceful and angelic as Cristiano peered into the cot to gaze at her. With her cap of sable hair, sweet little face and dimpled chin—a *definite* genetic inheritance from the Cordovas—she was absolutely enchanting. For disturbing seconds his head swam and his heart raced as he remembered another infant—had she lived, she would have been just like her. Then he recalled the fact that this was *Ramón's* baby, and that his cousin would never enjoy the privilege of gazing at his beautiful daughter as Cristiano was gazing at her now. Once again, sadness and regret bore down on him like a heavy iron cloak laid across his shoulders.

Glancing up, he solemnly studied the pale, strained features of the girl standing beside him. He could scarcely think of her as a woman at all—she appeared no more than a teenager.

'She is exquisite,' he remarked, the corners of his mouth lifting into a smile despite the terrible circumstances that had brought him here.

'She's a contented, happy soul. I can sense that about her already.'

Her guard down, Dominique ventured a smile back, and Cristiano thought he had never seen eyes of that vivid *heavenly* blue before. The mesmerising colour was tempting him to dive down deep into their iridescent crystal depths and lose himself completely. Young or not, there was something about her that affected him deeply, and the leap of hunger that suddenly flared inside him shockingly confirmed it.

'She must be—what? Around six…seven months old now?'

'Nearly seven, yes.'

'She is much changed from the picture you sent with your letter to Ramón.'

'I'd only just had her then. She was a tiny pink scrunched-up little thing, but she was still the most beautiful creature I'd ever seen!' Coiling her long honey-brown plait round her fingers, Dominique sighed and let it go again. 'It's such a shame that Ramón couldn't bring himself to acknowledge her. Not for my sake but for Matilde's. A child deserves to know her father, or at least something about him, don't you think?'

The statement had a doubly poignant resonance for her. Her own father had left her mother when Dominique was just a baby, and her mother had always refused to talk about him except to run him down. No matter how she personally felt about Ramón, Dominique would never do that to her own child.

Reaching inside the cot, she tenderly ran the tip of her finger across the sleeping baby's downy cheek. 'I think she'd make any man proud to be her father.' Her voice was an emotional whisper as her glistening eyes met Cristiano's.

'Yes…she would…'

Suddenly Cristiano realised he was weary right down to his marrow, and not as in charge of his emotions as he would like. Although no stranger to the deadening weight of grief, he had honestly forgotten how enervating it could be. Now tiredness and sorrow was draining him of the capacity to stay clear-headed and in control, and this girl with her flawless blue eyes and stubborn pride was disturbing things in him that he would prefer remained dormant.

His thoughts inevitably turned to his family. He knew that they were waiting anxiously to hear about the success of his trip so that they could make preparations for welcoming Dominique and the baby into their home. Despite Dominique's reservations about returning to Spain with him, Cristiano had no intention of disappointing them.

'It is getting late.' Glancing down at the gold Cartier watch that glinted expensively against his tanned wrist, he deliberately assumed a more businesslike manner to help put things back on an even keel. 'I need to book into my hotel and get a shower and some dinner. Tomorrow I will send a car for you, and we can meet to discuss the situation further when we are both feeling a little less emotional and overwrought. Do you agree?'

'I'll agree for Ramón's mother's sake,' Dominique replied, moving stiffly towards the door. 'But I'm not promising anything more than that.

Biting back his frustration, Cristiano reached inside his jacket pocket, withdrew his wallet, and then a small embossed card. 'This is the name and telephone number of where I am staying. If you should think of anything you need before we meet tomorrow…*anything* at all…I want you to ring me.

I will send the car at around ten a.m. Will that suit? The sooner we can talk again the better.'

'Ten is fine. I'm always up early with Matilde.'

'So…I will say goodbye for now, and look forward to seeing you again tomorrow, Dominique.'

He extended his hand to her and she took it reluctantly, slipping her palm away from contact with his as soon as she could, as if she was wary of his touch and his promises. Cristiano's shoulders stiffened. He nodded towards her rather curtly, to show his displeasure at this small act of rebellion, and ruefully made his exit.

Dominique asked for Cristiano at the desk and was stunned by the deferential response she received. No sooner did she mention his name than a smartly suited concierge arrived to whisk her personally up to the top floor in the spacious lift of the glamorous Mayfair hotel. He left her outside the door of his suite with all the respectful attention that any visiting VIP might receive.

Feeling somewhat overwhelmed, Dominique waited until her escort departed before she touched her knuckles to the walnut panelling and knocked. As she did so, she would have sworn that her heartbeat was far louder than the answering echo that seemed to bounce ominously round the wide, softly carpeted corridor. She had never set foot in such a smart, exclusive hotel before, and couldn't help but feel like an impostor. And the prospect of seeing Cristiano again after the turbulent encounter of last night was growing ever more daunting.

When the shiny black chauffeur-driven Jaguar had arrived to pick her up and bring her here it had sent Dominique's fears spiralling almost out of control. Now here, in these luxurious, opulent surroundings, her concerns about the power the Cordovas might potentially have over her were frighteningly confirmed. She'd hardly slept a wink for thinking about the Spaniard's visit. *Had Cristiano been telling her the truth when he'd said that Ramón's family would welcome her and Matilde with open arms?* What if it had just been a ruse to get her on Spanish soil where, with their money and power, they could bring the full force of the legal system to bear to ensure that Matilde stayed with them for ever?

'Dominique.'

Suddenly the man she'd come to visit was in the open doorway before her—a tall, dark clothed figure, lean-hipped and hard-muscled, the suggestion of reined-in power very much evident despite his casual stance. Like a cat ready to pounce at the first hint of danger. Glancing up into his compelling face, she saw that his eyes were as fathomless as a black night studded with stars, and his jet hair gleamed like a dark moonlit sea. Dominique's mouth seemed to instantly dry up at the sight of him.

'Where is Matilde?'

'I left her with my friend for a couple of hours…I thought it would make it easier for us to talk.'

'That is a shame. I was looking forward to seeing her again.'

Dominique felt both guilty and chastised. 'I'm not trying to stop you seeing her. I just thought—'

'It is early yet. Perhaps I can see her later on in the day?'

Cristiano studied her face intently for a moment, as though needing to discern whether he could trust her or not, and Dominique sensed he knew she had not brought Matilde along because her fears about the outcome of this meeting had not yet been allayed.

'You had better come in.'

The elegant drawing room she entered was decorated in a tasteful quintessentially English style, with antique furniture, inviting luxurious sofas and armchairs, and plush red velvet curtains finished with opulent swags at the windows. There was even a baby grand piano in residence, its polished ebony wood gleaming. Dominique felt like the little match girl, wandering in from the cold in her nondescript black woollen dress and slightly over-sized tweed coat. A room like this, she mused, called for nothing less than a tall elegant blonde clad in haute couture and diamonds—the kind that graced billboards, not a five-foot-five unconfident girl with nondescript brown hair and a deepening sense of dread.

'I've ordered us some coffee. It should be with us shortly. Please…let me take your coat.'

Embarrassed and then angry at the idea that Cristiano must guess that her well worn, less-than-elegant coat was a charity shop buy, Dominique handed it to him with an air of defiance.

'Sit down,' he told her, his dark gaze briefly skimming her figure in the unremarkable black dress…*another cast-off from a charity shop.*

It was impossible to know what was going on behind those extraordinary dark eyes of his, but everything about Cristiano Cordova reeked of class and money. Standing there in that elegant drawing room with him, Dominique was painfully aware of the discrepancy in their backgrounds. It was funny, but she hadn't felt that way with Ramón. Maybe it was because he had been younger and a little less sure of himself? There had been times in their short-lived relationship when he had definitely displayed what had seemed like vulnerability to her. In contrast, she had never met a man who appeared more certain of his place in the world than Cristiano

Cordova. No doubt he already *had* a tall elegant blonde in his life, Dominique mused.

'Make yourself comfortable,' he suggested. 'It is cold outside today, no?'

He didn't seem the type to casually discuss the weather, and she guessed that maybe he was doing it to try and help her feel less overwhelmed. But would a man like him be that considerate? A man who clearly knew what he wanted and would not let a little thing like somebody else's conflicting desires get in the way?

As she sank into one of the inviting armchairs, Dominique watched Cristiano take up residence at the end of the sofa nearest to her—which was far too close for comfort, if she was honest—and she swallowed hard.

'Yes, it is cold.'

'I can see that you are somewhat tense about this meeting, Dominique. I want to reassure you that I have asked you here only because I want the very best for you and your daughter.'

'That's all well and good, but I'm a little tired of everybody else being convinced they know what's best for me and Matilde!' she snapped, feeling her throat threatening to close.

'How old are you?'

'Twenty-one… Why? I suppose now you're going to tell me that I'm far too young and irresponsible to possibly know my own mind? Well, for your information I know *exactly* what I want for me and my baby, and I don't need anyone else to tell me different!'

A knock on the door heralded the arrival of their coffee and prevented Cristiano from immediately replying to her tirade. While the smartly attired steward arranged an exquisite silver tray on the low burnished wood table in front of them, Dominique tried hard to get her emotions back under control. *Why did the man get to her this way? Make her feel so defensive and angry?*

Watching him tip the steward at the door, she waited until he returned to his seat before she spoke again. 'I'm sorry—I lost my temper.'

'It is an emotional time for all of us. Let me pour you some coffee. Do you take cream and sugar?'

'Yes, please.'

He looked frighteningly calm and collected in comparison with the riot of nerves and emotions she was personally experiencing inside, and as Dominique accepted her drink, his gaze met and held hers for perturbing seconds.

'I spoke to my family last night and I explained to them why you are reticent about returning to Spain with me. They understand your concerns about your job, but—like me—do not see it as an obstacle that cannot be easily overcome. They have implored me to do my utmost to persuade you to come and join us for Christmas at least. You have had some time to think things over and now I would really like your answer, Dominique. What do you say?'

CHAPTER THREE

NO PRESSURE, then...

'I'm still unsure,' she replied. 'They've already organised the rota at the restaurant, and I've promised I'll work.'

'And, apart from working, how were you planning on spending the rest of the holiday?' Cristiano asked quietly.

The question was apt to make her burst into tears. Biting her lip, Dominique covered her distress by briefly raising her cup to her lips and carefully sipping at her drink. 'I was just going to spend it quietly with Matilde.'

'You were not planning on spending any time with your mother?'

Dominique tensed even more. 'She's going skiing with friends, like she always does at Christmas. I probably wouldn't have seen her anyway.'

Cristiano stared at Dominique in disbelief. *Her*

mother was going away with friends, leaving her daughter and grandchild to spend the Christmas holidays entirely alone? He understood that other cultures had different ways of doing things, but this was surely one of the most unnatural things he had ever heard!

Although offended on Dominique's and the baby's behalf, he quickly saw an opportunity for making his case even more compelling, and did not hesitate to take it.

'Christmas where I come from is a truly magical season,' he intoned softly, the edges of his lips lifting in genuine pleasure at the thought. 'At the centre of the tradition is the *belén*—what you call here the Nativity. The scene is recreated using all kinds of lovingly collected materials and passed down through each family, generation to generation. It is something we take great pride in. Sometimes whole communities get together to make the *belén*, and you will find them in many public places as well as in the churches. On Christmas Eve—what we call Nochebuena—the church bells sound joyfully, calling everyone to mass, and afterwards we all return home for a fantastic feast. When that is over we gather round the Christmas tree to sing carols. It is a time for warmth and community…not a time to be alone!'

Dominique's big blue eyes were round with

wonder. Gratified, Cristiano could see that he'd captivated her with the inviting picture his words had conjured up.

'My mother has never believed in making a big fuss at Christmas,' she sighed, her slender shoulders drooping a little in the plain black dress. 'In fact she's always dreaded it rather than looked forward to it. A "commercial rip-off", she calls it. That's why she prefers to go away rather than stay at home.'

'Your mother has her view on the matter and I have mine. But one thing is for certain…you and the little one cannot spend Christmas alone. Consuela would be beside herself if she heard such a thing!'

'Consuela?'

'Ramón's mother.' Cristiano leant towards her, renewed determination in his heart as he thought of the aunt he loved and adored as much as his own mother. 'Come back with me to Spain, Dominique. You will not regret it, I promise.'

'You mean for Christmas? What about my job at the restaurant? I might lose it if I don't work.'

He shook his head impatiently. 'If it comes to it, I will ensure it will not be a problem. I told you…from now on I see it as *my* duty and responsibility to provide for you, and instead of worrying about how to make ends meet if you stay in the UK you will be able to concentrate on the most important job of all in Spain…that of raising your child.'

'And if I decide to accept your offer and stay… what about your own immediate family?' she asked him reasonably. 'Do you have a wife and children? If so, won't they mind you inviting a complete stranger and her baby into your home?'

His body tensing, Cristiano waited for the inevitable feeling of sorrow and regret that pierced him to subside a little. The symptoms were like an illness that persisted, as raw as they had ever been, and he suspected he would *never* be free of them.

'I have neither wife nor child,' he replied, his jaw tightening. 'So the problem would hardly arise. In any case, I am head of the Cordova family and I am entrusted to make decisions that are best for all.'

'You mean…whatever you say goes?'

'If you want to put it like that…yes.'

'I see.'

'Was there anything else you wanted to know?'

She pursed her lips and gazed straight ahead of her.

Cristiano's brow furrowed. 'Dominique?'

'It's just that… Well, is it right that I should contemplate going to live with Ramón's family under the circumstances? I mean, when we'd already broken up and everything? It might have been different if we had been engaged to be married, but we weren't.'

'Did you *want* to marry him?'

'No. That was something I never fooled myself about. Even when he was with me he never stopped admiring other girls. I was well aware he craved his freedom and detested the idea of a long-term commitment. A marriage between us wouldn't have lasted five minutes!"

'That may unfortunately have been the case, but I have to tell you that you have *every* right to expect the support of his family, Dominique. It is Matilde's birthright we are talking about here! As well as my own responsibility towards her, Ramón had money and property that will naturally go to his daughter now that he is dead. Once you are established in Spain everything will be arranged legally.'

'Assuming I agree to go, of course!'

Assessing the proud lift of her head and the continued defiance etched into her small, perfect jaw, Cristiano could not help but smile. Victory was close, he sensed, but he would not risk jeopardising it by displaying arrogance at such a crucial juncture.

'I understand your concerns—it is unknown territory for you, and your fears about going to people you do not yet know are only natural. But you are an intelligent girl, and I think you are already aware that returning to Spain with me and the opportunities that would afford you if you decide to stay—as well as the family support you would receive—would surely make for a much better future than you could ever hope to enjoy here!'

She glanced away from him for a moment,

chewing on her lip, her gaze reflective. 'It's a big step…moving to another country. All right. I'll agree to go with you for Christmas, but after that…well, we'll see. My main concern is that I make the right choices for my child. Naturally I want her to be with people who'll love her as much as I do. And I'm well aware she probably won't have that if I stay here. My mother is too bitter and disappointed in me to ever be the kind of grandmother I would wish for Matilde…I realise that.'

'That is *her* loss—of that I have no doubt.'

Equal parts of anger and dismay clutched at Cristiano's vitals when he thought about Dominique's mother and her unforgiving, unnatural attitude towards her daughter. But he was also eager to ring home and give them some good news for a change. To let them know that Dominique and the baby *would* be coming back with him for Christmas would fill them with joy instead of the numbing sadness and grief they had been living with these past few weeks. A baby in the house would signify new life and a new beginning. *New hope.*

The thought laid a soft blanket over his own grief and despair, and he glanced at Dominique with genuine concern, seeing a young woman who clearly needed his protection and guidance. He could not let her down.

'When can you be ready to leave?' he asked her,

stirring his coffee and taking a satisfying sip of the dark sweet brew.

Her cup rattling a little in its saucer as she placed it on the table, Dominique sank further back into her chair and folded her arms. 'Well… I'll have to discuss it with my manager at work, but I'd say the earliest I could go would be in about two weeks' time. If I'm not going to be there over Christmas I'll probably have to put in some extra hours to make up for my absence. There'll be other things to arrange too…a medical check for Matilde, packing, and I'll have to ask my neighbour to keep an eye on my place for me while I'm away.'

'Two weeks is out of the question! I aim to be back in Spain in no more than a week, and I am not going back without you! You can arrange the little one's medical check, but as for your work—I will be only too happy to speak to your manager and put him in the picture. You should be entitled to compassionate leave at the very least!'

Once again Dominique was made aware of the iron resolve of the man sitting opposite her. She recognised his natural proclivity for taking charge of both situations and people—and could not help feeling resentful. She had had a bellyful of being told what to do! Her teachers, her mother… everyone pushing and prodding her to achieve their *own* ends, not hers. If she was going to become part of this new Spanish family that her daughter had inherited then she had to establish for Cristiano Cordova the fact that she had a mind and a will of her own, and would not be backed into a corner by anyone.

'That won't be necessary. I'm quite capable of speaking to my manager myself, thank you! And if you can't wait as long as two weeks, then why don't you go back as planned and let me follow on later?'

'No.'

Dominique had never heard such an intractable no in her life. Getting to his feet, Cristiano appeared suddenly restless, as if he had sat too long and was unused to such enforced inactivity.

'We will return to Spain together and I will not hear of any other arrangement than that! Over the coming week I will be totally at your disposal to help you with whatever has to be done—and it will be done, rest assured. And, talking of travelling, you have an up-to-date passport, I presume?'

Dominique nodded, her expression stunned.

'And Matilde?'

'Well, no,' Dominique answered. 'There's hardly been a need…'

'No matter—I can easily speed things up with a word in the right ear at the embassy. And as for packing—you will not need to bring much with you when you first come out at all. I will ensure absolutely everything you need will be provided once we arrive back home.'

'Can you turn water into wine too?'

He stared at her with a dark look in his eyes.

'Very amusing! I can see that it will take time for you to become used to how I operate, Dominique, but you will soon learn. When I say a thing should be done then it is done without question, and I want you to know that I will be completely unrelenting in my goal to have Ramón's daughter *and* her mother on Spanish soil sooner rather than later. I am absolutely adamant about that!'

Her cheeks twin beacons of indignant scarlet at his words, Dominique stubbornly refused to shy away from Cristiano's arrogant gaze. But an icy chill of warning slid down her spine. *Ramón had been right...his cousin was, indeed, formidable.*

'And I want *you* to know that whilst I may be young I'm no badly behaved five-year-old who needs to be told what to do—so don't treat me like I am!'

'Is that so? I will endeavour to try and remember that. I am beginning to see that Ramón certainly had his work cut out for him being with you, Dominique!'

To Dominique's complete surprise, Cristiano's steely-eyed glare was swiftly replaced by a teasing glance that made heat erupt inside her like a rip tide, scorching right through her centre.

Stunned by her disturbing response—and suddenly not feeling quite so defiant—she pushed to her feet. 'I need to use the bathroom,' she mumbled and, disconcerted that the smile had still not completely left her tormentor's lips, she hurried away in the direction he indicated.

Standing in the luxurious marble bathroom, in front of a huge antique mirror edged with gold-painted rosebuds and curlicues, Dominique surveyed her flushed, heated face with impatience and surprise. *What had just happened in there?* Why was the man getting to her so? Dropping her shoulders, she flicked her hair back over her shoulder and sighed. She was scared, that was all. Fear was apt to make her anxious and edgy, liable to react nervously to even the most inconsequential thing.

But how could she feel anything *but* scared about the possibility of going to live in Spain amongst people she didn't know, as well as putting herself under the daunting wing of a man like Cristiano Cordova? It hardly surprised her that he was a lawyer—no doubt a frighteningly successful one too. Once they were in his sphere, he would hold her and Matilde's futures in his hands as ruthlessly and single-mindedly as he controlled the fates of the people he represented in court, she was sure.

Yet, even so, Dominique realised that this was

the right thing to do for her child. She might not have had the chance to find out about her own father, or be close to his family, but Matilde *would*. And even though she could foresee that sparks would fly between herself and Cristiano—he would want to control her and Dominique would naturally want to resist being manipulated in any way—he had told her that his family were kind, loving people, and the picture he had painted so evocatively of the kind of Christmases they enjoyed had been compelling. Her heart had squeezed with longing for such an experience.

If only she could trust what he said, then maybe she could start to allow herself to hope that the future might not be so frightening as she feared. She *ached* to feel connected to the rest of the world again…not to be cut off by people who were so emotionally distant that they made Dominique feel like an island in a stark, cold sea. Her mother had scorned her for throwing away her future by having Matilde, but it was her emotional neglect that had driven her into Ramón Cordova's arms in the first place.

Ramón. Even though he had been thoughtless and wild, and in the end had rejected her, when they'd been together he had given her more attention and affection than anyone else ever had. He had shown her what it was to laugh too, to be young and foolish and not to take life so seriously.

Suddenly it hit her hard that he was dead—his vibrant young life ended before it had really begun, leaving his child without even the possibility of ever meeting him. She felt her whole body sag towards the floor, as if some strange irresistible force were dragging her down, down into a dark abyss, and tears welled up in her eyes like hot springs, rolling down her cheeks in glistening wet tracks. *Was she destined to be alone and unloved for ever?* She almost couldn't bear it.

'Dominique? Is everything all right?'

Cristiano's voice sounded from the other side of the door. Straightening in shock, Dominique ripped a tissue out of the chic box on the vanity unit, blew her nose and mumbled, 'I'm fine. I just need a minute, okay?'

'You are crying,' he retorted, his voice accusing.

'I suppose that's a hanging offence where you come from?' she burst out, unable to help herself.

'Do not be so foolish! I never said it was an offence to cry.'

There was a surprisingly gentle quality to his tone that Dominique had not heard before.

'But if you are upset I would like to help comfort you,' he added.

Comfort… Spiritual, emotional, physical… It was the thing she longed for, but somehow it always escaped her. The distressing events of the past year had all but ripped away her confidence and trust in everything, and on top of that her hormones were going haywire after having Matilde.

'You are the *last* person I would want to comfort me!' she heard herself rail, before she could stem the impulse.

There was silence outside for a long moment, then Cristiano spoke again, his voice low and his words measured.

'Maybe you would prefer it if it was my cousin standing outside this door talking to you? But as we both know that is not possible. You will simply have to make do with me. Open the door, Dominique.'

'I don't want Ramón!' she answered, her tears coming faster. 'Why would I want him? It was over between us a long time ago, and he walked out on me—remember? It's just such a waste, that's all—to die like that! A stupid, *stupid* waste!'

Glancing at her stricken expression sidelong in the mirror, Dominique gulped down another sob and dabbed feverishly at her reddened eyes.

'Sometimes it is hard to make sense of these things, even when one has faith… But life goes on, yes? And you have a beautiful baby daughter to remember him by. Not all is lost.'

Strangely comforted by his words, Dominique took a deep breath, then shakily released the latch and opened the door. The handsome visage that confronted her was both grave and concerned, and she didn't know why she should feel so guilty about yelling at him, but she did. He was, after all, throwing her a lifeline of sorts, as well as giving Matilde an opportunity to grow up knowing the family that had raised her father…

'There is a park close by,' Cristiano told her, dark eyes assessing her tear-stained face with intimate scrutiny. 'The day is bright and cold—I think we should take a walk together and get some air. What do you say?'

'I don't know. Yes…all right.' But even as she agreed, Dominique sensed her lip quiver uncontrollably and her face crumple. 'I'm just so *tired*!' she breathed mournfully, dipping her head. 'So tired of everything!'

In the next instant Cristiano had propelled her into his arms and was cradling her head against his chest, just over his heart. The steady, even throb of his heartbeat and the comforting sensation of warmth and strength that emanated from his hard, masculine body made Dominique curl her fingers into his fine wool sweater for added security, and she gratefully shut her eyes, feeling as if they stood together in the eye of a storm. She prayed it would soon pass. But her scalding tears would not be so easily contained, and they seeped from her eyelids in a steady trickle of pain and sorrow. *What was the matter with her?* After all this time of staying strong, telling herself she could cope come what may, she was suddenly falling apart.

'Cry all you want, *querida,*' the man who held her murmured in his compelling velvet-lined voice, his big hand cupping her head and stroking her hair as though tenderly giving consolation to a child. 'Expressing our sorrows is sometimes necessary rather then holding them inside. You should not see giving in to grief as something undesirable, or feel that you have to put on a brave face when you are feeling sad. That would not be good for you *or* the little one!'

For disturbing moments Cristiano felt as if his feelings were under siege as he held Dominique's slender quivering body close to his own. The scent of her honey-laced shampoo was inexplicably alluring as it drifted beneath his nose, and he had never touched hair of such fine silk as hers before. The sensation was *incredible*. He was aware too of the soft fullness of her breasts as they pressed intimately into his chest, and was shocked by the entirely inappropriate sensations that swept violently through his body as a result of that close contact.

It had been too long since he had held a woman in his arms, and no doubt *that* was why his body was reacting so strongly. All he had wanted to do was offer Dominique some comfort and reassurance, but now her body was awakening feelings in him that he'd thought long petrified. If the sensations were purely sexual he could handle them well enough—women had always been interested in Cristiano, and there had been no lack of opportunity for that kind of consolation since the tragedy that had stopped his world. But other, much more *dangerous* emotions were assailing him too, and Cristiano realised he would have to be on his guard against getting this close to the beguiling Dominique again. The risks were simply too terrifying to be contemplated…

CHAPTER FOUR

AS HER tears and sorrow started to abate, Dominique became disturbingly aware that she was actively *enjoying* being held in Cristiano's arms. Not just because he was giving her the comfort she sorely needed, but because his body was hard and warm and strong, and the contact made her feel *alive* and human again, after being shut off from those vital sensations for too long.

Now she knew why babies failed to thrive when they were denied the most basic necessity of all…that of being touched and held. Surely something similar must happen to adults? And it was with genuine reluctance that she uncurled her fingers from the soft weave of Cristiano's sweater and started to step out of the protective circle of his arms.

Just before Dominique disengaged herself completely, he took her hands in his and stroked the pads of his thumbs back and forth across her fine, delicately boned fingers. His dark gaze was almost brooding.

'It will get better, you know? You will find a way to manage it. I know it is hard to believe that right now, feeling the way you do, but you will. Every day the hurt will ease a little more. You are fortunate that you have little Matilde to draw comfort from.'

He sounded as if he knew intimately what it was to lose someone you cared for. Staring back into the black velvet night of his arresting glance, Dominique felt her hands alive with electricity from their contact with his. Her grief and despondency had been stunningly transformed into a fascination that perplexed and frightened her.

'I think I'll give that walk a miss, if you don't mind? I really ought to be getting back to Matilde,' she heard herself announce, her voice sounding remarkably even and calm in spite of her turbulent feelings.

Cristiano shrugged, his expression not easing in its disturbing intensity one iota. 'When can I see you again?' he asked.

Her heart momentarily stalled at the question—*for a second there he had sounded like an ardent lover, counting the minutes until he saw his paramour again*—and Dominique sensed heat rush into her face.

'Why don't you come and join me for dinner

this evening? You can bring the baby…I will see about a private room for us,' he suggested when she did not reply straight away.

'I can't. I'm working tonight.'

'Ring them and say that you are taking the night off.'

'Are solutions always so black and white to you?'

Dominique bet when this man dealt with clients he didn't suffer fools gladly, or grant any quarter to anyone who dared disagree with him. The world must seem a very different place when you saw the answers to problems with such enviable clarity!

'I'm already going to have to let them down when I tell them I can't work over Christmas as it is. It would hardly be fair for me to phone in at the last minute and say I'm taking tonight off as well!'

'I can see that you have a very admirable sense of duty, Dominique, and although I am disappointed you won't be joining me tonight I cannot fault it. So… We will meet tomorrow for lunch instead, yes? We can go for a walk in the park first, then have something to eat afterwards. Does that plan appeal more to your sense of fairness?'

His lips twitched teasingly upwards at one corner, and Dominique was transfixed by the blaze of light that humour brought to his otherwise smouldering dark gaze.

'It does.'

'So…if you insist you have to leave now I will ring down to Reception and organise a car to take you back home. I will send it again for you tomorrow at around midday.'

'Okay…thank you.'

'You are feeling a little better now?'

As he brought his hand lightly down onto her shoulder, Cristiano's touch almost made Dominique jump out of her skin.

'I'm sorry I lost it like that.' She grimaced, hardly daring to look at him and suddenly needing vital fresh air to help her breathe.

'There is no need for an apology,' he said quietly, devastatingly holding her gaze, even though everything inside her was clamouring to be set free from it.

When she could hardly stand the tension any longer, he gave a barely perceptible nod of his head and moved towards the telephone on the bureau just inside the door. Seconds later she heard him ring down to Reception to order the car to take her home…

Having spoken to his family and given them the news that they'd been waiting on tenterhooks to hear, Cristiano strode restlessly through the hotel and made his way to the park. As he slid his ungloved hands into the pockets of his camel-coloured cashmere coat and made his way down paths strewn with the untended debris of faded and dead autumn leaves his thoughts turned like a magnet to Dominique and the baby.

Both females were stirring things in him that he had rigidly striven to keep contained—an action that stemmed from his great desire to make himself impenetrable to hurt from another human being again. Up until Ramón's shocking death he had more than succeeded. But now the big blue guileless eyes of the woman his cousin had abandoned, along with her fierce pride and that gorgeous baby girl, were making inroads into the previously impervious wall he'd built around his emotions. He knew he would have to fortify it if he was to stay immune.

He didn't doubt for a moment that he was doing the right thing in taking them home with him to Spain—his sense of duty and familial loyalty confirmed it, if nothing else—nevertheless Cristiano knew that their unexpected presence in his life was going to test his resolve as nothing had before.

As he sighed into the frigid air, his warm breath made a curling plume of steam. A well-dressed couple strolling past from the opposite direction wished him good afternoon, and Cristiano politely inclined his head in acknowledgement. As he walked on, he was blindsided as his mind's eye caught and held the vision of another woman's beautiful face. The pain it wrought inside him almost made him stagger.

Unable to fight off the scene that unfolded in his head, he devastatingly recalled the passionate, loving words that woman had called out to him from her hospital bed just two years ago. A seemingly straight forward labour had taken an unexpected turn for the worse, and the next thing Cristiano had known was that his wife was fighting for her life—and their baby's. Just before the medical team had rushed her off to surgery Martina had called out to him. *'Te amo, Cristi! Te amo!'* Her stunning brown eyes had been full of tears and so had his own as he'd stood there, icy dread robbing him of all life and turning him to stone, nauseous with the realisation that he was in the middle of a nightmare he might never wake from…

All his faith, personal influence, professional know-how and wealth had served him to no avail that terrible day, and by the time he'd received the news that his wife and baby had not survived the emergency operation that had been undertaken to save them Cristiano had felt as if he had been driven to his knees by the most vicious, merciless storm imaginable.

The pain of it was as fresh now as it had been that day, despite the platitudes he had spoken earlier. Gritting his teeth, he lengthened his stride and began to head down a path that he saw led to a large wintry lake flocked by squawking birds, and with a determined upsurge of strength he managed to ride the crest of the terrible emotion that had so cruelly racked him. Eventually sensing it subside, he renewed his vow never to leave himself so vulnerable again.

Knowing they were going to the park, Dominique had hoped they would go by the lake, so she'd brought with her a paper bag full of stale crusts of bread to feed to the birds. Cristiano seemed quite happy to go along with this idea and, despite being dressed more appropriately for lunch at the Ritz than to take a casual stroll through the park, he walked alongside Matilde's pushchair closely enough to look as if he belonged there. It gave Dominique quite an odd feeling. And even odder was the fact that she realised she couldn't really imagine Ramón undertaking the same ordinary action and taking pleasure in it. He would have been too impatient to go on and do something far more exciting, and would probably have spoiled the outing with a sulk.

Guiltily Dominique pulled herself up short. *Was she being disloyal to the father of her baby by thinking such an uncharitable thing?* Disturbed, she pushed the thought away and glanced sidelong at Cristiano instead. This morning she'd woken with a strange fluttering sensation in the pit of her stomach and had realised it was excitement at the idea of going to Spain. Somehow this man walking beside her had persuaded her it would be a very good idea for her to go, and for some reason Dominique had started to believe him.

Whether it was the thought of spending a Christmas like the one he had so vividly described, amongst people who genuinely cared about her daughter's wellbeing, or just the opportunity to consider starting life afresh in a new country with a 'clean slate,' she couldn't have said for sure, but she knew she had to give it a try. There was certainly nothing holding her in the UK if she decided to move there permanently, and that included her mother. Talking of which…

'By the way, I spoke to my mother this morning and told her I was going to Spain with you for Christmas.'

'And how did she take the news?'

'She was strangely quiet, actually. Not the reaction I expected at all. She said we should talk when I get back.'

'Perhaps she has finally realised how selfish of her it is to leave you to your own devices during the holiday?'

'Why should she think that?' Shrugging, Dominique countered the sting of her mother's rejection of both her and her baby with a fresh spurt of anger. 'It's what she usually does! It would be a bit late in the day for her to develop a conscience!'

'You have never mentioned your father?' Interestedly, Cristiano glanced at her. 'I am presuming he is not in the picture any more?'

'He left when I was two. God knows where he is now! He never kept in touch, and I doubt whether my mother would have even wanted him to. She's been furious with him for most of my life! It's her main motivation for getting up every day…just so she can be mad at him all over again!'

Not commenting, Cristiano merely looked thoughtful, and Dominique concluded that he was obviously thinking what a screwed up family she came from!

Biting her lip, she tightened her hands a little round the handlebars of the pushchair.

Reaching the lakeside, Dominique carefully positioned Matilde where she had the best view and, checking that the cheerful knitted blanket to safeguard her from the cold was securely in place, she crouched down low beside her and laughingly threw the crusts to the accumulated feathered throng.

'Look, Tilly! Look at the lovely birds, darling! How happy they are to see you!'

Watching them both with growing fascination, and a secret pleasure he could not deny, Cristiano stood protectively by, his gaze moving now and again to the other small groups of families dotted round the perimeter of the lake, also feeding the birds. His connection to the young woman beside him was for once allowing him entry to an experience that they perhaps took for granted. He valiantly steered his mind away from the distressing recollection that had assailed him yesterday and concentrated instead on this new memory that Dominique and her sweet child were helping to create.

'Make yourself useful!' she chided him suddenly, passing him a handful of crusts and gazing up at him with teasing mirth in her brilliant blue eyes. 'I've literally got enough here to feed the five thousand!'

'If you ask me' Cristiano responded drolly, 'those birds already look overfed. Any more food and they will not be able to take off!'

'A sense of humour, Señor Cordova? I didn't expect that!'

'You think I am too serious?' he asked, frowning, not quite knowing how to take her criticism.

'Perhaps...I don't really know. It's just that you seemed like you were miles away, that's all.'

'I was merely observing the other people doing what you are doing and wondering how it is that a simple pastime such as throwing some bread to birds can bring so much pleasure.'

'When you do it with your children it's the best thing in the world!' Dominique announced, leaning into Matilde's pushchair to plant a sound kiss on her daughter's plump pink cheek. 'Isn't it, Tilly?'

Cristiano remained silent in bittersweet agreement, but as his gaze locked with Dominique's a palpable sensation of warmth seemed to flood his insides. His previous disquiet vanished and he knew he was staring. The icy wind that was blowing had stung her cheeks into two bright pink spots of colour, and some fine strands of honey-brown hair, freed from her plait, danced wildly across them.

She glanced quickly away, clearly discomfited by his intense regard. 'When we've got rid of all the bread, do you think we could go and eat?' she asked him, her gaze now firmly on the lake and the diving birds as they braved the near-frozen surface to reach the semi-submerged crusts.

Concerned that he had neglected his duties, Cristiano agreed straight away. 'Of course! Do you like Indian food?' he asked her. 'There is an exceptionally good Indian restaurant nearby, where I have reserved a table for us. If you do not like that particular cuisine then we can go somewhere you'd like better.'

'Indian is great…as long as you think I'm dressed okay? It's not somewhere really posh, is it?'

'No…it is not "posh".' His lips curved into an amused smile. 'It has an authentic Indian ambience, and you can go dressed casually—as we are.'

'What you're wearing is *casual?*' Now it was Dominique's turn to be amused.

Glancing down at his smart chinos, handmade Italian shoes, black cashmere sweater and three-quarter-length black leather jacket, Cristiano was genuinely perplexed by the question. 'My outfit is certainly not formal, if that is what you are suggesting!'

'No...perhaps it isn't formal, but it still looks expensive and classy. Whereas what I'm wearing definitely doesn't! Perhaps we ought to just go for a burger somewhere? I don't want to embarrass you.'

She was wearing denim jeans, boots, a bottle-green polo-necked sweater and the slightly over-sized tweed coat she'd had on yesterday. Very little make-up adorned her features, and she looked fresh-faced, young and beautiful. Why she imagined he would be *remotely* embarrassed to be seen with her appearing as she was Cristiano could not begin to fathom. He did not like the sense that her parents' emotional neglect of her—as well as his cousin's abandonment—had made such a harsh dent in her self-esteem.

'That is an entirely ridiculous notion, Dominique! You look perfectly acceptable to me. All I want you to do is enjoy the food and hopefully the company too.' He smiled wryly. 'Put your worries aside for a while.'

'And they won't mind at the restaurant if I feed the baby while I'm there?'

'You are feeding her yourself?' For a moment Cristiano sensed an intense tingling heat throb low in his stomach at the idea of Dominique breastfeeding, and he was furious with himself for feeling aroused when it was the most natural thing in the world for a mother to feed her baby that way. He noticed the colour in her cheeks bloomed even pinker at his question.

'No. I tried to feed her myself but I had to give up in the end. I wasn't very good at it.'

'But she takes a bottle quite happily?'

Dominique nodded.

'Then where is the problem? As long as she is able to take nourishment that is the main thing, is it not?'

Glancing towards the lake, Cristiano threw a handful of bread in the direction of a rather dejected-looking duck that was isolated from the rest, He shivered as a particularly icy breeze seared into his face just then. As pleasurable as this little outing with Dominique and the baby was, he was seriously missing the far friendlier climes of his own country. He was also concerned that it was too much for the child to be out in such hostile weather.

'We should go now,' he announced, swiping the remainder of the crumbs from his leather gloves. 'It is really far too bitter for Matilde. We should get her inside into the warmth.'

'You're probably right. Say bye-bye to the birds, Tilly! We'll come and visit them again another day.'

Rising to her feet, Dominique gave Cristiano a fleeting smile, and as she turned the pushchair round and started back up the path that had led them to the lake he automatically put his hand at her back, as if to guide and protect her…

CHAPTER FIVE

IT WAS going to be the last night Dominique spent in her bedsit for a while—at least until after Christmas, and maybe longer than that if she decided to take the monumental step of settling in Spain. She'd had a farewell drink with a couple of close friends, and Katie from across the landing, and now all she had to do was finish her packing. Thankfully Matilde was being an absolute angel and sleeping peacefully—tired out, Dominique was sure, from being cuddled and petted by the three girls who'd dropped in to say goodbye to them.

Tomorrow was the big day. She and Matilde were flying out to Madrid with Cristiano, and when they arrived his personal driver was going to meet them and transport them the seventy kilometres to the town where he lived. The thought was exciting, but somewhat overwhelming too. Cristiano kept telling her not to be daunted—that everything would work out perfectly—but Dominique could not help fearing it might not, and then where would she be? Back in this too-small bedsit with a growing infant and barely enough money coming in to make ends meet.

Pausing as she turned to the half-filled suitcase she'd hefted onto the foldaway bed that doubled up as a couch during the day, Dominique sighed heavily as she gazed critically round her. As optimistic as she'd tried to be when she'd first set eyes on the place, she'd be a liar if she didn't admit the rundown décor and general living conditions weren't depressing. If she hadn't had a baby to look after and a job to go to five nights a week perhaps she might have got round to doing some redecoration to freshen it up a little…

No…she was glad to be leaving this bleak, dreary environment to go somewhere warmer and more welcoming. The only thing that was really making her stomach roll over time and time again was the idea of going with Cristiano. Seeing him on and off over the past few days, for lunch or coffee, and walks in the park whenever she could grab an hour or two away from the demands of her week, had not lessened her heightened awareness of the man one jot. She had learned that he definitely liked to take charge, that he had certain old-fashioned views about men taking care of women, and that he could be brusque one minute then absolutely charming the next. With Matilde he'd assumed the role of a very fond uncle, and he loved to make a fuss of her and buy her little gifts—pretty dresses and baby toys that had clearly been purchased from the more upmarket department stores.

All in all, he did the things that most women would love their children's fathers to do for them, and Dominique sensed that her vow to distance herself from men in general after what had happened with Ramón was being seriously compromised by his appealing attentions. However, she knew that once back in Spain Cristiano would have his own very independent life to lead, and although he would be close at hand, she and Matilde would not command his attention half so much as they did here.

That was good, she told herself. She absolutely did not want to need or depend on him— She had learned too well how no one could be relied upon. But it would be very hard when she had become so used to his presence as well as his reassurance and advice. Somewhere deep inside Dominique sensed a warning that she knew she should seriously heed. She'd already been abandoned by her father, and the father of her child. Did she want to risk making the same catastrophic mistake again by becoming too attached to Cristiano? He was merely acting as a sort of guardian for her and Matilde until he got them safely back to Spain, and that was all. After that his life would resume as normal, and Dominique would be busy getting used to a completely new situation—as well as a whole new set of people on her own. The thought gave her serious butterflies.

The phone rang, startling her, and she scrubbed a hand round her face to help focus. Her tone had an unknowingly husky cadence as she spoke into the receiver. 'Hello?'

'Dominique?'

The sensually commanding Spanish voice that answered had become compellingly familiar, and an involuntary shiver rushed through her at the sound of it.

'I was wondering if you might ring,' she replied, shocked that the word she had actually been going to use was *hoping*. Feeling mild irritation at her foolishness, she was glad that Cristiano wasn't there in person to witness her telling blush.

'How is the packing coming along?' he asked, and she heard the smile in his voice.

Glancing down at the only half-full suitcase, Dominique grimaced. 'Actually, I had to take a break from it for a while. I had some friends round this evening to wish me bon voyage, and I've only just got Matilde off to sleep after all the excitement. I'm just about to carry on.'

'Do you need any help? I could be there in about half an hour.'

'No! There really isn't any need…thanks.'

Her hand was shaking as she threaded it through her hair. Right now she didn't need the added distraction of his presence, and besides, she was sure he had seen enough of her depressing bedsit. No, she would be far more relaxed packing her meagre belongings on her own rather than have Cristiano helping her.

'It won't take me long, and then when I'm done I'm going straight to bed. We have an early start in the morning, right?'

'I will be there to collect you at around eight-thirty. Our flight is at eleven. I hope the baby won't disturb you too much tonight…you will need your rest with all the travelling we have ahead of us.'

'I have a feeling she'll sleep through.'

'Good. I rang my family earlier, and they will definitely *not* be sleeping through,' he said ironically. 'They are overwhelmed at the idea that you are coming and they are going to see Ramón's daughter at last.'

'No more overwhelmed than I am at the thought of meeting *them*.'

'You have nothing to worry about.'

'So you keep telling me!'

'And what I am telling you is the truth. Anyway…I

think I should let you go now and finish your packing. *Buenas noches*, Dominique. Sleep well.'

'Goodnight…'

Suddenly saying his name seemed too intimate, so she chose to exclude it, but as she replaced the receiver on its rest it came to her that she was holding her breath…

Matilde had won over the airline staff as soon as they boarded, and during the flight in the first class cabin the steward and stewardess assigned to look after them took every opportunity to stop and make a fuss of the beautiful infant. In turn, her huge brown eyes and happy dimpled smile declared her definite approval of being the centre of so much attention.

Cristiano could not help but feel a strong wave of pride that the irresistible little girl had Cordova blood running in her veins, and he knew that when she was grown she would be a *magnet* for all the young men in the vicinity. He frowned, surprised by the worry this thought produced. Already protective towards her, he also sensed a definite possessiveness where her mother was concerned, and that perturbed him. Dominique was young and beautiful. Some day she would marry, and another man would assume the role of guardian and protector to her and her child. *And that was just as it should be.* Cristiano would be relegated to a far less important role in their lives and he would simply have to learn to accept it. His jaw tightened.

Glancing at Dominique now, as she stared out of the window at the clouds—just as he himself had been doing only a week ago on his way to meet her—he silently observed her classic, flawless profile and knew great pleasure in doing so. Matilde had fallen asleep on her lap, and the baby's head was snuggled into the groove of her arm. Together they made the most beguiling tableau.

'What do you see out there amongst the clouds?' he asked softly, leaning towards her.

Her dreamy blue-eyed gaze settled on his face in surprise. 'It's compelling, isn't it? It makes me wish I could fly...get away from everything troubling that's going on down there on the ground and escape up here into the silence and solitude. That would be amazing!'

A frisson of concern rippled through Cristiano. 'This world makes you wish to escape it?'

'Doesn't everybody feel like that from time to time? What's the matter? Have I said something wrong?'

'No. Of course not.' Determinedly releasing the tension that had gathered between his shoulderblades, Cristiano put aside the distressing notion concerning his cousin's death that sometimes plagued his mind and focused on the lovely face before him instead. 'It is just that I want you to know that you have everything to live for, Dominique. Life has been a challenge sometimes, yes…but now you are coming to Spain it will get much easier for you…trust me.'

'I do. I have to—or else I wouldn't have come, would I?' Her glance was brief but intense.

As she pulled her gaze away Cristiano almost wanted to command her to look back again. He touched her arm. 'You look tired,' he observed. 'Give me the little one and take a nap for a while.'

'Are you sure?'

'Of course.'

Carefully Dominique lifted the still sleeping Matilde into his arms and, feeling the slight but warm and pliable weight of the infant sag against him, Cristiano was again struck by how protective he felt towards the child. Settling back into his padded reclining seat with the baby held firmly against his chest, he sensed the kind of peace that he had not experienced in a very long while steal over him. And the truth was he found it almost too seductive for words…

The impressive edifice loomed up before Dominique like some intimidating Moorish citadel from the ancient past, and her blue eyes widened in surprise. When she'd thought about what Cristiano's home might be like she hadn't really known what to expect, and hadn't asked. But in her wildest dreams she would never have imagined something on the scale of grandeur and beauty she was seeing now!

Cristiano's driver—who had introduced himself at the airport as Valentín—smoothly drove the luxuriously upholstered black sedan up the twisting walled road that led straight to the entrance, and, craning to see out of the window, Dominique saw three women standing outside in the courtyard, in front of a huge double-fronted doorway. It was coming on to late afternoon, but the sun was still a banner of fierce brightness in the sky and she shielded her gaze with her hand from the stunning glare.

Sensing movement beside her, she turned as Cristiano's depthless sable eyes sought hers. 'We are here. And, as you can see, your eager reception committee is waiting.'

He smiled and there was something else in his glance besides satisfaction in reaching their journey's end that Dominique couldn't readily identify. Something that made her feel as though she was falling, with no glimpse of where or how she would land…

Her stomach turned hollow.

'Gaaa!' Wriggling in her baby seat, a now wide-eyed Matilde reached out to Cristiano with a gummy grin.

Catching the tiny plump hand that waved wildly in the air, he raised it to his lips and kissed it. 'The same to you, my little princess! Now, let us go and see who is waiting to meet you. May I?' he asked Dominique, and when she nodded agreement he carefully lifted the baby into his arms once more.

To tell the truth, Dominique was glad he had offered to take her daughter, because now it came to it she realised just how acutely anxious she really was about this meeting. Out on the gravelled courtyard the sun was still beating down with surprising force for December—and Dominique moved towards the little group that was waiting to greet them with Cristiano and Matilde just ahead of her, her heart galloping and her stomach turning uneasy cartwheels.

She prayed that any impending awkwardness that might surface would soon be behind her, so that she could at least try and relax a little, but her mind was racing with fear and doubt. *What if Ramón's mother believed that Dominique had somehow driven her son away? What if she blamed her or felt resentful that she lived while he had died?* She knew her wild speculation made no sense, but she couldn't seem to help herself.

In the group that was gathered there were two older women and one perhaps a little bit older than Dominique herself, and she saw that one of the older women was wearing black. For Ramón? she speculated. This, then, must be his mother. All the women were strikingly attractive, with the same midnight-dark hair as Cristiano, but in the two older women it was threaded with pure silver.

The woman dressed in black moved towards Cristiano and the baby with tears streaming freely down her face. Most of what followed speech-wise Dominique could not understand, not being familiar yet with the language, but she did hear 'Ramón' and *'la niña'* several times, and the emotion in the other woman's voice acted as a catalyst for her own. She swallowed hard to try and contain it, her heart full to overflowing as she watched the woman who must be Ramón's mother lift a curious-looking Matilde eagerly but lovingly into her arms. Then tears turned quickly to beaming smiles, and the baby was showered with kisses and more loving attention—not just from the woman who held her, but from the other two women as well.

Feeling somewhat redundant, yet strangely happy as she viewed the highly emotional scene, she glanced up in surprise as Cristiano stretched his hand out, indicating she should go to him.

'Dominique…' The pale, slender palm she slid into his was given a reassuring and firm squeeze that sent immediate goosebumps flying across the surface of her skin. 'Come and meet my family. This is my mother, Luisa.'

Warm eyes with the gloss of silky dark chocolate beamed back at her. Then, without further ado, she found herself being kissed soundly on both cheeks and pulled urgently against the other woman's ample bosom for a fierce, affectionate hug.

'Dominique!' she heard, in Luisa's halting, deeply accented voice. 'Words cannot describe what we are all feeling today. The baby—she is…she is so—so important to us, we cannot tell you! Cristiano… Please, my son, explain.'

'In my family,' he began, his dark gaze settling gravely on Dominique, 'my mother and Consuela are the only ones left. They have lost nearly everyone… parents, uncles, aunts…their husbands, of course. I am not married, and neither is my sister Elena. Therefore there were no grandchildren until Matilde. What my mother would like me to convey to you is that she is our hope for the future…and so she is very, very precious to us all.'

Dominique stared—first at Cristiano, then at Luisa, then at Ramón's mother, who was grinning from ear to ear as she jiggled a now laughing Matilde. *So much loss…* It was unbelievable. She was almost unbearably moved. For the first time since Cristiano had suggested it, she felt a sudden clear certainty that she had done absolutely the right thing in coming to Spain, and in that moment she knew she would stay. There was a lot of healing to be done here, and who knew? Perhaps her beloved child would help start the fragile process?

'Well…I'm very pleased to be here with Matilde, Luisa. Even though the circumstances are so sad.'

'You must call me Mamá,' Luisa instructed immediately, grabbing Dominique's hand and patting it. She glanced at her son, watching the proceedings with his usual quiet, dignified gravity. 'She is very beautiful, is she not, Cristiano?'

His pensive glance touched Dominique's for a long, disturbing second. '*Sí.* She is.'

'I am Elena.' The stunning younger brunette stepped away from Ramón's mother's side at that moment and gave her a quick, hard hug.

Her perfume was gorgeous, and no doubt expensive, but there was nothing stand-offish or superior in her manner, and for some reason, Dominique warmed to her right away.

'The baby is so lovely! We are all just so excited to have you with us in time for Christmas, and hopefully after that you will decide to settle here permanently! I am afraid that Consuela's English is not as good as my own, or my mother's, but she so wants to speak with you and I will be happy to translate.'

Addressing the woman who held the still smiling

Matilde so tenderly, Elena indicated she should come closer. Consuela stared deeply into Dominique's anxious gaze and spoke in a passionate, clearly emotional flood of Spanish.

'She says she is honoured to meet the mother of her son's child. She wants me to tell you that although her heart is broken because she has lost her beautiful son, she feels that she has been blessed by the Holy Virgin herself because you had his baby—even though he did not take care of you as he should have. Ramón was not a bad person…only troubled.'

Wary of the lump forming inside her throat, Dominique smiled and nodded to show Consuela that she appreciated what she said. She took a moment before she asked Elena to convey to her that there was no blame in her own heart for what Ramón had done, only a great sadness that he had not lived to see the beautiful daughter he had fathered.

All the while she was speaking, Dominique had been keenly aware of Cristiano listening intently to what was being said, and a big part of her wanted to go to him and lay her head on the broad, hard-muscled shoulder she was fighting so hard not to depend on. Reminding herself that she had to cultivate a distance from him emotionally—*not* get even more deeply involved that way—she leant forward and kissed Consuela affectionately on her cheek.

'Gracias,' she said softly. 'Thank you for inviting

me and Matilde to come and stay with you. I honestly was not looking forward to the two of us spending Christmas alone.'

As Elena translated, Cristiano moved closer.

'Let me take you and show you where you will be sleeping.' He put a hand beneath Dominique's elbow, and the expression on his bronzed handsome face was hard to decipher even as he bestowed a warm, tender smile on the other women. 'Consuela, why don't you take care of the little one while I show Dominique to her rooms?' he suggested.

CHAPTER SIX

THE house—if you could call it that—was like its own little kingdom.

Everywhere Dominique looked were soaring stone arches leading into door-lined corridors. But although it was certainly vast, somehow the family that lived there had cultivated a distinctly warm and welcoming ambience inside, instead of one that might so easily have been distant and intimidating because of its sheer dimensions.

There were homely touches everywhere. Family photographs in the most elegant frames sat atop classically designed furniture as well as on more native, unvarnished pieces. Vases of exotic blooms were plentiful, as were vivid and colourful tapestries adorning the thick earthen walls that were securely reinforced by tall brick pillars. Candles abounded, as well as a plethora of bookcases in different cosy alcoves, crammed with books of all kinds—and usually with a comfortable chair nearby, Dominique noticed, in which to sit and read undisturbed. Charmingly, every windowsill also housed a small, simply designed lamp of some kind.

But the thing that arrested her attention the most was the unique flavour of the country and its people that somehow permeated the atmosphere and wrapped itself round her enraptured senses as though casting a spell. Walking through that amazing building, with its mosaic-tiled floors, arabesque design work and compelling artefacts, Dominique had the sense that she was being somehow transported back through time. This might easily have been the palace of a sultan or an emir! An excited shiver ran down her spine. *It was strange...but now that she was here she didn't feel as alien as she'd thought she might.* In fact, she had the oddest sense of belonging that she couldn't explain.

Standing at the entrance to the most exquisite bedroom, after negotiating countless corridors and one grand sweeping staircase with Cristiano, Dominique likened herself to a shipwreck survivor who had somehow, by angelic intervention, been washed up on the shores of a beautiful island filled with every lush fruit known to man. As her brooding escort silently watched her, she was almost too overwhelmed for words by the sight that met her gaze.

The room she viewed was one of the two allocated to her, comprising a sitting room and bedroom, and was the most luxuriously appointed she'd ever contemplated staying in. Drawing the eye immediately was a very grand and magnificent four-poster bed, draped in gold and emerald-green brocade, and next to it was the most charming intricately carved wooden crib for Matilde. Dominique exclaimed her pleasure out loud when she set eyes on it. The little satin pillow and quilt inside looked hand-sewn, and were quite simply exquisite.

Sweeping her gaze round some more, she saw lush hangings made of silk on the walls, with embroidered scenes reflecting the fascinating mix of Arabic, Judaic and Christian legacies that Cristiano had informed her influenced this particular part of Spain. The antique chairs, occasional tables and clothes chests that furnished the rest of the room looked like the very finest. Her bedsit back in London resembled some Dickensian pauper's dwelling in comparison! *What must Cristiano have thought when he saw it?*

'This is just for me and Matilde?' she asked, hugging her arms over her chest in the thin petrol-blue sweater she wore with skinny black jeans. 'The pair of us could easily get lost in all this space after what we've been used to! What an amazing place you live in...I had no idea!'

'Ramón never talked about his home?' Cristiano's glance all but dissected her, it was so piercing.

Feeling a little uneasy, Dominique shrugged. 'Not really. He talked more about *you*, as a matter of fact.'

'Me?'

'He really looked up to you, you know? You were someone he admired and aspired to be like.'

Someone he'd admired and aspired to be like? Was he supposed to take heart from that, when since Ramón's death the thought had routinely niggled away at him that in the final analysis he had simply let his cousin down? *Just as he had let down his wife and child,* Cristiano reflected bitterly. He hadn't been able to save any of them. Even though he would have sacrificed everything—including his own life—so that they could live.

Frowning, he tried to push away the sense of hopelessness and futility that suddenly washed over him, but it was not easy. Finding himself staring at the slim but shapely young woman standing just a few feet away from him, with her tantalising silken rope of hair, dressed in the kind of plain and simple clothing that should not be remotely alluring at all yet somehow was, Cristiano almost swayed at the force of his desire to touch and hold her. It swept over him with all the power of something deeply primal.

Madre de Dios! What was happening to him? He was not supposed to feel this way about a girl he considered himself guardian and protector to! He knew right then that it would be extreme folly to give in to such an impossible and dangerous urge—that it would be like lighting the fuse to a most lethal explosive and the fall-out would be considerable. Everything inside him felt like a coiled spring, tightly bound, because he had to strive so hard to control his shocking impulse…

'My family were overjoyed to see the baby…just as I knew they would be,' he remarked, a slight catch in his voice.

There was an urgent need to change the subject to something lighter, to somehow tamp down this restless, potentially perilous desire that tormented him. It did not help his case to observe the huge four-poster bed, positioned only inches away from where Dominique stood.

'It is so good to see them smiling again.'

'They are incredible women! I did not realise they…and you…had lost so many of your loved ones. It's just so sad. If Matilde being here helps bring happiness into the house, then I am truly glad that I came.'

'Good.' His smile somewhat strained now, Cristiano moved towards the door that led back into the corridor. 'Why don't you familiarise yourself with your new surroundings for a little while, and I will go and arrange for your luggage to be brought up? Do not worry about Matilde…she has three doting women to take care of her now, and is perfectly safe.'

'Cristiano?'

'What is it?'

Suddenly she was there beside him, her peachy smell stirring the air and making his body tighten with almost shocking and violent demand as he glanced into the flawless blue mirror of her long-lashed gaze.

'Are you all right?'

'Of course. Why should I not be all right?' he answered tersely, confused that she should display such apparent concern towards him.

'It's just that I sense some tension in you. Won't you tell me what's the matter?'

She bit down on a temptingly plump lower lip that Cristiano would defy a *saint* not to want to taste and coloured deeply.

'You've been so good to me and Matilde during the past few days… If there's anything I can do to help you, you will tell me, won't you?'

To Cristiano's utter surprise, she reached out and laid her slender cool palm over his hand. Sensing what he was sure was simply meant to be comforting pressure, for a moment he was rocked to his very soul. The turmoil-inducing contact scorched along his nerve-endings like living flame.

'That is a dangerous offer, Dominique. And, trust me…it is one that you would be very wise to retract at this moment in time.'

His smile was almost bitter, as well as painfully rueful. Freeing his hand and opening the door, Cristiano stalked away from her without saying another word…

Joining them for a special homecoming meal which the women of the household—along with the housekeeper, María—had prepared for that evening was Marco, Elena's Italian boyfriend. They had recently become engaged, Elena had confided to Dominique earlier, her dark eyes glowing with excitement and pleasure. He was a slim-built and extremely handsome young man, and the couple seemed quite besotted with each other.

In fact, watching them from time to time as she hungrily tucked in to the delicious food that had been cooked in her and Matilde's honour, Dominique knew a pang of longing that wouldn't easily abate. *And it was worryingly heightened whenever she glanced Cristiano's way.* He was sitting at the head of the magnificent dining table to her left, and amid the magical glow of myriad softly flickering candles his dark eyes and sable hair glinted with the fierce sheen of polished jet.

Why had he reacted so bitterly to her offer of help earlier? His sudden unexpected coldness had hurt her. It might be wrong, and not very wise of her, but Dominique had started to see him as her friend…

someone she could trust above all. But now she indeed saw the danger of viewing such a powerful, charismatic man as him in such a way. When it came down to it he was as unpredictable and unknowable as he had been when Dominique had first met him. She was kidding herself if she dared to assume a closer bond than that.

Her stomach dived to her boots as she considered the thought that had been worrying her the most. *What if he was furious with her because he thought she'd been trying to come on to him in some way?* Reliving the scene when he'd made his terse remark, Dominique shockingly reflected on how her words might not have seemed quite innocent from Cristiano's point of view. Deeply perturbed, she reached out for the glass of ruby-red Rioja that was glimmering in the candlelight beside her plate, and almost knocked it over in her haste to lift it.

'Careful!'

Next to her, Cristiano's compelling rich voice throbbed out a warning.

Glancing up at him in alarm, Dominique grimaced. 'Sorry.'

'You do not have to apologise. You are enjoying your food?'

'It's wonderful! I'm loving it, actually… What did you say this casserole was called?'

'*Estofado de pescado.* This particular region is well known for its fish dishes.'

'Well, it's absolutely delicious!'

Across the long and magnificently laid table, Consuela caught her eye and bestowed an uninhibitedly warm smile on the younger woman. She had spent the rest of the afternoon and most of the early evening taking care of Matilde, and had even accompanied her to their bedroom to watch her settle the baby into the beautiful crib that Dominique was not surprised to learn was a family heirloom.

'Eat more!' she said, in her limited English, pushing another appetising dish in her direction. Then, turning towards her nephew, she addressed him in rapid Spanish, and it was obvious to Dominique that the conversation was about her.

'My aunt has heard that the food in England is terrible and is worried that you have been starving yourself because it is so bad!'

Cristiano grinned, and there was no strain about that sensual, rather beautiful mouth of his as he translated. Instead it was curved with genuine delight, and beneath its dazzling effect Dominique felt a little like a neglected plant that had been languishing in the shade too long and had suddenly been moved out into the sunlight.

'What?'

'She thinks that you need some more meat on

your bones, Dominique…and also that you need to be out in the sun more—because you are, in her opinion, far too pale!'

Knowing the older woman did not mean any insult, but was merely saying what she thought, Dominique sighed. 'Well, please tell Consuela that I have never starved myself in my life and never will! I certainly don't hold with all that rubbish the media push about skinny being best! And the food at home is not *that* bad! There's plenty of variety, at any rate, with all the different cultures that thrive there. As for being too pale…I'm sure the Spanish sun will soon change that—given time!'

Studying her intently for a moment, Cristiano translated what she'd said, and Consuela's concerned frown quickly turned into a pleased smile.

'Bueno!' She nodded and, reaching across the table, tightly squeezed Dominique's hand.

The other woman's care and attention was touching and, caught unawares, Dominique sensed the sting of tears prick the backs of her eyelids. *She had received more kindness in this household in one day than she had in years at home with her mother, and she almost didn't know how to handle it…*

'Tomorrow my aunt would like to take care of Matilde while I take you to lunch, and also show you some of the sights of our beautiful town. Does that plan meet with your approval?'

'Don't you have to get back to work?' Dominique asked Cristiano in surprise, blinking away the moisture that had helplessly surged into her eyes.

'I have made some phone calls and I do not need to be back in my office for another two days. Until then I will be here to help you settle in.'

'You don't have to do that. I'm sure you have more important things to do than play nursemaid to me and Matilde! I've already taken up too much of your time as it is.'

'What could be more important than bringing my aunt's grandchild home? And I would be very remiss in my duties indeed if I did not take proper care of you and your daughter while you are living under my roof!'

'I told you before,' Dominique retorted, dabbing her eyes with the corner of her linen napkin, suddenly feeling more vulnerable and exposed than she liked, 'I don't need anybody to take care of me!'

The truth was that something in her took great offence at the idea that Cristiano only viewed her as some kind of 'duty' he had to fulfil. His marked distance towards her since their arrival in Spain had left her longing for the return of the charming and attentive man who had walked through the park with them on a crisp winter's day, with his hand at her back, talking quietly about the many stunning vistas of Spain and the fragrant, sultry heat of his homeland that he was missing with a passion.

'Excuse me.' Politely inclining her head towards Consuela and Luisa, Dominique pushed back her chair and hurried out of the grand dining room, with its fabulous coffered ceiling and glowing candles, trying hard to get her bearings through her tears as she stood in a cavernous corridor illuminated only by the softest lamplight.

Footsteps from behind told her she had not been allowed to escape as easily as that.

'Everyone is concerned that you are not happy. What is wrong?'

Turning, she saw Cristiano walk slowly towards her, compelling and heart-stoppingly masculine, dressed in top-to-toe black, the lamplight making the carved contours of his face appear even more hauntingly arresting than usual.

'Today has been an emotional journey in more ways than one, that's all. And I'm very tired. I don't mean to offend anybody, but I'd like to go back to my room now and maybe have an early night. Will you please give your family my apologies?'

'That is not a problem. But I do not like to see you so upset.'

Before he could consider the wisdom of such a gesture, Cristiano raised his hand and touched his knuckles very gently to Dominique's tear-stained cheek. Her skin was very close to being as soft as Matilde's, and her blue eyes were so bewitching that he was in perilous danger of forgetting just why he had followed her out here in the first place.

'All I need is a good night's sleep and I'll be fine.'

'Will you, Dominique?'

His fingers slid down her cheek and under her chin. Lifting it a little, so that he had even better access to her beguiling gaze, Cristiano found himself studying her with an explosively insistent renewal of the desire he'd experienced earlier in her bedroom. His whole body was electrified by it.

'What do you—what do you mean?' Her soft voice fell to a bare whisper as she stared back at him.

Knowing he was locked in one of the fiercest battles for self-control that he'd ever experienced, still Cristiano could not help but lower his head towards the sweetly parted lips that tempted him so powerfully.

'I am not so sure a night's sleep would ease what troubles *me* right at this moment,' he said ruefully, his voice growing husky.

His mouth touched Dominique's long before he realised he had very definitely lost the battle he'd been engaged in—that in truth had been consuming him all evening…

CHAPTER SEVEN

DOMINIQUE was certain her bones were melting… As soon as Cristiano's lips had made their descent towards hers, her eyelids had closed of their own volition as she gave herself up to the sense of wonder and the most all-consuming excitement she could ever have imagined.

Divine, glorious, *essential*… These were the epithets that soared through her mind as she willingly surrendered to his kiss. Her hands held onto his lean waist, everything in her softening to welcome his opposing hardness, and she was shocked to discover what little resistance she had against this man.

The combustible contact probably only lasted just a few seconds, but in Dominique's mind it seemed to go on for ever…*perhaps because she willed it to?* In the end it was Cristiano who ended the kiss, not Dominique—even though she knew it probably should have been she who called a halt to the most devastating engagement of the senses that she'd ever had.

His dark, aroused glance reflected back to her the fact that he had been equally engaged and affected by the sensuality they had both just experienced.

'I probably should not have done that…but somehow I find that I cannot regret it. *Buenas noches,* Dominique. Sleep well.'

He turned around and strode back down the hall before Dominique even got the chance to reply, his heels hitting the ground in rhythmic staccato echoes.

Feeling even more disorientated than before, she glanced round almost dazedly at the terracotta walls with their glowing lamps, needing a moment to right herself again. She was finding it hard to believe what had just happened wasn't some astonishing dream she'd somehow conjured up because she was tired and emotional. She sighed softly and hugged herself tight…

'Tilly, Tilly! You are so silly!'

Blowing a loud raspberry on her daughter's perfectly plump little belly as the baby lay in the centre of the huge bed, arms and legs flailing in excitement and her sweet face wreathed in delighted dimples, Dominique sensed a wave of love so strong consuming her that it almost took her breath away.

Every day the bond between mother and child was growing ever more powerful, and the little girl meant the sun, moon and stars to her. Yet as she gazed lovingly down at Matilde, Dominique found herself wondering if her own mother had ever looked at *her* like that when she was so small and defenceless and had depended on her for everything. It was hard to imagine when all Dominique could recall was impatience and irritation.

Swallowing down the hurt this thought provoked, she asked herself what it was about her that was so *hard* to love. She'd always tried to do her best, to be helpful and thoughtful and not deliberately difficult. Yet even Ramón had not been able to love her…not even when he'd known she was carrying his baby. The fault surely *must* lie with her.

Her mind drifted cautiously to Cristiano's devastating kiss last night. Dominique had been trying to hold the intoxicating memory of it at bay from the moment she'd opened her eyes an hour ago and greeted the day, but now it filled her mind in glorious and vivid Technicolor, and something deep inside her ached hard with need. She was sure that in the cold light of day—despite what he had said last night—Cristiano *would* regret their passionate kiss. And now Dominique had to shore up her defences even more firmly against the growing attraction she felt towards him, and learn to keep her distance whenever she could. *She'd been hurt enough.* She did not want to be hurt so badly ever again…

'Come on, Tilly! There's a good girl. Let's put this lovely new dress on you, shall we? Your grandmother is looking after you this afternoon, and I think you should look your best for her, don't you?'

The knock on her sitting room door startled her. Glancing down at her pyjama-clad figure, Dominique reached for the robe at the end of the magnificent bed and quickly put it on. Thinking it might be her daughter's doting new grandmother, come to wish her grandchild good morning, she scooped the half-dressed baby up in her arms and hurried out to see if she was right.

But it was not Consuela Cordova who was waiting. It was her ebony-eyed, broad-shouldered and handsome nephew, dressed in crisp white shirt and jeans and looking unexpectedly and disturbingly more relaxed than Dominique had ever seen him.

'Buenos días!' He smiled, and his teeth were very white against his beautiful bronzed skin.

'Good morning,' she answered, a distinct husky catch in her voice.

'My mother and my aunt have already breakfasted, but I have been waiting for you and Matilde,' he explained.

Then, before Dominique could respond, he reached out his arms for the baby, who was busily chewing on her soggy drool-covered thumb as her mother held her.

Her daughter was completely at ease and smiling as she handed her over. Was there *any* female who wouldn't be similarly delighted to find Cristiano Cordova on her doorstep? Dominique wondered, a rogue shiver of pleasure rippling through her.

'*Buenos días* to you too, my beautiful little angel! Did you sleep well? Did you? We must have a little chat about all the sweet dreams you must have had!'

'You shouldn't have waited for us,' Dominique told him, flustered, as he swept past her into the room, murmuring baby talk to a clearly entranced Matilde.

'I wanted to.' Glancing away from the baby for a moment, fixing his attention on Dominique instead, he shrugged and then smiled again. 'Now, go and get yourself ready and I will wait here with Matilde.'

'I need to finish putting on her dress.'

'Give it to me and I will do it.'

His tone clearly brooked no argument, and with her legs stupidly trembling Dominique went and fetched the dress and brought it back to him.

'Now go! We will be perfectly all right here until you return—won't we, Matilde?'

There was something utterly sexy and compelling about a man who could be relied upon to take care of a baby, Dominique thought as she hurriedly showered and dressed. Then, guiltily catching herself, she remembered her vow not to get too emotionally attached to Cristiano unless she wanted to invite a whole mountain of trouble to come crashing down on her!

'Concentrate!' she exclaimed out loud.

Pushing her fingers irritably through her newly washed and dried hair, she quickly plaited it, then nervously surveyed the very spartan selection of clothing she'd brought that now hung in the huge antique wardrobe. Cristiano had said something about taking her to lunch. Dominique hoped it would be somewhere fairly casual rather than upmarket, because she didn't even *possess* an item of clothing that was what you could call dressy.

It occurred to her that she might be expected to wear something sombre, in deference to Ramón's death. The idea was too depressing to be contemplated—and surely Cristiano would have mentioned it if that were the case?

Telling herself not to get too hung up about clothes, she picked out a fairly demure knee-length dress with a colourful floral design and a band of blue ribbon that went around the ribcage, underneath her breasts. If the day were as warm as yesterday, then it would surely fit the bill? She could already feel the heat through the opened patio doors, and she paused to savour its sultry kiss as the evocative perfume of the new morning filled her senses. The house was on a hillside, not too far from a mountain range, and consequently the air was quite intoxicating.

'I'm ready. Sorry if I kept you waiting.'

Cristiano's heart slammed hard against his ribcage as Dominique walked back into the sitting room. He already knew she had a good figure, but in the pretty summer dress she was wearing he discovered it was actually quite sensational. Her legs were long and shapely, and thankfully not too thin. She had slender, elegant calves, and a tiny waist, and Cristiano realised that her shape was definitely more hourglass than straight up and down. Her dress showcased her attributes perfectly, and the scooped neckline of the bodice allowed a glimpse of cleavage that was simply...*arresting*.

Suddenly becoming aware that he had still not said anything but was just staring—like a schoolboy with a crush on his teacher—he pushed to his feet from the couch with Matilde in his arms, briefly inclining his head.

'Very nice. That is a very charming dress you are wearing, Dominique. It will not do a lot to help my blood pressure today, but still...I definitely appreciate it.'

He knew the look he gave Dominique to accompany his words was provocative, but Cristiano could not help himself. Waking up this morning with the memory of those sweet lips of hers pliant, warm and sexy beneath his, and now seeing her in that sultry little dress was doing nothing less than adding fuel to the fire that was already simmering inside him…

'If you think it's not suitable then I'll change into something else.'

'I did not say it was not suitable, and I do not want you to change. You have a beautiful figure, Dominique… You are young and lovely, and I do not expect you to dress like a nun!'

'Your mother and your aunt won't think I'm—' Frowning, she still seemed unconvinced about the dress. 'They won't think I'm being disrespectful? Wearing something so colourful, I mean?'

'Because Consuela is wearing the garb of mourning?' Slowly Cristiano shook his head. 'No. In years gone by it was customary for the widow or the mother of a man who had died to wear black for quite some time—even the rest of her life if she chose—but now it is up to the woman concerned, and clearly it does not apply to you, Dominique. Please…just relax. And now we should go down to breakfast. I am sure this little one is as hungry as I am!'

'She's had her bottle this morning, but I've also brought some baby cereal from home for her. I'll just go and get it.'

* * *

'I may have to hold your hand so that I do not lose you. It is very busy today because Christmas is so near.'

Before they went to lunch, Cristiano had decided to take Dominique to the gypsy market. The colourful stallholders sold their wares all over Spain, but in his opinion the market that was held in their own historic little town was one of the best. Smiling at Dominique as people bustled around them, eagerly examining the goods on sale—from clothing to jewellery, ceramics to shoes—he saw that his companion was completely transfixed by it all. *And holding her hand was not exactly something he found difficult,* Cristiano thought ironically.

Every time he glanced her way, and her clear blue eyes met his, he had to practically fight off the almost overpowering need to touch her. Not wanting to delve into the reason for this impulse too closely, he decided to simply enjoy the day and take the opportunity of seeing the places that were so familiar to him through Dominique's captivated eyes.

'I'll be all right,' she answered him, her gaze almost deliberately avoiding his. 'I'll make sure I stay close. Oh, look! They're selling Christmas trees!'

Gravitating to a large area where the most traditional Christmas decoration of all was displayed, in almost unbelievable abundance, Dominique stared wistfully at the trees for sale.

'Will *you* have a Christmas tree?' she asked.

'Of course. In fact I know that we have one being delivered to the house the day after tomorrow. Elena and my aunt usually decorate it together. They will also be putting out the *belén*—remember I told you about that?'

'The nativity scene? Yes…I remember.'

'And tomorrow night the Christmas lights will be turned on in all the towns and cities across the country. There will also be parades and processions, and the churches will be filled with people.'

'Do you think your family might let me join in when they decorate the tree?'

Dominique gazed at Cristiano with all the heartfelt yearning of a child long denied such a magical privilege, and he thought about the cold comfort her mother offered at Christmas and was disturbed by how angry he felt.

'We will all do it together,' he promised, his glance settling intently on her face and this time not allowing her to easily avoid it. 'Even Matilde must be included. I know my aunt will insist on it!'

'She seems to really love Tilly already.'

'She has loved her since the moment she learned of her existence! Her grandchild being here has made the world of difference to her. Instead of dreading the future, she now wants to live to a very old age so that she can see Matilde grow up to be a woman with a family of her own!'

'Thank you.'

'For what?' Cristiano's dark brows drew together in puzzlement.

'For bringing me to Spain and letting me be a part of all this…' Gesturing at the busy, colourful market around her, Dominique smiled, shy and tentative.

'You are most welcome.' He bowed his head towards her in a formal manner almost from a bygone age, and was silently delighted when her eyes widened to the size of dinner plates in response.

From time to time—inevitably, perhaps—Cristiano spied a face that he knew in the crowd, and immediately engaged in conversation. Inevitably too a curious gaze would go to Dominique, and he would have to introduce her.

Seeing how it made her uncomfortable to receive their condolences about Ramón, he made the decision to cut short their visit and leave for the hilltop restaurant where they were lunching instead. But as they prepared to leave the bustling market behind he spied the most exquisite sapphire-blue shawl on a stall displaying many beautiful silks and scarves—it was almost the same vivid hue as Dominique's eyes.

Steering the surprised young woman beside him towards it, he nodded at the plump grey-haired holder whose stall it was, and whose own generous shoulders were covered in a bright scarlet version. Gesturing towards the blue silk, Cristiano asked her how much it was and then bartered her down to a lesser, more reasonable figure, as was the custom. When the item had been wrapped and paid for, he drew Dominique to one side and gave it to her.

'It matches your eyes,' he told her, his voice lowering. 'And it will be perfect to wear later on, when the sun goes down and the evening gets cooler.'

As she accepted the gift he placed into her hands, he was touched to see her lips tremble ever so slightly as she received it.

'It's—it's too kind of you, and it's absolutely beautiful! Thank you, Cristiano.'

The way she said his name, in her reserved English accent, made his insides flood with warmth. He liked it. The trouble was he thought perhaps he liked it a little *too* much, and that immediately alerted him to the fact that he was not keeping his guard up against her charms as strictly as he should be.

Grimly, Cristiano made himself remember what had happened to Martina and their baby, and as ice flowed into his blood instead of heat he found his ardour for the pretty young woman beside him thankfully ebb…

CHAPTER EIGHT

AT THE restaurant they sat outside, like many other diners, enjoying the warmth of the sun and the stunning views of the mountains in the distance. Viewed from a stranger's perspective, Dominique was sure she blended in perfectly with everybody else…a tourist, perhaps, having a relaxing lunch with a handsome friend, husband…or *lover*… She flinched at that last too disturbing possibility. Yes, outside she might appear to be calm and at ease, but inside…inside she was in utter turmoil.

The gift of the stunning sapphire shawl from Cristiano had all but undone her. So had the comment he had made about her eyes. Coupled with his deeply stirring kiss last night, she barely knew what to do with the wildly impossible thoughts she was having.

'You are not eating.'

Glancing up, she tumbled headlong into the compelling velvet darkness of Cristiano's searching gaze. 'I'm just trying to take it all in…the beautiful day… that breathtaking view of the mountains…the fact that I'm here in Spain and Matilde has been reunited with a grandmother who loves her. I might have to pinch myself to check that I'm not dreaming!'

'So…you are happy?' A corner of his beautiful mouth quirked upwards into his smooth-shaven cheek. 'Happier at least than when you were in England on your own?'

'I won't pretend it wasn't tough. Being a single mother is hard enough, but to be honest I think there's a conspiracy of silence about raising children amongst those who have them! Because it's viewed as such an everyday event it's assumed it should be somehow easy, when actually it's probably one of the hardest things a human being could ever do!'

'But you do not regret having Matilde?'

'Never! How could I? She's the most wonderful thing that's ever happened to me! I'd die if anything happened to her!'

'Well…' Raising his wine glass to his lips, Cristiano's tanned brow creased thoughtfully. 'One day you will meet a good man, get married, and she will have the father she deserves.'

Why did his comment not cheer her in the way he obviously meant it to? Dominique reflected dolefully. Of course she didn't want to spend the rest of her life raising her daughter on her own, but after Ramón's desertion thinking about meeting someone else was the furthest thing from her mind. Yet when she was with Cristiano she sensed herself becoming more and more entranced by him. And seeing the way he was with his family—so caring and protective—and how he was so natural with a small infant like Matilde, didn't help her vow to keep her distance for fear of future hurt—but something told her it was already too late for that anyway…

'That will not be for a long time yet, I'm sure.' Laying her fork down beside her plate, she touched her napkin to her lips, inexplicably feeling her heart race.

'You are not the kind of woman who should be alone, Dominique.'

'What makes you say that? I've been managing all these years on my own, more or less!'

'But that does not mean you have to continue managing on your own.'

'Let's change the subject, shall we?' It was hard not to react defensively when Cristiano was touching upon the one issue that never made her feel very good. 'Relationships are unfortunately my Achilles' Heel, and that's just the way it is! No matter how hard I try, I'm just no good at them!'

'Be careful that doesn't become a self-fulfilling

prophecy,' Cristiano warned darkly, his expression without humour.

Why did Dominique get the curious feeling he was not just talking about her? What was his story? she mused silently. Why wasn't an amazing man like him married, with at least half a dozen kids to dote on? He was clearly devoted to family, and appeared to genuinely love children. *Yet there was something behind those fascinating eyes of his that Dominique had glimpsed once or twice that bothered her...something that suggested he had been badly wounded by someone too...*

'This is really very good,' she said, digging her fork into the fragrant rice dish in front of her, knowing she was deliberately trying to deflect further discussion about a topic that caused her more grief than any other. 'Though it's hard to concentrate on food with the fantastic view.'

'Yes,' Cristiano agreed, his steady gaze lingering long on Dominique's face. 'The view is...rather compelling...'

Later that evening Dominique found herself in the library. She had mentioned to Luisa that she had forgotten to bring a book to read, and the older woman had kindly brought her to this magnificent repository of books of all kinds—many, as she had proudly told Dominique, in English. Her husband had been a great reader, and so was Cristiano, and he often brought books back with him from his travels. After Luisa had left her to go and help prepare the evening meal, and while Matilde was under the protective wing of her grandmother in the sitting room, it was really pleasant for Dominique to have some time in which to relax on her own for a little while.

As she scanned the generously filled bookshelves, she was inadvertently distracted by a group of photographs that hung on the wall. Her interest piqued, she found herself gravitating there to inspect them more closely. But before she could do so the library door opened behind her, and the man she seemed to spend an ever-increasing amount of time trying not to think about entered the room. He was dressed casually but smartly, in another elegant white shirt teamed with black trousers tailored to perfection, and his dark hair looked glossily damp in the light that shone from the hall behind him. Dominique realised he must have recently showered for dinner.

Without saying anything, he shut the door behind him and slowly came into the room to join her. She sucked in a breath. When he was just inches away from her, he spoke. 'My mother told me I would find you in here. I do not mean to intrude upon your privacy, but I thought you might like some help navigating what we have. Tell me what kind of books you like and I will point you in the right direction.'

'Oh…I like all kinds of books. Biographies, novels, history… Do you have anything about the region where you live?'

Dominique's tongue briefly stole out to wet her suddenly dry lips. *Cristiano was standing way too close… She could barely remember her own name, let alone expound on what kind of books she liked reading when he stood so near!*

'*Sí.*' He shrugged those wide shoulders of his as though her answer amused him. 'Of course. We have *many* books on that subject. We have a fascinating history, as I am sure you can tell just by glancing at the architecture around you. But you surprise me, Dominique. I would have thought you were more in the mood for a novel of some kind. *A Christmas Carol,* perhaps, bearing in mind the season we are in?'

'Dickens is a wonderful writer, but honestly I don't think I have the concentration for a novel right now. My mind is all over the place!'

'Oh?' His gaze was seemingly transfixed on her lips, and Dominique froze. 'Why is that?'

'Wh-why?'

'I see that you are wearing the shawl I bought you,' he commented.

Disturbingly, he moved closer. So close that she

could see every minute detail of his arrestingly attractive face in sharp focus—from the coal-black sweep of his long lashes to the darker shadow of beard grazing his hard, lean jaw, with that Cordova dimple in the chin that Matilde had so charmingly inherited. She was startlingly aware too of the exotic tang of his aftershave which, combined with the seductive male heat he emanated, was putting her senses under extreme intoxicating duress. Dominique had no will to tear her gaze away for even a second.

'I was right. It perfectly matches the colour of your eyes.'

'It does? Well, I—'

She was stunned into silence when Cristiano placed his hands either side of her face, his hypnotic gaze holding hers with heart-pounding purpose, and Dominique knew what he intended long before the explosive touch of his lips on hers obliterated every coherent thought in her head.

This time it was no exploratory kiss—executed, perhaps, with the aim of helping her forget her worries for a while and relax… No. This was the full-blown, hungry kiss of a man caught in the grip of inflamed desire, and Dominique had never in her life been the recipient of such raw, passionate need.

His tongue thrust into her mouth with almost brutal command, and a heat started to burn inside her that made her shake and fear for her very sanity. Her hands reached out to steady herself against Cristiano, her fingers biting into the iron-hard flesh of his waist as her own escalating need suddenly outran any whispered caution in her head to stop this now and be sensible. It was simply heavenly to be wanted and desired this much, and Dominique started to kiss Cristiano back just as feverishly and wantonly as he was kissing her, her heart open wide and her senses more intensely alive than they'd ever been before.

Ramón had kissed her with the clumsily selfish needs of an over-eager boy, but Cristiano was without doubt kissing her like a *man*. And when his hand cupped her breast and he moved his thumb devastatingly back and forth across the rigid velvet tip beneath her thin summer dress, Dominique's hips felt as if they had melted right down to the bone. Her mouth slid away from his with a soft groan of pleasure as he ground his tight, lean hips against hers, the tender flesh of her cheekbone grazing against the harshness of his studded jaw. Impinging on her besieged senses was the shocking primal evidence of Cristiano's need, and Dominique's legs seemed to turn to liquid rubber that could not possibly sustain her upright position for long.

'I will lock the door,' Cristiano whispered against

her ear, brushing his mouth briefly but devastatingly across her tender lobe.

Before she could absorb the earth-shattering meaning of such a statement he left her to do just that. With the touch of a button he dimmed the lights too, and Dominique stared at him as he returned, wondering how a man as beautiful and perfect as he could possibly want an unconfident and ordinary girl like her, when he could probably have any stunning woman he wanted.

'Everyone is busy and will not miss us for a while,' he told her, and before she had an inkling of what he intended Cristiano slid his arm around her waist and lifted her bodily up into his arms.

Her heart was racing so fast inside her chest that Dominique seriously feared for her ability to remain conscious. Finding herself gently lowered onto a sumptuous red velvet chaise-longue that was positioned by the unlit fireplace, she stared wide-eyed and nervous up into the riveting handsome face that gazed down at her.

'I want to make love to you…I have been thinking about it all day,' he told her. 'In fact…the idea has been *consuming* me.'

Dominique reacted purely on instinct. Reaching up, she urged his face down towards hers. The time between kisses had been far too long, in her opinion, and she was unashamedly hungry for the taste of his lips again. He had a taste like no other man she'd ever known, and it was both intoxicating and addictive.

Her delightful blue shawl slid away from her shoulders, its delicate fringe brushing against the exposed flesh of her slender arms revealed by her dress. She heard the thud of Cristiano's shoes as they hit the floor, and a little throb of shock pulsed through her. Just before he touched his achingly seductive mouth to hers Dominique sensed the pleasure she'd been longing for about to sweep her away—as easily as some flimsy raft on a compelling sea. 'Please don't regret this…' she said softly. 'That's all I ask.'

For a moment his avid glance stole her soul. '*Nunca*… Never!'

His seductive reply was as fervent as Dominique had hoped it would be. Arms entwined around him, she felt Cristiano's muscular weight press her down deep into the velvet fabric of the couch beneath her. The hard, masculine warmth of his body seemed to seep into her marrow, making everything inside her tense so hard with need that she felt she might snap in two.

Shifting his position slightly, he started to touch her intimately with his hands and his mouth…exploring, kneading, tasting…and Dominique could not contain the uncontrollable tremors that were the result of his devastating sensual attention.

'You are so soft…so incredibly beautiful,' he whispered against her ear as his hands—which had been moving back and forth across her pelvis—finally moved lower, dragging up the hem of her dress and, with destroying purpose, cupping her through the flimsy cotton of her panties.

Even as Dominique felt her breath catch, Cristiano inserted his finger into the heat and moisture that drenched her there. Pushing her dress up further, he let his hot mouth fall upon her aching breasts contained by the simple white cotton bra, his lips and tongue giving them equal attention as his fingers worked their irresistible magic between her thighs. Dominique felt herself drowning in the erotic pleasure that consumed her like hot, licking flame ripping through a tinder-dry forest.

A harsh gasp left her throat and, captured by the sound, Cristiano diverted his attention from her breasts to her mouth, claiming it passionately as his fingers moved rhythmically faster and deeper inside her.

Learning intimately what the expression 'seeing stars' meant, Dominique bit down hard on her lip to try and contain her cry as she climaxed, shutting her eyes against a pleasure so wild and yet so profound that she couldn't help but release tears.

'Dominique? Look at me.'

Her eyes flew open again at the huskily voiced

request, and her already fast-beating heart galloped even more when she saw the expression of primal need and hunger etched into the striking contours of Cristiano's bronzed face.

'What is it?'

'You are crying… Is it because I caused you pain?'

His concern was such that Dominique's heart stalled. She hurried to reassure him.

'No. No—of course not! I just…' Hesitating over what she had been going to say—because she did not want to refer to Ramón and the intimacy she had shared with him, which had been nowhere *near* as satisfying—Dominique tried to explain her feelings another way. 'I was crying because what you—what you did gave me such pleasure, Cristiano! It made me feel a little emotional…that's all.'

'Do you know how much *more* pleasure I want to give you? I am almost in physical pain with the desire to be inside you!' Cristiano's voice was rough with need as he slid his hand behind Dominique's head and angled it towards him, his voracious glance devouring every inch of her startled face. 'But I realise this is not the place for me to join with you as I long to! Tonight…after everyone has retired and Matilde is fast asleep…I will come to you. Leave your door unlocked…*sí*?'

Should she come to her senses and say no? All Dominique knew was that she ached down to her very soul to have him possess her in the way he so candidly described, and to refuse him would be like denying herself vital oxygen to breathe. She wasn't about to do any such thing.

'All right,' she whispered, tenderly cupping his face.

He kissed her passionately then, as if to brand her with his taste and leave her with the tantalising promise of what lay ahead in the night to come…

CHAPTER NINE

THROUGHOUT the delicious meal that had been placed before him Cristiano merely toyed with the food on his plate. It was as if some strange exotic disease afflicted him, making him feel light-headed almost to the point of dizziness. His heart raced and his stomach clenched as if it was trapped in a vice. *And the symptoms were heightened whenever his gaze happened to alight on Dominique.*

Dominique…the bewitching young woman that his irresponsible cousin had got pregnant and abandoned without even the most basic financial assistance with which to raise his child. The woman Cristiano had sworn to protect and watch over until such time as some other man…her future husband… took on the responsibility. The woman he now lusted after as he had lusted after no other woman before… Even his *wife*, God rest her soul.

He could hardly believe what was happening to

him. Before he had pledged himself to Martina, Cristiano had enjoyed seducing women just as much as any other red-blooded male. But his need to be near Dominique—to know where she was when she wasn't in his sight, to hear her voice, to gaze at her and wonder what it would feel like to have that long unbound hair of hers trickle freely through his fingers, to have her unique scent saturate his senses—it was like some unstoppable force of nature that he scarce had any control over.

For the past two years he had steered clear of romantic entanglements like a driver taking an immediate detour whenever a potential traffic jam loomed on the horizon. Nothing could have prepared him for the powerful feelings running through his body and mind whenever he even *thought* about Dominique—let alone spent time with her. And this afternoon, when he had deliberately sought her out in the library, locked the door and engaged her in the most *intimate* way… Cristiano almost had to suppress a groan as he recalled the experience.

As though sensing his passionate discomfort, Dominique glanced across the table at him just then, and he saw the surge of colour that tinted her cheeks to a most delightful rose-pink. Dry-mouthed, he let his glance fall to the scooped neckline of the dress she was wearing, and the enticing shadow of cleavage it revealed. She had the most lush, perfect breasts...*breasts that Cristiano's mouth had become acquainted with only a few short hours ago.*

When he thought of the night that lay ahead he tried to quash any qualms that arose in his mind about the wisdom—or lack of it—of what he was anticipating by fiercely asserting that he would not be reckless. He would absolutely protect Dominique against another situation like the one that had manifested itself with Ramón. And he reassured himself that their being together the way he yearned for could not be wrong when she had made it so clear to him that it was what she desired too...

Dominique had lain in the bathtub for ages after Matilde had gone to sleep. She had scattered a handful of fragrant rose petals in the steamy hot water—a gift that had been left in a beautifully presented jar, along with many other expensive toiletries on the marble surround for her exclusive use. Lounging back in the gently lapping perfumed water, she felt as close to the legendary Cleopatra as a girl could get. She might not be bathing in asses' milk but this luxurious alternative was seriously hard to beat!

As soon as she started to relax, one subject asserted itself in Dominique's mind above all the rest. *Cristiano and his promised visit.* Even though the air was filled with steam, she sensed a shiver of delicious anticipation quiver through her. Their encounter this afternoon in the library had been beyond words, but it had left her hungry for more of his thrilling touch.

Her excitement was only dampened by one question… *Was she the biggest fool that ever lived where men were concerned?* Why didn't it seem to be an even halfway viable option to resist Cristiano's devastating attraction? *It was a dangerous game she was playing.* And she was the one who was going to get hurt—not him.

Her disquiet increased. He had already mentioned that he expected that she would meet someone else one day and get married. Surely the subtext of that assertion was that she would then be off his hands, leaving him free to enjoy the bachelor status Dominique guessed he guarded so jealously? And why wouldn't he, when he was rich, gorgeous and successful? Who could blame him if he wanted to play the field instead of settling down? All that was probably on the cards with him for Dominique was a brief, intense affair.

A frustrated sigh escaped her. *If only Cristiano hadn't been so persistent in trying to help her!* If only he hadn't acted so honourably on his cousin's behalf and brought her back to Spain, united her daughter with her grandmother and given Dominique the opportunity for a far better life than she'd ever known before! All these amazing things had worked their magic on her sensitive heartstrings more than anything else—even more than the sizzling attraction that now flared between them. And now her situation was as precarious as a novice trapeze artist balancing on a high wire…

By the time she'd vacated the sensually fragrant bath serious doubt had set in about the whole affair. And once she'd dried herself off, put on a short cotton nightdress and climbed into bed, Dominique told herself that when Cristiano showed up she would tell him she'd changed her mind about them being intimate. That she'd decided it was best if they just stayed friends rather than risk spoiling everything if they became lovers…

But midnight came and went, and there was no sign of the man whose visit she'd anticipated with such nervous excitement and trepidation. Hurt that he'd obviously come to the conclusion himself that their nocturnal assignation wasn't a good idea, Dominique switched off her bedside lamp and lay back in the darkness, feeling slightly ill. *Why hadn't he come?* Had he recognised somehow that she was too needy and been put off? God knew she had tried so hard to contain her emotions and feelings around him, tried to let him see only that her intention was to be independent and not depend upon *any* man again!

But then she had been so eager when he had kissed her, touched her. She had hardly pushed him away!

Oh, God...why couldn't she ever get it right? Turning her face dejectedly into the pillow, Dominique reluctantly closed her eyes. As profound disappointment and an inevitable sense of rejection washed over her, she prayed she would soon escape her distress in the dreamy avenues of sleep…

'*Buenos diás,* Dominique.'

Everything in her tightened at the sound of that arresting rich voice, but she did not glance round. In the large but homely kitchen, giving her daughter her breakfast, Dominique was halfway to Matilde's mouth with a spoonful of oatmeal when Cristiano finally put in an appearance. The other members of his family had long since eaten and gone out again, leaving her with some precious time to spend alone with Matilde. She wondered that Cristiano had the *nerve* to wish her good morning after so casually standing her up last night, but told herself that whatever happened she mustn't let him see how upset she was.

'Morning.' Dominique murmured the word beneath her breath, and was startled when Cristiano dropped down onto the bench opposite her at the long pine table, ruefully tunnelling his fingers through his midnight-black hair. There were dark smudges beneath his eyes, as if he had hardly slept, but she steeled herself against feeling the slightest bit of sympathy for him.

'I am sorry about last night,' he ground out, the huskiness in his voice making her spine tingle.

'Are you?' Scooping another spoonful of cereal from the cheerful yellow bowl in front of her, Dominique briskly popped it into Matilde's eagerly waiting mouth. 'I'm not. With hindsight I can see that it would have been the very *worst* of mistakes, and you not showing up has thankfully helped me come to my senses!'

'Please do not say that!'

When Cristiano would have reached for her hand, Dominique deliberately moved it out of his way.

'I *wanted* to come to you…more than you can even imagine!' he insisted. 'But I asked myself if I was being entirely fair to *you*, Dominique. You have already had cause to doubt the integrity of one Cordova…I did not want to put you in a similar position again. I did not want you to think that I was taking advantage of you simply because you are staying in my house and we have developed an attraction for one another.'

'Well…whatever your reasons, you did me a big favour, Cristiano! I'm obviously too damn trusting for my own good! This latest incident has only confirmed that. There's no need for you to give it another second's thought. Let's just put it behind us and carry on as normal until I leave to go back to England—okay?'

'*Como?* Since when did you decide that you *were* going back to England?'

Even as he asked the question, everything in Cristiano clamoured silently in violent protest. *Fear of risking his heart and his soul had kept him out of Dominique's bed last night, and this was the price he was to pay for it! Dios mío!* He had wrestled with the twin demons of fear and desire *all* night, and now he realised his decision not to go to her was going to drive her away. He could see by the hurt and confusion on her lovely face that she had taken his non-appearance as nothing less than pure rejection, and he could hardly blame her.

'Since I woke up this morning! Anyway…I told you I wasn't sure if I would stay on after Christmas. It doesn't mean I won't keep in touch with Consuela and the rest of the family. I'll come back for visits whenever I can.'

'No! That is not good enough!'

His fist came down on the table and rattled the crockery. Matilde's lips trembled and she stared at Cristiano in obvious trepidation. Seeing her sweet little face very close to tears, Cristiano was immediately contrite—though no less angry with Dominique for her disagreeable announcement.

'I am sorry, *mi ángel*...I did not mean to frighten you,' he murmured to the baby and, leaning towards her, tenderly stroked her cheek. Lifting his gaze to Dominique, he ruefully shook his head. 'Do not punish my family because you are mad at me,' he said gruffly. 'They want you to stay...*I* want you to stay!'

'Matilde needs a wash. Excuse me.'

Getting to her feet with the baby in her arms, Dominique barely glanced at Cristiano. Again he silently cursed himself for making her distance herself from him like this when secretly he craved anything *but* distance between them!

'Come back and have a cup of coffee with me?' he suggested lightly.

He could see by the look in her blue eyes that she was torn for a moment, and Cristiano felt hope flare in his heart. But then she wrenched her glance free and walked to the door.

'I have some Christmas cards to write,' she murmured. 'I'll see you later.'

Back in the library after dinner, still brooding over what had happened the previous night, and still hurt that Cristiano had not sought her out for a private conversation for the rest of the day since their encounter at breakfast, Dominique found herself once again drawn to the group of photographs she had been going to examine yesterday.

One large colour portrait dominated all the rest. It consisted of three men in a formal family pose. In the centre was an older man, with thick greying hair and rather kind dark eyes, and on either side of him stood Ramón and Cristiano. The picture must have been taken a good seven or eight years ago at least, Dominique reflected, because Ramón looked not much more than a boy. Her heart squeezed as a shaft of pain went through it. *It was hard to believe he was dead.*

But, despite her sorrow at a young life taken too soon, it was Cristiano's image that drew her gaze the most. It was almost a shock to see him apparently so relaxed and happy—happier than Dominique had ever seen him. And what caught her eye too was the glint of gold on what would be his wedding finger. Her stomach executed a dizzying somersault. What had happened to his wife? Why was she never mentioned by anyone? Were they divorced? Had she had left Cristiano for another man? Such a scenario seemed hardly conceivable!

Behind her the door creaked open, and with a frisson of surprise she saw the man she'd been contemplating in the photograph standing there in the flesh.

'I have been looking for you,' he told her.

'Have you?' Wary of letting her guard down

around him again, Dominique shrugged. 'And I thought you'd been avoiding me for most of the day!'

'Then you thought wrong.' He sighed. 'That was taken about seven years ago,' he commented as he walked towards her, his glance leaving her to settle on the photograph she'd been studying. 'The man in the centre is my father, José. I suppose you have been looking at Ramón?'

Drawing the vivid blue shawl that Cristiano had bought her at the gypsy market more securely about her shoulders, Dominique glanced up at him, and she was certain her heart missed a beat. The pain in his voice as he'd asked the question was palpable, and her sudden need to help ease it in some way was intense.

'Actually…I was looking at *you*,' she confessed, her blue eyes directly meeting his.

'Oh?'

'You look—you look so content… And I noticed that you're wearing a wedding ring?'

Before she'd spoken Cristiano had appeared as though he was going to smile at her, but the instant Dominique mentioned the wedding ring his face changed completely. The deeply contoured slashes that denoted his cheekbones were sucked in sharply, and the broad banks of his wide shoulders seemed to visibly tense in what appeared to Dominique to be a potentially explosive cocktail of pain and anger.

'That was another life. One that I do not particularly want to discuss in casual conversation!'

Stung, Dominique retaliated. 'Just because I mentioned the fact you were wearing a wedding ring doesn't mean that I treat the idea of your marriage remotely "casually", Cristiano! Anything *but*! Something told me when we first met that you had been badly hurt by someone. Until last night I thought that we—that we were becoming *close*… that you might trust me enough to confide in me. Don't you think it's absolutely normal that I might be interested in your past? It's not my intention to hurt you by bringing it up!'

'You do not have to intend hurt… Talking about that particular phase in my life inevitably *does* inflict pain, Dominique!'

Sensing the debilitating tightening in the area of his chest that always responded thus at the memory of his wife and baby, Cristiano fought to get past the waves of grief so that what he said would make some sense. Strangely, he suddenly realised that he did not feel as vehemently opposed to discussing what had happened as he usually did. *Was that because he did indeed feel that he could trust Dominique with knowledge of the most tragic event of his life and knew she would not abuse that trust?*

He had come in search of her because he could barely stand another second of being without her company, and he'd wanted the opportunity to try in some way to heal the rift that had come between them since this morning. Cristiano did not want to give the appearance of rejecting her again by refusing to be drawn about his past.

'Martina and I were married for three years. Just over two years ago she died, giving birth to our baby. Our child did not survive. The surgeons could not save either of them.' He had automatically crossed his arms over his chest, as if subconsciously protecting his heart, and he sensed Dominique's little sigh of shock feather softly over him. Cristiano grimaced. 'She knew she was taking a huge risk in becoming pregnant, given her history—but she kept the knowledge from me until it was too late.'

'Cristiano—I'm so sorry!'

Her lovely blue eyes were glassy with tears, and instead of dwelling on his own tragedy, Cristiano found himself wondering how *anyone* could thoughtlessly cause this incredible woman pain when she clearly had a heart wider than any ocean on the map?

Suddenly the need to have her in his arms became overwhelming, and he closed the gap between them in one stride, drawing her urgently against his chest. Before Dominique could utter a word Cristiano desperately sought her mouth, claiming a hard, hot kiss that he honestly wished could go on for ever. But at some point he did come up for air, and when he glanced down into Dominique's flushed, beautiful face, he registered the piercing need her features revealed with a bone-deep ache unlike any he had ever known before...

'Tonight,' he murmured, unable to deny her need any longer. 'Will you allow me to come to you?'

Equally unable to deny him, despite the heart-break of the night before, Dominique nodded her acceptance...

Her heart seemed to be breaking with sadness. She was dreaming of snow and Christmas trees, and her mother not loving her, and a tear slid from beneath her lashes and dampened her cheek. Something gentle brushed it away and a soft sigh escaped her.

The wonderful sensation of warm hands cupping her face made Dominique suddenly turn rigid as she realised this was no dream, and her eyelids flew open in shock. In the moonlight that filtered into the room through the partially opened drapes, Cristiano's dark eyes gleamed back at her, and his sensual lips curved into a smile that was as seductive as it was concerned.

'You were crying.' His rich velvet voice was pitched deliberately low in deference to the baby sleeping peacefully in her crib.

'A bad dream...' Husky with sleep, Dominique's

reply was barely above a whisper, but to her own hypersensitive hearing her heart beat loud enough to awaken the whole household.

'Will you let me help chase the bad dream away?'

'I thought you'd changed your mind again…that you weren't going to come…'

'I am sorry about that, *mi ángel*.' His rueful sigh feathered over her. 'Consuela knocked on my door and wanted to talk. She is overwhelmed by the knowledge that her grandchild is here with her at last, and was feeling somewhat emotional. Naturally she wanted to discuss Ramón too. I did not want to hurry her away.'

'Of course not!'

'But at the same time I could barely contain my frustration at not being with you! I want you so much!'

Thrilled to hear him say it, Dominique was about to tell Cristiano she felt the same—but found her declaration shockingly silenced by the hungry press of his warm, tantalising lips against hers. At the first inflammable touch of that erotic satin mouth heat poured through her body like liquid fire. Actual tremors rippled through her.

It was as she feverishly pushed the satin quilt aside to let Cristiano join her that Dominique realised he was naked to the waist and that the only clothing he wore was a pair of silk mulberry-coloured boxer shorts. As far as male bodies went, his definitely had the 'wow' factor—in spades. She saw for herself the strongly delineated collarbone and the wide, powerful shoulders above a hard-muscled bronzed torso and stomach where not a single ounce of spare flesh found a home. No wonder his clothes looked so good on him!

Helplessly transfixed, Dominique noticed too the erotic coating of silky dark hair dusting his nipples, and as her feverish gaze dared lower, past taut, lean hips, she saw the way another fine smattering led a provocative trail into the waistband of his boxers.

But there was little time for her appreciative perusal of his mouthwatering masculinity when, with a harsh groan of need, Cristiano suddenly took command of her mouth like a man presented with his first proper meal after being released from solitary confinement. He devoured her as if he would never get enough, and *never* be satisfied… And with his ravishing velvet tongue he introduced Dominique to a wild eroticism she hadn't even known existed until then. There wasn't a corner or crevice of her mouth that he didn't plunder with destroying command and brand with his addictive masculine flavours.

Lying beneath Cristiano's hard, lean and muscular body, she felt like butter left out in the sun, inexorably melting.

All of a sudden he levered himself away from her

and sat back on his haunches. 'What are you doing?' she asked, her mouth going dry at the thought that he had changed his mind and was going to leave.

'I want to look at you,' he replied, and ran his gaze hotly over the feminine curves that she knew were easily revealed by the thin cotton fabric of her nightdress.

She'd put on a little weight since having Matilde, but she knew it suited her...made her more *womanly*, somehow. Dominique scarcely took a breath as Cristiano hooked his thumbs under the flimsy shoestring straps and skimmed them hungrily down over her breasts. Exposure to the air hardened her aching, tingling nipples almost to the point of pain, and she was so turned on by the ravenous glance he gave her that she could swear she was suddenly on fire with a fever. Her thighs trembled and her nipples puckered tighter still, as though he had drawn ice cubes across them. Everything in her was almost unbearably sensitive to every glance, every touch, and she wanted him so much she almost cried.

'Undo your hair for me,' he commanded, his voice sounding as if it rolled over gravel.

With shaking fingers, Dominique slipped off the band from the end of her plait and with long practice deftly released the entwined silken skeins of honeyed brown so that they spilled across her shoulders like a river of tarnished gold. Catching her hair in his hand, Cristiano turned it over again and again to examine it, as though he could not quite believe what he was seeing. Then he raised his glance to meet hers, and in that moment Dominique truly felt as though she was the most beautiful and desired woman on earth—because his dark smouldering gaze told her that she *was*.

Bending his head, he touched his lips to every exposed inch of flesh on her body, then employed his fingers to seductively caress the place where Dominique longed for him the most. Just before he took her to the very cliff-edge of her resistance he peeled off his boxers and used the protection he had brought to sheath himself.

Clinging on to the hard bunched muscles at the tops of his arms as Cristiano inched inside her, Dominique realised her own muscles were almost rigid with tension at the idea of accepting his full, impressive length into her body. She feverishly wondered if her post-baby condition would give him enough of the pleasure she wished for him.

Sensing her anxiety, he went still for a moment as he regarded her. 'Try to relax, *mi ángel*...I realise it has probably been a long time, and that you might be sensitive, but if you relax it will be easier...*sí?*'

Hearing the genuine concern in his voice, Dominique sighed and stroked her hand down over his chest, the tips of her fingers lingering for a moment on one of his hard, flat nipples.

'I'm only afraid I won't be able to—that because of the baby I might not be so—'

Even now, in the most *intimately* vulnerable situation she could find herself in, she still managed to blush. Leaning forward, Cristiano touched her face, his dark gaze brooding and possessive.

'Everything about you is already giving me the most unbelievable satisfaction and pleasure, *mi ángel*... Nothing about your incredible body could possibly disappoint me. Now, let me return the compliment...'

His hard-trained muscles quivering with the effort of not letting his desire overcome him, Cristiano finally thrust inside Dominique to the hilt, and sensed her hot, silky muscles enfold him like the most exquisite tight glove. His heart all but unravelled at how good it felt being with her like this, and his doubts—for now at least—were jettisoned firmly away.

Tussling with his conscience all evening—even *after* his revelation about Martina to Dominique in the library—he had been plagued by many guilt-ridden thoughts. Thoughts that he would be 'betraying' his cousin's memory or letting his family down in some way should he be with Dominique the way he longed to. But most of all Cristiano had worried that by succumbing to the physical attraction that flared so hotly between them Dominique might ultimately believe he was just *using* her. After all… what could he offer her but uncertainty? What had happened to Martina and their baby had scarred him irreversibly, and he was hardly in a position to promise Dominique anything relationship-wise.

However, in the end, *wild horses could not have kept him away from her.* His desire for her was simply beyond all reason.

Dominique moaned low, her incredible blue eyes glazed with uninhibited sensuality as Cristiano drove himself into her again and again with increasing need and passion—certain he could not hold out against this almost unbearable barrage of the senses for much longer without reaching the destination his whole body was primed for. Sensing the sudden rapid constriction of the soft velvet enclave that held him, Cristiano saw Dominique squeeze her eyes shut tight, and passionately he went deeper as she climaxed, causing her to clutch his hips tight and release his name in one of the sexiest-sounding sighs he had ever heard.

Unable to hold back any longer, his will-power and desire finally sent him hurtling upwards into a vortex of pleasure so profound that Cristiano sensed himself unravelling as though he might never stop. The sensation was like the most heart-pounding ride through dizzying white water rapids that he could ever imagine.

'Madre mia!'

'Are you all right?'

The ravishing girl in his arms was looking slightly concerned, and Cristiano smiled at her wryly, thinking whimsically that she resembled a beautiful fairy princess from tales of myth and legend with her long rippling hair and bewitching eyes. *She had certainly woven a spell around him...* There could not be many men alive who would resist such shimmering and innocent beauty given the chance, Cristiano speculated.

'All right?' he answered, his glance gently mocking. 'Do you know how you have made me feel? *Estupendo!* Wonderful! Like I could climb a mountain or walk the Great Wall of China non-stop without rest! You have made me a slave to your beautiful sexy body, Dominique, an addict for the taste of your sweet honeyed lips... And most of all...' He sensed the catch in his throat as he coiled some of her dazzling hair round his fingers. 'You have made me hungry for more!'

I think I'm in love. Regarding the gorgeous sable-haired Spaniard who had just made love to her with all the passion and wild beauty that her wounded heart could ever have hoped for, Dominique had the stunning revelation that that same heart was even more vulnerable than she'd feared. Because it was too late now for regrets, or to rein in her emotions where Cristiano was concerned—even if he expected her to. And how was she supposed to stay here in his house, with his family, knowing that her love for him would probably never be reciprocated? That his heart belonged for ever to his wife and baby who had died so tragically?

Anguished, she knew she had probably landed herself in the deepest hot water that she had ever been in—and that *included* becoming an unmarried mother. She'd thought she had found a safe haven at last from all the past hurt that had wounded her, and the thought that she might have to leave that haven practically as soon as she'd arrived made her feel sick to her stomach.

All she could do was leave the outcome to a greater force than her own mere will. Learning to trust again was not something that came easily after what she had been through, but why not give it a try for once? she thought.

As the moonlight beaming in from the open window touched Cristiano's head and shoulders with an almost ethereal glow—and with Christmas just around the corner—she asked herself if there had ever been a better time in which to make a heartfelt request of the Divine?

CHAPTER TEN

THE sensation of a silky hirsute leg rubbing up and down one of her own bare legs beneath the bedclothes caused Dominique's eyes to ping open in heart-racing shock. Caught between the land of sleep and wakefulness, for a moment she forgot where she was.

As the beautiful bedroom with all its fine antiques and luxurious furnishings came into view in the softly smudged morning light—instead of the shabby bedsit she'd grown used to—reality hit with a vengeance. And—more importantly—the reality of just *whose* leg was rubbing up and down against hers.

Turning her head, Dominique came face to face with a pair of smouldering dark eyes that would warm up a statue on a freezing winter's night. And right now, with the look Cristiano was giving her, Dominique was anything *but* an inanimate block of stone…

'Buenos diás.' He smiled, placing a deliberately sexy little kiss on her startled mouth.

'I thought—'

'What did you think?' He cupped her face and his leg inserted itself silkily between her thighs.

The melting sensation that made her feel like marshmallow was stealing through her body again, and Dominique struggled to give her thoughts voice. 'I thought—I didn't expect to find you still here,' she admitted, and there was a husky cadence to the words that finally emerged.

'Did you want me to leave?' he asked, tanned brow furrowing.

'No… It's just that…' Struggling to contain her embarrassment, Dominique sighed. 'I thought you might not want anyone else to know… That we were together, I mean.'

'Why would you think that? Do you imagine I am ashamed of being with you?'

'No… But—what will your family think when they find out, Cristiano? What if they think that I deliberately—?'

'Seduced me?' he interjected, his dark brows wriggling comically like a pantomime villain.

Despite her anxiety, Dominique couldn't help but smile. 'I just want them to know that I'm not some manipulative little gold-digger. I would die if I thought they believed that for even a second!'

'If you *were* a gold-digger, do you think you would even be here right now? Do you not think I would have recognised that right from the start? You did not even want to *talk* to me when I first came to your flat! Much less try and get money from me!'

'As long as your family know I am only here because of Matilde…because I don't want her to miss out on having a family who really love her.'

'I do not even have to tell them that… They can already see for themselves the kind of woman you are, Dominique.'

'And they do know that I didn't deliberately get pregnant to try and trap Ramón? It was an accident, you see. He—'

'I do not want to talk about Ramón!'

The anger in Cristiano's voice as well as the tension that rolled off his body, made Dominique recoil for a moment.

'I am only too aware of how my reckless cousin could behave. You do not have to draw me a picture! I am sorry if it hurts you to hear it, but it is a wonder he did not father many more children out of wedlock than just Matilde! Deep in her heart Consuela knows it too.'

'It doesn't hurt me.' Her slender shoulders lifted and fell in a weary shrug. 'Not any more. Please don't be angry because I brought up the subject. I just want things to be out in the open…for there to be no doubt I'm here for all the right reasons. I was just afraid of what Consuela and the others would think if they found out we had slept together. You must understand my fears?'

Driving his hand through his already tousled black hair, Cristiano looked thoughtful for a moment. 'No one is going to think any less of you, Dominique. You will have to trust me on that. In fact, I know they will be glad that I have such a close bond with you. There is nothing to worry about. Truly. Now, come here… Have I not said that I will protect you and take care of you?'

He dropped another lingering kiss on her softly parted lips, as if to seal his assertion, and a sigh of pleasure helplessly left her. But at the back of Dominique's mind she wondered exactly what Cristiano meant by vowing to protect and take care of her. After making passionate love to her for most of the night, did he still view her welfare as something he was interested in merely out of a sense of duty and honour, because his cousin had made her pregnant and her child was a Cordova?

Even though his arm was lying possessively across her middle, Dominique moved to push up into a sitting position. *If the truth were known, Cristiano was probably just as commitment-shy as his cousin.* Doubly so because of what had happened to his wife… Her stomach turned over in dismay. Her wish that there might be a chance for them to enjoy a proper relationship was probably just a foolish pipedream, and one she should quickly put aside unless she wanted to make herself thoroughly miserable. It was nearly Christmas, and she at least wanted the opportunity to try and enjoy the season in this magical place before she had to face any more heartbreaking reality.

'What are you doing?'

'I need to put the bottle warmer on for Matilde's feed.' She glanced down at the wristwatch she wore out of habit most nights. 'She'll be waking up soon.'

Grasping the swathe of silken hair that spilled down over her breasts, Dominique started to swiftly plait it. At the same time, she glanced over to where her baby lay in peaceful slumber.

Cristiano slid his arm coaxingly round her waist. 'She is not awake yet. There is still time to wish each other good morning properly…*sí*?'

His warm lips found the spot between Dominique's shoulder and neck and his teeth nipped gently. Her treacherous body responded immediately, her breasts growing heavy and her nipples stinging with avaricious need to feel his hands and mouth there. But, as delicious as Cristiano's seductive touch was, she knew she was going to have to distance herself a little today out of sheer self-preservation. *Making love with him had left Dominique much more vulnerable to being hurt by him than before, when their relationship had been purely platonic…* He had rocked her world to its innermost core, and the repercussions were already making themselves felt.

'I'm a little…tender,' she told him. It was no contrived excuse. Her lover had been mindful of her welfare, but at times passion had dictated he was not always as gentle as he might have been.

'I am sorry if I hurt you, *mi ángel…* Forgive me.' Cristiano's glance was rueful. 'Next time I will try not to be so demanding. But I cannot minimise the passionate effect your beautiful body has on me, Dominique… Not when every touch makes me burn for more and robs me of the desire and will to even get out of your bed today!'

Thrilling at hearing him say there would be a *next time*, Dominique stored away the little bubble of joy that burst inside her and scooted to the edge of the bed.

'I'll go and sort out the bottle warmer, then get a quick shower before Tilly wakes.'

'Very well.' Behind her, Cristiano lay back on the pillows with his arms over his head, deliberately—or so it seemed to Dominique's hungry eyes—*not* pulling up the sheet to cover his awesome bare chest, as if to show her what she was missing. 'If you *must* desert me I will lie here until my other favourite girl awakes!'

* * *

Everyone seemed in particularly high spirits that morning, and Cristiano was no exception. Being with Dominique and Matilde—or Tilly, as her mother so affectionately called her—affected him profoundly. Apart from arousing his deepest male instincts to take care of them both, just being in their presence lifted him out of the dour and humourless mood that for too long a time since Martina's death had been an unhappily frequent visitor.

Now, as he instructed the crew that were so carefully carrying the huge Christmas tree into the family living room as to where the tree should be placed, he found himself anticipating Dominique's childlike awe when she saw it with mounting pleasure. And when he was alone again after the men had gone, and his mother, aunt, sister and Dominique were all in the kitchen, helping to prepare food for the family's special 'arrival of the tree' lunch, Cristiano allowed himself a few moments of quiet reflection about what had occurred the previous night.

In Dominique's arms he had not just found the physical satisfaction his body craved, he had also found a woman who—although she had been badly betrayed—had not closed the door on being with a man again, and had given him a tantalising glimpse of what it could be like if Cristiano were to commit to her on a permanent basis. His nights would be filled with the most intensely passionate loving, he didn't doubt. And his days—his days would be filled with thoughts of going home to her loving arms whenever he was away from her, and when he was with her he would not want for anything but her and sweet Matilde.

The idea was temptation personified... Yet even as he considered it Cristiano knew a most terrible dark fear as well—the fear of losing Dominique and Matilde as he had lost Martina and their baby, and also Ramón, another family member he had vowed to watch out for and protect. *What if he failed Dominique and her child as he had failed them?* It did not bear contemplating. Cristiano knew he would be drained of everything if that happened. Every positive, hopeful aspect to his life would be gone. He had already been down one of the darkest roads of life, and he did not want to go down one as soul-destroying again. For the sake of his sanity he could not risk it. He simply could not...

'Your mother told me I could come and take a peek.'

The woman Cristiano had been contemplating with such passionate fervour arrived in the room with her baby in her arms, and the vivid blue eyes that could rarely conceal her feelings were already alight with wonder at the sight of the magnificent Christmas tree.

'Oh, Cristiano! It's so beautiful—and the smell

of pine is just divine! But it's so high! How on earth are we going to put the fairy or the star on the top?'

His arm automatically sliding round her slender waist, Cristiano grinned, planted a loud kiss on the baby's downy cheek and then did the same to her wide-eyed mother. 'Some poor idiot will no doubt have to risk a broken neck to climb up a ladder and place it there—that is how!'

'Oh!'

'You may well say oh, *señorita*!'

Unable to resist her adorable expression, Cristiano kissed Dominique again—only this time his mouth moved over her lips instead of her cheek and lingered there. They had the completely ravishing taste of vanilla and honey combined, and he passionately wished that he could take her back to bed and stay there for the rest of the day.

'Cristiano?'

'Hmm?'

'I have a favour to ask…'

'Of course.'

At that moment Cristiano would gladly have given this woman the world if he could. Glimpsing both hope and excitement in her otherwise serious expression, he felt a flare of warmth fill his belly.

'I need to buy some gifts…for your family. Would you be able to take me somewhere so that I could do some Christmas shopping?'

He was about to easily agree when he remembered something.

'Elena is going into town this morning…she mentioned it to me earlier. And we are having a late lunch today, as opposed to an early one, so there is plenty of time. You should go with her. She would be glad to take you, and it would be nice for you to spend some time together on your own. Matilde can stay here with me. Here…let me take her.'

Having no qualms whatsoever about taking care of the infant he was becoming more and more attached to as the days went by, Cristiano put out his arms for the smiling baby. When Dominique released her, Matilde babbled away at him as though certain he understood her perfectly. After positioning her small body safely against his chest, he reached down into his back pocket for his wallet.

'You will need some money,' he said, taking out several notes and holding them out to Dominique.

'No, I won't!' She looked aghast. 'At least, not yours! I do have some money of my own, you know! Do you think I would seriously contemplate buying your family presents with money *you* gave me?'

Knowing she had her principles about things—one of them apparently being to take as *little* as possible from Cristiano—he slowly and reluctantly returned the notes to his wallet and placed it back in his pocket. But, again, he needed to let her know that it was her *right* to be supported and helped by him.

'I did not mean to offend you, *querida*...I merely wanted you to have what you needed without worry. Tomorrow, when I return to my office, I want you to come and meet me for lunch. Elena will bring you. When you are there I will take you over to the bank and set up an account for you to use straight away. I will also get you to sign some legal documents which will give you access to Ramón's money and assets, which—as I explained before—you and Matilde are now entitled to.'

She flushed at that, and Cristiano sensed the mental tussle going on behind those clear blue eyes about accepting something she perhaps believed she did not deserve. He personally knew plenty of people—especially in his line of work—who were definitely *not* possessed of such admirable humility when it came to taking what they believed was due to them. *They could learn a lot from Dominique, he was certain...* Frankly, it still astonished him that she expected so little from her baby's father's family.

'Are you sure you'll be all right with Matilde?' Capturing the end of her plait and staring down at it for a moment, she obviously thought the whole situation was too awkward to comment on further. 'I've left her bottle in the kitchen with Consuela, and there's also a bag with all her baby stuff in. Everything you'll need is there.'

'We will be absolutely fine…won't we, *pequeña?*' Gently he drew the pad of his thumb across the deep little cleft in the infant's chin and grinned with delight when she grabbed his thumb and tried to chew it. 'Just go and enjoy your Christmas shopping, and I will look forward to seeing you at lunch.'

'All right…and thank you.'

'You are most welcome.' His gaze met and held Dominique's with sudden unguarded longing and, seeing by her rapt expression that she felt the same exquisite demand in her body too, he willed her to go find his sister before he dispensed with common sense entirely and persuaded, even *begged* her to come back to bed with him instead…

'It is very sweet of you to want to buy my family gifts for Christmas, but they really do not expect it, you know!' Stirring her coffee, Elena studied Dominique with a concerned frown as she sat across the table from her in the small busy café.

Glancing down at the two shiny carrier bags at her feet, Dominique sighed contentedly. She had taken enormous pleasure in spending the small amount of cash she had kept by for just this purpose, and would not be denied the satisfaction it gave her. The Spanish town was littered with the most individual and interesting little shops, selling everything from ceramics and lace to wood carvings and swords. The art of sword-making had not died out with their Moorish ancestors, Elena had told her. It still thrived today.

Browsing alone for a while, when Elena had left her to do some shopping of her own, Dominique had loved the sense of freedom and excitement it gave her. For once she was anticipating Christmas with something close to joy. Apart from being with Cristiano, she would also be spending it with people who genuinely desired her and her baby's company and cared about their welfare. The small, inexpensive items she'd bought would not bowl anyone over, but it was the thought that counted, and Dominique had wanted some way of saying thank you for the hospitality and total loving acceptance that had been accorded her and Matilde since their arrival.

'It's just my way of thanking all of you for welcoming me and my daughter into your home.'

'You were Ramón's girlfriend and Matilde is his child… You are family whether you wish to be or not!' Elena's dark eyes twinkled. 'And I am also very happy to see that you and my brother are getting along so well too. It has been quite some time since I have seen his eyes light up the way they do when *you* walk into the room, Dominique!'

Feeling her face grow hot beneath the other

woman's teasing and if she was honest surprising observation, Dominique stared.

'It doesn't bother you?'

Elena's smile ebbed away and her expression became more serious. 'Why should it bother me that my brother appears to have found something to make him smile again after so long of being so unhappy it would break your heart?'

'He told me about what happened to his wife and baby.' Lowering her gaze for a moment, Dominique hoped she had not transgressed some unspoken family code by mentioning it. But Elena did not look put out in any way.

'The loss utterly devastated my brother,' she confided. 'And since losing our father he has felt much responsibility for everyone…*too* much. When Martina and the baby died he somehow believed he could have done something to prevent it. I told him, "You are not God! You do not have the power to say whether someone should live or die!" These things happen, and it is terrible for those who are left behind, but perhaps it was Martina's time…you know what I mean? Perhaps it was Ramón's time too. Who knows?'

Shrugging her shoulders in her navy linen dress, Elena sighed, and the deep sadness in her demeanour was palpable. Inside, Dominique's mind and heart were under serious siege at what she had just heard. It was heartbreaking enough that Cristiano had lost his wife and baby in such a shocking way, but to be living with such guilt for what had happened was almost *more* heart-rending.

No wonder he had seemed initially so reluctant to discuss his marriage when Dominique had been studying the photo in the library and had seen him wearing a wedding ring! He had received a great emotional wound and was obviously still in the process of trying to heal. How that healing must be hampered by the idea that he could somehow have prevented his wife's death—and Ramón's death, as Elena had mentioned? How would his poor heart ever heal if he thought their deaths were due to some imagined fault or lapse in his vigilance? What a terrible burden for *anyone* to be carrying round!

'I can't believe what you've just told me, Elena.' Dominique reached out her hand for the other woman's and held it for a few moments in silent solidarity. 'Your brother is a wonderful man, and he doesn't deserve for the rest of his life to be so unhappy because he feels responsible for the people he loved who have died!'

'We have tried telling him that so many times but he does not listen!' Shaking her head a little forlornly, suddenly Elena looked straight at Dominique. 'Perhaps…because it is clear that you and little

Matilde have won a special place in his heart… perhaps he will listen to *you*, Dominique? Do you think you could try talking to him about this?'

CHAPTER ELEVEN

She had never seen such a lovingly decorated and beautiful Christmas tree before. Dominique was certain. Standing in front of it that evening with Matilde, the sparkling lights and glittering baubles shiningly reflected in her baby daughter's eyes, Dominique shook her head in silent awe.

The rest of the family had dispersed after a happy and companionable couple of hours dressing the tree, and she welcomed these few minutes on her own to simply just stand and admire it with Matilde. All those difficult and emotionally sterile Christmases she'd spent with her mother faded away in the light of Dominique's feelings now. *Perhaps it was time to forgive and forget?* If there was ever a time to extend forgiveness then this was probably the season in which to do it. She would write her mother a letter…or, better still, phone her. Life was definitely improving, she would tell her, and perhaps she would be pleased? With some distance between them, maybe some of the tension that was normally prevalent in their relationship would have eased a little?

'You look deep in thought.'

Startled by that compelling deep voice—she hadn't even heard him enter the room—Dominique let her gaze fall into Cristiano's. As was becoming a habit whenever she saw him, her heart seemed to skip a beat.

'I was just enjoying a quiet few moments with Matilde.'

'Then I am disturbing you?'

He started to back away, and before she knew what she intended Dominique had laid her hand on his shirtsleeve to stop him.

'You're not disturbing me at all.'

She'd spent most of the afternoon thinking about what Elena had told her, about him feeling so responsible for his family tragedies, and she'd longed for an opportunity to talk to him alone.

'But you are *definitely* disturbing me.' He moved in closer, smiling ruefully. 'But then…you always do, Dominique.'

'Can we talk?'

'Something is troubling you?'

'Not exactly. I just—'

'Come and see something with me.'

'What?'

'You will see. Come.'

Finding herself led back out into the cavernous hall outside the huge drawing room, Dominique sucked in her breath at the candlelit nativity scene that had been arranged there. Even Matilde stared at it, her little face alive with interest in the small perfectly made figures—both human and animal—amid the straw. Feeling Cristiano's arm slip very naturally round her waist, Dominique knew a stunning moment when everything in her life seemed to suddenly mirror the most exquisite perfection. With her baby in her arms and the man she loved beside her, she was very close to crying with happiness—not to mention relief and joy.

'It's one of the most beautiful things I've ever seen,' she sighed.

'Sí,' Cristiano agreed, a faint smile touching his lips. 'This, for me, is what Christmas is all about… this and being with my family.'

'Family is very important to you, isn't it?'

'Of course.'

'Cristiano…Elena mentioned to me today that you've been carrying around so much guilt about what happened to your wife and Ramón. I was sad to hear it. You have no need to feel guilty in any way.'

Her heart was beating so loudly that the roar of it was like an ocean in Dominique's ears. It was too late to take back the statement, but in one sense she wished she could—because, seeing the forbiddingly angry expression that had stolen over Cristiano's face, she knew that the exquisite moment she'd been blessed with just now had suddenly been relegated to bittersweet history. Now she clearly saw the bleak landscape that resided in his compelling eyes, instead of the calm sea that had previously been there, and when his arm left her waist Dominique was utterly bereft.

'So this is what you discussed during your shopping trip?' His mouth tightened in distaste. 'I did not realise it was open season on casual discussion of my feelings!'

Horror-struck, Dominique tightened her arms round her baby's small body, afraid she might drop her because she was trembling so. 'That's not how it was at all! The subject only came up because we care about you, Cristiano! Elena has obviously seen what you've been going through first hand, and she's concerned at how you've been coping.'

'I do not need anybody's concern! What happened was a terrible tragedy and I am coping with it in my own way—a way that does not require anyone else's help or opinions on how I should be dealing with it! I am getting on with my life and I am doing my best to put the event behind me. I would ask that you would respect both my privacy *and* my feelings, Dominique, and not raise the matter again!'

When Cristiano looked as if he might underline his angry statement by walking away from her, Dominique steeled herself with new resolve. She cared about this man far too much to leave him be and let him deal with his tragic loss in isolation, and worse still *blaming* himself for it. After all…he hadn't left *her* alone when she'd insisted she didn't need his help, had he? Whether he knew it or not Cristiano needed her love and support, and she would get that point across if it killed her!

'Are you going to blame yourself for your wife and Ramón's death for the rest of your life, Cristiano?' she burst out.

'Who knows?' He shrugged, his expression bleak as a Siberian winter. 'Maybe I *deserve* to feel guilt? Did you ever ask yourself that…huh? My wife clearly felt she could not confide in me and so the fault *is* mine! Somehow I must have put out the message that she could not have trusted me with the knowledge of the risk she was taking by becoming pregnant…that I would have used the information against her!'

'And would you have?'

'*Sí!* I would! If it meant that she would have had her life, of course! But I am not a tyrant! I knew how much she wanted a baby. If she had told me the truth we could have explored other avenues…like adoption. I wanted children too, but I would not have had her put her life at risk to bear my child!'

'Of course you wouldn't! I know enough about you to realise that, and your family does too!' Her throat aching at the pain he must be feeling, Dominique found it almost too hard to speak. 'Your wife was an adult and she made her own decisions. You have to somehow make your peace with that and absolve yourself of all blame and guilt. I am certain she would have wanted that for you!'

'And what about Ramón?' Moving restlessly away from her, Cristiano walked down the corridor and back again.

'*What* about Ramón?'

'He needed help. He needed *my* help! But I was always too quick to judge him. I always expected the worst, and so what could he do but live up to my limited expectations? He was not a bad person. He was just a boy who missed his father and grew up amongst women who doted on him because they loved him and perhaps spoiled him a little too much. I could see that it grieved him that he could not please me the way he wanted to. He was so hungry to be what the world thought of as a success, and he was not happy that instead he was viewed as a spoiled rich boy who had neither sense nor morals! I have thought many times about his accident…I have wondered if in a state of depression he might have deliberately driven his car too fast that night along that treacherous road… That he might have—'

'Taken his own life?' Her eyes widening, Dominique vehemently shook her head. 'Ramón would never have done such a thing! No matter what might have been going on with him, he loved life far too much to want to end it! Cristiano, you must have been driving yourself crazy with all these wild imaginings! You've got to let this go…please! For your *own* sake if not for your family's! Because it would be a terrible shame—and not only that such a tragic waste too—if you were to continue to burden yourself with all this useless guilt!

'Who knows how much time any of us are given when we arrive in this world? Crippling ourselves with "if onlys" is futile when we don't ultimately control *any* of it! I am sure you were an amazing husband to Martina, and the best of cousins to Ramón—but you had nothing to do with the reasons they died! And if they loved you—as I am certain they must have—do you think they would want the rest of your life to be blighted with unhappiness because you believe you could have done something to prevent their passing?'

'It is not so easy to just let go of the guilt, as you suggest.' His dark eyes glittering, Cristiano's sculpted features were taut with pain. 'When my father died it fell to me to take on the mantle of head of the family. That entails being someone they can rely and depend on! They told me at the hospital afterwards that Martina had always carried a high risk of having complications in childbirth—she had pleaded with the doctors not to tell me about it! Can you imagine? She carried that burden all by herself, when if she had shared it with me I could have—'

'Saved her?' Dominique didn't know how she dared even say the words when the man in front of her seemed so furious, but say them she had to. 'Think about what you're saying, Cristiano… please! You are a wonderful man, dependable and reliable—the kind of man anyone would want on their side—but that doesn't mean you have the power to control every single event that happens in your loved ones lives or your own! I'm sure your wife only wanted to spare you pain by not telling you about her condition. She must have loved you *so* much. Ramón too. He had a car accident, Cristiano. Accidents happen every day. How could you possibly have had anything to do with that? It was in his nature to take foolish risks sometimes, with no regard for his safety! I knew him too, remember? But you, Cristiano…you have the whole of the rest of your life ahead of you, and you have to forgive yourself for the imagined failings in your past and move on… Just as *I* am learning to move on.'

Silence fell. A silence broken only by the harsh drawn-out breaths that came from Cristiano. Praying she hadn't somehow made things worse by speaking out, Dominique could only wait in soundless anguish for the outcome of their passionate exchange. In her arms Matilde wriggled, and then let out a sharp cry. Her attention diverted, Dominique tenderly touched her lips to her baby's velvet-soft forehead.

'What is it, my darling? Are you hungry? Is that what's wrong?'

'Go and feed the child.'

The tiniest flicker of a smile raised the corners of Cristiano's mouth. He looked resigned and a little weary, perhaps, but not angry any more. A shaft of the most dizzying hope raced through Dominique's insides.

'Will you come with me?' she asked.

He sighed heavily. 'Not right now. I need some time alone to think. But we will talk again later, I promise.'

Wishing fiercely that he would change his mind and join her, Dominique tried to corral her frustration and give him a smile. 'Well…when your thinking is done, perhaps you'll come and find me?'

Giving her an enigmatic smile in return, Cristiano turned his back and walked away down the corridor…

* * *

He drove for miles, hardly paying attention to where he was going. Somehow the act of driving, of steering the car and working the controls, helped free his mind so that he could think with more clarity. It was said that Einstein had had his best and most creative thoughts when he was shaving. Cristiano allowed himself a small grin at this, one of the more obscure facts he'd collected over the years. Then, as a bundle of dried grasses rolled by in the warm gusty wind, his expression grew more serious again.

The emotionally charged encounter he'd had with Dominique while admiring the belén *had struck a loud chord inside him.* For a man who had once given absolute credence to the idea that there was a purpose and a meaning to every life it was amazing how he could have gone so wildly off course with his guilt-ridden beliefs. Dominique, his mother, Consuela and Elena—they had *all* been right in their assertion that the power to control events did *not* lie with him…as it did not lie with *any* man or woman, for that matter. That being the case, there *was* no blame.

He had always done his best for the people he loved. *Always.* If it still nagged at him a little that perhaps he should have made himself more available to talk to Ramón than he had done then

Cristiano told himself it was about time he let that thought go and realised that even if he *had* spent more time with his troubled cousin he probably would not have been able to change anything. Just as knowing what Martina had faced would not have changed anything either. His wife had always longed for children. Even if Cristiano had persuaded her that with the risks involved it was probably not a good idea for her to become pregnant she would have fought him tooth and nail to get her own way. And if he had tried to stop her she would have been dreadfully unhappy, possibly even blamed him for not letting her try to have a baby.

In the end, it was just not meant to be… Letting out a deep sigh to free the sensation of tightness in his chest, Cristiano focused on the dusty road ahead, the glorious sight of the sun-struck mountains giving a little ease to the painful emotions that beset him. Dominique was right. *She had learned some hard lessons in her own life and had not emerged from them without gaining some valuable insight.* Nobody knew how much time they were allotted on earth. All one could do was live each day in the best way that they could and trust that there was indeed a plan for everyone.

To Cristiano's mind it now seemed somewhat ungrateful to waste another day of the life he had been given in guilt and regret. Especially when his future could possibly be *far* brighter than he had ever dared to hope…

A wave of tiredness hit her later on that afternoon, and Dominique went to have a lie-down in her bedroom. At Consuela and Luisa's insistence she left the baby with them while she rested.

All she could think about was Cristiano and whether, after what they had discussed, there would be room in his life for her and Matilde after all. Not just as their 'guardian and protector', but as something deeper and more meaningful…something that would require him to make a more lasting commitment to them than he might have envisaged?

If such a thing could not be achieved, then Dominique would have no alternative but to return to England after Christmas and just pay a visit now and again, as she had suggested once before. It was too bad if he did not like that plan. She needed to survive too, and she could not do that if she was around Cristiano without the deep connection between them that she craved…

Worn out with thinking and hoping, she eventually dozed off.

When she came downstairs about an hour later, she found the women gathered together in the drawing room, talking companionably. There was no sign of Cristiano. Elena had told her earlier that he'd gone out for a drive, and Dominique's stomach had been tied up in knots at the idea that he was driving to try and get away from the deep unhappiness that consumed him. *What if he never resolved the guilt and regret that dogged him about his wife's death? What if he remained a widower for the rest of his life, never allowing himself the chance of being with someone new? Someone who adored him with every fibre of her being? Someone who wanted the opportunity to show him how good life could be again?*

Dominique tried for a smile as Consuela dandled Matilde on her knee and made the baby laugh, but she knew it was a half-hearted effort at best.

'You have a nice lie-down?' the older woman asked in her halting English.

'Lovely…thank you. I feel revived.'

Her gaze fell upon the small overnight case that was at Consuela's feet. Recognising it as her own, Dominique frowned.

Observing her quizzical glance, Consuela lifted it by its leather handle and held it out to her. 'You go with Cristiano,' she said, smiling.

'Cristiano?'

'I have been waiting for you, *querida*,' a familiar voice said from behind her.

Standing in the doorway, with a bone-melting smile, dressed in dark trousers, white shirt and a stylish chocolate-brown suede jacket, he was the most devastatingly handsome man on earth, and Dominique's heart all but leapt into her throat at the sight of him.

'I don't understand…'

'I am taking you to Madrid for a little trip. I own a small hotel there. We will stay the night and drive back tomorrow.'

'I sneaked into your room and packed your bag while you slept. I hope you do not mind?' Rising to her feet from her armchair, Elena went to Dominique and gave her a brief but affectionate hug.

'But—but what about Matilde?'

'Need you ask?'

Cristiano grinned, and Dominique looked round at the three women, whose love for her child was shining in each pair of twinkling dark eyes…

'This is all a bit sudden, isn't it?' Her legs were shaking as she realised she was the unsuspecting target of a somewhat tender conspiracy.

Cristiano released a heavy sigh and scraped a hand through his gleaming dark hair. 'Are you going to stand there looking bemused for the rest of the day? Or are you going to come with me and find out what this is all about when we get to Madrid?'

Dominique swallowed hard. 'I think I'm going

to go with you,' she replied, her voice a little husky with emotion.

'*Bien!*'

As he held out his hand, Cristiano's dazzling smile was like sunshine after a prolonged period of rain, and he enfolded her small, slim palm protectively in his own…

'A small hotel, you said?' With her head on one side as she surveyed the sumptuously appointed bedroom in their suite, Dominique glanced wryly at her good-looking companion as he dropped his bag and her overnight case on a chair. 'Define "small", Cristiano?'

'Okay.' He shrugged. 'So I am prone to being a little modest. It is hardly my worst fault!'

'Now that you've mentioned it, what *is* your worst fault?'

Walking slowly towards him, Dominique knew the expression on her face was deliberately provocative. The answering gleam in Cristiano's black eyes made her heart race.

He put his arms out as she reached him and caught her in a possessive embrace. 'Perhaps it is that when I fall in love I fall too hard and too fast?' he said, smoothing the pad of his thumb across her cheek.

Dominique thought she glimpsed a momentary flash of pain cross his sculpted features. 'Has it happened often?' she asked softly.

'No…only twice in my life.' He was staring at her as though she were some kind of priceless treasure just unveiled to him. 'And you?' he enquired, his expression suddenly more intense. 'Were you in love with Ramón?'

'It's like I told you when we first met. I thought I was for a time…' She grimaced at the bittersweet memory. 'But really I just—I just needed someone, and for a while he was there for me.'

'So you have never really been in love?'

'Not until now. No.'

Silence was the answer to her nervously voiced statement, and inside her chest Dominique's heart squeezed with love and longing for the man who was holding her so tenderly and yet at the same time with a grip like steel that promised not to let her easily escape…

'Something inside me died when I lost my wife,' Cristiano told her, and for a long moment she held her breath. 'I truly believed I would never find another woman to replace her…let alone lose my heart again. But you have proved me wrong, Dominique…*so* wrong! I find myself as foolish and as hopeful as a schoolboy when you are around, and all I can think of is taking you somewhere we can be alone together so that I can make love to you!'

'I feel the same! Oh, Cristiano, I love you so much!' Thrilling at his words, yet impatient for him to stop talking so that she could feel that heavenly mouth of his against hers, Dominique put her hand up to his gleaming black hair and gently smoothed a lock of it away from his temple. 'You have become the most important thing to me and Matilde. I don't even want to *imagine* living the rest of our lives without you!'

'Then do not!' Cristiano growled passionately against her ear.

Sensing his hands move down to her hips and drag her hard against his pelvis, Dominique felt the steely hardness of his desire brush urgently against her and her limbs flooded with glorious liquid velvet. 'Take me to bed...*please,*' she whispered back to him.

They undressed urgently, but Cristiano's movements deliberately slowed as he undid Dominique's coiled hair as though unwrapping the most precious of gifts. This was not a task to hurry or take lightly. It was one of the erotic privileges he had so often dreamed of since Dominique had come into his life.

A wave of fierce masculine pride assailed him as he sensed her quiver hard with excitement at his touch. *He was quivering too.* All his senses were wild with joy, and with the hot, restless need to unite his body with hers once again.

The only covering Dominique had when he was finished was her glorious mane of rippling spun gold hair, its dark honey brushing temptingly against the aroused tips of her beautiful breasts as it cascaded down to her slender but nicely rounded hips. Unable to resist touching her a moment longer, Cristiano put his mouth to those delectable rigid points and sucked hard. The sensation caused even more heat to flood straight to his loins, and his erection was so tight with arousal that the line between pleasure and pain was only separated by the slimmest of threads.

Sliding his hand through her hair, he pushed Dominique's head gently down to the plumped-up pillows behind her. When she was lying supine, he moved back down her body, parted her long smooth thighs and slid his fingers across the hot, silky nub at her centre. She immediately jerked, and panted out his name. Caught up in the fast-flowing river of his growing desire, Cristiano delved deep inside her with hungry fingers, and then, when he was drenched in her honeyed heat, he put his mouth to the place where his fingers had caressed her.

Her thighs moved helplessly wider apart, and Dominique's hands gripped the satin eiderdown beneath her with a groan as Cristiano's tongue moved rhythmically back and forth across the core of her femininity. Just when she thought she would break like an overstretched harp-string if she didn't have the release she ached for Cristiano used that wicked instrument of seductive torment upon her with deliberate erotic slowness, and drenching waves of glorious heat swept over her in tingling succession, endowing her body with the most profoundly wondrous delight it had ever known…

When he glanced up at her with the most toe-curling satisfied grin Dominique had ever seen, desire consumed her again almost in an instant. Fastening her hands on the iron-hard slopes of his broad muscular shoulders, she urged him urgently towards her.

'Now you,' she breathed. 'I want you to have the same pleasure you have just given to me!'

'*Mi amor*… You will not find me arguing with that!'

He slid into her body in one smooth but sure thrust, and Dominique felt her muscles grip him tightly and quiver hard with delight. Her hunger and arousal reached barely imagined peaks of joy as Cristiano drove into her like a man intent on making her remember this amazing connection always. She ran her hands over his back and felt her nails dig into his slick, taut muscles as the feelings inside her grew close to the point of explosion.

When they had both cried out at the same time, their gazes meeting in shared wonder, they slowly returned to earth together, holding on to each other fast.

'I want you to be my wife.'

Without preamble, Cristiano spoke his thoughts aloud.

'Was it your intention to ask me that when you brought me here?' Dominique inquired, her pulse accelerating with the wildest joy.

'Yes, it was.'

'And does your family know you were going to ask me this?'

He shook his head and smiled. 'No. I would not tell them what was in my mind until I spoke to you, *mi ángel*.'

'Are you sure, Cristiano? You'd be taking on a lot, you know. Me *and* Matilde.'

'I love your daughter as if she were my own…I want to be her father, Dominique, but that does not mean I will not tell her anything she wants to know about Ramón when she gets older. Of course I also want *us* to have children together too…maybe three or four…'

'Three or four?' Dominique gasped.

'At *least*!'

'You plan to keep me busy, then?'

'Very!'

With a wicked smile, Cristiano claimed her lips for long, satisfying seconds, and for a while Dominique simply let herself bask in the luxury and delight of his amazing kisses. Then he lifted his head, glancing down at her with a frown.

'You have not said whether you will accept my offer of marriage yet. I beg you not to keep me waiting any longer!'

'Didn't I just give you my answer with my eyes, Cristiano?' Her voice soft with emotion, Dominique slid her palm across his slightly roughened cheek and caressed it. 'Of *course* I will be your wife! I want the chance to show you that life can be good again…for us both. We won't forget the past, but for now we will put it behind us. Our memories will be like a library we visit from time to time, but they will not be where we *live*!'

'*Sí*…I like that.'

And to show her how much he concurred with her statement, Cristiano once again showered his wife-to-be with the kind of kisses that meant they would be most fervently occupied for a considerably long time indeed…

Christmas Eve…

Standing outside Cristiano's study door, Dominique glanced down at her green satin dress with a little spurt of pleasure. Her fiancé had bought it for her only yesterday, insisting that she had to have something special to wear on one of the most celebrated of nights in the Spanish calendar.

In the kitchen, the housekeeper and the rest of the

Cordova women were busily engaged in putting the finishing touches to the splendid feast that was in store—a menu that had been planned with a precision and attention to detail that wouldn't have shamed an army campaign. The house looked absolutely stunning, and it was as if everything around Dominique were holding its breath in anticipation of what was to come. It was indeed turning out to be the kind of Christmas that Dominique had longed for, and one she would remember for ever…

Knocking lightly on the heavy oak door, she felt butterflies immediately assail her insides at Cristiano's almost curt, *'Adelante!'*

'It's only me,' she announced shyly as she stepped over the threshold into the impressive high-ceilinged room.

Seated behind a huge desk, Cristiano glanced up and gave the smile that never failed to turn her legs to jelly. His hungry gaze made no bones about the fact that he very much liked what he saw, and he pushed to his feet and moved across the room to join her.

'*Hola…*"it's only me"!' he teased. 'I like what you are wearing, by the way. Whoever bought it has impeccable taste!'

'I wanted to give you your Christmas present.' Her closed palm opened to reveal the small package it had been concealing, and Dominique gave the small silver-wrapped box to Cristiano.

She twisted her hands together a little nervously as she watched him peel off the glittery paper and then open the lid of the cardboard container that was inside. As he withdrew the perfectly oval silver frame, he studied the photograph it contained with an almost grave expression on his face. Then he looked up, and Dominique saw that his eyes had a sheen that hadn't been there before.

'Do you like it?' she asked anxiously. 'I couldn't think what else to give you.'

'I love it, *mi ángel!* You could not have given me anything more precious. I will put it on my desk at work, and whenever I need some inspiration I will look at this picture of my two beautiful girls and know that I can accomplish anything if they are by my side…*anything!*'

'I'm so glad you feel that way.'

'Never doubt what I say…I mean *every* word. And now I have something to give to you.'

Walking back to his desk, Cristiano put down the photograph with its wrapping and opened a drawer. Removing something, he walked slowly back to where Dominique stood. Opening what she now saw was a tiny black velvet heart-shaped box, he took out the most dazzling ruby and sapphire ring and, taking Dominique's left hand in his, he placed the glittering jewel on her wedding finger.

'Now you are officially my fiancée!' He beamed

and, pulling her close, kissed her with lingering thoroughness. When he had freed her lips once more, he cupped her face in his hands. 'And soon that ring will be joined by another one…a *wedding* band. Happy Christmas, Dominique. Know that I love you more than I can say. You and Matilde have given my life a meaning I thought never to have again.'

'When we first met, your words drew the most captivating picture of what Christmas was like in your country, and I so longed to experience some of the magic you conveyed! But nothing could have prepared me for the miracle of *you*, Cristiano… *nothing!* Happy Christmas, my love!'

CHRISTMAS BRIDE-TO-BE

BY
ALISON ROBERTS

Alison Roberts lives in Christchurch, New Zealand. She began her working career as a primary school teacher, but now juggles available working hours between writing and active duty as an ambulance officer. Throwing in a large dose of parenting, housework, gardening and pet-minding keeps life busy, and teenage daughter Becky is responsible for an increasing number of days spent on equestrian pursuits. Finding time for everything can be a challenge, but the rewards make the effort more than worthwhile.

For Carol, who's not a Christmas baby but is still very special. With love

CHAPTER ONE

THE sound was threatening.

A low growl that made the hairs on the back of Jillian Metcalf's neck stand on end.

She froze, the sealed sharps container she was about to deposit in the designated bin suspended in mid-air.

The sound took her straight back to those horror movies she and her friends had loved to be terrified by. Way back, when they had been too young to be allowed too much freedom and the only Friday night entertainment had been a video at one of their houses. They had sat in the dark, clutching each other and shrieking…like when the werewolf had been just about to launch a gruesome attack.

Just after it had growled.

Cursing her overactive imagination, Jill straightened her spine, albeit cautiously. Werewolves did not hide out behind the rubbish bins of a small rural hospital. And they weren't known for surprise attacks in the blazing midday sun.

Tilting sideways so that she could see between the tall green recycling bins beside the large skip, Jill pushed back the blonde curls that the breeze was playing with and peered into the shadows. The gleam of bared white fangs accompanied by another growl might have continued to seem threatening but as her eyes made the adjustment from the glare of the white pebbles paving this courtyard area to the gloom of the shade, Jill could see the eyes of the wolf.

Sad eyes.

She put down the yellow plastic sharps bin and dropped to a crouch.

'Hey,' she said softly. 'What's the matter, girl? Are you hurt?'

The growling stopped, replaced by rapid panting. It didn't matter that Jill was a doctor and not a vet. She knew the animal was breathing too fast. She watched as the bared teeth disappeared and a long pink tongue hung out.

'You're hot and thirsty,' she informed the dog. 'And no wonder! I'm not surprised you've tried to find some shade. Want to come out and find a drink instead?'

The answer seemed to be in the negative. Jill eyed the gap between the bins. It had never bothered her unduly that she had the solid build of a country girl but there was no way she could fit in that gap. She could wheel all the recycling bins out of the way but they would be heavy and it was a very hot day. Unless it was too injured, it would be much easier to coax the dog to come out.

'Don't go away,' Jill advised. 'I'll be right back.'

It was a quick trip to the back door of Ballochburn Hospital's kitchens.

'I need a bowl,' Jill announced.

A large woman banged the door of an oven shut and then peeled a teatowel from where it had been looped through her apron string. She mopped a very red face.

'Where are your manners, Jilly Metcalf?'

Jill had to bite her lip to kill the grin. Never mind that she was temporarily in the position of being one of the doctors in charge of this hospital and technically Maisie Drummond's boss. She may as well have been ten years old again and stealing gooseberries from the back of the Drummonds' orchard.

'Please?' she added obligingly.

Maisie sniffed thoughtfully but Jill knew better than to appear impatient. The portable radio on the window-sill filled the silence with the New Zealand version of 'The Twelve Days of Christmas'.

'And a pukeko in a ponga tree...'

'And what would you be needing a bowl for?' As expected, Maisie had made her decision in Jill's favour. 'I thought you'd finished your ward rounds.'

'There's a dog,' Jill explained. 'Hiding behind the bins. I think it might be hurt and it's too scared to come out. And it's thirsty,' she added firmly. 'It needs water.'

'I'm not surprised,' Maisie muttered, mopping her face again. 'Must be over thirty degrees out there.'

'Hotter in here,' Jill said sympathetically. 'There's a nice breeze outside, though. Why don't you open some windows?'

Maisie muttered something almost inaudible about it being a totally inadequate form of air-conditioning and that nobody else would put up with her working conditions, but she moved to pull up one of the heavy wooden sash windows. The cord had clearly been broken long enough for the positioning of a brick to keep it open to be automatic. The breeze had picked up and both women turned their faces towards the welcome cooler air.

'A bowl, you said?'

'Yes, please, Maisie.'

'For a dog.'

'Yes.'

'Whose dog?'

'I have no idea.'

'This is a hospital, Jilly, not a veterinary clinic.'

'I know that. I'll take it home until I can find its owner.'

'It's unhygienic,' Maisie grumbled as she opened a cupboard. 'You can't go using people bowls on dogs. Not in a hospital.'

'I'll put it in the steriliser.'

'You'd better.' Maisie turned on a tap over one of the vast stainless-steel sinks and filled the bowl with cold water.

Jill skirted a trolley set out with lunch-trays. Beautiful trays with sandwiches and Maisie's famous home-made chocolate cake and peeled slices of fruit. The trays all had names on them and Jill could see the one labelled for old Mrs Hinkley. The sandwiches were full of egg and parsley. The crusts had been removed and the slivers of fruit were thin enough to eat even if she was refusing to put her teeth in again.

How many hospitals in the world would there be where patients got this kind of individual attention? Mind you, how many hospitals only had four or five inpatients and too many eerie rooms containing empty beds and had managed to survive this long without being shut down?

It was probably the last of its kind and it would be a sad day when it disappeared like all the others.

Jill pushed the thought away somewhat guiltily. It was partly her fault that it might eventually close. Finding doctors to live and work in rural areas was increasingly difficult and she herself was a prime example of one of the new generation of doctors who preferred to work in a large city with services that covered after-hours care and the immediate back-up of the specialist skills and resources a large hospital could provide.

She held out her hands to take the bowl of water but Maisie didn't hand it over.

'I'm coming, too,' the older woman said.

'There's no need. You're busy—it must be time to deliver the lunches.'

'I've been doing this job for thirty years, young lady. I was doing it the day you got born upstairs and I'll still be doing it when you swan off to Australia and that exciting new job you've got lined up. Don't you go telling me how I should be doing *my* job.'

'Sorry.' Jill had no desire to step on any toes and she certainly didn't want to spend the time listening to one of Maisie's prolonged lectures. The poor dog outside had already been waiting too long for a drink. She turned towards the back door. 'It's just out here.'

'I do know where the bins are.' Maisie stomped along behind Jill. 'I'm just coming to make sure it hasn't made too much of a mess. And that it doesn't have rabies.'

'We don't have rabies in New Zealand, Maisie.'

'Always a first time,' Maisie warned. 'You sure it's not just a big possum? They carry tuberculosis, you know.'

'It's definitely a dog.'

A very hot, frightened dog. Jill pushed the bowl well down into the space between the bins.

'There you go, girl,' she said soothingly. 'Nice cold water.'

The dog didn't move.

'Don't worry,' Jill added. 'Nobody's going to hurt you.' Her voice was soft, almost a croon. 'It's just water. Nice and cold. Because you're thirsty and hot, aren't you, sweetie?'

A snort came from Maisie's direction. 'You've always been barmy about animals, you have. Always dragging home some poor hedgehog or bird or anything else that couldn't get away from you. Drove your poor mum and dad up the wall, you did.'

'Did I?' Jill turned to raise her eyebrows at Maisie. 'They never *seemed* to mind.'

From the corner of her eye, she could see the dog taking advantage of the lack of direct attention. It slunk forward on its belly. Seconds later they heard the sound of vigorous lapping and Jill beamed.

'Good *girl*,' she said approvingly. 'Are you going to come out now and let us have a proper look at you?'

'It's probably a boy,' Maisie said. 'And it'll probably bite you.'

'No-o-o.' Jill poked her hand into the gap and let the dog sniff the backs of her fingers. 'You wouldn't do that, would you, darling?' She could see the faint movement of a shaggy tail. An apologetic sort of wag. 'I think it's hungry, Maisie.'

'I'm not cooking lunch for a dog and that's *that*.' Maisie folded her arms.

'Come on, girl.' Jill scratched an ear hiding in matted, shaggy hair and then moved backwards. 'Out you come.'

It came. With its tail firmly between its legs and a drooping head, but it moved out of its hiding place to slink closer to Jill.

'It's not wearing a collar. I reckon it's lost.'

'Dumped, more likely. And no wonder!' Maisie stared at the dog. 'That's the ugliest mutt I've seen in all my born days. What *is* it?'

'Might be a farm dog. There's a bit of bearded collie in there, I would think, to give it such long hair.' Jill grinned as she eyed the tawny tufts of hair that sprouted in all directions. 'You're just having a bad hair day, aren't you, sweets?'

'Got spaniel eyes, if you ask me,' Maisie pronounced. 'Pathetic-looking thing, isn't it?'

'It's so thin.' Jill chewed her bottom lip. 'I can feel all its ribs.'

Maisie sighed wearily. 'I'll see if there's a few scraps in the fridge.'

'And it's...' Jill was running her hands gently over the matted coat. 'Oh, boy!'

'What?'

'I think it's pregnant. The tummy sure doesn't match the state of the ribs.'

'That'll be why it got dumped, then.' Maisie tutted her disapproval. 'People can't be bothered paying for kennels when they want to go on their Christmas holidays, and if they *can* be bothered, I'll bet kennels won't even take dogs that are about to whelp.'

'Well, there's room at *this* inn.' Jill stepped away and patted her leg. 'Can you walk, sweetie? I'll take you home. It's not far.'

The dog needed no encouragement. It moved in order to stay in contact with Jill's leg.

'I won't be long,' Jill told Maisie. 'I was planning to drop home and have lunch with the folks, anyway. I'll be back to do the clinic at one and tell Ange I've got my pager on if she wants me for anything on the wards.'

Maisie waved her off. 'Don't forget to wash your hands. You don't know what you might catch from that mutt.'

It wasn't a long journey.

There was an apartment within the old hospital complex for a resident doctor, but thirty-five years ago the newly married Dr James Metcalf had purchased an old villa adjacent to the hospital grounds. The hinges of the gate he'd put in the back fence had almost rusted through but it was still used often enough to keep it serviceable and the track that led beneath the century-old oak trees and through the carpet of bluebells in springtime was so well worn it would probably be there for ever.

The dog cringed at the loud creak of the rusty hinges and Jill stooped to pet the animal.

'You're safe now,' she said. 'It's OK, honest!'

The swing at the bottom of the garden was surrounded by apple trees laden with half-formed fruit. A cacophony of cicadas sang about summer and the only weeding being done in the oversized and neglected vegetable patch was courtesy of several black and white spotted Wyandotte hens.

'Rule number one,' Jill warned the dog, 'don't eat the hens.'

A hugely fat ginger cat eyed the newcomer warily from its position in the sun at the top of the steps.

'Rule number two,' Jill whispered, 'be nice to Marmalade.'

The screen door leading into the kitchen banged shut as it always had.

'Hi, Mum!' Jill called. 'I'm starving! What's for lunch?'

The silence was unexpected but not worrying. As the wife of a small community's only long-term doctor, Hope Metcalf was involved enough to keep her very busy, especially this close to Christmas. She was probably caught up in a choir practice or helping to set up for pets' day at the local primary school or she could just be working out the front in the riotous cottage garden that was her pride and joy.

There was no sign of Jill's father either, but he'd had a few house calls to make that morning and, given the area the practice had to cover, it could have taken a long time.

'Never mind,' Jill told the dog. 'I'll make myself a sandwich. Wait till you taste Mum's ham. It's fabulous.'

Ears that had been as droopy as the tail pricked up. Liquid brown eyes fastened on Jill with an expression that squeezed her heart. She bent down and patted the dog again.

'You're a darling, aren't you? I'm sure you haven't really been abandoned. Who would do something like that?'

She sighed unconsciously as she straightened. It wasn't that she was out of touch with the reality of what went on in the world, it was just that bad things seemed to have a sharper focus here.

This community, this house, her family were Jill's rock. The solid foundation her life had been built on. Familiar, predictable...*safe*. A haven she carried with her even when she was a thousand miles away in Auckland. She'd missed it desperately two years ago when her marriage had crumbled.

Yes, she had made a mistake. But she knew she wasn't mistaken in believing that the kind of relationship she wanted *did* exist. That it was possible she could still find it...one day. She'd just be more careful next time. Look a lot harder before she leapt.

The timing of this, her first long visit to the trusted reality of home since she'd left to go to medical school, couldn't have been better, given that her final divorce papers had arrived in the mail the very day she had been packing to leave on her way to a new life. She'd actually been finally able to pull off that wedding band. To leave it behind.

Even the mess on the scrubbed Kauri table in this huge kitchen was comfortingly familiar. A whole week's worth of newspapers neatly folded and stacked. Bills that needed attention. A sugar bowl and salt pig made of crude clay coils that had been Jill's own creations in pottery class at primary school when she had been ten years old. Never mind that they wobbled and the glaze had been patchy. Mum said they were rustic and she loved them and they'd been on the table for nearly twenty years now.

The mess on the faded pink Formica bench was a lot less comforting. If there was one thing her mother hated, it was a dirty bench. She would never leave the house with her work-space looking like that unless…

Unless something disturbingly out of the ordinary had occurred.

The bang of the screen door was a relief, until Jill turned to find it was her father entering the kitchen.

'Where's Mum?'

'Isn't she here?'

'No.'

Jim Metcalf frowned. 'But she knows what time clinic starts. I've only got half an hour for lunch.'

'She must have gone somewhere in a hurry. It's not like her to leave dishes not done.'

Jim's gaze raked the cluttered bench but then dropped. 'Good Lord, what's *that*?'

'A dog.' Jill bent to provide a reassuring scratch for the head pressed anxiously against her knee. 'A stray dog.'

'Looks like a doormat on legs. Put it outside.'

The grumpy tone was familiar enough to ignore. 'Mum didn't say anything about having to go out early. I wonder why she didn't leave a note? I hope Aunty Faith isn't sick or something.'

'Doubt it. If I'm half as healthy as she is when I'm ninety-three I'll be more than happy.' Jim was still staring at the dog.

'That animal stinks. What *is* it with bringing home waifs and trays? You're just like your mother.'

Jill was taken aback by the edge of vehemence in his tone. Had Maisie been right? Had she driven her parents mad with the various animals she had 'rescued' all those years ago?

'I'll give it a bath,' she offered.

Jim grunted. 'I suppose you've already given it a name.'

'No.' Jill smiled with relief. She had only imagined the air of real grievance. It had always been the stamp of her father's acquiescence, if not approval, to bestow a name on any new additions to the family. 'Any suggestions?'

'Fly. It's bound to attract a few, smelling like that.'

'She won't smell when she's had a bath.' Jill looked down at her feet. 'I think she's beautiful. I might call her Bella.'

Her father's expression suggested she was as barmy as Maisie had accused her of being, but whatever he was about to say was cut off by a strident beeping.

'It's me,' Jill said unnecessarily.

'Must be a PRIME page, then.'

Jill was the only one of the two doctors wearing a second paging device. With rural ambulance services manned by well-trained but voluntary crews, providing medical back-up for emergency callouts was just another part of a country doctor's workload. Having come straight from a run of working in a large emergency department, Dr Metcalf senior had handed Jill the pager on her first day as his temporary locum.

'You're far more qualified to wear this than I am,' he'd said. 'The Jeep's got a full kit in the back.'

Jill went straight to the wall phone at one end of the kitchen bench. She scribbled information on a piece of paper and hung up within a minute.

'There's been a light plane crash,' she told her father. 'It was aiming for the airfield but came down a few paddocks early on Bruce Mandeville's farm. Only one occupant but he's unconscious.'

'You'd better get your skates on, then.'

'It's miles away. The ambulance is out on a long-distance transfer and it'll take awhile to get the other truck on the road.' To find crew for the old back-up vehicle in Ballochburn's emergency vehicle fleet could mean pulling people in from fruit-picking or sheep-shearing duties. 'I'll be late for the clinic.'

'I'll do the clinic.'

'You sure?' Jill was already heading for the door. She barely noticed the dog shadowing her every move.

'Of course I'm sure.' Her father sounded remarkably like Maisie had a little earlier. 'How the hell do you think I've been managing for the last six months?'

'Sorry.' Jill pulled open the screen door. 'I'll see you later, then.'

Was she still missing something here? A level of tension that was causing the people she loved the most to snap and snarl at each other?

Or was she overreacting? Allowing the new tension that this emergency call had created to infect everything else happening around her?

Jill opened the door of the Jeep. She stuck the magnetic light on the roof and plugged its cord into the cigarette lighter inside. It would start flashing bright orange as soon as she turned the vehicle on. Nobody would ticket her for exceeding the speed limit.

About to jump into the driver's seat, Jill noticed the dog.

Just sitting. Clearly expecting to be abandoned again. There was no time to find a safe place to leave it.

'Hop in, Bella,' Jill ordered. 'We're going for a ride in a fast car.'

CHAPTER TWO

HE WAS conscious now.

Jill could see the man sitting in the long, dry grass on the side of a slope, his shoulders hunched, his head in his hands. A very dejected picture.

And no wonder!

Below him—upside down—was a small, gleamingly new-looking, two-seater aircraft with a seriously bent propeller.

Bruce Mandeville was standing beside the plane, rubbing the back of his sunburnt neck. Three black and white dogs lay at his feet, tongues lolling. Bella, who had been looking out the window of the Jeep, saw the farm dogs and slid down to cringe on the floor behind the two front seats as Jill brought the vehicle to a bumping halt, having hit yet another rabbit hole.

With his black singlet, baggy shorts that matched the ancient khaki hat, short woolly socks and stout workboots, Bruce looked every inch the sheep farmer that he was.

He also looked suitably impressed.

'Nice little bird, isn't it?' he greeted Jill. 'Must've cost a pretty penny.'

Jill opened the back door of the Jeep to extract her kit. 'How's the pilot doing?'

'He's alive.' Bruce glanced towards the motionless figure on the hillside. 'And not very polite. Hardly my fault he chose to land in a mob of sheep, is it?'

Jill paused for a moment. Any information Bruce could give her might be helpful in assessing her patient. 'How long was he unconscious?'

'Not long. I was working in the next paddock and saw him come down. Sounded like his engine had conked out. Sheep ran in front of him and he headed for the hill but the wind must've caught it and it flipped. He woke up just after I called for help.' Bruce patted the mobile phone clipped to the pocket of his shorts. 'Never did think much of these newfangled things but I guess they have their uses.'

'How did he get out of the plane?' Jill had started walking towards the man. 'By himself?'

'Yep.' Bruce was staying where he was. 'Sure didn't want my help. Rude blighter if you ask me.'

He's probably got a head injury, Jill thought. Tends to make people seem rude.

'G'day,' she said aloud. 'I'm Jill Metcalf. I'm a doctor.' Taking hold of his wrist, she was pleased to feel a strong, steady pulse.

'Good for you.' He didn't look up.

Jill could see blood oozing between the fingers of the hand cradling his forehead. She unzipped her kit, pulled on a pair of disposable gloves and reached for a dressing and a pouch of saline.

'Are you having any trouble breathing?'

'No.'

'Anything hurting apart from your head?'

'No.'

'What about your neck? Is that sore?'

'No.'

Jill tore open the pouch of fluid and used it to dampen the large gauze pad. 'Let's have a look at the damage.'

'I'm fine.'

'Hey, I'm the doctor here.' Jill kept her tone light. Friendly. 'I'm the one who gets to decide that.'

He resisted for only a moment when she took hold of his hand and lifted it away from his head. She looked at the still bleeding, deep, four-centimetre laceration on his temple.

'You're going to need a few stitches in that.' She put the clean dressing over the wound. 'Hold this on for a tick while I find a bandage.'

The rapid response to her instruction was reassuring. Nothing wrong with his motor skills. With his verbal responsiveness and eye opening good, it put his level of consciousness at normal. She fished in the kit for a crêpe bandage.

'Where the hell am I?'

'Don't you know?' His GCS might need to be amended down a point if he wasn't oriented to time and place. And that could indicate a more serious head injury.

'I didn't notice any signposts, no.'

'Do you remember what happened?' Jill used her teeth to rip open the plastic covering on the bandage.

'I had engine trouble. I was making a perfectly controlled forced landing and a tribe of bloody sheep got in the way, that's what happened. Next thing I knew I was upside down.'

He had a lovely voice. Rich and deep. His clear enunciation suggested a good education.

'You were knocked out,' Jill told him. 'Bruce found you. OK, you can take your hand away now. I've got it.' She held he end of the bandage in place over the dressing and made a oop to secure it. 'Do you know what day it is?'

'Yes.'

Jill continued bandaging in silence for a moment. 'You oing to tell me, then?'

'Why? Don't *you* know?'

It should have been irritating, having an uncooperative atient, but there was a hint of humour in the dry tone and it vas at that point that the man tilted his head and looked up nd Jill could finally see his face properly.

A very striking face. He hadn't shaved for a day or two and here were smears of blood on olive skin that had a hint of allor but nothing could detract from a pair of absolutely orgeous, deep brown eyes.

Eyes that reminded her, remarkably vividly, of a pair she'd een not very long ago, hiding behind some rubbish bins.

Not that they looked anything like dog's eyes, of course. wasn't even the colour. It was the hint of a haunted look that id it. As though this man, sitting on a hill in a remote sheep addock, was feeling as lost and abandoned as the dog had een. As though…he had been trying to hide from something hat scared him?

Crazy. Her imagination had always been way too keen to in away with her. Jill ignored the way her heart had squeezed i response to the idea that this person was in trouble. Instead, ne finished her bandaging, using the little metal clips to ecure the end, and focussed on that glint of humour she'd etected. She even smiled cheerfully.

'Yes, I do know what day it is. I'm just trying to find out ow well your brain is functioning after the knock you've had n your head.'

'It's the 23rd of December. Two days before Christmas
And it's approximately 12.30 p.m.'

'Closer to 1.30 p.m. now but that's OK. I guess you'r
oriented. You just don't know where you are.'

'Apart from it being somewhere closer to Wanaka tha
Dunedin? No.'

'So you were heading for Wanaka?' It was a popula
tourist spot.

'Yes.'

'On holiday?'

'Not exactly.' He was looking down. Avoiding both ey
contact and the sharing of any personal information. Ji
wanted to see his face properly again.

'What's your name?'

'Jack.'

'Really? Hey, I've never met a Jack before.'

'And why is that funny?' He was staring at her with
faintly bewildered air.

Jill did her best to wipe the grin off her face. Maybe she'
been wrong about that sense of humour. 'It's just that…well…
I'm Jill, remember?'

The penny dropped quickly enough but he clearly didn
find it amusing and the look Jill received made her feel lik
an idiot. Hardly professional to be distracted by the childis
association their names had with a classic nursery rhym
was it? Any remnants of her smile vanished and Jill cleare
her throat in a businesslike manner.

'I'm going to give you a quick check and then I'll take yo
back to the hospital so I can sew up your head.'

'Just a ride to town would be good. I need to sort out wha
to do about my plane.'

'We can deal with that later. There'll be someone at the aero lub who'll know what to do.' Jill shone a penlight into Jack's yes, checking pupil size and reaction. 'You got a headache?'

'Yeah.'

'Feel sick?'

'No.'

Jill felt his head and then his neck. Strangely, it felt like an ddly personal thing to be doing and she'd been a doctor for ng enough not to feel like that when treating patients. Was because of the strange environment—being out in a sheep addock instead of an emergency department?

Or was it the fact that this Jack was not only an extraordi- arily good-looking man but that he'd dropped out of the sky nd seemed to be hiding something? It wasn't just her over- ctive imagination. He was hardly forthcoming in sharing formation, was he? He was monosyllabic. Withdrawn. aciturn, even.

'Let me know if anything hurts,' Jill told him.

Apparently nothing did. With no evidence of any other trauma nd his vital signs all within a normal range, Jill was happy to t Jack climb to his feet. She had realised he wasn't a small man ut it was disconcerting to be looking up this far. He had to be ver six feet tall because Jill's head barely reached his shoulder.

'Take it easy,' she warned. 'I might not be able to catch you you're too wobbly.'

'I'm fine.' Jack followed her towards the Jeep. He paused eside the plane.

'Thanks,' he said to Bruce. 'Sorry to be nuisance. I'll get e plane out of your paddock as soon as possible.'

Bruce tugged on the floppy brim of his hat. 'No problem, ate. I could give Wally a bell, if ya like.'

Jill came to the rescue in the perplexed silence. 'Wally' in charge at the aero club. He's a retired aircraft engineer s he'll probably be able to help with whatever needs sorting o your plane.'

'Oh…' Jack was staring at the crumpled blade of the pro peller. 'That'd be great.'

'He can get hold of Jack at the hospital,' Jill told Bruce 'We'll be keeping him under observation for a while.' Sh didn't allow any time for a protest from Jack. The vacant wa he was staring at the aircraft was a bit of a worry. 'Let's g then, shall we?'

'I need my bag. It's in the luggage compartment.' Jac took a step towards the plane but stumbled. Jill caught his arm

He pulled himself upright and shook off the support. 'I'r all right,' he muttered. 'Just a bit dizzy.'

'Come and sit down, then. In the Jeep,' Jill ordered.

'I'll get your stuff,' Bruce offered.

'There's a pack,' Jack said reluctantly. 'And a camera ba I really need that.'

Jill made a phone call to cancel the back-up ambulance whil Bruce hauled things out of the side compartment of the sma plane. The camera bag was large and professional-looking.

'Are you a photographer?' Jill asked.

'Yeah.'

'Freelance?'

Jack was doing up his seat belt. He glanced up at th question and Jill could have sworn he was puzzled. Havin trouble coming up with a response. If she was inclined t be uncharitable, it would have been easy to decide that thi man was not telling the truth. Then again, he'd had enoug of a bump on the head to knock him out. He had admitte

) a headache. Maybe he was having trouble with his
emory as well.

'Are you on assignment?' she prodded helpfully, 'for a
agazine or newspaper or something?'

'No. I'm just working for myself.'

'But you hope to sell your pictures?'

'Um...yeah, I guess.'

Jill gave up. The engine roared into life and she waved at
ruce. As the Jeep bumped back across the paddock away
om the farmer and his dogs, a shadowy shape appeared from
ehind the front seats. Bella's head poked through the gap and
he lifted her nose to catch the breeze from the open window.

'Good grief! What's *that*?'

'A dog,' Jill said crisply. 'Her name's Bella. For now.'

She was getting another of those odd looks. 'Do you often
hange your dog's name, then?'

Jill laughed. 'No. She's just a lost and lonely dog that came
ito my life about an hour ago. She needed a name.'

'Why Bella?'

'Because she's beautiful.'

Jack gave Bella one of those cautious kind of looks. 'Right.'

'It's OK. She won't bite. At least, I don't think she will.'
ill pulled to a stop and opened her door. 'You stay there. I'll
et the gate.'

Bella climbed into the driver's seat while she was out of
he vehicle, opening the gate, and when Jill went to get back
1 she slunk sideways, onto Jack's knee.

'Oof,' he said. 'She doesn't smell very beautiful, does she?'

'Get off, Bella,' Jill ordered. But the dog was still sitting
1 the same place when she got back from shutting the gate
ehind them. As they picked up speed, she stood up and thrust

her head out the window. Disreputable tawny tufts of ha
were instantly plastered against her head. Her rear end wa
plastered against Jack's chest.

'I could shove her in the back with the kit,' Jill offered.

'I'll survive,' Jack said faintly. 'Takes my mind off m
headache, anyway.'

Score one for the mystery man, Jill decided. Not man
people would be prepared to have a smelly dog standing o
their knee.

'You never told me where I am.'

'Ballochburn,' Jill supplied. 'Heart of stone-fruit countr
We're famous for peaches, apricots and cherries. Shee
farming out of the valley. And we've got a lovely rive
Favourite holiday spot for hundreds of people. Oh...' Ji
braked suddenly. 'And rabbits. We've got millions of rabbits

Having avoided squashing the creature, Jill picked u
speed again. The new silence was a little disconcerting. An
unusual. Jill never had any trouble chatting to anyone but sh
felt inexplicably wary of this stranger.

She cast frequent glances in her passenger's directio
trying to gauge whether his level of consciousness might b
dropping or his wound still bleeding. No eye contact wa
made. Jack was staring, as best he could, over Bella's bac
and through the front windscreen.

They were getting into the irrigated land that supported th
fruit orchards and it was green and leafy and gorgeous.

'Nice,' Jack murmured.

'It is, isn't it? I haven't been home nearly often enough i
the last few years. I forget how glorious it is.'

'You grew up here, then?'

'Yes.' Jill rewarded this voluntary attempt at conversatio

with a beaming smile. It was a good sign that her patient wasn't feeling too bad. 'Born and bred. My dad's been the doctor here for thirty-five years.'

'So you're following in his footsteps.'

'Being a doctor? I guess.'

'I meant being here. Is it your turn for the next thirty-five years?'

Jill pulled a face. 'Are you kidding? Fate worse than death in my book. I'm a city girl now. Trained and worked in Auckland and I've got a fabulous job lined up in Melbourne to start in the new year. In Emergency,' she added proudly.

Jack made a sound that fell well below being impressed. 'You like drama, then. Blood and guts.'

'Love it,' Jill said firmly. Somehow, it was disappointing that he wasn't impressed. That he sounded almost derogatory about her chosen passion. 'The bloodier and gutsier, the better.'

No. That made her sound like some kind of trauma vulture. Needing the misfortune of others to spin her wheels.

'I was going to be a GP,' she said more soberly. 'I figured that would fit in with raising a family and stuff down the track, but when I did a run in ED, I just fell in love with it.' Mind you, that could well have had something to do with the fact that her dreams of a settled future and family had been crumbling at the time. No. There was more to her passion than escapism. 'The variety of work is amazing,' she added a little defensively, 'and you actually know that you save a life sometimes.'

'And sometimes you don't.' Jack's tone was flat. Curiously lacking in expression. 'How do you deal with that?'

An odd question. Zeroing in on something negative like that. Was this man haunted and miserable-looking because he had a problem with depression?

'As best you can,' Jill said easily. 'You try and focus on the good stuff.'

Another silence fell but Jill was happy enough to let it continue. Jack's speech was fine. Clear and not repetitive, which could have suggested concussion. He may be unimpressed and negative but his brain seemed to be functioning perfectly well and he wasn't looking nauseated despite the twisting road or the smell wafting from Bella's coat.

He could probably cope if the journey was extended by just a few minutes.

'Would you mind if I stopped up the road here for a tick? There's someone I'd really like to check up on.'

Jack shrugged. 'I'm hardly in a position to object, am I?'

'How are you feeling?'

'Fine.'

'Headache?'

'Hasn't got any worse.'

Jill slowed as the exuberant blooms of a tall rosebush hedge came into view. Sure enough, on a cobbled area in front of some ancient stables, she could see her mother's car parked. She would feel a lot happier if she could reassure herself that all was well with her family.

'I won't be long,' she promised.

She parked in the shade of the hedge, near the black wrought-iron gate that closed a narrow passageway beneath an arch of the roses. Aunty Faith's house had certainly been an original settler's cottage but it had been lovingly restored and added to over the decades and was now nestled in grounds that made it as picturesque as a dwelling could be. It had attracted more than one article in house and garden magazines.

The wide-brimmed straw hat, bobbing amongst the tall

delphinium spires at the back of one of the herbaceous borders, was instantly recognisable. And welcome. There couldn't be too much wrong with someone who was out working in their garden.

'Aunty Faith?'

Jill hurried along a brick path skirting a lawn that looked like a bowling green. She would need to get a lot closer to have any chance of being heard, but she didn't want to give Faith Metcalf too much of a fright. Not when she was ninety-three and could fall off her perch any time.

As if!

Jill was grinning as she rounded the metre-high stand of Shasta daisies and dodged the range of a sprinkler. Nothing frightened her great-aunt. The opposite was far more likely. And how on earth did she stay so immaculate? Her cream gardening gloves looked as unsoiled as her crisp white linen trousers. The Christmas lilies she was clipping with her secateurs wouldn't dare spread their yellow pollen. They were being laid with careful precision to nestle in a long shallow cane basket.

'Hello, Aunty.'

'Jillian! What a lovely surprise.' Faith tilted her cheek to accept a kiss. 'Why aren't you busy doing the clinic?'

'Dad's doing it. I had to go out on a call to an accident.'

'Oh, dear! Nobody badly hurt, I hope?'

'Not too badly. I'm just on my way back to the hospital with him. He needs a few stitches.'

'And you've stopped to say hello?' The tone suggested that Jillian was being remiss in her duties. There was a protocol to almost everything in life as far as Faith was concerned, and it needed to be followed.

'I had to pop in just for a minute,' Jill said apologetically. 'To make sure you were all right.'

'Of course I'm all right. Why wouldn't I be?'

'But Mum's here, isn't she?'

Faith picked up her basket with a sigh. The heady scent of the huge fragrant white lilies floated past Jill's nose. A Christmas smell. These blooms were probably destined for one of her aunt's amazing arrangements that would grace the church or maybe the hospital foyer.

'She's in the gazebo,' Faith confirmed. 'Having a bit of time to herself for once. I'm going to make us some lunch in a minute.'

'I'll just say hello, then.' Jill couldn't shake the vague sense of disquiet the apparently innocuous words had envoked. Since when had her mother hid away in order to have time to herself?

'Didn't you say you had a patient waiting to go to hospital?'

'He's fine for the moment. I've parked in the shade and I'll be really quick.'

He'd fallen into a parallel universe.

One filled with sunshine and birdsong and happy people.

Not that Bruce, the sheep farmer, had been particularly happy but that was understandable as he himself hadn't been all that polite, having found himself hanging upside down in the middle of nowhere.

Great start to a new life. The voyage to rediscover himself and find something meaningful to hang the rest of his life on.

Ha!

The fates had decided to rub salt into his wounds, Jack decided, opening his eyes now that the fresh wave of pain and nausea had subsided. The smelly dog had moved, thank goodness. It was curled up on the driver's side. On a seat that was probably still warm from happy, golden Dr Jill's bottom.

A woman who looked like a Christmas angel masquerading as a medic, with that halo of shining blonde curls around blue eyes and a smile that lit up her whole face. Way too happy. And too sure of what path she was following in life. Too capable of dealing with what Jack had failed to deal with so spectacularly.

He blinked, peering out the window as movement caught his peripheral vision. He could see the young doctor walking with a much older woman who was carrying a basket of flowers. He kept staring as the women moved out of view.

He'd been dropped into an environment that looked far too perfect to be real to someone who'd lived in large cities his whole life. Right now he was looking through the bars of a wrought-iron gate at a stone cottage surrounded by an astonishingly colourful garden—a scene that could have graced the front of any coffee-table book or calendar.

It was picture perfect.

So maybe he ought to be taking a picture of it.

He *was* a photographer now, wasn't he?

Yeah….right!

On the other side of the cottage was another smooth green lawn. A stream ran beneath willow trees on the far side and tucked under the graceful foliage was a round trellis structure. A figure got up from the cane chair in the shady interior of the open room.

A woman of about the same height as Jill's petite five feet two but with a much more solid build. Cuddly.

Except she didn't look cuddly right now. Her mother's eyes were swollen and red and her face blotchy. Jill was shocked. The alarm bell that had sounded faintly at the sight of that cluttered bench at home was sounding again with a far more strident note.

'Mum! You look awful! What on earth's the matter?'

'Everything!' Hope Metcalf burst into tears.

'Not a very tactful thing to ask, Jillian,' Faith pointed out mildly.

Jill put her arm around her mother. 'Sorry. I just don't understand. What's going on?'

'I'm sorry,' her mother sobbed. 'I never meant this to happen when you've only just got home, but I can't do it any more…I just can't!'

'Can't do what?'

'Live with your father.'

Jill's jaw dropped. Her parents having marital problems? It was unthinkable. They were two parts of a single unit. The core of Jill's rock. The kind of relationship she had confidently expected to find herself, where the chaff of small irritations could always be blown away to reveal the wheat of what was real and important. Could it be that Jill's rock had a previously unseen crack? Her head moved in a small, decisive shake that deemed the notion of a major upset ridiculous.

Her great-aunt seemed to agree. 'It's a storm in a teacup,' she said calmly.

'What is?' The guilt of leaving her patient waiting a little longer had to be squashed. Jill needed to get to the bottom of this.

'He shouted at me,' Hope said miserably. 'Just because I couldn't find his car keys.'

Jill almost smiled. This was hardly the stuff of divorce. Her father had never been able to find his car keys. Or clean socks. Or cufflinks or stamps or any of a hundred other things. For someone who had such a focussed and decisive mind when it came to any matters medical, he had to be the archetypical domestically challenged male.

'And he should have told me years ago how much he resented the children. He always said if it made me happy then it made *him* happy.'

'Of course it did,' Faith said soothingly. 'He didn't mean it, Hope. James has always been very proud of the lengths you went to to help all those children.'

Jill had thought so, too. Or had that been an illusion? Like her parents' marriage being rock solid and unshakable?

'No.' Hope pressed a damp handkerchief to her nose. 'He said he's never had a home to call his own. It's always been full of waifs and strays and troublemakers. He said, just for once, he'd like to have the house to himself for Christmas. Well, that's what he's going to get.'

'Oh…' Jill took a deep and somewhat shaky breath. She hadn't thought for a moment that dropping in here would be lifting the lid on a giant can of worms.

Totally unexpected worms that she couldn't begin to try and unravel right now.

'We need to talk about this, Mum, but I can't stay right now. I've got a man in the Jeep who needs stitches in his head. What time will you be home?'

'I'm not coming home.'

Faith patted Jill's arm. 'You go, my dear. Look after your patient. I'll look after your mother.'

'But…'

The pat became pressure. Jill found herself moving along the path towards the front gate, accompanied by both her great-aunt and her mother.

Her mobile phone rang. She looked at the call display a little helplessly. Did her father have any idea of how much he'd upset his wife?

'Hi, Dad,' she answered warily.

'Where the hell are you?'

'I'm on my way back. I just stopped to make sure Aunty Faith was all right as I was going past.'

'Do you have any idea where your mother is?'

'Yes.' This was good. Maybe he wanted to apologise for whatever outburst had triggered this unprecedented disharmony. 'She's right here. Do you want to talk to her?'

Her mother was glaring as she shook her head firmly. Her father sounded even more determined.

'No, I don't,' he said furiously. 'Just tell her that she'd better get home. That blasted woman from Invercargill just turned up with four children she wants to leave here. *Four!*' The call was cut off abruptly.

Judging by the shocked look on Hope's face, she had heard the angry words quite clearly.

'It must be Margaret,' she said in dismay, 'but I told her this morning I would have to think about it. That I'd ring her back after I'd talked to Jim. That's what started all the trouble and then I was so upset I forgot all about it.'

'It's not the best time to have a whole family that needs fostering, is it?' Jill chewed her lip anxiously. 'I'll talk to Margaret when I get back.'

Faith didn't appear to be listening. She was frowning as she neared the gate. 'Who is that?'

Jill's eyebrows rose. 'That's my patient. From the plane crash.'

'What's he doing?'

'Looks like he's taking photographs.'

'Well, obviously, Jillian. I may be old but I'm not senile. I'd just like to know why he's taking photographs of my house without asking my permission.'

'He's got a head injury.' Jill felt obliged to defend Jack. 'He probably forgot.'

Introductions seemed to be in order, although it felt very strange when this man was a patient.

'This is my mother, Hope Metcalf,' Jill said cautiously, 'and my great-aunt, Faith.' She turned to her family. 'This is Jack…'

The pause was unavoidable. An introduction to someone without a surname would not be up to scratch. Sure enough, Faith stared down her nose.

'Jack who?'

'Sinclair,' he provided, willingly enough. 'Pleased to meet you, ma'am.'

Nice manners, Jill thought approvingly. Might help if he smiled sometimes, though. She noted the faint bloodstain on the bandage around Jack's head. It was high time she got him back to the hospital and fixed that wound properly. She'd better remember to ask when he'd last had a tetanus shot as well.

'You're taking photographs of my house,' Faith was saying sternly. 'Why?'

'It's an extraordinarily beautiful house,' Jack responded. 'I've never seen anything like it.'

Faith was only partially mollified. 'What do you intend doing with those photographs?'

'Nothing.' Jack put his camera back into the bag. 'But I'm sure I'll enjoy seeing it again. I could send you some copies if you like.'

'Hmm.' The sound was suspicious. 'What do you normally take photographs of, Mr Sinclair?'

Jill expected a vague answer like the one she'd received when trying to quiz Jack about his profession, but to her surprise Jack's lips quirked into something hinting at a smile as he met her great-aunt's steely gaze.

'I was planning to do a series about Christmas,' he said. 'To see if I could capture something unique. Traditionally Kiwi, you know? I'd like to try and record what makes it special.'

'He was heading for Wanaka, Aunty,' Jill put in. 'But his plane crashed.'

'It didn't *crash*,' Jack corrected her. 'I was making a perfectly well-controlled forced landing…'

'And then you crashed.' Jill wasn't going to let him avoid the truth. She'd have to watch that he didn't make light of any symptoms that could point to a head injury that needed investigation.

'Hmm,' Faith said again. It was a thoughtful sound now. 'You do look a bit pale, Mr Sinclair. I think you'd better get to the hospital and let Jillian sort you out.'

Her mother, who had been struggling valiantly to look happy and interested in meeting Jack, couldn't control the wobble of her bottom lip. 'And the children, Jilly. Please, tell Margaret I'm dreadfully sorry but…'

Faith linked her arm through Hope's and turned her away from the gate. 'Jillian's more than capable of sorting everything out. It's high time we had a cup of tea, my dear.'

Bella reluctantly made room as they got back into the Jeep.

'It's not far now.' Jill tried to sound cheerful which wasn't easy, given the new crisis brewing that she was supposed to sort out on top of the shocking revelation that her parents were a lot less than happy with each other. She started the engine and pulled back onto the road. 'Less than ten minutes. I must apologise for that.'

'Why?'

'Hardly very professional to go visiting when I'm effectively driving an ambulance. I've…ah…got a small family crisis going on.'

Jack grunted. 'Your mother certainly didn't look very happy.'

'No.' For a wild moment Jill was tempted to tell this stranger everything. To spill out how disturbing it was to have a crack appearing in her rock. But that would be even less professional than going visiting during a patient transport, wouldn't it? Besides, Jack looked as though he had problems of his own. He couldn't possibly be interested in having someone else's dumped on him.

But it was Jack who broke the silence that fell. 'So why isn't she happy?'

Maybe he *was* interested. Maybe if she was open with him, he might reciprocate. You shouldn't expect to receive more than you were prepared to give, should you?

'Things are a bit stressed,' she said carefully. 'The practice here covers a fairly vast area and there's a population of around three thousand people, which goes up considerably over the summer holiday period. It needs at least two doctors to manage but the last locum left six months ago and Dad's been coping on his own. He's sixty-five now so he should be thinking about retiring, but he can't. Not unless he can find a replacement and that's not going to be easy. Bad enough having a huge general practice with no after-hours relief, but there's the hospital to run on top of that.'

'What size is the hospital?'

'Not big at all. It used to have a thirty-bed capacity and facilities for minor surgery and stuff, but it's been downgraded. There's always a few elderly, recuperative and maternity patients, though, and the locals are determined not to lose the service. Anyway, I think Dad's tired and overworked and he's managed to upset Mum, which is a bit of a worry. Not what I expected when I came home for a happy family Christmas.'

'I guess not. And now you need to smooth things out for your siblings?'

'I don't have any siblings.'

'Your mother said something about the children. About telling Margaret how sorry she is.'

'Oh… Margaret's a social worker. From Invercargill. The children will be cases who need fostering. Mum's been taking in foster-children for ever.'

'*You* were a foster-child?' Jack sounded stunned.

'No, but I was supposed to be the first of about six, and that didn't happen. When I was about eight or nine Mum got interested in fostering and we've had extras in the house at times ever since.'

Waifs and strays and troublemakers.

A crying baby sometimes. A toddler marching around on fat little legs at other times. Quiet children and surly teenagers. They had stayed anywhere from a few days to a few months usually, though Maria had been there until the age of sixteen—even after they'd discovered she had been stealing drugs from the surgery and trying to sell them on the internet.

'They weren't all troublemakers,' she said aloud. 'And it was hardly continuous. Ballochburn's well off the beaten track so my parents weren't at the top of any list of available foster-parents. I suspect what's happened is that there's been a request for a placement over Christmas and, on top of the workload, it's a bit much for Dad right now. The children will just have to go somewhere else, I guess.'

Jack grunted again. He didn't sound interested any more and Jill drove in silence, giving up the hope that he might want to start talking about himself. It was curiously disappointing. Almost embarrassing. She was too open sometimes, wasn't she? Too trusting of people. She should have learned her lessons by now and yet she still got overruled by her instincts about people. The need to get involved.

Jack Sinclair clearly didn't want to let her into any part of his life. She may be rescuing him and on the way to patch up his wounds, but that would be it. He would exit her life, leaving an air of mystery behind him.

But again it was Jack who broke the silence. With another question that was a little out of left field.

'So your real name is Jillian, huh?'

'I hate it,' Jill said, with feeling. 'But I really can't complain.'

'Why not?'

'Because I narrowly escaped being called Glory.'

He had to think about that for a second and then he huffed. The sort of sound someone might make if they had no intention of being amused but couldn't help it.

'Right…an aunt Faith and a mother Hope. Yeah…you *were* lucky.'

This time the quirk of his lips was nearly half a smile. Jill turned her head at just the right moment to catch it and she was startled. If this man *really* smiled, he would be… gorgeous.

Absolutely, stunningly gorgeous.

An odd sensation pierced her gut. A weird *ping* that, unfortunately, Jill recognised only too easily.

Uh-oh!

There was something seriously attractive about Jack Sinclair.

Danger signs flashed with neon brightness in her head. It was as much a part of who she was as her overactive imagination and her willingness to trust others. Not that she felt that attracted to many men—quite the opposite, given that it had only happened a very few times—but when it did, it was like a runaway horse. She could fall in love so hard it blinded her, and by the time she found she'd been attracted to the wrong person, it was way too late.

It was *not* going to happen again.

No way.

Jill's fierce grip on the steering-wheel only eased as she pulled into the hospital car park.

'Here we are,' she said with forced brightness.

At least distraction was at hand. Beside a station wagon marked with the insignia of the southern health region's social welfare department, an anxious-looking woman stood talking to Jill's father.

Behind the woman were four children.

And three of them were crying.

CHAPTER THREE

THE misery of the children must be contagious.

Jim Metcalf had obviously caught it. He glared at his daughter.

'Where's your mother?'

'She can't come.'

'Why not?'

Jill's look told her father that she was far enough in the loop to know that he knew the answer to that question perfectly well. He looked disconcerted but then frowned. Jill groaned inwardly. Whatever the argument had been about, her father had decided he was in the right and she knew just how stubborn he was capable of being about backing down. Her mother could also be stubborn. No wonder she hadn't been able to escape that particular family trait.

'If I could just talk to her,' the anxious-looking woman said. 'I know I shouldn't have just come but I thought if she *met* the children…'

Jill looked at the wall of children. The only one not crying was the oldest—a sulky-looking boy of about nine or ten. Dark-skinned, with black hair, he was nothing like the smaller boy, who had red hair, or the girl, who had blonde hair but blazingly red cheeks. She was clutching the hand of a toddler who had virtually no hair at all and who was shrieking loudly enough to have brought Maisie out from the kitchens.

'What on earth is all this racket about?' Maisie demanded.

Jill was aware that Jack had climbed out of the Jeep. This was embarrassing. Not only was her passenger not particularly interested in any stress her family was under, he'd been less than impressed with the direction she was taking her medical career and he was now going to stand and watch her try to sort out what could only be described as a small circus happening in the car park of this sleepy rural hospital.

'It's OK, Maisie. I'll sort it out.' Jill tried to sound confident.

Maisie snorted.

Bella had climbed out of the vehicle to follow Jack. The toddler's shrieks made her cringe but she slunk closer to Jill and sat down on her foot. For a skinny dog, she was surprisingly heavy.

So was the heat of this summer's day. Jill could feel it pressing on her head like another weight. Heavy enough to cause discomfort that threatened to turn into a nasty headache. No wonder the children all looked hot and miserable. It would have been a drive of several hours to bring them here from Invercargill.

Something had to be done.

'Could you take the children into the kitchen and give them all a cold drink, please, Maisie?'

The cook blinked at Jill's firm tone but then gave a small nod, as though pleasantly surprised. She began to herd the children but couldn't resist a look over her shoulder.

'Have you fed that poor dog yet?'

'No.' Jill looked down at her foot. 'Bella, go with Maisie. She'll find you some food.'

Another snort was heard from Maisie's direction but the oldest boy paused and turned to stare at Bella. Bella stared back.

'Go on,' Jill urged. 'There's a good girl.'

The boy tapped his hand on his leg. Bella gave Jill a questioning look and Jill nudged her with her foot. 'Go on,' she encouraged.

Bella disappeared in the wake of the procession heading for the kitchens. Jim cleared his throat and looked longingly at the direction he needed to take to get back inside the main hospital building.

'I really ought to get back to my patients,' he grumbled. 'I've got Judith Cartwright in there with chest pain.'

Jill gave her father another look. Judith Cartwright was probably hyperventilating from stress. Again. It was hardly life-threatening. 'Could you show Jack where the waiting room is?' Jill gestured towards the man standing silently to one side. 'He was KO'd and could be concussed. He's also got a laceration that needs suturing.'

'It'll be a while before I have time to deal with that.' Jim ran his fingers through his thick salt-and-pepper hair, ruffling it enough to rival Bella's tufts. 'I've got a packed waiting room as it is.'

'I'm fine,' Jack said. 'There's absolutely no rush.'

'I'll do the suturing,' Jill promised. 'And I'll be able to help with the rest of clinic. Just give me ten minutes to sort things out.'

'Good.' Jim nodded and gave Jack a curious glance. 'I'll leave you for Jill to look after, then.' He smiled, nodded at Margaret then turned with obvious relief to march purposefully off towards the main doors.

'I'm so sorry,' Margaret said. 'I really didn't mean to cause such a problem. It's just that Hope's always been so helpful and I was desperate. There's no way I can keep this family together if we have to place them in town.'

Jill eyebrows rose. 'They're from one family?'

'Yes. They've all got different fathers.' The social worker sighed. 'I've known the mother for quite a while. She died this morning quite unexpectedly.'

'Oh, that's awful! What happened to her?'

'She overdosed on her antidepressants. We're trying to trace her family but they've gone on holiday somewhere in Europe so it's proving difficult. It could be a week or more until we can make proper arrangements and it seemed a bit tough to separate the children at Christmas.'

Of course it was. Jill chewed her lip. She could offer to take them home herself but that was hardly going to help sort things out for her parents, was it?

'I wish I could help,' she said slowly, 'but the problem is that Mum's not at home at the moment.'

'When will she be back?'

'I really don't know,' Jill answered honestly. 'I'm not sure she knows herself.' She avoided looking at Jack to see how he was reacting to her evasion. He knew her mother wasn't far away. Would he think her completely heartless, sending these children back to the city to get separated and sent to different foster-homes? He was already unimpressed with her. Seeing disappointment would be even worse.

Margaret sighed. 'It's not your fault, dear. I knew it was a gamble. I'll just have to take them back to town. Poor things, they hated the drive up. In fact, they haven't stopped crying since the police collected them all this morning.'

'I'm not surprised. They've just lost their mother.'

'The little ones don't really know what's going on but I'm worried about Jarred—the oldest. He's only nine and he's been holding that family together for a long time. He'll be devastated if they get split up.'

'I hope you can find the family soon.'

'So do I.' Margaret didn't sound very hopeful and Jill had to fight the urge to try and make everything all right. To say that, of course, her mother would love to help. But that was impossible. There was no way she could make this all right for everybody concerned.

Instead, she cleared her throat. 'I'll show you where the kitchens are,' she said. 'Jack? You may as well come with us and get out of this sun. I'll take you through to the surgery when we've found the children.'

Maisie was standing in the middle of the kitchen, her arms folded. 'If you ask me, these children are sick,' she said indignantly. 'You could fry an egg on the head of that baby.'

'Really?' Jill moved swiftly to lay her hand on the wispy hair. 'You're right, Maisie.'

She turned to the girl whose tear-stained cheeks were still flushed scarlet, despite being out of the sun. 'Hello, sweetheart. What's your name?'

'J-Jade.'

'Are you feeling sick, Jade?'

'I want Mummy,' the girl sobbed.

The oldest boy, Jarred, was crouched beside Bella, who was licking the base of a stainless-steel basin. He looked up.

'We've all been sick,' he said sullenly. 'We've got spots.'

'Oh, Lord!' Margaret sank onto a chair beside the long table. 'I had no idea.'

Jack stayed near the door he had just entered. He put his bags down and was watching the scene with apparent interest.

'What sort of spots?' Jill asked. 'Can you show me?'

'I can.' The red-haired boy hoisted up his T-shirt. 'I've got the most.'

Jill stared at the skinny pale chest on view. A chest that was marked by the outline of ribs but also by a lot of angry red dots. She moved closer. Some of the dots had little blisters on them.

'Oh…' Jill took a deep, even breath. 'And you've all got these spots?'

'Nat hasn't got any,' Jarred said, pointing at the toddler. 'And mine are starting to go kind of scabby now.'

'I've got more than Jarred had,' the redhead proclaimed. 'And they're really, really itchy.'

'Chickenpox,' Maisie announced triumphantly. 'I'd know those kind of spots anywhere.'

'What's your name?' Jill asked. Why hadn't she noticed the spots among his freckles earlier?

'Mel.'

'After Mel Gibson,' Jarred said. A rather adult tone of disparagement was clear. 'Mum thought he was hot.'

Jade's sobs increased in intensity. 'I want *Mummy*.'

Margaret looked ready to cry herself. 'Is that what it is? Chickenpox?'

'Yes.' Jill was nodding thoughtfully. 'It's chickenpox all right.'

'This is terrible,' Margaret said faintly. 'We can't place the children in private homes if they're contagious.' She paused and gulped audibly. '*Are* they contagious?'

'Very,' Jill said. 'The infectious period is from one to two days before the appearance of the rash until it's fully crusted.'

She smiled at the children. 'But don't worry. You'll all feel better in a few days.'

'But….' Margaret was clearly at a loss. 'What am I going to do?'

Jill smiled again. What needed to be done was crystal clear as far as she was concerned.

Maisie looked at Jill and sighed deeply.

Jack was also watching her. It seemed likely that he'd guessed her thoughts, judging by the suggestion of an incredulous smile that was tugging at his mouth.

He *wanted* to smile properly, didn't he? It was almost as though he'd forgotten how to.

'These children are sick,' Jill said calmly. 'They need to stay together and they have nowhere to go. I'm going to admit them all to hospital.'

'In Invercargill?' Margaret queried. Her eyes widened at the prospect of another long journey with a carload of children she now knew to be unwell.

'No,' Jill said. 'Here. In Ballochburn.'

Maisie made an 'I knew it' grumbling sound.

'We've got plenty of empty beds,' Jill said firmly. 'And we can call in some extra staff to help.'

Maisie's grumble took on a 'you'll be lucky' tone now.

'They can all stay together,' Jill continued, unable to prevent sounding pleased with herself. 'We'll open up one of the four-bed wards next to Maternity. I'll just call one of our nurses and get the beds made up.'

'How long will they need to stay in hospital?'

'Until they're not contagious. Could be anywhere from five to ten days. At least a week, anyway.'

Long enough for Margaret to have a chance to sort a

suitable and more permanent arrangement. Long enough to keep the children together, at least for Christmas. The social worker caught Jill's eye and smiled.

'Thank you,' she said softly. 'You're an angel.'

'Why did you do that?'

Jack was walking beside Jill along a quiet central corridor. The hospital had been built in an era that had taken aesthetics into account as much as any practical considerations. The high plaster ceilings were decorated with ornate roses along the edges. The floor was of deep brown polished wood and the long, wide space was punctuated at regular intervals with moulded wooden archways. Tall sash windows afforded a view into a well-tended garden.

'You didn't have to,' Jack added. He sounded curious rather than disapproving. Puzzled, even.

'It was the perfect solution.' Jill gave a satisfied sigh. 'Dad can hardly object—not when they're sick. He's good with sick people—especially children.'

'One would hope so,' Jack murmured.

'And Mum will be delighted. She'd feel terrible letting Margaret down and she'd move heaven and earth to help children in that sort of predicament. This way, she can help look after them but they won't be at home so it can't make things any worse there.'

'Things are bad at home?'

'Ah…' Jill had allowed her pleasure at solving one crisis to loosen her tongue more than she'd intended. 'Not really. Like I told you, there's a bit of stress around at the moment, that's all. It's nothing major.'

At least, she hoped it was nothing major. She slowed, glad

of a reason not to think about her mother's tear-ravaged face. 'Come in here. We've got a good treatment room next to X-Ray. It should have everything we need to fix up your head.' She grinned up at Jack. 'I'll spare you the trauma of going through the waiting room and being the subject of avid interest to all our locals.'

'Small town, huh?'

'Yes. Although we get quite a few strangers at this time of year. The camping ground is a real favourite and it's amazing how many people can get sick or injured on holiday. Not really fair, is it? A hospital is the last place you'd want to be when you're on your summer holidays.'

A hospital was the last place Jack wanted to be, full stop.

The corridor had been OK. So unlike the kind of hospital environment Jack was used to that it hardly registered.

But here, in this treatment room, it felt like the walls were closing in. Everything was so familiar. Too familiar. The oxygen and entonox cylinders, the trays of IV gear, the boxes of disposable gloves. Even the smell.

Jack climbed onto the bed that Jill was patting. He lay back and closed his eyes with a faint groan.

'You're not feeling great, are you?'

What an understatement!

'Not particularly,' Jack said through gritted teeth.

'Head hurting?'

'It's OK.'

'Feeling sick?'

'No.'

'What's making you feel so bad, then?'

She sounded like she cared. Really cared. But Jack didn't

want her sympathy. Didn't need it. He almost laughed. Life, he felt like saying. The fact that I'm so burnt out I'm dead inside. I have nothing left to give so why should I expect to be given anything myself?

Christmas. The season of giving.

And Jack had landed in the middle of nowhere to find a Christmas angel who seemed to be spreading magic.

That smelly dog thought so, anyway.

And four hot, miserable, itchy children.

And that worried-looking social worker from down south.

It was crazy and Jack was miserable enough to find the good humour and altruism irritating. So was the confidently expectant silence from Jill.

'I just don't like Christmas,' he growled finally.

'Ooh!' He could hear the smile. 'A real live Grinch. Cool!'

She obviously wasn't taking him seriously. He could hear a kind of hum as she moved around, collecting what she needed. A Christmas carol he vaguely recognised. Was it intended as a reproach to his 'Bah, humbug' comment? Jack focussed on the other sounds. Packages being ripped open. The clink of things dropping onto a tray or kidney dish. The sound of water running as Jill scrubbed her hands. Then he could sense her coming closer. Could feel her warmth and smell the faint scent of something like strawberries. Could feel the gentle touch of her hands as she began unwinding the bandage from around his head.

'Do you have any medical conditions I should know about, Jack?'

'No.' Except maybe post-traumatic stress syndrome. Or possibly good, old-fashioned, everyday depression.

'Are you taking any medication on a regular basis?'

'No.' They'd been offered, of course. Advocated strongly,

in fact, but Jack had been horrified. He'd take time out first, he'd said. Six months or a year. See if he could sort out his head himself. And his heart.

'When did you last have a tetanus booster?'

'About ten years ago.' He'd had one when he'd started working in an emergency department, hadn't he? Along with the course of hepatitis vaccine. You could take precautions against some of the potential dangers of working on the front line, couldn't you?

Shame there wasn't a vaccine to prevent getting too involved emotionally.

Getting wrecked.

Dying inside.

He could have carried on. Like the consultant he'd worked under, Jack could have functioned so that medicine had just been a job. No involvement. No caring. No fallout when things went wrong because that was just part of the job. You won some, you lost some.

But that had been, quite simply, unacceptable.

If he was incapable of becoming involved—in a controlled fashion so that he, at least, cared about what he was doing—then he would get out completely.

For ever.

Right now it felt like he could never be involved on any level. There was nothing left to give.

Just an empty space.

Sucking in a sharp breath was involuntary but Jack actually welcomed the sting of the fluid in his wound. It made him feel alive.

'Sorry,' Jill said. 'I'll put a bit of local in now. You'll feel it stinging a bit.'

It did sting.

And then there was just numbness.

The kind of numbness he was almost getting used to on an emotional level.

Jack cracked his eyes open far enough to catch a glimpse of Jill as she worked.

She was gorgeous—even with no hint of that merry smile creasing her face. Concentration on her task had intensified the blue of her eyes so that they reminded him of the tall delphinium spires he had seen in her great-aunt's garden. He could see the freckles dusting pale skin and decorating a cute snubbed nose. And the enchanting way her bottom lip was caught, just at one side, between small white teeth.

At any other time in his life Jack would have found this woman astonishingly attractive.

Right now he would have welcomed an indication of a response that was more than purely intellectual in the same way he'd appreciated the sting of the local anaesthetic. But it was like looking at a photograph. An attractive picture of something he had absolutely no connection with.

Being this close let him notice that pale band of skin on the third finger of her left hand where it was obvious a ring had been worn for a long time but had now been removed, suggesting that Jill was single again. Even that couldn't prompt any more than a vague surprise that she'd had a relationship that hadn't worked out.

Fear threatened to step in again.

The fear that he might have lost the ability to connect with anybody.

And what made that so terrifying was the knowledge that

the ability to connect was the only thing that could give life any real meaning.

Jack had to close his eyes again. To try and focus on the painless tugging he could feel happening to the skin on the side of his forehead. It was easy to imagine himself standing behind young Dr Metcalf, watching what she was doing.

Putting the needle in far enough from the edge of the wound to prevent the suture from tearing through the skin.

Releasing the needle holder and grasping the tip of the needle with forceps to pull it out of the base of the wound. Inserting it into the base of the opposite side and pushing it to the surface.

Pulling the suture material through and looping it twice around the needle holder. Grasping the short end and pulling it through the loops.

He could feel the wound edges being drawn together as the first knot was tied.

Stay focussed, he warned himself.

Don't step back any further.

Because, if he did, he would see the bigger picture of the young, vibrantly alive woman caring for an empty shell of a man.

And Jack didn't want to see that man. It wasn't him.

If he didn't sink into the fear, he could hold onto the hope that he could find what he'd lost.

He could find himself again.

CHAPTER FOUR

'WHAT have you done with that plane-crash fellow?'

'I got Maisie onto him.' Blonde curls bounced as Jill shook her head ruefully on entering the consulting room. 'I had to take extreme measures. He wasn't about to take my advice and rest quietly for a few hours.' She grinned. 'I finally told him I didn't have time to do the paperwork until I'd helped you with the clinic and if he scarpered I'd get into big trouble. The hospital might get its licence revoked and I was sure he didn't want to be responsible for having Ballochburn's iconic medical facility closed down. Besides, he needed a cup of tea and something for his headache.'

'Could do with a cup of tea myself, 'Jim grumbled. 'I popped into the kitchen a while back but Maisie was nowhere to be seen.'

'Mmm.' Jill tried to sound both surprised and sympathetic but she knew perfectly well that Maisie would have been upstairs, helping to make up beds for the new inpatients her father clearly didn't know about yet. Time to change the subject. 'Who would you like me to see?'

Her father finished the sentence he was scribbling in a patient's file. Jill could see the pink paper of an ECG trace sc he must have taken Judith's chest pain seriously enough to investigate it properly.

'Check with Muriel that nothing urgent has come in. If not, young Aaron Baker's got a sore arm. Doesn't look broken so he wasn't top of the list but he's been waiting awhile. If you sort him, I'll get on with all the repeat prescriptions. Sue's coming in as well. She's running a bit low on morphine.'

'Oh, I must catch up with Sue. I feel terrible I haven't had a chance to get out to the orchard yet.'

'I'll tell her you're here. She needs her friends right now and no mistake. She's having one tough year.'

'I know. We saw a lot of each other when she was up in Auckland with Emma.'

A tiny silence fell. A look shared that made Jill swallow hard to get rid of the sudden lump in her throat. What could you say when your best friend was facing the final Christmas her small child would ever have?

She managed a smile. Hopefully one that let her father know she understood how tough his part in the story was. That she was aware of the stress levels and that the grumpiness that might have upset the apple cart at home was forgivable. That she loved him for the depth of involvement and the genuine care he gave his patients. A quality she'd thought she'd found in the man she'd married, only she'd been very wrong. He had cared far more for himself than anyone else.

Many of those patients were still crowding the small waiting area. Jill had a quick word with Muriel, the receptionist, and then took Aaron and his mother and a melted bag of frozen peas through to the treatment room. Jim took Mrs Briggs into the consulting room. There were still half a dozen people sitting patiently, thumbing through magazines that were probably years out of date. Except for the large girl in the corner, who was sitting motionless, her head down and her long hair screening her face. But Jill couldn't respond to the subtle warning bell ringing in the back of her head. Not when there was obviously nothing life-threatening going on.

'Your dad was a friend of mine,' she told six-year-old Aaron. 'I went to school with him and I seem to remember him hurting *his* arm once. He fell off his motorbike. You're not into motorbikes yet, are you?'

Aaron's mother groaned. 'He would be if he got half a chance but, no, this time it was Rambo's fault.'

'Rambo?' Jill lifted the small boy to sit on the edge of the bed that Jack had been occupying only minutes previously. The tray of things she'd used to suture that laceration was still sitting on the bench, waiting to be cleaned up.

She could still feel his presence.

That odd sensation of too personal a contact that had come from touching him.

The curiosity about why he didn't like Christmas.

'Rambo's my lamb,' Aaron said proudly. 'We were practising.'

'It's pets' day tomorrow,' his mother said. 'Rambo's supposed to walk nicely for the judging and in the parade only he's grown like a weed and he's a bit strong for Aaron now. He pulled him over.'

'Where does it hurt?' Jill asked.

'Here.' Aaron pointed at his forearm.

'Can you wiggle your fingers?'

Small and very grubby fingers waggled.

'Can you squeeze my hand?'

'Ouch!'

'Show me where that hurts.'

Jill made a thorough examination of the limb. 'I don't think anything's broken,' she concluded. 'It's a bit sore but it isn't too swollen and it's not restricting his movement too much. If it gets worse we'll need to take an X-ray but I'm confident it's just a sprain. A bandage and some rest should do the trick. The bag of peas was a brilliant idea—it would have helped a lot.'

'Can I still take Rambo to pets' day?'

'Can Mum or Dad help you when it comes to the parade?'

'I don't *want* help. I'm not a baby.'

Jill nodded. 'Of course you're not. You'd have to be careful not to let him hurt your arm any more, though. Maybe you could just let him go if he pulls too hard, instead of trying to hang onto him.' She smiled at Aaron's mother. 'I guess the worst thing that could happen is that Rambo will run amok and cause chaos.'

'Which half the pets will be doing anyway!'

'Yeah.' Jill's smile broadened as she opened a crêpe bandage and began winding it around the small wrist.

She had to push aside the memory of winding another crêpe bandage so recently…around Jack's head. She had to stop letting him enter her mind so often or it could get out of control. Given her track record, her imagination could run amok far more wildly than Rambo ever could. She'd be having visions of walking down an aisle on Jack's arm soon. Admiring the wall of professional photographs he'd taken of their six beautiful children. Having the anticipation of seeing him smile to help get her through the worst of any working days.

Oh, *help*! Just the thought of seeing that smile was enough to make her feel gooey inside. This was threatening to be a bad dose.

'I took a pet lamb to school one year,' she said, a trifle desperately. 'Someone's dog started chasing it and they went right into the classrooms.'

Aaron's eyes widened. He was impressed. 'Did you get into trouble?'

'Not really. I had to clean up the little present he'd left for the teacher, though.'

Aaron giggled. 'What was *your* lamb's name?'

'Minty.' Jill wasn't going to elaborate. It had been her father's idea to call the orphan Mint Sauce. Lamb Chops had been the previous year's model.

'Are you coming tomorrow?'

'I'll certainly try. What time is the parade?'

'Two p.m.,' Aaron's mother supplied. 'And then there's the barbecue and school break-up.'

'That would bring back a few memories.' Jill sighed happily. ' I hope I can make it.'

'Will you bring a pet?' Aaron asked.

'I haven't got one at the moment. Although…' Jill taped the end of the bandage into place. 'I did find a dog today. If I brought her to school, someone might recognise her and I could find her owner.' She lifted Aaron back to the floor. 'Mind you, she'd need a bath first. She's a bit stinky.'

'So's Rambo.' Aaron looked up at his mother. 'Can we give *him* a bath?'

'No.'

'Please?'

'He's a sheep, Aaron. Sheep don't get in the bath.'

'But he's my *pet*!' Aaron's lip wobbled. 'And I want him to *win* and I can't wash him by myself because I've got a sore *arm*...'

Aaron's mother sighed deeply. 'We'll see...'

Mrs Briggs was coming out of the consulting room, clutching a prescription, as Jill waved the Bakers off.

'My Wally's coming in later,' she was saying to her doctor. 'There's a Friends of the Hospital meeting this evening.'

'Is there?' Jill's father didn't sound thrilled. Yet another evening to be taken up with professional responsibilities.

'Yes. Six-thirty p.m. You will be there, won't you, Dr Metcalf?'

'Probably,' Jim said gloomily.

'I'll be there,' Jill said. 'Did Wally get the message about that plane, Mrs Briggs?'

'Yes. He went to have a look at it after he dropped me off here.'

'I'll bring Jack to the meeting, then. He can have a chat to Wally.'

'And Hope will be there, of course?'

'Don't ask me,' Jim snapped.

'I'm sure she will.' Jill shot her father a warning glance as Mrs Briggs's eyebrows shot up. 'She wouldn't miss the Christmas meeting. Not when you always bring those wonderful mince pies of yours.'

Mrs Briggs sniffed. 'Yes, well, Wally'd better hurry up so I can get home to bake them. I'll look forward to seeing Hope later, then.'

'Mmm.' At least her mother wouldn't be too far away from the meeting venue. The quick phone call Jill had managed earlier had set wheels in motion so easily it only confirmed that she'd done the right thing. Hope would be upstairs somewhere right now, getting those children settled and happy. Finding pyjamas and toys and books. Probably a television set and videos. Planning on how to help Maisie feed them all.

Very satisfying.

Apart from the unexploded bomb of her father not being consulted about admitting four cases of chickenpox to his hospital.

Jill avoided his eye. 'Who's next, then?'

'Can you take that girl in the corner? I have no idea who she is.'

Doreen Briggs peered over her spectacles. 'Not a local,' she pronounced. 'Must be a camper.'

The girl's name was Elise. She followed Jill though to the treatment room without taking her eyes off the floor in front of her feet.

'Are you here on holiday, Elise?'

'Nah. I just got a ride with some people who were going camping here.'

'Where have you come from?'

'Dunedin.'

'Does your family know you're here?'

'Nah.'

The tone made it clear that the line of questioning wasn't welcome. Jill backed off.

'How old are you, Elise?'

'Eighteen.'

The eye contact was fleeting but defensive. She didn't look eighteen. Had she picked that as an age in order to stop someone trying to contact her family?

'And what's brought you in here today? Are you not feeling well?'

'I'm fine.'

Yet again, Jack popped into Jill's head. He'd kept saying he was fine when it had been painfully obvious he hadn't been. This girl was giving off a similar kind of vibe, too. Something sad. Something they were hiding…running away from.

'So how can I help?' she asked gently.

'I had a job in Dunedin,' Elise said. 'I was a nurse aide in an old folks' home. I've got a reference.'

'That's good.' Jill smiled, encouraging the girl to keep talking. To tell her what problem had brought her to seek medical assistance.

Elise looked up. She hesitated but then smiled back and for a moment the misery in her face vanished. If she washed her hair, Jill thought, and got a bit of sunshine and a healthy diet, and some clothes that weren't baggy enough to look like sacks, she would be a stunning-looking young woman.

'So, will you give me a job, then?'

'Ah…' Jill hadn't expected that. 'Is *that* why you're here?'

'Yeah. I really need a job.'

Jill nodded slowly. Lots of young people flocked to Central Otago for summer employment. There were always vacancies at the orchards.

'But why here?' she said aloud. 'In a hospital? Why not outside in one of the orchards? Or in a packing shed where there'd be heaps of kids your age?'

'I like hospitals,' Elise said. 'I want to be a nurse one day. You wanna see my reference?'

'OK.' Jill was trying to buy thinking time. She'd already

landed her father with a virtually one hundred per cent increase in the number of inpatients. If she started hiring casual staff behind his back, he would have just cause to regret asking her to help out as his locum. Not to mention that he was feeling aggrieved at the way waifs and strays had peppered his life. Elise had to fall into the stray camp. She was a bit solid to be a waif.

But Maisie had been looking for part-time help in the kitchens for ages.

They needed extra help for a few days at least to care for all those children.

And by all accounts, Elise was very good with old people.

'It's a wonderful reference,' Jill said warmly. 'It's not up to me whether you can have a job but I'll see what I can do. I might not be able to talk to anyone until we've finished seeing our patients. Can you wait for a while?'

'Sure.'

Blow the paperwork.

Escape was definitely in order.

He'd find the woman who'd given him that nice cup of tea and that melt-in-the-mouth home-made shortbread and ask about getting a taxi. Find a motel, maybe. He could always drop in on his way out of town tomorrow and give Jill any details she needed for her database and the government's accident corporation claim forms.

He didn't need to be in hospital but he wasn't stupid enough to be planning a long-distance drive immediately. His headache was bad enough to suggest mild concussion and, anyway, he couldn't take off and leave his pride and joy upside down in a paddock with sheep nibbling the brand-new paintwork. With Ballochburn being the size it was, the cook was bound to know who Wally was and how he could get in touch with him.

But where was she? Having given him the afternoon tea in the kitchen and told him in no uncertain terms he was to sit and take things quietly until further notice, she had sailed off like a battleship with a flotilla of little tugs.

It was about time someone sorted out these poor children, she'd said.

And, no, the dog was not allowed to go upstairs.

The aromatic mutt had gone somewhere, though. Jack was alone in the vast kitchen. His bags were still sitting near the door—a reminder of the nomadic life he'd embarked on. A clear statement that he didn't belong here and it was time to move on. With an effort Jack got to his feet, picked up the bags and left the comforting smell of baking behind.

He'd been down this corridor a couple of times now, on his way to and from the treatment room. He didn't want to bump into Jill or her father so he avoided going left. Looking straight ahead, he could see an atrium-type area with a sweeping staircase and an ancient lift with wrought-iron gates. Presumably the corridor to his right led towards the back door he had entered in the first place but his head felt too fuzzy to remember clearly and this rambling old building was like a rabbit warren.

Cautiously, Jack took an exploratory walk. Between a pair of the tall sash windows were some French doors he hadn't noticed before. They were open and they led onto a veranda and then into the manicured gardens. Somebody was sitting on a bench in the shade of a huge old tree.

Somebody that might know where the battleship woman had gone.

'G'day.'

The boy didn't bother to look up at Jack and he made no response.

'Jarred, isn't it?'

'Yeah.' The admission was reluctant.

Jack sat down on the bench. Even the short walk from the veranda had been enough to make his head pound and the shade was very inviting.

'I'm Jack,' he said politely.

There was no response. Jarred was sitting with his head down. His fingers were buried in the shaggy coat of the smelly dog.

The silence was a little awkward so Jack tried again.

'How's it going?'

'It's not allowed inside. The big lady said so.'

'No.' Jack looked down at the dog. 'I guess that's fair enough. It *is* a hospital.'

'I hate hospitals.'

'So do I, mate.'

'Why do *you* hate them?' It sounded as though it was Jarred's prerogative to hate everything. Jack was encroaching on ground where he wasn't welcome.

'Long story.' Jack leaned back and closed his eyes. 'Do you know where the…ah…big lady is at the moment?'

'She's upstairs with some other ladies. They've found some green stuff for a bath. It's supposed to stop you itching.'

'Right. I guess she's busy, then.'

'She said she'd come down soon. I have to stay here. She sounded cross.'

'I don't think she is cross.' Jack cracked an eyelid half-open. 'She sounded cross when she said I had to stay in the kitchen but I reckon she was just being kind. I'll wait for a bit until she comes down.'

The silence wasn't awkward this time, which was good. What wasn't so good was the feeling of kinship with this kid. Hardly surprising, though, was it? Easy to remember what it was like to be nine years old and feel all alone in the world.

Not that Jarred needed anyone to feel sorry for him. He wasn't really alone. He may have lost his mother but at least she had died and not just gone off because she hadn't wanted him. And he had siblings. A family. And he was going to be looked after by the Metcalfs. To have a Christmas in the parallel universe.

The kind of Christmas a nine-year-old Jack could have only dreamed of.

The kind of fostering that had never come his way—even for a few days.

No. He didn't need to get involved. Or tell the boy any of his own sob story. Jarred was lucky. And it wasn't his problem, anyway.

'What's in the bag?'

'Clothes and stuff.' Jack prodded the back pack with his foot.

'I meant the other bag. The black one.'

'Oh… That's my camera.'

The symbol of his new career. Not that Jack really expected to earn a living from his photographs. He knew it was escapism. What better way to take time out and observe life from a safe distance than to be behind the impersonal lens of a state-of-the-art digital camera?

'Can I see?' Jarred made it sound as though it was of no importance if the request was refused—in fact, he fully expected it to be refused—but Jack remembered that particular defence mechanism only too well.

'If you want,' he said casually. 'I could show you how it works and you could take a picture of Bella.'

The French doors were open.

Jill could hear voices as she hurried towards the kitchen and the deep rumble of one of those voices was already familiar enough to create a warm tingle.

A dangerous but, oh, so delicious tingle.

She paused on the veranda for a moment, caught by the picture in front of her. The two dark heads, close together, with the dappled light from sunshine filtering through leaves creating an almost halo effect.

Bella sat pressed against the boy's leg, her head flat on his lap, looking up with an adoring expression.

Much the same expression as was on Jarred's face when he stole an upward glance at the man sitting beside him. The looking was fleeting, his attention quickly refocussed on the object Jack was holding.

'It's a very good camera,' Jack was saying. 'Lots of professional photographers use it and lots use digital rather than film now. This is the latest model—ten point two mega-pixels.'

'What's a mega-pixel?'

Jill knew she should keep moving and not stand there, eavesdropping, but it was irresistible. Jack sounded different somehow. As though his guard was down. He was also talking to Jarred in a man-to-man fashion and Jill was loath to break into something that was clearly a good distraction from the chaos the boy's life had been plunged into. Heck, it was probably the most exciting thing that had happened to this lad in a long time. She wouldn't pass up the opportunity to have a serious discussion about something—anything, really—with Jack so why should she take it away from someone else?

'A mega-pixel is a measure of how big the CCD is,' Jack said. 'That's the bit of a camera that captures the image. Bottom line is, the more mega-pixels you have, the better quality the picture. You can make it bigger without losing any of the definition.'

'Is ten point two big?'

'Huge.' Jack sounded satisfied. He must love his photography, Jill decided. Was that part of his attraction? A sort of tortured artist quality? 'These pictures are the best you can get.'

'So you could make this one bigger?'

'Yeah. Big as a wall.'

'Can I have one?'

'Sure. Maybe not that big, though. The paper gets awfully expensive. I could make you an ordinary-sized one.'

'When?'

'As soon as I can find a computer to print it out on. I'll post it to you.'

'But I want to show Mel and Jade. And that lady.'

'Well…' Jack was hesitant. Reluctant. 'I guess we could show them on the camera, before I go.'

'When are you going?'

'As soon as I can, mate.'

'Why?' Jarred asked.

Yes, echoed in Jill's head. *Why?* What's the hurry?

'I hate hospitals, remember?'

'Oh…yeah…'

Jill could understand the disappointment in Jarred's voice. More than understand. She could feel it herself. She didn't want Jack to disappear, either.

And he wasn't allowed to. Not just yet.

'Hi,' she said brightly, bouncing down the steps as though she had just emerged in a hurry from the corridor. 'I found you!'

Sitting with his bags by his feet. Looking as though he couldn't wait to escape.

Why did Jack hate hospitals?

And Christmas?

'Jack took my photo.' Jarred sounded nothing like the sullen child she'd left crouching in the corner of the kitchen. 'Me and the dog.'

'Can I see?'

She peered at the screen on the back of the camera and Jack scrolled through several pictures. Some were terrible—just parts of a dog and one of Jack's left foot.

'I took those,' Jarred said proudly.

But then there were several more. Of Jarred and Bella and one in particular made Jill catch her breath. The boy and the dog were looking at each other. Very seriously. There was a kind of amazement caught in that moment. Like a recognition of finding a soul-mate. The very beginning of a love affair.

Jill's heart gave one of those bitter-sweet squeezes. 'That's really lovely,' she whispered. 'I'd like a copy of that one.'

'Sure.' Jack was offhand. Did he not realise the magic he'd captured?

'He can post you one,' Jarred said importantly.

'What sort of computer do you need to print one out on?'

Jack gave her a suspicious glance, as though the possibility she had been eavesdropping had occurred to him. She managed a perfectly innocent smile that said everybody knew about digital cameras.

'Do you need special paper?'

'I've got some paper,' Jack said warily. 'In my bag.'

'We could find a computer, then,' Jill said happily. 'I still need to do that paperwork on you, Jack. There's a good computer in the office.'

'Can I come, too?' Jarred's surly tone was back again. He didn't expect to be included.

'Of course,' Jill said. 'And then we can take your photos up to show the others.'

'Can the dog come?' Still surly. Pushing the boundaries.

'Her name's Bella,' Jill said.

'For now,' Jack put in.

'And she can't come inside a hospital.' Jill tried to sound firm.

'I hate hospitals,' Jarred said. 'So does Jack.'

Jill couldn't help glancing at Jack. He just shrugged. 'They're not usually anyone's favourite place.'

'I'll put her in the gardener's shed for the moment,' Jill decided. 'That way she'll be safe.'

Jarred followed Jill and Bella. 'Does Bella live in the shed?'

'She doesn't live anywhere at the moment. She's a stray.'

Jarred gave a very adult sigh. 'Like me,' he muttered.

Jill put her arm around a skinny set of shoulders and gave him a quick hug. 'Kind of, I guess. She's a bit lost so she needs someone to help look after her for now.'

Jarred's body was stiff. Unresponsive. He pulled away from the hug. They walked in silence for a minute as they headed back to the tree where she could see Jack putting his camera away in the black case.

'I could look after her,' Jarred announced somewhat defensively. 'I like dogs.'

'That would be cool.' Jill tried to sound casual but it was heartbreaking, the longing she could hear beneath the words. Even if it was just a temporary anchor, at least she could offer something to this child. 'You might be able to help me give her a bath later.'

'Mel's having a bath. It's green.'

'That'll be Pinetarsol. It helps stop itching.'

'That's what the lady said.'

'The lady's name is Mrs Drummond,' Jill told Jarred. 'Might be a good idea if you remember that one.'

Jack was watching them now. He had his camera bag over his shoulder, waiting to follow them inside to find the office. He had pushed his backpack under the bench, clearly planning to leave it behind. Jill smiled. This was good. She didn't have to think about his exit from her life just yet.

'Come with me,' she invited. 'Let's go and find that paperwork. And that computer.'

Jack nodded. 'I'll remember Mrs Drummond's name, too,' he said. 'I need to tell her how good her shortbread is.'

'Who were the other ladies?' Jarred enquired. 'Do I need to know their names?'

'That's easy,' Jill told him. 'They're both called Mrs Metcalf.'

'Why do they have the same name?'

'They're in the same family. Like you and Jade and Mel and Nat.' Jill paused. Maybe these children didn't have the same surname, given that they all had different fathers. 'I'm a Metcalf, too,' she added hurriedly. 'Jill Metcalf.'

Jarred thought about that for a moment as the three of them walked along the silent corridor. Then he cast another of those shy glances up at the man walking on his other side.

'That's funny,' he said. 'Isn't it?'

'What is?' Jill responded obligingly.

'Jack and Jill.'

Their gazes caught over the top of Jarred's head.

Jack raised an eyebrow. 'Went up a hill,' he murmured.

Jill grinned. 'Jack fell down and broke his crown. Well, that fits—you got a good bump on the head, anyway.'

He smiled.

Really smiled. The corners of his eyes crinkled and a spark of something gleamed in their dark depths. For just a tiny moment his face came alive.

Jill felt the axis of her world tilt sharply.

And Jill came tumbling after....

She liked him.

He could feel the warmth.

The *giving*.

And it was so seductive. Like the smell of roasting meat to a man who hadn't eaten properly for way too long.

She was just too good to be true, this happy, golden woman.

She would probably give even if she got nothing in return, but that would never be good enough. It would be as bad as being a doctor when you couldn't give a damn about the outcome of any cases you treated.

Jack wished he had something to give.

Anything.

Just enough to let her know that it was good there were people like her in the world. That she was special.

All he had to offer was a smile.

At least she couldn't know how rusty a gift it was.

And, curiously, it seemed to be enough.

CHAPTER FIVE

JUST occasionally, paperwork could transcend being a chore.

It could almost seem exciting.

'Full name?' Jill queried in a brisk, professional manner.

'Jack Sinclair.'

'No middle name?'

'Not that I know of.'

Jill could only frown at Jack's back because he was hunched in front of the computer on the other side of the office, having attached a cable to his camera and slotted shiny paper into the printer. Jarred sat beside him, staring at an image of himself and Bella now filling the screen.

'Cool,' Jarred breathed. He seemed to grow an inch or two as he sat up straighter.

Jill moved on from the unsatisfactory gap on her report form. 'How old are you, Jack?'

'Thirty-three.'

'Home address?'

'Haven't got one.'

'Oh, come on!' This really wasn't good enough. 'You must have an address.'

'Nope.' Jack's tone didn't allow for any further contradiction. 'And I don't have any next-of-kin either, if that's what you're about to ask.'

'Are you an orphan?' Jarred asked.

'Yeah.' The hesitation was noticeable. If Jack Sinclair did have any family, he wasn't about to admit it. Definitely running away from something, Jill decided. Like that girl, Elise, who was probably still sitting in the waiting room, having a life crisis that needed help to sort out. She began scribbling a quick history and treatment summary for Jack.

'I guess I'm an orphan now.' Jill looked up at the quiet words, in time to see Jarred shuffle his chair just an inch or two closer to Jack's.

The mystery man. Jill gave up on the paperwork.

He'd come from nowhere, had no family, hated Christmas and hospitals.

Jill had to resist the urge to go and put her arms around the man. To offer comfort.

Friendship.

Fortunately, she was as distracted as Jarred when the prints started emerging. Jack had made several copies, postcard-sized.

'Hey…thanks!' It was the first time she had seen the boy smile.

'You're welcome.' Jack wound up the cable and tucked it into the camera case. 'I guess I'll be heading off now.'

'No!' The word popped out before Jill could prevent it. 'You can't.'

Jack just raised an eloquent eyebrow and Jill blushed.

'I said you'd come to the Friends of the Hospital meeting tonight,' she offered by way of an explanation.

'The *what*?'

'It's a community group. It got formed years ago when the

hospital was first under threat of closure. It's what's kept us going. They do all sorts of things to cut costs, like the committee that looks after the gardens. And they fundraise. My Aunty Faith is the chairperson.' Jill knew she was babbling but hopefully she was hiding any more personal reasons for not wanting Jack to disappear just yet. 'She does the most. She even provides Christmas dinner for any inpatients and all the staff. It's a real treat.'

Jack had been listening in amazement. Now he was scowling. 'And what on earth does that have to do with me?'

'Wally Briggs is the treasurer of the Friends. He's been to see your plane and I said I'd bring you to the meeting so you could talk to him.'

'What time is the meeting?'

'About 6:30.'

'So I'll come back. I need to find somewhere to stay.'

'There isn't anywhere.'

'There must be.' Jack's tone was an echo of Jill's when he'd failed to provide a home address. 'A pub or motel or cabin in the camping ground or something.'

'Everything's full at this time of year. Even the camping ground. There are waiting lists for people who want to come here for their holidays. They book years in advance sometimes.'

There were empty bedrooms in their parents' house. Rooms that would not be taken up by children needing care.

'I'll go into town and have a look for myself, anyway,' Jack said.

'It's a long walk.'

'I'll get a taxi.'

'We don't have a taxi service.'

'I'll rent a car, then.'

'In Ballochburn? You've got to be kidding.' Jill winced as Jack's scowl deepened. Any second now he would just march out the door and off into the sunset. 'Besides, I want to give you another neurological check before I discharge you.'

'I wasn't aware you'd admitted me.'

'I hadn't.' But Jill smiled thoughtfully. 'That's not a bad idea, though. It would give you somewhere to stay for the night.'

'I'm not staying in a hospital.' Jack emphasised his words by walking towards the office door. Jarred watched, his face empty of expression, the precious photographs clutched in his hand.

Jack's exit was very effectively blocked, however, by the solid form of Maisie Drummond.

'So here you are!' Maisie took in the scene and sighed. 'I've been looking everywhere for you, young man.'

Both Jarred and Jack managed to look guilty.

'It's your turn for a bath,' Maisie pronounced.

Jack looked relieved and earned a frown. 'And Faith wants to talk to you.'

'Who's Faith?' Jarred asked nervously.

'One of the Mrs Metcalfs,' Jill whispered.

'Why does she want to talk to *me*?' Jarred whispered back.

'She doesn't,' Maisie said patiently. Jack was pinned by her stare now. 'She wants to talk to *you*.'

Time was doing odd things in the parallel universe.

This had to have been the longest day in Jack's life and it wasn't even over.

Maybe his perception had been altered by his head injury. That might also explain why he was now in the position he found himself in.

Trapped.

Swept along by a tide he'd had no power to resist.

Faith Metcalf was a force to be reckoned with, that was for sure. When she decided something was going to happen, woe betide anyone who stood in her way.

Jack had tried. 'I'm not the person you need,' he'd said, very firmly. 'And I can't stay.'

'You can't go anywhere. Wally tells me it'll take days to get the parts he needs to fix your plane. Did you realise you had a faulty fuel gauge? That you'd been running on empty?'

'No.' Jack had been horrified. 'The plane's brand-new.'

'Hmmph. Age doesn't necessarily equate to lesser ability to perform, Mr Sinclair.'

'Call me Jack,' he'd said wearily. 'And I'm sorry, but I can't stay. I'm told there's no accommodation available.'

'You can stay right here. For heaven's sake, haven't you noticed how many empty beds there are? There's a whole apartment set up for a locum doctor. You could be perfectly independent.'

'I'm not a locum doctor.' It had been hard to keep the desperation out of his tone.

'You can consider it reimbursement.'

'But I have no experience. I know absolutely nothing about making calendars.'

'What's to know? You can take photographs. Very good photographs.' Faith peered at the picture she was holding of Jarred and Bella and nodded with satisfaction. 'You can capture the spirit of Ballochburn and its hospital. It will be the best fundraiser we've ever managed. We'll be able to afford to attract a permanent doctor.'

'I have to be in Wanaka. Or Queenstown.'

'Why?' Faith was good at making a subtle but exasperated clicking sound with her tongue. 'To capture the spirit of a Kiwi Christmas? You've got it wrong, Mr Sinclair. Those places are far too commercialised now. If you want to capture the genuine article, you've landed in exactly the right place.' Her gaze seemed to penetrate any defences Jack could have mustered. 'And you'll be helping others as well as achieving your own goal.'

How could he refuse without advertising himself as a low-life? A bit of pond scum that didn't give a damn about the rest of humanity?

And if he'd thought his smile had been enough to make Jill happy earlier, it was nothing compared to the joy he saw when she came back from whatever mission she'd taken off on when Maisie had virtually frog-marched him off for his audience with Faith.

'Oh!' Listening to her great-aunt's brilliant plan had made her face positively glow. 'It's *perfect*!'

'No.' Jack's voice was a low growl. 'It's not.'

But Jill had simply ignored the negative noise. 'We've got everything. Cherry orchards and carol singers. Pets' day at school and Christmas dinner and presents. Families camping and barbecues and kids swimming in the river. It's the best place in the world to be for Christmas, Jack. You'll love it.'

No. He wouldn't. He'd be watching the joy of others from behind the lens of a camera. Cut off.

But wasn't that what he'd been planning to do all along?

Yes, but totally anonymously. Not with a nine-year-old boy who was gazing at him with something like hope in his eyes.

Or a golden woman who looked like she was being given the best gift she'd ever had.

Or an ancient matriarch who expected nothing less than compliance, thank you very much.

He should be taking to the hills. Getting as far away from this crazy place as possible. What was it about these people that was exerting a pull Jack felt powerless to fight?

It was more than the sum of the individual personalities, even if he threw in that grumpy cook with the heart of gold, or that large girl she now had in tow as her assistant—Elise. Or Wally, the man with a walrus moustache and a booming voice who was rising to the challenge of an aircraft repair job with military efficiency.

Or Jill's parents. Her mother was clucking over the chickenpox children with obvious contentment. Her father had been seen not long ago stomping off for a walk, muttering that he obviously wasn't needed and nobody was listening to him anyway.

It was more to do with the forest than the trees. The glue that held this community together. Jack could feel his feet sticking to it. He could rationalise his decision to comply with Faith's request by saying he had no means of going anywhere else for a few days but the truth was he didn't want to leave.

Instinct was telling him that fate had brought him there for a purpose. That it was possible he could find what he was looking for right there in Ballochburn.

And now, as the heat and sunshine of this strange day finally faded into a glorious summer dusk, the chorus of birdsong was interrupted only by the peal of laughter coming from outside the apartment window.

The locum doctor's apartment didn't have the best view. It was above the kitchens and its single window looked out not on the gardens but into a courtyard area where there were vehicles parked and a whole bunch of rubbish bins.

But it was the best view.

One that made Jack reach for his camera and position himself, propped against the frame of the open window for stability.

Jill was in the courtyard. Along with Jarred and a large steaming bucket and a stack of what looked like hospital-issue towels. A hose that was running and a dog who was shaking off the foam of the shampoo as fast as the woman and boy could make it lather.

Jill was saturated already. Her hair dangled in damp, curly strands. Her bare feet splashed in the accumulating puddles and her T-shirt stuck to her skin. Jarred held the hose. He fiddled with the nozzle, trying to make it spray. Jill was hanging onto the miserable-looking dog and she was laughing.

The camera shutter clicked and clicked again. It caught the dog shaking a storm of rinse water from its shaggy coat, disappearing under vigorously moving soft towels, emerging to roll ecstatically on the white pebbles and then bark with excitement and go head down, tail up in a puppyish invitation to play.

And it caught a moment that Jack knew was something special even before he scrolled through the collection. A back view of the woman and the boy as they stood admiring the clean dog. As Jill's arm stole around Jarred's shoulders and he'd turned to look up at her…and smile.

Jack may have been cut off by distance and the barrier of his camera. He wasn't an acknowledged part of that scene at all and yet he could feel both sides of that smile. The happiness that had been given to a boy who had far too much of the world's weight on his shoulders.

The happiness of the woman who had, probably unconsciously, given it.

He sat looking at the image for a long time before he tried to sleep that night.

Then he scrolled through the rest of the pictures from Bella's bathtime and it was another image that made him pause, lost in thought.

One of Jill. With her head tilted back as she laughed. With her sopping T-shirt clinging to her body. Cupping her breasts. The quality of the photo was amazing—even her nipples were clearly outlined. Jill wouldn't thank him for a photograph that made her look naked and Jack knew he needed to delete it.

But then he felt it. The curious sinking sensation like an electric shock that originated in his belly and then swooped lower.

Physical attraction.

Not an intellectual appreciation of how attractive Jill Metcalf was.

This was physical.

And *real*.

And it felt like a tiny part of him had sprung back into life.

It didn't matter that it couldn't grow. That he might never be ready to risk hurting himself or others by submitting to involvement. What mattered was that it was there at all. That he was still capable of feeling it.

That he wasn't as emotionally dead as he'd feared.

He could respond to an image. More importantly, he could recognise an image that evoked a response. Not that he would ever use that one of Jill, of course. He deleted it with only a brief flash of regret. The other one of Jill and Jarred was the prize he *could* use.

Maybe he could make this calendar. Capture that glue that made this place magic, Do something that could help others but didn't require any real involvement on his part. He could do that and then just walk away when it was finished.

Jill had been right.

This *was* perfect.

CHAPTER SIX

'GOOD grief! You're doing the dishes!'

Jim didn't turn around from the kitchen bench. 'Don't you start!'

'Start what?' Jill's spirits dropped a notch. Her father didn't sound any happier than he'd been last thing yesterday.

'Going on about how I never do anything to help around the house. I'm perfectly capable of doing whatever *needs* doing.'

'I know that, Dad. It's just a bit of a surprise to find you doing housework at six-thirty in the morning.'

'It's going to be a busy day. I've got patients to see, a mountain of paperwork to do and I'm expected at the school this afternoon to judge a pet rock competition or some such nonsense.'

'Oh, yes, it's pets' day. Cool.' Jill stood on tiptoe to plant a kiss on her father's cheek. 'And I know you love it. You've still got the pet rock I made on your office desk. I saw it yesterday.'

Her father looked tired. Maybe he hadn't slept well, which might explain his early and unusual activity. He looked miserable as well. Clearly he hadn't done anything to try and sort out the impasse with her mother but that was a subject Jill felt she should probably avoid for the moment. Jim's reaction to the news she'd admitted four children with chickenpox and that Hope was helping to care for them in the hospital hadn't exactly helped matters.

'She got what she wanted, then,' Jim had growled. 'Don't know why she bothered asking what I thought in the first place.'

Did her father feel neglected? Like he wasn't as important in Hope's life as the children she helped? Did her mother feel taken for granted? Like she was only important as a housekeeper? Had her parents become so caught up in their own interests they had just gradually drifted apart?

No. Jill refused to believe this was anything more than a minor disturbance. And she had a feeling Aunty Faith was right in saying it was something they had to sort out for themselves. She shouldn't interfere so she couldn't help feeling a trifle guilty at the unspoken accusation that she had taken sides by aiding and abetting her mother as far as the homeless children were concerned. It created tension that was unsettling.

'I'm going to take Bella for a quick walk before breakfast,' she said. 'And then I'll get on with a ward round.'

'Good. You admitted all those children so they can be your responsibility as well.'

'Of course.'

'Keep an eye on them. People think chickenpox is just another run-of-the-mill childhood illness like an ear infection or a cold, but you can get some nasty complications.'

'I know. Secondary bacterial infection of the skin lesions, cerebellitis, transverse myelitis, even pneumonitis or encephalitis in patients with abnormal T-cell immunity.'

Her father finally smiled. 'I'm glad to see you paid attention at medical school.'

'Anything else you want me to put on my list for the morning?'

'If you can. Sue couldn't make it in to pick up that morphine yesterday. I told her one of us would drop it out.'

'I should be able to fit that in.' Jill nodded. 'In fact, I'd love to. I've been trying to get out to see them for days and I was planning to take Jack. He needs to visit a cherry orchard to get some photos for Aunty's calendar.'

'Bloody calendar,' Jim muttered. 'Where does she get her ideas from?'

'I think it'll be great.'

'I can't say I approve of that plane-crash fellow staying in the doctor's accommodation either. What if I get a new locum turning up?'

'Hardly likely, this close to Christmas, but if we do, Jack can come and stay with us.'

'Ah, yes…' Jim dried his hands on a teatowel. 'The Metcalf Motel. Free to anyone who needs a bed.'

'It's only for a few days, Dad. This isn't like you. Where's your Christmas spirit?'

'Gone west,' he said gloomily. 'Like your mother seems to have.'

'Where did you say we were going?'

'To the Wheelers' orchard. Dave might not be there. He's probably at school with the boys for pets' day. The orchard manager won't mind if you take pictures, but they'll be very busy getting the final Christmas orders picked and packed. There'll be teams picking outside and probably chaos in the packing sheds. Very Christmassy.'

'The chaos or the cherries?'

'Both. I can never see a bowl of cherries without thinking of Christmas. And the chaos is part of the fun, isn't it?'

'If you say so.'

'And it's very Ballochburn—cherries. Along with peaches and apricots, of course. And apples in winter.'

'Nice healthy place.'

'Mmm.' Jill couldn't help her ironic tone. 'I could wish it was a bit healthier right now.'

'Why?'

'This house call I'm making. I'm dropping off a supply of morphine for a terminally ill patient.'

'Oh…'

It wasn't her imagination. Both the tone and the way her passenger visibly stiffened in his seat suggested discomfort. He didn't want to know.

Well, tough! If Jack was going to get into the real spirit of her home town, maybe there were some things he needed to know.

'Sue Wheeler is my oldest friend,' Jill told him. 'The only one left in Ballochburn, at any rate. We went right though school together but she never wanted to escape like the rest of us. She fell in love with Dave at high school and all she ever wanted was to live on his family's orchard and raise a family. They got married at nineteen and Sue was already pregnant.'

They were on the road that led past Faith's cottage now but Jill barely spared a glance for the eye-catching rosebush hedge.

'They had three little boys in the space of four years. The oldest one is nearly ten but Sue always wanted a daughter so they tried one more time and they had Emma almost three years ago. They were so happy.' Jill sighed. 'And then it all turned into a bit of a nightmare eighteen months ago.'

'She got sick?'

'Yeah. Nothing specific to start with, but Sue just knew something wasn't right. Dad listened, as he always does, and he went the extra mile to try and find what was wrong. They couldn't have diagnosed the cancer any earlier but it wasn't enough to save her.'

'What sort of cancer?'

'Abdominal. Something incredibly rare. Sue blamed herself for a while. She thought maybe it had something to do with the sprays they use in the orchards but there's no evidence. It's just one of those tragic stories.'

'How long has she got?'

'Not long. The family's hoping to have this last Christmas together. She's not in too much pain and there's any amount of support from the community for them all. It's wonderful that she *can* be at home. It's just really, really sad.'

'Yeah…' Jack was staring through the side window. Jill could almost see the barrier he'd erected around himself.

It was disappointing that the story hadn't touched him but, then, he didn't know these people, did he? If you took on board the sadness of every stranger that crossed your path, it would drag anybody down.

Jill stole another glance at Jack a moment later, however. It wasn't enough of a reason. Had she imagined the glimpses of warmth she had seen in this man?

Like when he had smiled at her over the amusement of being 'Jack and Jill'?

Or when she had seen him, shoulder to shoulder with Jarred, giving him the self-esteem of being talked to man to man?

Had she seen those glimpses because she had been looking for them? Hoping to find them because it would give a depth to her attraction to him and make it more meaningful than something purely physical?

Perhaps it would be just as well to be proved wrong. It

would make it easier when Jack picked up his bags and disappeared from her life.

He was still staring out of his window.

'Don't worry,' Jill said a little flatly. 'You don't have to come into the house. I'll be half an hour or so. You can get some pictures in the orchard and stuff.'

They were only a few minutes from the Wheelers' orchard when Jill's pager sounded.

'It's a PRIME page,' she said aloud, pulling the Jeep onto the wide grass verge. 'I need to call the emergency services control centre and see why I'm needed.'

'The Jefferson orchard?' she said moments later. 'Yes, I know where it is. I'm actually just down the road.'

She finished the call, pulled the Jeep into a U-turn and picked up speed rapidly.

'It's an accident,' she informed Jack. 'The neighbouring orchard to the Wheelers' which is a bit lucky. Someone's fallen from a cherry picker.'

Jack had to catch hold of the doorhandle as Jill put her foot on the brake and then turned onto a shingle road with a skid of tyres. Bella fell over in the back with a thump.

'Whoops! Sorry, Bella.' But Jack caught the flash of a smile. She was enjoying the adrenaline rush of an emergency response.

Jack wasn't. He would rather not be feeling it at all but he couldn't stop it, any more than the automatic action of leaping out of the vehicle as soon as it came to an abrupt halt by the waving figure of the orchard manager.

Or scanning the area, to see the empty basket of a cherry picker several metres from the ground. The supine figure beneath it and the group of shocked-looking young people standing around.

Jill's gaze had swept the scene, making the same assessment. Now she focussed on the man who'd met their vehicle.

'So he fell from that basket?'

'Yes.'

'Was he knocked out?'

'Yeah, he landed on his head.'

'Is he conscious now?'

'Yes.'

'Nobody's tried to move him, have they?'

'No.'

'That's good.'

Jack agreed silently. Given the mechanism of injury and the way the lad had landed, a spinal injury had to be very high on the list of suspected trauma. The inclination to step in and take over—to make sure any injury wasn't exacerbated by incorrect handling—was strong.

Too strong.

Jack had to remind himself he'd given up the practice of medicine, at least for the time being. It wasn't as though his skills were needed. Jill was the doctor here. And as far as she knew, he was simply a photographer. What would she think if he told her the truth?

She'd think she had been deceived, that's what. That he was an untrustworthy person. Jack didn't want Jill's opinion of him to lessen. He clamped his mouth shut. He stayed where he was beside the Jeep as Jill hoisted the pack from the back and moved off towards the victim.

But then she looked over her shoulder.

'Jack? Could you come, too, please? I might need a hand.'

She crouched beside their patient a moment later. 'Hey,' she said. 'I'm Jill Metcalf. I'm a doctor.' She took hold of the youth's wrist, feeling for his pulse.

It was the same introduction she had used with *him* yesterday. When he had been sitting in that sheep paddock, feeling like he'd stepped from one disaster in his life straight into another. Jack could remember that touch, too. The connection with another human that he hadn't wanted because it had carried an obligation. You shouldn't accept something when you had nothing to give in return.

'What's your name?' Jill asked.

'Nick.'

'How old are you, Nick?'

'Eighteen.'

'Can you remember what happened?'

'It was an accident.' One of the teenagers standing nearby was white-faced. 'I didn't think it was going to move that fast and I didn't know Nick was leaning out so far.'

Jill was gently moving Nick's head and neck into a neutral position. 'Jack? Could you come here and hold Nick's head? It's very important that it's kept still.'

'Sure.' Jack knelt by Nick's head. He knew exactly what he needed to do but he let Jill take his hands to position them, palms against Nick's cheeks, his fingers supporting his chin, his thumbs cradling the back of the skull.

'Does anything hurt, Nick?'

'Yeah... My back...and my neck.'

Jack's fingers stiffened a little as he concentrated. His support could be crucial right now.

Jill continued her questioning. 'Are you having any trouble breathing?'

'I…don't think so but I…can't move my legs.'

'Can you squeeze my hands?' Jill frowned slightly after she slipped her hands into Nick's. 'Harder?'

'I've got, like, pins and needles in my fingers.'

The indications were certainly there for a serious spinal injury. Jack could almost see the wheels turning in Jill's mind. He wanted to help. To make sure nothing was forgotten. A collar, a bag mask nearby in case assistance was needed if Nick's breathing became affected. Back-up that could provide the board and foam cushions and body straps needed for complete immobilisation. Baseline vital signs. IV access. He wanted to know if rural protocols allowed for a loading dose of steroids that could reduce the damage from inflammation of the spinal cord.

But Jill clearly didn't need his input and she certainly wasn't expecting it. The same kind of list had to be running through her head and she was acting on every thought. She knew what she was doing, too. The neck collar was positioned with the utmost care and strapped into place.

'I still need you to hold his head, Jack. You're doing a fantastic job.'

The brief smile she gave him was very different to the impish grin he was getting used to, but it included him in this incident and made him feel appreciated.

The smile and reassuring words she had for Nick were more than just professional. They held a sincerity and warmth that Jack knew was as important for this terrified young man as any medical intervention.

'You've hurt your back,' Jill told him honestly, 'but we can't know how serious it is yet. What we need to do is look after you very carefully and get you to the experts. I'm going to see if a rescue helicopter is available rather than try and move you by ambulance. Where's home for you?'

'Dunedin. I'm at varsity there.'

'We'll try and make that the first stop, then.' She moved away a little to make a call on her mobile phone but snatches of the conversation floated back to Jack.

'Paralysis, both legs… Paraesthesia, both arms… KO'd but GCS is now 15…'

An ambulance pulled up a few minutes later as Jill deftly slid an intravenous cannula into place in Nick's forearm. A middle-aged man climbed from the emergency vehicle as she finished taping the line securely and began setting up a bag of saline.

'Hi, Ted,' she called. 'Could you grab an oxygen cylinder for me, please?'

Jill handed the bag of fluid to one of Nick's friends to hold and adjusted the flow of the fluid to no more than a slow drip that would just keep a vein open. Jack nodded inwardly. The low blood pressure of 80 systolic she had already recorded on Nick was probably due to vasodilation caused by the shock of the injury. If she pumped fluids in to try and raise the pressure to a normal 100 instead of 80, she could risk complications from over-hydration. He was also pleased to note her care in administering pain relief. The potential effects on breathing from narcotics was something that needed experienced monitoring.

'I'm cold,' Nick said.

'Want a foil sheet?' The ambulance officer asked Jill.

'Yes, please, Ted. And the life pack. And a small towel. I want to roll it up to protect the neck lordosis.'

'Scoop stretcher?'

'No. We've got a chopper on the way and they'll have their

own gear. I might just use your radio and see if they can put me in contact with the pilot. I'll find out how far away they are.'

She did more than that. Jack listened to her giving the precise GPS co-ordinates for the orchard after checking a notebook she had taken from her pack. She chose a suitable landing site at one side of the packing shed that had no obstacles like power lines and, having finished the call, she directed some of the young bystanders to shift vehicles and check to make sure no loose debris was in the vicinity that could get sucked up into the helicopter rotors.

Her orders were concise and firm. Nobody was going to argue with anything she said. Including Jack. There was nothing he could have been doing to improve the management of this case.

To say he was impressed was an understatement.

His first impression of Jill Metcalf had been of a Christmas angel masquerading as a medic. But this was an angel with attitude. No wonder she loved working in an emergency department. Performing under pressure.

The noisy arrival of a large helicopter and the fierce blast of air from its rotors only a short distance away might have seriously ruffled Jill's shoulder-length curls but it did nothing to her level of calm assurance.

Her handover managed to convey everything the paramedics needed to know without alarming Nick. She continued to reassure him as she helped to immobilise him onto the backboard.

'These guys are the best,' she told him, 'and they'll be able to give you something more for the pain as well.' Her glance caught the flight crew leader. 'I've got morphine drawn up but he's only had 5 milligrams so far. I'd rather wait till you've got him hooked up to your monitors before giving him any more.'

She went with them as far as the helicopter to help load their patient. Jack made himself useful by tidying up the medical kit and putting it back in the Jeep. He nodded at Bella, who was sitting on his seat and hadn't tried to get out of the open door.

'You're a good dog,' he told her. 'Thank you for looking after my camera.'

A glance upward showed him that preparations for take-off were almost complete. The doors were shut, Jill had run back from the makeshift landing site and the rotors were picking up speed again.

Jack reached for the black bag on impulse and took his camera out. He was just in time to get a brilliant photograph as the rescue helicopter took off.

The force of the air from the rotors flattened the leaves on the cherry trees, exposing bunches of fruit as glossy and red as the paintwork on the chopper.

The group of young workers stood together, some with their arms around each other, watching the helicopter take off, concern for their friend in their faces.

Jill and the ambulance officer, Ted, were in the shot as well, also looking upwards, but their expressions suggested satisfaction in a job well done and hope that the outcome would be good.

If Faith wanted a picture that spoke of the vital role the town's doctor and volunteer ambulance service played in this remote community, this would be a winner.

Surprisingly, Jill seemed a lot less than satisfied as they got back into the Jeep to carry on with the original house call they had been diverted from.

'I'd rather be at the other end,' she confessed. 'With things like X-rays and CT scans on tap. With a neurosurgeon to call in and a theatre and intensive care unit in the same building.'

'Perhaps what happens on scene like that is just as important as far as the final outcome goes.'

Jill gave him a surprised glance. 'Gosh, you sound just like my dad. And it's true, I guess—for any major trauma in an isolated place. I suppose I'll just have do what Dad does and ring the hospital later to follow up.' Then she smiled. 'I do like helicopters, I must admit. You don't get a bit of excitement like that in any emergency department.'

There was no point trying to take pictures at the Wheelers' orchard. Having heard about the accident next door, the workers were subdued. Doing their jobs because the work had to be done. Or maybe the atmosphere was a little grim because of what was going on in the homestead that swallowed Jill up for at least thirty minutes.

A home that should have excited children preparing for Christmas, not facing the loss of their mother.

No wonder Jill look even more subdued than the workers when she finally emerged and put her kit back in the vehicle. She said nothing as they drove away and the silence continued until Jack began to feel uncomfortable.

Something needed to be said. Not that Jack had any desire to get involved, but it was a worry. He may not have known Jill for very long but he knew that it was wrong for her to look this deflated.

Even Bella sensed something wrong. She poked her head between the seats and gazed up at their driver.

Finally, Jack couldn't stand it any longer. He gritted his teeth.

'Are you OK?' The rhetorical question was gruff.

'No.'

The gears crunched roughly as Jill pulled off the road a few seconds later into a deserted rest area. There was a wooden table with built-in bench seats and a three-sided concrete box with a blackened interior that had been used for many a barbecue. The Jeep bumped past the table and down a steep track through trees and Jack caught his first glimpse of Ballochburn's river.

It was a typical New Zealand braided river, with both deep and shallow channels running past shingle islands. At some distance downstream he could see people. Faint shouts of glee and splashing reached them from youngsters who were jumping from a rock ledge into a deep swimming hole. High-school students on holiday, perhaps. It could be a good place to get photographs.

Later.

He couldn't suggest it, though. Not when Jill was sitting, gripping the steering-wheel with white knuckles even after she had brought the vehicle to a standstill.

To Jack's horror, tears were rolling down her cheeks.

He could understand her pain. She had to be so involved with a patient who was also a dear friend. She had to deal with feeling impotent, as if all the years of training and accumulated knowledge was useless.

No point in reminding her of her own blithe statement that you could deal with the downside of this career by focussing on the good stuff. He knew better than anything how inadequate that could be. He also knew the depths of despair it could pull you into and he didn't want to go there again because of Jill's unhappiness.

But he couldn't sit there and do nothing. He could feel her pain and as much as he didn't want to get involved, he already was simply by being there.

Awkwardly, he touched her arm, trying to convey at least the comfort of companionship.

'I'm sorry,' he said, his voice still gruff. Reluctant. Somehow his hand trailed down her arm and he felt his fingers being gripped. They were holding hands. Or rather Jill was holding *his* hand. Tightly enough to make it impossible to pull away.

'I'll be OK.' She sniffed wetly. 'Sorry. I just need a minute to pull myself together.'

She could do that? How?

'It's beautiful, really,' Jill said a few moments later. 'It's just Sue and Emma in there cuddled up, watching cartoons. Emma just adores them. They've set up a bed for her in the living room and they have videos running almost twenty-four hours a day for her.'

'Emma?' Jack felt something cold and nasty slide down his spine. Involuntarily, his fingers tightened around Jill's. 'It's *Emma* who's dying?'

Jill nodded. She sniffed again and scrubbed her nose with the base of her thumb. 'Where's a tissue when you really need one?' she asked with a watery smile.

Jack didn't even try to smile back. 'The little girl?' he queried slowly. 'The daughter your friend wanted so much?'

Jill nodded again. 'She's gorgeous. I've got to know her pretty well this year because they were in Auckland for months. They've been to the best paediatric specialists in the country over the last eighteen months. Everything that could have been tried has been tried but they can't stop the cancer. The tumour's the biggest part of her now and it hurts to move her, but as long as she's still and she has her family around her, she's actually happy.' Another tear escaped but got brushed firmly away. 'She's got the most incredible smile, Jack. Everyone who meets Emma just falls in love with her. And everyone is making the most of every moment she's still with us.'

Jack was transfixed. Still holding her hand. Searching Jill's face as though he expected to find something he was looking for. It wasn't that he felt drawn into the tragedy of the little girl. He felt nothing but an intellectual appreciation of how sad it was.

He couldn't get involved.

But Jill could. She was in it up to her eyebrows. She must know how to cope.

'How can you do it?' he asked quietly. 'Be so involved—as a friend *and* a doctor—knowing what has to come?'

'It's part of what medicine is all about,' she answered. 'It's one of those jobs that is a lot more than a career, you know? I suppose it defines who you are as much as *what* you are.'

Jill took a deep breath and blinked hard, several times. She stared through the windscreen at a river she probably wasn't seeing.

'I think it's a relationship as much as a job. It takes over your life and sometimes it can interfere with other relationships. I think that might be what's going on with my parents at the moment. But Dad has to give as much as he does to his work. That's who he is. Who *I* am, too.' She paused and swallowed. Jack could see the movement of her throat. Could sense her gathering her thoughts.

'It's like any other relationship,' she continued softly. It was almost as though he wasn't there and she was just thinking aloud. 'You get back only as much as you're prepared to give.

If you don't feel the pain of cases you can't help—like wee Emma—you can't feel the joy of all the cases you can help.'

Jack said nothing. In a parallel universe that was probably true. It hadn't worked where he'd come from, though, had it?

'The joy nurtures you,' Jill said finally. 'It gives you strength to deal with the other bits.'

'And that's enough?'

'Not always. The bad bits suck.' Her smile was stronger now. 'Like now. This is the kind of time I need the people who care about me. Like my family.' She eased her hand from Jack's as though she knew he wasn't one of those people. His hand felt cold. Empty. He reached back and scratched Bella's ear in the hope of erasing the emptiness, but it didn't quite work.

Was that why he hadn't coped? Because he'd never had a family? But he had stopped needing one long ago. When he had been about Jarred's age, in fact, and had known that he had to rely on himself to survive.

Jill was looking at the river now. Seeing it. She watched the children in the distance for a moment. 'It's my rock, this place,' she told Jack. 'It's where I get my strength. If I'm lucky enough to find a life partner, I might be able to cut the umbilical cord but until then my heart is here.' She gave a final sniff then started the engine. 'Sorry. I didn't mean to get so heavy. It's probably the last thing you need.'

Jack shook his head but Jill was reversing and didn't see. He wanted to say something to reassure her. Even to say that it might be exactly what he *did* need, but his mouth refused to cooperate.

Something held him back from saying anything because he knew if he started, he might not be able to stop. To tell Jill everything would mean opening a door he had spent the last months trying to close. And lock. Suddenly he was feeling confused. As though he had just realised he must have taken a wrong turning but had no idea how to get himself back to the last signpost. If there had even *been* a signpost.

The opportunity passed before he had any chance of weighing up whether or not to grasp it. They were driving on the road again and Jill had, indeed, pulled herself together.

She was looking forward, not back.

'The pets' day parade is at two o'clock. We'll need to try and get there a bit earlier than that so you can get some good photos. We'll have to hope there aren't any more emergency callouts but if there are, I'll leave you at the school and go by myself.'

Jack had to share the hope there wouldn't be another callout.

What if Jill ended up sitting beside a river and crying all by herself?

With no one to hold her hand?

She'd cope, he reminded himself. Angels with attitude could cope with anything. It wasn't as if he was going to be around for long. Jill wasn't even going to be around for that long. She'd be off, heading for a brilliant career as an emergency physician. She'd find a partner for life with no difficulty whatsoever.

Jack was left wondering how someone who could have been lucky enough to have won Jill—married her, in fact—had managed to mess it up. Had he not recognised how incredibly special this woman was?

CHAPTER SEVEN

BALLOCHBURN school's playing field was awash with colour.

Crowded with people that represented a large proportion of the community. Babies in front packs and pushchairs, proud grandparents wielding cameras, equally proud but somewhat anxious parents. And children. Dozens of children and their pets.

Ponies, calves, lambs, dogs, cats, even hens and an alpaca were being led, carried, positioned or played with. The sound of the children calling to each other, scolding their pets, laughter and the occasional wail of a baby made a cacophony of sound that took Jill back in time instantly.

So did the smell, where frying sausages and onions were competing fairly successfully with the more earthy aroma the pets were providing.

'I haven't been to a pets' day since I was twelve years old,' she told Jack.

'Looks like a circus.'

'Yeah,' Jill agreed happily. 'Isn't it great?' She attached a lead to Bella's new collar and anchored her to the towbar of the Jeep. 'People will be able to see you here,' she told the dog. 'Who knows? Someone might know where you belong.'

Jack took another glance over his shoulder as they walked into the school playground. 'I think she's decided she belongs to you.'

'I can't keep her.' Jill resisted the urge to look back. She knew Bella would be staring longingly in her direction. 'I'm not going to be here very long and I could hardly take her with me to Melbourne, could I?'

'I guess not.' Jack lifted the camera that was hanging around his neck and began taking pictures.

Jill was happy to keep pace with her companion, pausing frequently, just soaking up the atmosphere as they got closer to the action.

Good times.

If strength could be found in happy memories then the traditional country celebration of school pets' day was exactly what Jill needed today. It marked the end of the school year. The beginning of the long summer holiday and it was easy to remember how endlessly it had stretched ahead of her as a child. So full of sunshine and the promise of good things.

Not that she was feeling anything like as bad as she had just after the visit to the Wheelers that morning. It should be embarrassing that she'd cried all over Jack's shoulder but, curiously, it wasn't. It didn't matter if she saw her at her worst, did it? In a couple of days he would be gone and probably wouldn't even remember her. Just as well he had no idea how drawn to him she was. How comforting she had found his presence.

How right it had felt to be holding his hand while she'd spilled out her grief. Weird that she could feel this close to a stranger.

Being a family celebration, it seemed only proper that all the Metcalfs were in attendance. Making a slow circuit around the playground, Jill spotted the classroom set aside for displaying the sand saucers. Hope was in there, judging the miniature gardens that had been made by using flowers, leaves, small toys and lots of imagination. Jack looked amazed at the creations when Jill took him inside and he began snapping photographs.

'Hi, Mum. Did you bring Jarred to help you?'

'He'd never heard of a pets' day. I thought it would be nice for him to have an outing.' Hope sounded a little defensive. 'You did say he wasn't infectious any more.'

'I think it's a great idea. Are you enjoying it, Jarred?'

The boy dragged his gaze from where Jack was leaning over a desk, getting a close-up shot of a tiny farm scene in a saucer, where leaves were trees and tiny plastic sheep grazed beside a lurid-looking pond made from a toffee wrapper.

'It's OK,' he said. 'Where's Bella? I thought you were going to bring her. That's why we gave her a bath, wasn't it?'

'She's tied up to the Jeep, which is parked under an oak tree near the bike sheds. You can take her for a walk later, if you want.'

'We won't be staying too long,' Hope said. 'I just came to judge the sand saucers. I told Jade and Mel I'd take some sausages back for them.'

'Who's looking after them at the moment?'

'That new girl that Maisie's training up. Elise. She's marvelous with young children. She's been helping in the wards with the oldies as well. And in the kitchens. I suspect she's a treasure.'

Moving on, they found Jill's father in the neighbouring classroom, trying to grade pet rocks, some of which were quite large samples of river stones painted to look like animals.

'Oh, I love the hedgehog!' Jill grinned at the round stone

that had had long tree thorns superglued all over it. 'Wish I'd thought of that.'

There were sleeping cats, mice, birds and quite a few rocks that had just been painted bright colours and given faces. Jack went around the room with her but had to stop when a small girl tugged on his elbow.

'It's fallen off,' she said with a wobbly lip. 'Can you help me, mister?'

'What's fallen off?'

'Spot's bow.'

Spot appeared to be a shapeless stone that had felt ears glued on the top and a blob of black paint for a nose. The tartan ribbon that had created the impression of a neck was in the girl's hand.

Jill watched, fascinated, as Jack tried to reattach the bow. He was fumbling but she didn't want to offer to help. The care he was taking, and the automatic way he'd responded to a child's plea, had captured her. The threat of tears had receded completely. The girl was beaming at Jack's efforts.

She hadn't been wrong about his warmth. Behind those barriers lurked a very *nice* man.

Jill needed to turn away then. To pretend she was absorbed with the artistic endeavours on display.

'These are wonderful. Rather you than me, picking the best, Dad. And have you seen the sand saucers? They're amazing, too.'

'No,' her father said shortly. 'I haven't.'

At least her parents were in separate classrooms, Jill thought. Faith was probably the only other person present who would realise that Jim and Hope still weren't talking to each other.

Her great-aunt appeared as calm and dignified as ever. Jill spotted her as soon as they left the pet rocks behind and headed for the grass of the playing field. In a silk dress, with her wide-brimmed hat and an ebony cane that was her only concession to advanced age, Faith was in the company of Bruce Mandeville, carefully inspecting a long row of pet lambs.

'Dr Jill! Over here!'

'Hey, Aaron! How's the arm?'

'Getting better. We gave Rambo a bath. Come and smell him.'

Jill obligingly crouched and buried her nose in soft white wool. 'Mmm. He smells like passionfruit.'

'My conditioner,' Aaron's mother said wryly. 'A whole bottle of it, no less.'

There were so many animals to admire. So many people who wanted to say hello.

'Jilly! Haven't seen you for far too long. How are you?'

'I'm fine, Don. And you? How's the hip?'

'Better than new. I'm glad your dad talked me into having that operation. I can almost keep up with the grandkids now.'

And only a minute later, 'Jillian! Is that really you, dear?'

'Sure is, Miss Reynolds. Aren't you glad I haven't brought a pet lamb this year?'

'At least you cleaned up the mess it made.' The grey-haired teacher was eager to hug her former pupil. 'I've been keeping up with your news through Hope.'

'You're still in the choir, then?'

'Oh, yes. We'll be at the hospital tonight for the carol service. Is it true you've got a job at Melbourne's biggest hospital?'

'It is.'

'And you fought off hundreds of other applicants? Congratulations, dear.'

'I'm sure my parents have been exaggerating.' This *was* embarrassing, to have Jack overhear such admiration. 'It is an amazing job to be going to, though.'

'Well deserved, my dear. I always knew you were going to turn out to be something rather special.'

Jack didn't appear to be listening to the fulsome praise. He was taking a photograph of Aaron proudly holding the red satin sash designating first place over Rambo's head while trying to stand on the rope to anchor his pet. It wasn't hard for the large lamb to pull free. Aaron fell over backwards and for the first time Jill heard Jack laugh aloud.

'Fantastic,' he said. 'What a shot!'

'Ow!' Aaron wailed. 'Rambo, come back!'

'Go and chase him,' his mother ordered. 'Quick!'

'You must know everybody here,' Jack commented as they watched Aaron chasing his pet, the red ribbon fluttering from his fist.

'Just about.'

'Everybody seems to know everybody.'

'It's a small community.'

'More like a big family.'

'I guess. It's not always this rosy a picture, though. We get our fair share of upsets.'

'Like a family,' Jack repeated. 'It must have been hard to leave.'

'Not really. I had no choice. I had to grow up and leave home. I did my last couple of years at a boarding school in Dunedin. That made it easier.'

'But you said your heart's here. Don't you want to come back?'

'Not to live. I couldn't.'

'Why not?'

'I'd always wanted to be a doctor. I just grew up knowing that's what I'd be. Like my dad.'

'Being here hasn't stopped him practising medicine.'

'It's different for a woman. I couldn't practise here, even if I wanted to.'

'Why not?' Jack asked again.

'You remember what I was talking about this morning? About medicine being a kind of relationship?'

'I'm not likely to forget.'

'Oh…' Jill bit her lip. 'Sorry. You seem to be a bit too easy to talk to.' She looked away, at the parade lines that were now forming. If Jack didn't want to talk on a personal level any more, that was fine.

'I'm not complaining,' he said. He had raised his camera and was taking shots. 'Talk away.'

'Well, it's not the only relationship I want in my life, you know?'

'So you said.' Jack turned from the camera for a moment and raised an eyebrow. 'Good for you. A lot of people are put off when they've been badly hurt by a relationship that's gone wrong.'

For a minute they watched the parade in silence. Children rode past on their ponies, others dragged reluctant lambs and one boy was stuck with a calf that was firmly refusing to move. Jill's curiosity got the better of her and she interrupted the photographic session.

'How do you know I was badly hurt?'

'How long ago did your marriage end?'

'More than two years. My divorce is all finalised.'

'And when did you take your wedding ring off?'

'Oh…' Jill looked down at the third finger of her left hand. The pale mark where her ring had been was pretty obvious, wasn't it? 'Yeah, I guess it did take awhile to come to terms with it. I finally took it off as a kind of symbol of leaving my old life behind. I had kept it on so long as a kind of warning, I think. To remind myself to look before I leap. Not to trust so easily or completely. I was really naïve.'

'And you're not now?'

'No.' Jill shook her head confidently. 'I know what I'm looking for and I'd never be able to find it in Ballochburn.'

Jack didn't have to ask why not again. It was written on his face.

'I'd be marrying a sheep farmer or an orchardist if I stayed here,' she elaborated. 'They'd have to understand and deal with the kind of commitment it takes to be a good doctor. The time involved and the way it can interfere with family life. Especially somewhere like here, where there's no after-hours service and you're practically permanently on call.'

'Your parents made it work.'

'Did they? I'm beginning to wonder if that's a big part of what's wrong at the moment. They've drifted apart. How much has that got to do with the practice?'

'But you were married to a doctor before and that didn't work.'

Jill was silent for a moment but her response came easily enough to surprise her. 'He was only a doctor on the outside. At a deep level he cared about himself more than anyone else. I can't operate that way. If nothing else, the failure of my marriage has shown me how important that caring is. I think it's a gift. Like being able to paint or sing or—' she smiled at Jack '—to take great photographs.'

'But doctors are more likely to have it?'

'No, of course not. But maybe people who have it are more likely to go into careers that are people-oriented. Caring professions.'

'So a sheep farmer or orchardist might well have what you're looking for. You shouldn't write them all off.'

'That's true.' Jill's grin was mischievous. Deliberately lightening the conversation. 'OK, maybe there just isn't anyone in Ballochburn that I fancy the socks off. Oh, look!'

Jarred had Bella in tow. They had gravitated to where the dogs were being judged before they joined the end of the parade. Miss Reynolds was handing out the prizes. A red ribbon went to a girl who had a small fluffy white dog that had a Christmas decoration attached to its head.

'I have an extra ribbon,' Jill heard her old teacher announce as they drew nearer. 'I think it should be for a special visitor. Jarred, isn't it?'

Jarred ducked his head shyly but another boy gave him a nudge with his elbow.

'Go on—it's just a ribbon and your dog's cool.'

It wasn't just a ribbon, though. Jill could see the way it was still clutched in his fist after he'd taken part in the small parade around the playground. Like the way he had held onto that photograph Jack had taken of him. She could also see the longing gaze he gave the other boys when Hope came to tell him she had finished judging sand saucers and it was time to go.

'Leave him with us, Mum,' Jill said. 'We'll bring him back later.'

They joined the queue for sausages wrapped up in bread with lashings of tomato sauce. They watched the races start after lunch when parents joined in with their children for sack and egg-and-spoon races.

'Do you think I could go in one?' Jarred finally asked.

'I'm sure you could,' Jill answered. 'Let's go and ask Miss Reynolds.'

The only race left was a three-legged one where children had to be paired with an adult.

'I could do it with you,' Jill offered.

Jarred shook his head slowly. His gaze slid sideways—towards Jack.

'I need to take photos,' Jack said apologetically.

'I could take a photo of this one,' Jill suggested. 'But have you ever been in a three-legged race?'

Jack looked at Jarred and the hesitation was so slight she was probably the only one to notice.

'Sure I have,' he said.

The white lie was obvious from the first step they tried to take with their inside legs bound together with an old rugby sock. They were out of step and fell over in a tumble of mismatched limbs. Jill could see the agony of mortification on Jarred's face.

Then she saw the way Jack helped him up and put his arm around the boy and she felt something melt inside her. She completely forgot to take any photographs, watching the moments he took to figure out how to make the race work and explain it to Jarred. Tentatively, they tried again and took a successful step. And then another. They picked up speed but it was way too late and they were last by such a big margin that they got a bigger clap than the winners. And they both looked even more delighted than the winners had.

It really was time to go after that and it became something

of a rush as Jill realised she was late to help her father with the general practice clinic due to run from 4 p.m. till 7 p.m. The hassle of putting up the extra seat in the back of the Jeep so that Jarred had a safety belt was a nuisance but Jill declined Jack's offer of assistance other than to move the medical gear out of the way.

'It's tricky but I know how to do it,' she told him. 'I have to release this clip here and hold it up and the rest kind of flips open.'

Like an extra-strong deckchair. The seat folded out and then the metal bar that provided its support flipped down to lock into the catch on the floor. It folded easily enough. The bar sprang open with alacrity. Unfortunately, Jill let it go a moment before it reached the catch and the mechanism snapped shut again. Even more unfortunately, Jill had her hand in exactly the wrong place and the fingers of her right hand got crushed between the two bars.

She gasped with shock.

'Oh, no!' Jack dropped the pack he was still holding and wrenched the bars apart. 'Are you hurt?'

'Um…' Jill stared at her hand. Her middle finger had an odd dent around midway between the knuckle and the joint and the whole finger was white. Then the pain message finally reached her brain and instinctively she put her uninjured hand over the other and cradled it to her chest.

'Let me see,' Jack demanded. He lifted her hand away. 'You *have* hurt yourself!'

He sounded outraged, Jill thought in vague wonderment. As though he really, really didn't want her to be injured. Or maybe he felt guilty. Did he think it was his fault because he hadn't insisted on doing the task himself? She opened her mouth to reassure him but couldn't say anything. The pain was overriding the ability to put any words together coherently.

'What's happened?' Jarred sounded frightened.

'Jill's hurt her finger.' Jack's voice was calm. In control. 'Can you go and find someone and ask if they've got some ice? There might be a fridge in the staffroom.'

'OK.' Jarred ran off, with Bella loping at his heels.

'Can you move it?' Jack asked.

'I don't think so. Not yet, anyway.'

'Can you feel me touching the end?'

'Yes.'

'Are these other fingers all right?'

'Yes.' Jill could feel his touch. Oddly, she trusted him not to hurt her any more, even when he touched the injured finger. She was quite happy to let him examine her—as though he knew what he was doing. Had he done a first-aid course of some kind or was it just a combination of common sense and caring?

Because he *did* care. She could feel it all the way into her bones. His touch. The tone of his voice.

The way he was looking at her.

'I hope it's not broken,' he said.

He was holding the eye contact and Jill couldn't look away.

'Even if it is, there's not much that can be done. I'll just have to strap it to the next door finger and keep it still for a while.'

'The ice should help, if Jarred can find some.'

'Yes.'

They were still staring at each other. He was still holding her hand.

They were so close. Only inches separated their faces. If Jill stood on tiptoe and tilted her face, she would be in the perfect position to be kissed.

She *wanted* to be kissed.

'I'll bet it hurts like hell,' Jack said.

'Yes.' But Jill wasn't thinking about the pain. She was busy drowning in Jack's eyes. Falling deeper.

Don't look at me like that.

The plea formed on Jack's lips but he couldn't utter the words.

A maelstrom of emotions were warring inside his head. In his heart.

The horror of seeing Jill hurt herself.

The fierce wish that he'd been able to protect her from harm. He *could* have. He should have.

The desire to make the pain go away. To make everything all right. And the frustration of knowing he couldn't.

The awakening of feelings he'd thought he couldn't have any more. Of caring too much.

Of letting people down.

If Jill kept looking at him like this, he would be unable to keep any distance at all and if he got any closer—even a hair's breadth—this woman was going to fall in love with him.

He could fall in love with her. Too easily.

And he would let her down because he wasn't capable of caring enough. He couldn't trust himself to commit to caring about anything because at some point it could become too much again. It would threaten to destroy him and he would have to stop caring. He would become a person like her ex-husband. A doctor just on the outside.

And that would destroy her.

'I can't do it,' he found himself murmuring aloud. 'I can't give you what you need, Jill.'

She didn't look away. Even as Jarred ran back towards

them with Miss Reynolds, who had a bowl of ice in her hands, and Faith, who was carrying a stack of teatowels.

'But I'm not asking for anything, Jack,' she said softly. 'Maybe I can give you something.' She even smiled. 'It's Christmas after all. We're allowed a little bit of magic.'

CHAPTER EIGHT

DR METCALF senior took one look at Jill's finger and groaned. 'This is a disaster!'

'It's not that bad, Dad. The colour and capillary refill are fine now and the sensation's almost back to normal. I don't think it's broken. Look, I can move it.' Jill managed to bend her finger a little. 'Ooh, ouch!'

'We should X-ray it.' Jim gave a resigned sigh. 'Have you seen how many people are in that waiting room?'

The noise had been impossible to ignore when they had trooped in minutes before. Muriel had been looking harassed as she'd filled in new patient forms and tried to establish order. Jack had taken one look and disappeared rapidly to tie Bella up in the garden and take Jarred upstairs to show off his ribbon to his siblings.

'Most of them are one family,' Jill said. 'Campers, I think, and it looks like the children all have a nasty dose of sunburn. A gallon of Calamine lotion and some paracetamol should do the trick. I can still deal with something like that.'

Jim was still staring gloomily at the offending finger. 'We'll strap it and give you some anti-inflammatories. If it's not any better later tonight we'll X-ray it. You can't be too careful with hands—especially when it's your dominant one.'

'I'm not planning on being a surgeon. Or a concert pianist. It can wait.' Jill held her breath as her father splinted her finger by strapping it to its neighbour with narrow sticky tape.

'It's not just the waiting room. Maisie called a few minutes ago. She's worried about one of your chickenpox kids. The youngest.'

'Nat?'

'Apparently he's spiked a fever and he's pretty miserable.'

'I'll go and have a look at him.'

'And then there's Betty. Angela says she didn't eat any lunch and seems very quiet. She's only a week post-op. She could be brewing an infection. Or a thrombus.'

'I'll check her out, too.'

'How are you going to manage? It'll be a bit difficult to look in that lad's ears or feel Betty's belly one-handed.'

'I'll manage. It feels much better now it's strapped.' Jill wiggled her hand experimentally. 'If I can't manage, or if I find something I'm worried about, I'll give you a call, OK?'

Jim just nodded. 'Send in that sunburnt family on your way out, would you?

Armed with her stethoscope, a tympanic thermometer and an otoscope, Jill made her way upstairs towards the wards.

Towards where Jack had gone.

Would he still be there? The tingle of anticipation at the possibility was too pleasurable to try toning it down despite a new misgiving.

She had seen that flash of fear in Jack's eyes back in the Ballochburn school's car park.

The need to offer reassurance had been overwhelming, which was why Jill had said she wasn't asking him for anything.

And she wasn't.

Yes, she realised she was falling in love with Jack Sinclair and she would desperately *like* him to kiss her.

Or more.

OK, a lot more.

But Jill knew this was just a blip in her life. An interlude that was going to last a few days at the most. A bit of Christmas magic.

Would it hurt to make the most of it?

Maybe Jack had been dropped into her life to let her know it was possible to feel this way again. Part of the reason she'd kept that wedding band on for so long had been as protection. To stop anyone trying to get close because she hadn't been anywhere near ready to try again.

She felt ready again.

Jack could be a little practice run. Training wheels before launching herself back into life properly.

At the top of the sweeping staircase, Jill paused for a moment, looking out the window to see if she could spot where Bella had been tied up. She was in the shade, which was good. Just beside that bench where Jack and Jarred had been sitting—had it only been yesterday?

Her breath escaped in a long sigh. She was kidding herself, wasn't she? The real truth was that she wanted a lot more than a set of training wheels. She couldn't have anticipated feeling this drawn to someone because, despite her ability to fall head over heels in love, she had never felt quite like *this* in her life.

Jack was amazing. Gorgeous. Kind. Mysterious.

She was suspicious, of course, that it couldn't come to anything, but what if caution stopped her even investigating? What if Jack left and she hadn't found out if the possibility of something was there? If she looked so hard she put herself off leaping even a tiny bit? It could be something she might regret for the rest of her life.

Jill turned away from the window. Jack probably wasn't even with the children any longer and she had work that needed to be done.

Her finger throbbed. Right up until she entered the disused four-bed ward that had been transformed into a nursery. A cot had been slotted in for Nat and the fourth bed was being used by Elise, who was keeping an eye on the children overnight. Hope was sleeping along the corridor in another empty ward.

The large girl was there now, joggling a red-faced, miserable toddler on her lap. Jade and Mel were sitting on another bed, discarded toys and games littering the floor around them. Jarred was teaching them a song.

Faith, Hope and Maisie were all watching with varying degrees of admiring smiles as the younger children chanted the words of the song Jarred must have picked up from his new friends in the school grounds.

'We three kings of Orient are

One on a tractor, two in a car...'

Jack was taking photos but he looked up as Jill entered and gave her a half-smile that made her heart trip and then speed up noticeably.

'One on a scooter, tooting his hooter

Following yonder star...'

Hope clapped her hands, beaming.

Faith nodded approvingly. 'A very famous man wrote that song. John Clark, his name was, except most people called him Fred Dagg.'

Jarred ducked his head. 'I can't remember the rest.'

'I can.' Jill grinned and then opened her mouth to sing. *'Oh, oh... Star of wonder, star of light. Star of bewdy, she'll be right...'*

Jack was chuckling now. A rich, joyous sound that widened Jill's smile further. Had he never heard the iconic Kiwi Christmas song?

'Star of glory, that's the story... Following yonder star...'

'Do it again,' Jade begged.

'Can't, sweetie. I've come to visit Nat, 'cos he's feeling sick.'

'He's getting the spots now,' Mel said.

'I thought he might be. How are *your* spots?'

'Itchy.'

'Getting scabby yet?'

'One of them is. Does that mean I can go out to play now?'

'Soon. When they're all scabby, like Jarred's.'

'Faith told me about that finger.' Hope was frowning sympathetically at Jill's hand. 'How's it feeling?'

'I'd actually forgotten about it,' Jill said in surprise. Amazing how a pleasant emotion could cancel out a negative one. She stole a glimpse at Jack, who was packing away his camera.

'It's only one more sleep till Christmas,' Jade said importantly. Then her face creased anxiously. 'Do you think Santa will know where we are?'

'Of course he will.' Hope exchanged a glance with Faith and Jill realized they had everything under control. These children would be getting some treats for Christmas. She disguised her pleased smile by directing it at Elise, who was holding Nat up towards her.

'No, you keep holding him, Elise. He seems happy enough for now.'

But Nat's face crumpled ominously as Jill approached so she looked over her shoulder at the older children. 'Hey, could you guys sing to Nat again? It might distract him while I take his temperature and try to look in his ears.'

To a much more confident rendition of their version of 'We Three Kings', Jill examined the toddler, who was entering the most miserable phase of this illness. Jill managed to listen to his chest and get enough of a glimpse into his ears and throat to be happy enough that he wasn't developing any sinister complications.

'We need to get his temperature down a bit and do something for this rash. I'll give him some paracetamol and then I think a bath with lots of lotion will be the best we can do for the moment. I'll come back and check him again after I've done a ward round.'

Jack chose to head off at the same time but when Jill went to veer into the geriatric and recuperative ward, he was spotted by the charge nurse, Angela.

'Just what I need,' she called. 'A *man*!'

'Ooh, your number's up,' Jill whispered.

'I hope not,' Jack whispered back. 'She must be sixty at least!'

'I can't reach the top of the tree,' Angela explained as she hurried to meet them. 'Even with the stepladder, I'm too short.' She peered over her half-moon spectacles at Jill. 'And you'd have to fly to get there.' With a warm smile she held out a large sparkly star to Jack. 'It'll only take a minute,' she said winningly.

Except that it took a lot longer, of course.

Who could fail to spot the photo opportunity of old arthritic hands busy attaching decorations to the lower limbs of the oversized pine tree? As far as these patients were concerned, being the potential pin-up models for a calendar was the most interesting thing that had happened for a long time.

Enid Hinkley was mumbling enthusiastically but nobody could understand a word.

'You need to put your teeth in,' Jill reminded her. She glanced over Enid's shoulder to where she could see Betty sitting in an armchair beside her bed, just watching the others.

She didn't see Enid pick up her walking stick but she heard the result as the elderly woman leaned forward to poke Jack.

'Oof!' he said. 'What was *that* for?'

'Enid!' Angela said disapprovingly. 'You know you're not supposed to poke people. It isn't polite.'

Enid mumbled more loudly.

'She wants to make sure you take *her* photo,' Angela translated for Jack, who was rubbing the back of his thigh.

Smothering a giggle, Jill went over to Betty—a woman in her seventies who had recently undergone a bowel resection and had come back to Ballochburn to recuperate.

'I hear you're not feeling so good, Betty?'

'Her temperature's up a bit.' Angela had followed Jill. 'Only 37.4, though.'

'How's the tummy feeling?'

'Not so bad,' Betty said. 'I'm all right. Just having an off day.'

'Let's get you up on the bed so I can have a proper look at you.'

It wasn't easy, examining a patient with the middle fingers of her right hand strapped together, and it was some minutes before Jill went to the phone on Angela's desk, near where the tree was being decorated. The silver and gold baubles were much thicker on the lower branches and tinsel was now being applied generously.

Jill dialled an internal extension number. 'You still busy, Dad?'

'Is the Pope Catholic?' She heard a faint sigh. 'I think I might have got rid of the last patient for now. Hope so, because Muriel reckons she's cooking up a migraine. I've just got a mountain of paperwork to do. How's the lad?'

'OK for now. A bit sad but I can't see anything worrying that's brewing. I'm hoping to get his temperature down, which should cheer him up.'

'And Betty?'

'Mild pyrexia. Heart rate's up a bit. Blood pressure's stable. She's got a bit of abdo tenderness, though, and the incision is definitely more inflamed than it was yesterday.'

'Infection?'

'Probably. I'll get a urine sample and we need bloods for a white-cell count and cultures, but I'll get her started on antibiotics stat.'

'Good. Sounds like you've got things sorted.'

'Yes. Um…'

Her father chuckled. 'You need me to take that blood sample, don't you?'

'Yes. Sorry, Dad. I know how busy you are. I'd ask Angela but she doesn't get much practice these days and Betty's veins aren't the best. And I certainly wouldn't be doing her any favours by trying it left-handed.'

Jack looked up from his position only a few feet from where Jill was standing. He opened his mouth as though about to say something but when Jill raised her eyebrows, he gave a subtle headshake and his gaze returned to the screen on his camera. Enid was in front of him, beaming toothlessly as she looped a long strand of tinsel over the end of a branch. What was that about? Jill wondered.

'I'm on my way,' Jim was saying. 'Have things set up, could you? Someone else could well arrive down here any minute.'

'Sure.'

It was no problem to collect the tourniquet, alcohol swabs needle and test tubes. By the time Angela had filled in the labels, Jim had arrived on the ward. He looked out of breath

'Are you OK, Dad?'

'I'm fine. I just ran up the stairs a bit fast, that's all.' Jim picked up the needle and smiled at Betty.

'This will hurt you more than it hurts me.'

'Get away with you.' Betty smiled. 'You wouldn't hurt a fly.'

'You haven't lost your touch, have you?' Jill commented seconds later. 'There's a lot of GPs out there who would have trouble with veins like Betty's.'

'It's one advantage of being run off your feet with a rural practice, I guess.' Jim handed the tubes to Angela. 'You don't get a chance to lose your touch. Let's put a plaster on this.'

He still seemed out of breath. Jill frowned. 'Are you sure you're feeling all right? You look pale.'

'Stop fussing, Jillian. You're as bad as your mother.' Jim smiled a farewell at Betty. 'I'll see you later when I come up to enjoy the carol singers.'

Heading for the door, Jim frowned at his daughter. 'Stop staring at me. I'm *fine*.'

But he didn't look fine at all. He looked a bit grey, was breathing too quickly, and had beads of perspiration on his forehead. Jill followed him, exchanging an anxious glance with Angela. The senior nurse gave her head a quick shake as though she agreed something wasn't right. Should Jill be more insistent or would that make things worse by getting her father's back up?

He was hardly likely to take any notice of her. Jill wished the last locum, Andrew, was still there. He'd have to listen to another doctor if it wasn't his child. She gave a 'What can I do?' kind of shrug and Angela looked as helpless as he felt.

Jim had reached the desk now. Jack had his black bag on the desk as he put his camera away. He was staring at the older doctor as Jim scribbled a note in Betty's file.

'What's wrong with your jaw?' Jack asked, after watching Jim scrubbing it with the knuckles of his free hand.

'A bit of toothache,' Jim growled. 'Don't *you* start!'

'Any chest pain?'

Jill had come to a halt beside her father. She stared at Jack. How on earth could he know that tooth pain could be an expression of cardiac problems?

'No,' Jim said.

'But you're short of breath.' Jack had a very intent, focussed look on his face. Jill felt invisible. 'Have you had anything like this happen before?'

'I just ran up the stairs too fast. I'll be fine. I'll sit down for a minute.'

Silently, Jill pulled out the chair from behind the desk and watched her father sink onto it. Jim's hand went into his shirt pocket as he sat down.

'Oh, my God!' Jill exclaimed. 'What's *that*?'

'GTN.' It was Jack who answered. 'You're having an angina attack, aren't you, Jim?'

'I know what it is,' Jill snapped. 'I just want to know why Dad's carrying it around with him.' She glared at Jack. 'How do you know what it is, anyway?'

But Jack's attention was completely on Jim. 'Have you seen a cardiologist?' he queried.

Jim shook his head. 'Don't need to.' He pulled the cap from the spray canister and raised it to his mouth.

'Hang on a tick.' Jack reached for his wrist. 'You don't want to be taking GTN if your blood pressure's low.' He nodded a second later. 'OK, your radial's fine—you can go ahead. Are you taking aspirin?'

'If I remember.' Jim scowled at Jack. 'You're a doctor, aren't you?'

'Not any more.' The headshake was decisive. 'But I can tell you what you need to do right now, and you might listen to me more than you would to your daughter.'

So he had stepped out of the closet because he'd seen her frustration at trying to get her father to admit something was wrong?

She wasn't about to appreciate his assistance, however. She was as stunned by the revelation as she was worried that her father might be having a heart attack. 'You don't just stop being a doctor. Or were you struck off?' Jill put her hand on her father's shoulder. 'I'm not sure you *should* be giving my dad any advice. I'll look after him.'

'I wasn't struck off,' Jack said quietly. 'Do you have a twelve-lead ECG machine available? Benchtop testing for cardiac enzymes, by any chance?'

Jim had taken two puffs of his spray under his tongue. He was leaning back in the chair with his eyes closed. 'It's easing off now,' he said.

'You still need an ECG. And bloods.' Jill managed to sound ery firm. She could take over now.

'And don't forget the aspirin,' Jack added. 'Where's your ECG machine?'

'Downstairs. In the outpatient clinic.'

Jack looked at Angela. 'Do you have a wheelchair we ould borrow?'

'You're not putting me in any damn wheelchair,' Jim nuttered.

'We could put you into bed here, then,' Jack suggested almly. 'And bring the machine up here.'

Jim glanced up to find Enid Hinkley grinning toothlessly t him. 'Oh, all *right*. I'll use the damn wheelchair.'

Jill had every intention of pushing the chair herself but ouldn't help wincing as she put pressure on her injured hand. The chair started to turn in a circle.

'Let me push,' Jack offered.

'I can manage.' Jill gritted her teeth and straightened course. For some reason she didn't have time to try and analyse, Jack's evelation that he was a doctor and not a photographer wasn't tunning her any longer. It was making her angry.

Very, very angry.

'I can help,' Jack insisted.

'I can *manage*,' Jill snapped back.

'What about the ECG?' Jack queried politely. 'Can you ttach all the leads one-handed? Can you take a blood sample rom your father more easily than you could from Betty? Or et an accurate blood pressure even?'

Jill fumed in silence. She knew if she opened her mouth he would be as ungracious as her father in accepting assis-

tance. She also knew, as well as he did, that assistance wa
necessary right now.

If Jim noted the grim silence in which he was trundle
down to the clinic, he probably assumed it was because ther
was something to worry about. The tension only increased a
they found people waiting there.

They stared at the trio, at the older man in the wheelchai
the young woman with a bandage on her hand and finally
with some relief, at Jack. 'Are you the doctor here?'

'I am,' Jill responded. 'I'll be with you as soon as I can
She tried to smile reassuringly at Muriel, who was sittin
behind her desk with her mouth open, staring in conserna
tion at Jim. She could hardly tell her father's faithful recep
tionist not to worry, though, could she?

Not when she was worried sick herself.

It came as a huge relief to everybody that Jim's EC
showed no indication of a heart attack.

'There's not even any ST depression to speak of,' Jack note
'If you were having an angina attack, it seems to have resolved

Jim pulled his oxygen mask off. 'I don't need this, then
Didn't think so.' He sat up and swung his legs off the bed. 'Th
GTN is more than enough.'

'You need investigation,' Jack told him. 'A cardiac cathe
erisation, an echo and an exercise test would be a good ide
I think.'

'Maybe. If and when it gets any worse.'

'No Dad,' Jill said. 'You need to do it as soon as possibl
I'll set it up.'

'Can't,' Jim said stubbornly. 'I'd have to take at least a whol
day off. Probably two. I'll do it when I've got a new locum.'

'*I'm* your new locum,' Jill reminded him.

'Temporary.'

'Long enough. I'm here for weeks. There shouldn't be any problem setting up an appointment in that time.'

Jack nodded, as though the problem had been solved. 'What's your lipid profile like?' He smiled wryly at Jim's expression. 'You have no idea, do you? Doctors really do make the worst patients. What's your family history as far as cardiac disease goes?'

'How long has this been going on?' Jill interrupted. 'And why didn't you *say* something?'

'It's no big deal.' Jim sighed and took hold of Jill's uninjured hand, which he patted. 'I'm sorry, love. OK, I've had a bit of a niggle now and then and GTN fixes it so I've realised it's probably angina. But it seems to be stable. The same sorts of things bring it on, it's responsive to medication or rest and I'm not getting associated symptoms, so I'm sure I haven't had an infarct.'

'You were short of breath today.'

'I ran up the stairs.'

'You were grey and sweaty.'

'It's a hot day. I didn't get a chance to get one of those sausages at school and I forgot to get something later. I feel great now. No pain. No shortness of breath.'

Jill was unconvinced. 'You need to rest. I want you to lie in here and stay on that monitor.'

'No. There are patients waiting out there.'

Jack looked from father to daughter and back again. 'It might be a good idea,' he told Jim. 'At least for an hour or two. I've got the feeling your daughter is just about as stubborn as you are.'

Jim chuckled, the lines of tension finally leaving his face. 'She's worse, believe me.'

'I can help with any patients that turn up, if need be. My practising certificate is perfectly current. It's in my wallet, if you want to see it.'

'I'll trust you,' Jim said. 'You seem to know what you're talking about. And you're right—it's not worth the fight I'd have to have with Jill. I'll stay here and behave—but just until the carol singing. I wouldn't want to miss that.'

The thought of the choir reminded Jill of something else. 'Does Mum know you've been getting chest pain?'

'No. And you're not to say anything.'

Jill's lips folded into a mutinous line.

'She's been going on for years about the hours I work. This would give her the ammunition to try and force my retirement and you know I can't give it up.' There was a silent plea in her father's eyes that made Jill feel inexplicably sad. 'It's my life, Jilly. You—more than anyone—must understand that.'

'Let's get this blood sample. If we can get it to town, we should get a result by tonight. If it's normal, I won't say anything. Just yet.'

The same effort to hold her tongue was not going to apply to Jack Sinclair.

With the reassurance that her father wasn't in any imminent danger the anger Jill felt towards Jack resurfaced. And now she knew why she felt so angry.

Betrayed, even.

On an instinctive level, she had trusted this man. As much as her father trusted the fact he was a qualified doctor.

And Jack had not been honest with her.

She told him precisely that after they'd left her father under strict instructions to stay put and rest. In the short corridor that led to the waiting area, Jill paused, folded her arms and glared at Jack.

'You lied to me. You're not a photographer.'

'I am now.'

'It's not as if you didn't have the opportunity to tell me the truth. Good grief, you let me position your hands to show you how to stabilise that boy's neck as if you had no idea what you were doing. And up on the ward, you were thinking about offering to take Betty's blood sample, weren't you? When you heard me apologising for dragging Dad up there.'

'I made a decision to stop practising medicine. I need to stick to that.'

'So why didn't you "stick to that" when it was obvious Dad was having an angina attack?'

'I could see he wasn't going to listen to you. That you needed help.'

Jill wasn't going to let the fact that Jack had been trying to help her count for anything. 'You just couldn't help yourself, that's the real reason. You don't just stop being a doctor.' She gave an incredulous huff. 'There I was, blathering on about how it's more to do with who you are than what you do for a living. You knew exactly what I was talking about, didn't you?'

Or had he? He hadn't been interested in hearing Emma's story. Jill could recall the disappointment that he hadn't seemed to care. Her tone became scathing.

'I suppose you were one of those medics who do see it as just a job. The ones who can stay as uninvolved as possible.'

He flinched visibly. He even had the nerve to look outraged. *'No!'*

'So you just got bored, then?' It was easy to direct the

anger at allowing herself to fall in love with another wron person—another person who wasn't trustworthy—toward Jack. To make this *his* fault. She could get over this nice an quickly. She could just dump her disappointment and frustration and even her worry about her father's situation righ where it belonged.

On top of Jack Sinclair.

'What sort of doctor *were* you, Jack? A dermatologist Pathologist? Psychiatrist?'

'An emergency physician, if you really want to know.'

'No, I don't think I do.' Jill turned away with a dismissiv flick of her curls. 'I doubt that I'd believe what you said, an what does it matter anyway? You'll be gone in a day or two.

Jack's voice behind her was quiet. Controlled. 'Would yo rather I left now?'

Jill had to turn back. 'So you'd be happy to take off an let people down? How's Jarred going to feel when he think you're here for Christmas Day? What about Aunty Faith? Yo agreed to take the photographs for that calendar she's s excited about.' Jill dragged in a ragged breath. 'Not that I'n surprised. If you can just give up medicine, I don't suppos it matters to you if you let people down.' This time she wasn' going to turn back. She gave Jack one last, supremely disappointed look. 'You just don't give a damn, do you? If you wan to go, that's fine by me.'

CHAPTER NINE

IT WAS hardly surprising that Ballochburn's interdenominational church choir had traditional red robes and frilly white collars. Or that they held matching candlesticks that glinted from fresh polishing.

With Faith as their conductor, things were being done properly.

Jill's mother was in the middle of a semi-circle arranged according to height. To one side, Judith Cartwright sat bolt upright in front of a small portable electronic keyboard. The choir sang perfectly in tune and there was no nonsense about pukekos in ponga trees or wise men on scooters. The old favourites of 'Silent Night', 'Away in a Manger' and 'Hark the Herald Angels Sing' filled the ward.

Jarred sat on the floor beside Enid Hinkley's armchair, staring in fascination at the movement of Wally Briggs's moustache as he added a gloriously rich baritone to the range of feminine voices.

Jack stood to one side, camera in hand, staring in equal fascination at the play of candlelight on Jill Metcalf's golden curls. She was still deliberately avoiding his gaze. Still furious with him, no doubt.

The image of the Christmas angel she had represented had receded rather sharply since the verbal attack he had been subjected to. This woman was quite capable of being stubborn and intolerant. Why had he thought she would understand if he'd spilled his guts, as he'd been tempted to do when they had been sitting beside the river? Just as well confusion had helped him hold his tongue. He'd been wrong to think that Jill had all the answers.

This was *his* problem.

Something he had to work through in his own time and in his own way.

Why did it matter so much that Jill's opinion of him was now so low?

Why had he stayed to continue his obligation to take these damned calendar photographs?

The knot in his gut was anger, that's why. A familiar resentment that he'd somehow been dropped on the wrong side of the bed at birth or something. The confirmation that nobody would ever bother getting to know who he really was.

Or care enough about that person.

What was really holding him back was that there was someone else who was in danger of feeling the same way. A nine-year-old boy who was coming out of his shell thanks to the illusion of the parallel universe.

Jack wasn't going to be the one to bring reality crashing in around Jarred. Not today, on the eve of Christmas. Not in the midst of the magic of candlelight and music and the brightly wrapped parcels that had mysteriously appeared under the twinkling tree.

He had been wrong to think that he had nothing to give

anyone. He could talk to Jarred. Tell him he was a terrific kid and how important he was going to be to his brothers and sister in the years to come. That things would get better in time. Give him something to hang onto during the tough times that were sure to come.

Because things would get better. For himself as well. Maybe this was all an illusion but it had shown him he was capable of feeling again. He cared about Jarred. Given a chance, he could have cared about Jill.

Too much.

It wasn't meant to be but it had demonstrated that it could be possible. With someone. Some time.

He had been given the kind of hope he'd like to give Jarred. And he knew just how valuable a gift that could be.

The carol service finished at 9 p.m. Quite late for the three young children who had been given the treat of gathering in the corridor, well away from the ward, to listen to the carols.

Nat had fallen asleep on Elise's shoulder, which was a good sign he wasn't feeling too miserable any more. His colour was also looking better, Jill noted with satisfaction.

Maisie detached herself from the small group as she saw Jill coming out of the ward, with the choir and other spectators trailing behind her.

'You get these kiddies to bed,' she directed Elise. 'I'll bring you up some hot chocolate when the choir's had their supper.'

Jarred hung back, shifting from foot to foot, waiting for Jill to finish the call she had just answered on her mobile phone.

'Can I go and say good night to Bella? Please?'

'I'm sorry, hon.' Jill had to refuse the request. 'I have to go out on a call.'

'What's happened?' Jim turned from the conversation he was having with Wally Briggs.

'It's Sue,' Jill said simply. 'She's asking for me.'

'Oh…' The sound of comprehension hung in the air and conversation around them trickled into silence.

'I'd better come, too,' Jim said heavily.

'Poor wee mite,' someone said sadly, 'I was really hoping she'd last until Christmas Day.'

Jill had to swallow hard. She put her hand on her father's arm and gave it a squeeze. 'There's no need.'

There was no need to say anything else. People with sombre faces made way for Jill. She could hear Jarred behind her, sounding bewildered but brave.

'I could go by myself. I know where the shed is.'

'It's OK, mate.' Jack's voice. 'I'll come with you. I could do with some fresh air.'

Long after Jarred had gone to bed, after the walk with Bella and the long talk they'd had, Jack was still up. Sitting in the dark, quiet garden. A glance at his watch showed him it was after midnight.

Christmas Day and here he was, in the last place he could have expected to be—a hospital.

Feeling things he had never expected to feel.

Concern for Jarred. Empathy. Satisfaction, almost, that he *could* feel that empathy and offer hope for a future. And, curiously, an extraordinary release in having told someone else about his own childhood.

He'd been sitting here for nearly two hours, just experiencing these emotions.

Feeling alive again.

Not that everything he was feeling was positive. Far from it. Jack had had to remember things he'd vowed to put behind him for ever. To share them with a nine-year-old boy who'd left, looking at him as though he was some kind of hero.

So different from the way Jill had last looked at him. As though he had disappointed her too much for it to be tolerable. The way her ex-husband had disappointed her?

That hurt.

It hurt so much he could add it to that background anger of feeling misunderstood because nobody—especially Jill Metcalf—cared enough to try and find out who he really was.

But it was his own fault, wasn't it?

How could anyone know who he was when he had locked it away so completely?

He'd never tried to find out if someone could care about him because he'd never revealed who he was—to anyone. He'd been hiding his whole life.

Fearing rejection.

Sabotaging any relationships he'd ever tried. Preventing anyone from getting too close. Protecting himself.

Right now, the person who knew him the best was sleeping in a room with his younger siblings. Probably dreaming about a life that included a scruffy dog he'd fallen in love with.

Jarred hadn't rejected him. He'd been stunned to hear about Jack's history. Disbelieving at first and then…overawed. The way the boy had gathered his own courage and strengthened himself to face the future had actually been visible in the way those skinny shoulders had straightened. In the very adult eye contact that had expressed both amazement and gratitude.

Love, even.

Jack had promised he'd stay in touch. He was going to give

Jarred his mobile phone as a Christmas gift. He would get himself a replacement and then they could stay in contact. He would keep Jarred's phone topped up and they could communicate by text messaging or calls. For as long as Jarred needed a mentor. A parent figure if he wanted one. One that wasn't going to disappear from his life.

The thought of what the gift would symbolise gave Jack the best feeling. A glow that stayed with him as he made his way through the darkened corridors of the old hospital. Up the sweeping staircase and past the wards to get to the apartment over the kitchens.

The large, shadowy shape lurking upstairs gave him a fright.

'What the *hell*?'

They were too trusting in this neck of the woods. Doors weren't locked. No security. A middle-aged nurse on duty in the geriatric ward and a teenager watching over a roomful of children. One pint-sized female doctor who was currently miles away and another doctor who was at least minutes away in his own house and was way past running to protect anyone from a low-life who might be on the search for drugs.

But it wasn't a low-life. It was the teenager, Elise, and in the faint glow of moonlight Jack could see she looked far from happy.

'What's wrong, Elise?'

'I've got a sore tummy. I think it must have been those mince pies I had for supper. I've just been to the toilet.'

'Did that help?'

'No.'

Jack took hold of the girl's wrist. Her pulse was racing. 'Where does it hurt, exactly?'

'All over.'

'Is it there all the time or does it come and go?'

'It's there all the time but it gets worse and then a bit better. Kind of in waves.'

'Can you describe the pain? Is it sharp? Dull? Did it come on suddenly?'

'It's just been getting worse and worse. It's like a really bad cramp.'

'Like period pain?'

'Yes. Only worse.'

'Have you had anything like this before?'

'No.'

'Are you feeling unwell in any other way? Hot and cold, maybe? Have you been vomiting?'

'No. It's just my tummy.'

Her skin felt damp and Jack could hear the faint gasp of over-rapid breathing. Whatever this pain was caused by, it had to be significant. Appendicitis? Ovarian cyst or torsion?

'I'm going to take you downstairs,' he told Elise. 'I need to see what's going on. Have a look at your tummy and take your blood pressure and things.'

'But—'

'It's OK. I'm a doctor.'

'But I can't leave the children. I felt bad enough, going to the toilet.'

'I'll wake Hope up and tell her what's happening.'

He was back within a couple of minutes. 'All sorted. Do you think you'll be able to walk?'

Elise nodded. 'It's not so bad again now.'

But she had to stop halfway down the stairs. To sit down, doubled over, groaning with the pain. By the time Jack got

her as far as the surgery and flicked on some lights, he wa
really worried.

He should call Jim. Hand over the responsibility of this un
expected patient.

Except he couldn't. Jim was, hopefully, sound asleep
Resting. The last thing he needed was the stress of an emergenc
that could bring on another angina attack. Or worse, given tha
they couldn't know how serious his heart condition was.

He should ring Jill on her mobile but he couldn't do tha
either. Not when she was with her best friend who had jus
lost her small child.

Elise was reluctant to climb onto the narrow bed. 'It hurts

'I know.' Jack put his arm around the girl to assist her. Hi
hand was in contact with her belly. It felt rigid.

Peritonitis? An appendix that had already burst? But sh
hadn't seemed unwell. Hadn't been running a temperatur
or complaining of any abdominal pain. She had seemed fin
when she'd been holding Nat as Jill had examined th
toddler earlier.

And her stomach didn't feel rigid by the time she wa
lying flat on the bed.

It felt…odd.

'Elise?' Jack took a deep, steadying breath. 'Is there an
chance that you're pregnant?'

The silence was unnerving. So was the way Elise refuse
to meet his gaze.

'How far along are you?'

'I don't know.' Elise burst into tears. 'My boyfrien
dumped me when he finally found out, just like I knew h
would. And my mum threw me out.'

Was she anywhere near full term? Jack felt her abdome

more thoroughly. Elise wasn't small by any means. She could easily have concealed a pregnancy for months. He could feel the shape of the baby beneath a thick layer of flesh. It seemed to be well down. Engaged. And then the muscles beneath his hands contracted again.

Elise groaned and the sheet beneath her bunched as she grabbed fistfuls of the white cotton.

'I've got to get these track pants off you,' Jack said tersely. 'And see what's happening. You're in labour, Elise.'

'Oh… *No-o-o!*'

Jack had to agree. This was hardly appropriate—undressing a teenage girl in a deserted clinic.

And if she was giving birth to a premature baby, there were far too many things that could go wrong. And they were far too far away from any back-up.

Jack did not want to be doing this. He could feel beads of perspiration breaking out, along with the grim realisation that he had no choice.

But then he forgot about himself. The sight of a crowning infant's head drove any personal baggage into oblivion. He could only hope that nothing would go wrong. Check that the umbilical cord wasn't around the baby's neck. Support the tiny body as it emerged and keep it head down to prevent fluid getting into its lungs.

Astonishingly, it seemed to be a good size. It opened its mouth and took a first breath. Let it out in a warbling cry.

'It's a girl,' Jack said.

'Oh…' Elise struggled to prop herself up on her elbows. She saw her baby and burst into tears again. 'Oh, my God!'

'She's absolutely fine.' Jack was watching the baby pink up and move its limbs. He could feel a strong, rapid heartbeat.

The crying had stopped by the time he clamped and cut the cord but the baby still looked fine. It seemed to be watching him with eyes so dark they looked black. Watching and…trusting.

He helped Elise sit up against the pillows and placed the infant in her arms. 'I need to find some towels,' he said. He frowned as he saw how Elise was shivering violently in the aftermath of giving birth. 'And some blankets.'

He opened cupboard doors but couldn't find what he needed. 'I'll be back in a tick,' he said.

He opened the door to the surgery and almost walked straight into the figure of Jill Metcalf.

She looked pale and drawn. And also very worried. 'I saw the lights on,' she said sharply. 'What's going on?'

The baby gave another cry behind him and Jill's jaw dropped.

'Elise,' Jack said succinctly. 'She's just given birth. Can you show me where you keep your towels?'

'I just don't believe it.'

'It was a surprise, that's for sure.'

Jill stopped walking. Despite the fact it was 2 a.m. and she had agreed to go home and sleep, she was reluctant to leave the hospital grounds. Maybe that reluctance had been why she hadn't refused Jack's offer to accompany her through the gardens.

They had only got as far as the big tree with the bench underneath it. The one Jill would always think of as being Jack and Jarred's bench from now on. Without thinking, she sat down.

'Life's so weird sometimes, isn't it? I come from a family who's just lost their precious daughter and find a new life in the world. Another little girl.'

'Life does go on, I guess, even if we don't feel ready for it.' Jack sat down beside her. 'Was it terrible at the Wheelers'?'

'Yes and no. The grief is dreadful, of course, but the strength of that family is amazing. The love they have for each other will get them through this. I didn't need to stay. I...couldn't...'

Jack simply nodded. 'Sometimes it's too hard, isn't it?'

Jill sat silently for a moment. She could feel the comfort from Jack's presence—the way she had when she had first told him about Emma—and it drove away any residual anger from the way he'd lied to her.

Jack understood. He had to know exactly how hard this was. She shouldn't have said those things about him just being a doctor on the outside. It wasn't true. It didn't matter what he chose to do for a living for the rest of his life, he could only understand because he was capable of feeling this way himself.

Of caring. *Really* caring.

'Why did you give up medicine, Jack?'

'I lost the capacity to care about what I was doing.'

'I don't believe that. I saw the way you looked tonight when you were holding Elise's baby. And the way you couldn't help yourself taking care of my dad yesterday afternoon. You're a born doctor, Jack.' She touched his hand. 'You care a lot.'

He moved his hand away from her touch. 'It's easy enough to care when things don't go wrong.'

Jill thought about that for a minute, aware of the peaceful warmth of a summer's night enveloping them. Of the intimacy of sitting together like this, with only the croak of frogs and the rustle of a nearby hedgehog to break the silence.

Until she spoke very softly. 'What went so wrong for you?'

Jack sighed. 'Lots of things. Too many bad cases. Seeing things that shouldn't have happened. Feeling responsible.'

'Like?'

'Like the guy who had chronic back pain and had made it worse by trying to dig a tree stump out of his lawn. Seemed like an uncomplicated case. I took his history, gave him pain relief and organised X-rays and a scan.'

'Exactly what I would have done.' Jill nodded.

'And how would you have felt when he died an hour later from an undiagnosed triple A?'

Jill swallowed. 'Terrible—of course. But it happens, Jack. Especially with something like an aortic aneurysm that can rupture catastrophically. Even if you'd known exactly what it was, he might well have not made it.'

'I know. And if a GP hadn't sent one little kid home with his sore ears it might still have been too late but it was me who got him in ED a few hours later. Comatose from meningitis. He died before we could get him anywhere near Intensive Care.'

'You can't take responsibility for cases like that. It would break anyone.'

'I know that, too. I learned to step back from getting too involved. I had a great role model in my senior consultant. He was one of those doctors you mentioned—the ones who don't give a damn. The ones who see medicine as just a job.'

Like she'd accused Jack of being. How wrong had she been?

'I thought that was the way forward. The way everybody copes.'

'No,' Jill said quietly. 'Not people like my dad.'

'Or you.'

'I don't think it worked for you either, did it, Jack?'

He snorted. 'No.'

'So what happened? What was the last straw that made you give it all up?'

'A five-year-old boy who got clipped by a truck when he ran out onto a pedestrian crossing. Multi-trauma. His mother was so hysterical we had to send her out of Resus.'

Jack leaned forward, his forehead resting on his hand as he continued speaking. Slowly at first. Quietly. As though talking to himself. Jill had to resist the urge to touch him again. To take hold of his hand. She didn't want to break what felt like a spell of connection. A mystery unfolding.

'I had him on oxygen. Fifteen litres a minute but his sats were only eighty-nine percent. I listened to his chest and there was no sign of a pneumothorax. I bag-masked him and got the sats up to ninety-eight percent, no problem. He needed intubation to protect his airway and give him adequate oxygenation.'

Jill just listened. Jack cleared his throat and spoke more rapidly, as though remembering the urgency of the situation.

'I couldn't visualise the vocal cords. Sucked out a heap of blood and tried again but there was obviously trauma. The sats were dropping again so I bag-masked and called for back-up. My consultant arrived. He asked me if there was a pneumothorax and when I said no, he told me to try again with the intubation. I said I was worried about the possibility of laryngeal trauma and oedema and queried calling Anaesthesia for an emergency tracheotomy. He said we didn't want to chop a hole in the kid's neck unless it was absolutely necessary.'

Jill could sense the impending disaster. She found she was holding her breath.

'I'll cut a long story short,' Jack said bitterly. 'The attempt at intubation failed again. The kid's condition deteriorated. Finally, my consultant gave a bored kind of shrug, reached for some gloves and ordered someone to get him a tracheotomy kit.'

He took a long, slow breath. 'It was too late. I had known it would be too late. I watched the nurse swab that little neck and the consultant take his time identifying the landmarks. The child had been without oxygen for too long by then. Even if he survived he'd be brain damaged. And it took way too long to do the procedure. There was a lot of damage and too much bleeding. The boy went into cardiac arrest well before the tube got placed. I was doing compressions. I knew it was futile but I had to try and do *something*.'

'That's horrible,' Jill murmured.

Jack glanced up. 'You know what the worst thing was?'

'What?'

'There I was, doing the compressions, and I look down and this kid had a plaster on his knee. One of those cartoon character ones with someone like Goofy or Donald Duck on it. It really hit me that someone loved this boy. Looked after him. I thought of all the grazed knees I'd had that had never got a plaster put on them.'

A wave of shock hit Jill.

This wasn't just about a man who had been unable to cope with the emotional pressure of being a doctor.

It was about someone who was thirty-three years old and had never been properly loved.

She hadn't imagined that haunted look the first time she had seen his face. It hadn't just been a flight of fancy when his eyes had reminded her of those belonging to a lost and frightened dog hiding behind rubbish bins.

This wasn't the familiar squeeze of compassion Jill could feel gripping her heart at this moment. It was more like a cramp. Painful and raw.

'We worked on that kid for forty minutes.' Jack had returned to speaking quietly. To himself. 'And finally my consultant stripped off his gloves, threw them in the bin and called the time of death. Then he turned to me and said, "Go and tell the mother."'

'Oh, *God*,' Jill whispered in horror.

'I did it,' he said flatly. 'I even held it together. Gave the poor woman the usual spiel about how we'd done everything possible and how sorry we were, but it wasn't true and I didn't feel that I had. I couldn't feel anything at all. It was like I'd died inside when I'd noticed that plaster. I knew then that I had to get out and it's been that way ever since.'

'You're not dead inside, Jack. Not by a long shot.'

'Maybe not. I've certainly been feeling things again since I arrived here. There's something about this place.' Jack looked up properly for the first time since he'd started talking about himself. He caught Jill's gaze and held it. Picked up her hand and held that as well.

'Something about you, I think,' he added with a gentle smile. 'I suspect it's magic. You and this place together.'

Jill squeezed his hand. 'It's not really magic. It's just that this place is my rock. You've never had a rock, have you, Jack?'

He shook his head. 'I guess that's what I need to find.'

I could be your rock, Jill wanted to say. I could love you and nurture you and give you the strength you need to be who you really are.

Because she knew that was a person it was more than well worth being.

The words remained unuttered, however. A rock that was forced into your hand could just become a dead weight, couldn't it? It was something you had to choose for yourself. Something you recognised the value of enough to want to keep it with you for ever. They had only just met each other. It seemed crazy that she could feel so sure. She certainly couldn't blame Jack if he had no inkling of a similar feeling.

Instead, she nodded agreement. 'A rock is an emotional bank. You can take what you need out but you have to have an open account and you have to put funds back whenever you can. You're just bankrupt at the moment, Jack, that's all. You've given too much and nobody's given enough back to you.'

She wanted to cry. It was easy enough to adopt a stray dog and give it love and find it a home. Her mother had proved how you could help the kind of children Jack must have been, at least temporarily. But did she have the right to offer anything to Jack? When she wasn't even going to be in the country for much longer?

'You'll find it, Jack. It might be a place—like this one.'

'There aren't any other places like this.'

'It could be a person. Someone you'll fall in love with who feels the same way about you.'

Would he say something? Even a hint that he might see her as a contender for that person?

She didn't have to leave. It didn't take a huge stretch of her well-polished imagination to think of staying here.

With Jack.

Taking over from her father—as a team.

Why would she need to leave the place her heart belonged if everything she could want was right here?

A career as a doctor.

A man she could love with her whole heart.

A family of their own somewhere down the track.

Jack had a lump the size of Africa in his throat. He couldn't swallow. Couldn't speak.

He knew exactly what he needed as his rock.

Jill.

But she deserved so much better than damaged goods. Why would she look at someone like him who couldn't guarantee he could cope with commitment? Why would she trust him when he couldn't trust himself?

Maybe, one day, when he had sorted himself out properly, he could risk rejection and offer her his heart.

But not now. Not when he was in the painful process of a kind of rebirth. It would take time to deal with all this emotional stuff again and not feel so vulnerable.

'It's time I went,' he said finally. He withdrew his hand from Jill's and stood up.

'What?' Jill gazed up at him in dismay. 'You're going to leave Ballochburn? *Now?*'

Jack grinned. 'Actually, I just meant it's time I went to bed.' Then his smile faded. 'But it is time I left Ballochburn. If I don't start looking, I'm never going to find my rock, am I?'

'Not today,' Jill said with an audible gulp. 'Not on Christmas Day.'

'No. I can't leave on Christmas Day. I have a present I want to give someone. Jarred. I'm going to give him my phone so we can stay in touch.'

'Oh-h-h…' Jill got to her feet. She was smiling as she stood on tiptoe. 'That's so nice.'

And then her arms were around his neck and she seemed to get taller. Or was Jack leaning down? Whatever. She kissed him. Or he kissed her. Just a gentle brush of their lips.

They pulled apart instantly. Just far enough to look at each other. Jill's eyes were wide and shining. Her lips were parted. The invitation was, quite simply, totally irresistible.

Jack lowered his head and kissed her.

Properly.

CHAPTER TEN

'SHE had *what*?'

'A baby, Maisie. A dear little baby.'

'Who had a baby?' Jim must have been drawn to the smell of bacon filling Ballochburn Hospital's kitchens.

'Elise. Last night, just after midnight.' Jill threw her arms around her father. 'Merry Christmas, Dad!'

'I'm not sure what's merry about it so far,' Maisie grumbled. 'That lass didn't even tell me she was expecting.'

'You're miffed because you didn't spot it for yourself,' Jill teased. She went to steal a piece of bacon from the large cast-iron pan but got her fingers smacked.

'You can just wait your patience, Jilly Metcalf. I've had that girl lifting piles of linen and scrubbing floors, *that's* what I'm "miffed" about.'

'Didn't do her any harm. She's fine,' Jill reported happily. 'And so's the baby. All seven healthy pounds of her.'

'Who delivered it?'

'I did.' Jack walked into the kitchen in time to hear Jim's question. 'Nice, straightforward delivery, if somewhat unexpected. No complications.'

Maisie was appalled. 'What do you think you're doing, Jack Sinclair? Going round delivering people's babies?'

'Jack's a doctor,' Jim told her. 'A very good one, I suspect.'

'No!' Maisie looked more than miffed now. She looked hurt at the apparent size of the loop she'd been excluded from.

'I got there just a few minutes later,' Jill added soothingly. 'And none of us knew Jack was a doctor until yesterday.'

'Why not?' Maisie asked.

Good question, Jill thought. Not that she was about to answer it. She couldn't quite meet Jack's gaze either. For a moment all rational thought deserted her and all she could think of was that kiss they had shared last night. Or rather in the early hours of Christmas morning.

A kiss like no other Jill had ever experienced. One that she might not be lucky enough to ever experience again.

Hungry. Gentle. Passionate. Asking questions she had been only too happy to answer. Except she hadn't given the right answers, had she? Why else would Jack have walked away? Come back to place one more tender kiss on her lips? Then he had really gone, with a smile but without saying a single word of farewell.

'Why didn't someone call me?' Jim demanded.

'You needed to rest,' Jack reminded him. 'How are you feeling this morning, anyway?'

Maybe there hadn't been anything more Jack could have said after that kiss. He'd already said so much. Did he regret revealing as much as he had? Letting her in somewhere that Jill suspected no one else had ever been invited?

'I'll feel a whole lot better when I've had some breakfast,' Jim muttered.

'You'll have to eat fast,' Maisie warned. 'There's a heap to do round this place if Christmas dinner's going to make it to the table.'

Jim was still muttering as he sat down at the table. 'It's not right, waking up to an empty house on Christmas morning. First time it's happened in thirty-five years.'

'Sorry, Dad, but you weren't up and I *had* to nip over and see how Elise and the baby were doing.'

'She's doing just fine.' Hope came into the kitchen, holding a bundle of fluffy towelling. She peered down at the tiny face in the middle of the bundle. 'Aren't you, darling?' Hope glanced up at her husband. 'Merry Christmas, Jim.'

'Merry Christmas,' he returned gruffly.

The greeting was strained, but it would be, wouldn't it? They were the first words this couple had spoken directly to each other in days.

Jack had his camera out to catch the tiny starfish hand that had escaped the swaddling and seemed to reach out to the appreciative audience.

'Has she got a name yet?'

'No. Elise says she's a Christmas baby so she needs a special name.'

Jill looked at her father. He was the one who always had the original ideas when it came to names. But Jim was more interested in the plates of bacon and eggs and mushrooms that Maisie was delivering to the table.

'Eat up,' she ordered, 'while I get the trays up to the wards. And I've got a job for everybody after that.'

'But, Maisie, I've got a Christmas present for you,' Jill said.

'It'll have to wait,' Maisie said firmly. 'It's almost 7:00 a.m. and I'm not delivering a cold breakfast on Christmas Day. Faith would have my guts for garters if there were any complaints.'

* * *

Right on cue, Faith arrived.

'I hope those children didn't wake up too early,' she said. 'Come on, Jillian. It's time for Christmas.'

'Coming.' Jill stuffed a last crunchy piece of bacon into her mouth. She was still chewing it as she picked up the bag of gifts Faith and Hope had hurriedly put together yesterday. The toys and games weren't new but it would hardly matter to a bunch of children who had nothing, would it?

Jack followed, camera still in hand. 'Wouldn't be Christmas without the kids,' he said to no one in particular, 'and this is going to be a Christmas calendar, isn't it?' He had that small package for Jarred ready, Jill noticed—using up space in his camera bag.

Hope was already back in the children's room, helping Elise as she fed the infant. Nat was bouncing up and down in his cot in the corner and Jarred was still asleep. Jade and Mel were sitting up in bed, rubbing sleep from their eyes, staring at the small Christmas tree in the corner of their room. A tree that looked just as empty underneath as it had when they'd gone to sleep last night.

Faith poked her head around the door. 'Are you ready, children?'

Silent, wary nods. Jarred woke up, swung himself out of bed to rush to the tree and then stopped abruptly, an expression of resigned disappointment on his face.

'Told you he wasn't real,' he said to Mel and Jade.

Mel looked shocked. Jade's eyes filled with tears.

'Who said I wasn't real?' boomed a masculine voice. The tall figure, in full red regalia, black boots and an oddly rectangular shape to his huge belly, stood framed in the doorway. The walrus moustache didn't quite match the snowy white beard but who was going to notice? Jill could just make out Jack in the background, camera poised.

'Ho, ho, ho!' said Santa.

The children shrieked gleefully. Jarred couldn't quite manage the nonchalant air he was striving for. He managed half of it, with a suspicious scowl and his hands in his pockets, but then he saw the sack bulging with gifts and his eyes widened as he grinned.

'Awesome,' he said.

'Sorry I'm a bit late,' Santa boomed. 'Ballochburn is a bit out of the way, you know.'

Jim Metcalf slipped into the room as the children excitedly tore into parcels. The Friends of the Hospital had done themselves proud and there were plenty of new gifts of toys and clothing for the family. Nat was more interested in the wrapping paper than the contents of the gifts, apart from the floppy pink rabbit that had been one of Jill's childhood favourites. Already soft and worn with one eye missing, the toddler pressed it against his cheek as though greeting a long-lost friend.

It was Nat that Jim headed for.

'Thought I'd better pop up and see how the young fella was doing,' he said offhandedly to Jill.

'He's a lot better.' Jill scooped up both Nat and the pink rabbit for a cuddle. 'Still running a fever but paracetamol is wonderful stuff.'

Jim's grunt was satisfied but he didn't leave the room. He watched, along with the other adults present, as Jade tried on a pair of angel wings and fitted the headband with the tinsel halo over her wispy blonde hair.

'I'm the Christmas angel,' she announced. 'Jack! Jack! Take my photo!'

But Jack was busy, crouched beside Jarred, explaining the workings of the mobile phone to him.

'It's OK,' Jarred said. 'I know how to use a phone. Everybody does.'

'Cool. As soon as I get my new phone, I'll text you the number.'

Jarred just nodded. A casual observer might have thought he was less than impressed with the gift, but Jill saw the shy look he gave Jack a moment later.

The smile that passed between man and boy suggested a bond no one else would ever share.

A bit like the smile Jack had given her, just before he'd finally turned and walked away after that kiss.

She wished she had a gift for Jack.

She did—a huge gift—but would he want to accept it?

Her instincts had not been wrong this time. Jack was a lot more, rather than less, special than the man she had fallen in love with. His problem wasn't that he didn't care. He did. Too much.

Would he want to care about her? Would he consider accepting the gift she was prepared to give?

Her heart and soul. To have and to hold. From this day forward…

Probably not, Jill decided, which was why he'd walked away in silence last night. He wasn't ready for such a gift. He had things he needed to sort out for himself first. Having to blink the threat of tears from her eyes, she found it helpful to focus on her father as he moved further around the room.

To where Elise sat in an armchair, feeding a baby that was now sucking like an expert.

'Everything OK?' he queried casually.

'I guess. I'm sorry I didn't tell you I was pregnant when

you gave me the job, Dr Metcalf. I didn't think this would happen while I was here.'

'Just as well it did. I don't care what they say these days, a hospital is still the best place to have a baby.'

Elise looked down at her infant. 'She's beautiful, isn't she?' She looked up at Jim. 'I can't believe she's mine, you know? Someone I can love who will love me back.'

Jim cleared his throat and Jill could see the way he blinked. Exactly the same way she had a moment ago, when she had been thinking about Jack. Go, Elise, she applauded silently. Hit him in that soft spot and you'll have a job for life here if you want it.

Elise seemed to catch her thoughts. 'I know it won't be easy,' she said, 'but I reckon I can make it work. I've got a job already…that is, if you'll let me keep it for a while.'

'I'll see what we can do.' Jim was silent for a moment. 'I hear you're thinking of a Christmas name for this wee dot.' The casual tone didn't fool Jill. Acceptance was definitely on the agenda here. Love for her father made her eyes decidedly misty. A glance at her mother showed that Hope was also listening to the exchange. She looked misty-eyed, too.

'Mary's a bit boring,' Elise said. 'And I don't like Ivy. Or Joy, particularly. Angel's too cheesy. Holly's nice but lots of people call their babies Holly these days.'

'What about Carol?' Jim suggested.

'Like a Christmas carol? I hadn't thought of that.' Elise looked down at her baby again. She bent to brush a soft kiss on the downy head. 'I like it,' she said. 'A carol's a kind of song and songs are always happy.'

Jim smiled. He sighed with satisfaction. 'I'd best get going,' he said. 'I need to make sure Santa hasn't found a supply of medicinal sherry or something. We'll see you later, at lunchtime.'

He didn't seem to notice the way Hope stared after him as he left, blinking away tears of her own.

Jill was tempted to rush after her father. To drag him back and insist that he sort out the silly disagreement with Hope, which had grown out of all proportion. How could they let it continue? On Christmas Day?

It was only the stern look from Faith that prevented Jill following her impulse. Yes. Her parents did need to figure out what was important all by themselves or it might not be meaningful enough.

Just like Jack needed to do.

Her heart sank more than a fraction. It was going to be a bitter-sweet Christmas by the look of things. Tears and laughter. Joy and sorrow.

She would just have to try and make the most of the joyful bits.

A call out to the camping grounds just after Maisie had presented Jill with a bucket of fresh peas to shell seemed anything but a nuisance. Jill positively beamed at Jack.

'Hooray! I was wondering when we'd find time to get you to the camping grounds today. Grab your camera and come with me. It just wouldn't be a Ballochburn calendar without pictures of the campers.'

'It doesn't sound too serious,' she added a minute later as she held the back door of the Jeep open for Bella to jump inside. 'Someone's burned their hand in the kitchen. They've got it under running water so I told them I'd go there rather than having him brought to the hospital.'

She was still avoiding looking at him for more than a second, Jack realised with dismay. Here they were with the first opportunity they'd had to be alone since they'd parted in the middle of the night and Jill was cheerfully talking—non-stop—about anything but that.

Going on about the unique Christmas feel the camping grounds had. How families came back year after year because they loved it so much. How there were now people bringing their children who were using the caravans or camp sites their own grandparents had used.

Was she avoiding the topic because it was unwelcome?

Thank goodness he had managed to control himself last night. Not to try and take that kiss any further.

God knew, he had wanted to.

The taste and scent of this woman. The first touch of his lips on hers and he had plunged into another time and space. A place of unimaginable excitement. Pleasure. Sheer…*warmth*.

A place of total acceptance. Even after he'd confessed his dreadful, dark secret, Jill hadn't rejected him.

She had, instead, given him the answer he'd been seeking.

It was simple, really, wasn't it?

In the emotional bank, his account was overdrawn and in order to top it up, all he needed was someone to give him the funds. Or rather, someone he could earn the funds from because he wasn't a charity case.

Jill was the most giving person he'd ever met. She just gave to everybody, no questions asked. She didn't seem to ask anything in return but she clearly received as much as she needed for her own account to stay firmly in the black.

She would give to Jack if he asked, but he wasn't going to ask. Not unless he had something of equal value that he could give in return. And maybe Jill didn't want anything more from him. Maybe that was why she was avoiding the topic—and any significant eye contact.

Jack let Jill's chatter wash over him, making noncommittal but encouraging noises when required. Trying to pick up any signals, verbal or otherwise, that Jill might want to talk about something more personal.

Like that kiss.

Hadn't she said they were allowed a little bit of Christmas magic?

That was before she knew you were a doctor, Jack reminded himself. Before she knew that you'd lied to her. Or how emotionally bankrupt you are.

It wasn't a very long journey to the camping grounds down in the valley beside the river.

Not nearly long enough to convince himself that he had anything worth offering Jill.

The manager of the camping ground met the Jeep and directed Jill towards a concrete block building that housed the showers at one end and the kitchens at the other.

'Is it OK if Jack, here, wanders round to get some photos?'

'Sure. Is this for the calendar I was hearing about in the pub last night?'

'Yes.' Jack nodded at the man. 'I hear it wouldn't be complete without having the camping ground in it.'

'Too right, it wouldn't. Feel free, mate.'

Jack wandered around as Jill disappeared into the kitchens. He hadn't expected such a Christmas feel to a makeshift settlement of tents and caravans so he was astonished at what he found.

Tents that had decorations tied to their poles. Caravans decked out in coloured lights. People wearing Christmas hats and umpteen over-excited children. Some were already on the river, trying out new inflatable toys and a canoe or two. One was trying to Rollerblade on grass and several teenage girls were sitting together, madly texting on shiny new mobile phones.

The way Jarred would be before too long.

The image of the look on the boy's face that morning would stay with Jack for ever. The gift had meant so much. Not the phone—that had been just the bit that could be wrapped. They had both known what the real gift was. Support. Having someone in the world that cared about you.

He could give *that* to Jill.

Hell, he could give her all the love that had been bottled up inside him all his life.

He could share her laughter.

Hold her when she needed to cry.

Make sure her account was overflowing even if she was a world away from this magical place she'd grown up in.

Jack's step felt almost urgent as he made his way to the camp kitchens. Jill was still in there and things couldn't be too serious, judging by the laughter and loud, cheerful voices.

Several families were using the facilities to prepare their Christmas dinners by the look of it. Women with champagne glasses nearby were making salads. Men held cans of beer and poked at basins full of marinating meat.

'Pete'll do anything to get out of the cooking,' one was shouting.

'Nah.' Someone else laughed. 'He *was* doing the cooking. He got his fingers mixed up with the sausages.'

'Yeah—easy mistake!'

Jill was using damp teatowels to wrap the man's scorched-looking palm. 'We'll keep it cool until we can get you to th surgery and put a proper burn dressing on it.' She spotted Jack 'First-degree burn,' she told him. 'Painful but not serious Anyone want to come with Pete and give him a ride back here?

'Nah.' A man lifted a beer can in salute. 'Walk'll do yo good, mate!'

'That's my beer you're drinking, Wayne!'

'So it is! Guess I better come along and be the taxi, then

'Pete can ride with me,' Jill said. 'Could you take Jack We're a bit short on seats in the Jeep.'

No chance to talk to Jill about anything personal on the wa back to the hospital, then, and goodness knew what kind c chaos was brewing for the rest of the day. Jack could hav been disheartened. Probably would have been except that Ji looked at him. Caught his gaze properly for the first time th day. And she smiled at him.

That warm, loving kind of smile she was so good at.

Just for him.

Jack followed Wayne to his car with a seed of hope takin root. Blossoming even.

It didn't need to be ruthlessly weeded out, the way nine year-old Jack had learned to do in order to save the disappoint-ment at seeing it wither and die before it could bear fruit.

No. This was it.

Fate had dropped him from the sky because the answer ha been waiting for him, right here in the heart of stone-fru country.

And he had found it.

* * *

It didn't take long to sort out a suitable dressing for Pete's hand and supply some pain relief.

'You'll need to keep it dry,' Jill warned. 'And I want to see it again tomorrow.'

'Won't be able to wash the dishes after dinner, then.' Pete grinned. 'Shame!'

'He won't need those pills,' Wayne joked. 'A few tinnies should anaesthetise that hand pretty well.'

'Go easy.' Jill smiled. 'And have a good rest of Christmas.'

'You, too,' the men chorused.

'We won't,' Jill informed Jack, 'unless we go and do our bit in the kitchen. Aunty Faith might provide all the food and the tablecloths and silverware and so on, but there's a lot to do to make it as perfect as she expects. I'll bet those peas are still waiting to get shelled.'

They were. It was nearly midday and Christmas dinner was due to be on the table at 2 p.m.

Not that the youngest patients in Ballochburn Hospital were expected to wait that long. Maisie had roasted a chicken for them.

'We'll say it's a small turkey,' she said, as she set the trays. 'Jarred can eat with the rest of us. He's not infectious any more and he's old enough for grown-up food.'

The grown-up turkeys had been in the ovens for hours now. A huge glazed ham sat waiting on a silver platter. Brussels sprouts filled a vast stainless-steel pan and a row of plum puddings sat like decorations on a side bench. Hope was making cranberry sauce. Wally was peeling a huge mound of potatoes, his Santa hat still in place, though slightly skew. He was delighted to see Jack.

'Grab a peeler, lad, and come and tell me all about that plane of yours. Latest model Cessna, isn't it?'

'Yep. A Skyhawk SP.'

'Wouldn't mind taking it for a bit of a spin.'

'You'd be very welcome, as soon as it's airworthy again.

'Won't be long, lad. The parts turned up on the bus las night. I'll get onto it first thing in the morning. Civil Aviatio still has to do their little investigation bit but I'm sure tha won't be a problem. You'll be up and away in no time.'

Up.

And away.

Jill stopped eating the peas she was shelling and starte putting them in the pot like she was supposed to.

Would Jack come back when he had found the answers h needed?

Would she still be here?

She had to find a way of trying to let him know that sh would welcome him back into her life if he chose to come Whenever that might be and wherever she was. He woul be able to find her whereabouts by asking someone i Ballochburn. Her family would always be here.

Jill looked at her mother's back as she stood stirring th sauce and then at her father, busy sharpening a wicked-lookin carving knife by swiping it on a steel. She didn't realise sh had sighed aloud until she felt her great-aunt's gaze.

'I hope you're not eating too many of those peas, Jillian.' Fait picked up a stack of linen napkins and silver serviette holders 'I'm just going to help finish setting the tables,' she said. 'I' send Judith Cartwright down for the crackers and then—'

Whatever was next on Faith's agenda remained unknowr The clatter of the heavy steel dropping on the tiled floor mad everybody jump.

'Jim!' The colour drained from Hope's face. 'Whatever is vrong?'

Peas fell from Jill's suddenly numb fingers. Her father's ace was a dreadful shade of grey with an unnatural shine of perspiration. He had a fist pressed to the centre of his hest—the classic sign of someone suffering from unbear-ble chest pain.

This was no simple angina attack. GTN and oxygen were ot nearly enough to combat the pain.

'He's having an infarct, isn't he?'

Thank goodness Jack was here. He and Wally carried Jim hrough to the surgery. Even if Jill's hand hadn't been injured, he would have had difficulty attaching the ECG electrodes. Dr drawing up the morphine he needed.

This was her *father*.

And he could be dying.

'Looks like an inferior.' Jack added the pink twelve-lead CG trace to the folder of notes. 'How far away is that he-icopter?'

'Shouldn't be long now.'

Hope hadn't left her husband's side since he'd collapsed n the kitchen. She was still clutching his hand.

'Don't you dare die on me, Jim Metcalf!'

'I thought you were sick of me.'

'How could I be sick of you? I don't see you often enough o get sick of you, you silly man. How many times have I told ou you work too hard?'

'Not hard enough,' Jim mumbled. 'I should have been round to help you more.'

'I don't need help,' Hope sniffed. 'All I needed was to get oticed sometimes.'

Faith didn't need to come into the surgery to tell them th
rescue helicopter had been spotted. They could all hear th
welcome sound of the approaching transport that would hope
fully get Jim to emergency care and treatment before to
much of his heart muscle was damaged.

'I'm coming with you,' Hope declared.

'Of course you are,' Jim agreed. 'Wouldn't be able to liv
without you, Hope. Wouldn't want to.'

'I'm coming, too.' Jill smiled at her mother and handed he
some tissues.

'You can't,' Jim said. 'We can't leave Ballochburn withou
a doctor.'

'What's wrong with Mr Sinclair, then?' Faith queried. 'O
Dr Sinclair, so I've been told. ' She eyed the syringe Jack wa
holding as he prepared to top up Jim's level of pain relief. 'H
certainly *seems* to be living up to his new reputation.'

Jill had seen that kind of fear in Jack's eyes before thi
When she had offered to give him some Christmas magic. H
wasn't ready to have that much asked of him. It could be a
much of a disaster as Jill asking for some kind of commitme
before he'd had a chance to get to know her. And trust her.

'I'll stay,' she said quietly.

The relief on Jack's face didn't last long, however. It barel
registered before the door of the surgery flew open.

'Help! Someone, *help*!'

Maisie had a small limp body cradled in her arms.

'It's Nat,' she cried desperately. 'He's *choking*!'

CHAPTER ELEVEN

'HE roar of the rescue helicopter landing in the car parking rea directly outside the surgery was deafening.

Nobody inside the room took the slightest notice.

Jack had taken Nat from Maisie's arms. 'What happened?'

'He was eating chicken off Mel's plate…' Tears streamed own Maisie's fat red cheeks. 'He was really hungry, poor wee amb. He stuffed it in and…and then he stopped breathing…'

Jack was sitting down in the chair beside the desk as Maisie obbed out the history. He tipped the toddler face down over is knees, supporting his head with one hand. With the heel f his other hand, he delivered rapid and forceful blows etween Nat's shoulder blades.

Then he turned the child face up, keeping his head lower an his chest. Jill could see the awful blue tinge to the lips. 'here was no sound or sign of any air movement. There was omplete airway obstruction and Nat was clearly unconscious.

'Try chest thrusts.' Woozy from the morphine and his voice uffled by the oxygen mask, Jim was struggling to sit up on e bed. Hope clung to his arm, trying to keep him from etting up.

'Stay where you are, Dad.' Jill pulled a laryngoscope fror its case on a shelf and snapped the blade open to turn on the ligh

'Can you open his mouth?' she asked Jack. 'I'll see i anything's visible.'

Something was. Lodged too far back in the toddler's mout to reach with fingers, and Jill wasn't about to try. She coul end up pushing it further down and causing more damage.

'Where are your Magill forceps?' she asked her father.

'With the bag mask…side pocket of the life pack.'

'There's no time,' Jack snapped. 'He's blue.' He bent dow placing his mouth over Nat's, holding his nose shut and tryin to push air in with mouth-to-mouth ventilation.

'I'm barely getting anything in,' he said grimly, seconds late

At that moment the still open doorway to the surgery wa filled by new arrivals.

Two paramedics and behind them Faith and Jarred.

'What the hell's going on?' a paramedic queried. 'I thoug we were coming for a cardiac patient.'

'This kid's choking,' Jack informed them tersely. 'Yo qualified to do a needle cricothyroidotomy?'

'Yes, but the kit's still in the chopper.'

'It won't be enough,' Jill said urgently. Creating an airwa with a wide-bore needle was a temporary solution. Even they could remove the obstruction in the time they bought, th likelihood of swelling and repeat closure of the airway mea that a longer-term solution was vital. 'He needs a surgic airway,' she added decisively.

'Get on with it, then,' Jack said. 'We're losing too muc time.' He tried to deliver another breath to Nat.

'I can't, Jack!' Jill held up her right hand with the stra ping on the two middle fingers. 'You'll have to do it.'

* * *

Time seemed to freeze.

Jill could see the enormity of what she was asking Jack to do.

To face his worst nightmare.

To revisit the appalling incident that had driven him away from practising medicine.

To take full responsibility for trying to save a child's life.

She could feel her eyes filling with tears as she crouched beside the man on the chair, still holding the unconscious child. She laid her hands over his.

'Jack,' she whispered. 'You can do this. *Please.* Do it for Nat. For me…for *yourself.*'

Then the frozen moment was gone and all hell broke loose.

A paramedic ran for gear. Jack laid Nat on the floor. Jill scrambled to find what they needed.

Jim could only watch from his bed, with Hope's arms around him.

Faith had her arms around Jarred.

'It'll be all right,' Jill heard her say over and over again, like a mantra. 'It'll be all right.'

Jack had never felt anything like this.

Such sheer panic.

Holding the utterly limp child in his arms. Looking up to see Jarred's gaze fixed on him from the corner of the room the boy was wedged into.

Do something, he seemed to be yelling silently. You've got to *do* something.

Feeling Jill's hands gripping his. The transfer of warmth. Strength.

Hearing her voice. The belief that rang through in her words.

He *could* do this.

He *had* to.

For Nat. For Jarred. For himself. But perhaps most of all for Jill because she believed in him. Because she touched his soul in a way no one had ever touched him.

He would do anything she ever asked of him.

Even take a scalpel to a tiny child's throat. Cut into it. Reverse his hold and insert the handle of the scalpel into the incision and rotate it to open the airway.

It was Jill who held out the smallest-size endotracheal tube to be inserted and a paramedic who had the suction equipment ready. It was Jack who connected the bag-valve device and secured the tube with fingers that still weren't trembling. He attached the bag mask and gave Nat his first full lungs of oxygen in what seemed like far too many minutes.

And it was Jack who took the Magill forceps now that they had time and opened Nat's mouth. He held the tongue out of the way with the blade of the laryngoscope and shone the light on the obstruction.

It was a sharp piece of bone hiding inside the chicken meat. Jack had to work very carefully to ease it out without doing any further damage. He held it up a minute later, still gripped in the forceps, for everybody to see.

'You got it!' Jim sank back onto his pillows, closing his eyes in relief.

'He's breathing for himself,' Jill cried. 'Look!'

Seeing the small chest rise and fall without the assistance of the paramedic holding the bag mask was a joy, but Jack wasn't going to let himself relax just yet. Even when the monitor clipped onto Nat's tiny finger revealed that the oxygen saturation was up to one hundred per cent.

'There could be a lot of swelling from that obstruction. I can't see how much damage there is. He's going to need the airway for a while.'

He needed rapid transport as well. Intensive monitoring with surgical back-up if necessary. Expert assessment and enough time to gauge whether his brain had been deprived of oxygen long enough to sustain permanent damage.

Or maybe the time needed would not be as long as Jack feared.

Nat was stirring. Regaining consciousness. His eyes opened and he gazed in dismay at the strange and frightening environment he found himself in. His face crumpled as he began to cry soundlessly. His gaze roved, seeking a more familiar face than the medics still crouched over him.

Jim gave Hope a gentle push. 'He needs you, love.'

'So do you.' Hope was clearly reluctant to let go of her husband. 'He knows Maisie as well as me.'

'It's OK,' Jim murmured drowsily. 'As long as I know you're close. They need you as much as I do, my love. All those children have. For years.'

So Hope crouched on the floor and cuddled Nat as best she could while preparations around them gathered momentum.

'Jack had better go with you,' Jill said. 'To keep an eye on Nat.'

'That'll still leave Ballochburn without an able-handed doctor,' Faith pointed out. 'What if something else happens?'

'But Nat needs a medical escort. So does Dad, for that matter.'

'So what's wrong with these paramedics?' Faith asked bluntly. 'Don't they train these people to manage situations like this?'

'Indeed they do, ma'am.' The paramedics exchanged amused glances. 'I think we can safely transport both our patients here. We're running a bit short of space in the chopper as it is—unless Mrs Metcalf wants to stay behind?'

'No,' said Hope.

'No,' said Jim.

Nat's little fists closed on the fabric of Hope's clothing as a silent testimony to his own wishes.

'I guess that settles it.' A paramedic nodded.

'Of course it does,' Faith said crisply. 'We need Jack *and* Jill here. They're a perfect team.'

Within minutes, everything was organised. Jim was loaded into the helicopter, his pain relief topped up, oxygen on and continuous ECG monitoring in place.

Nat was loaded as well, to travel in Hope's arms, also with oxygen on, although his oxygen saturation and his colour were perfectly normal.

All those left behind watched the helicopter take off and Jill was grateful for the firm grip with which Jack was holding her good hand.

'We'll give it a couple of hours,' Jack said. 'If we haven't heard from your mum by then, we'll ring the hospital and find out what's happening.'

How on earth was she going to get through this dreadful period of waiting?

Hearing Maisie sobbing behind her wasn't helping.

Faith appeared to agree.

'This is not your fault, Maisie Drummond, and that little lad is going to be fine. Our Dr Sinclair saved his life.'

Our Dr Sinclair. Miraculously, Jill felt a smile tugging at her lips. She looked up and caught Jack's gaze.

Her Dr Sinclair. She held his hand more tightly.

'We've got a ward full of people waiting for their Christmas dinner, Maisie,' Faith said sternly. 'I think the plum puddings could spare a little of their brandy and when we've fortified ourselves, we'll get on with doing what needs to be done.'

Maisie rallied and sniffed bravely.

Jill squeezed Jack's hand again as Faith led Maisie away.

'You did it, Jack,' she said quietly. 'You *did* save Nat's life. I'm so proud of you.'

I love you, she wanted to say. But maybe she didn't need to. The way Jack was looking at her right now made her feel as though she had already said the words.

That he'd said them right back to her.

'You believed in me,' Jack said softly. 'You have no idea how much that means.'

'Oh, I think I do.'

'And Jarred—did you see the look on his face?'

'No.' Jill turned to where Faith and Maisie had almost reached the door. 'Where *is* Jarred?'

'Oh, Lord!' Faith turned back, completely losing her customary air of calm assurance. 'He ran away when Jack was about to put that tube into Nat's neck. With everything else happening, I clean forgot to go looking for him.'

'We'll find him,' Jack said.

Faith looked at the way he was still holding Jill's hand. At how closely together the two of them were standing. Her face relaxed noticeably and she nodded.

'Bring him back in time for dinner,' she instructed. 'And, Jack?'

'Yes?'

'We'll need you to carve the turkey, seeing as James isn't here.'

The children's room was quiet.

Elise lay on her bed with Carol sound asleep beside her in the plastic crib borrowed from the maternity ward. Cuddled under each arm she had Jade and Mel. Now worn out from a morning's excitement, they lay listening to Elise read them one of their new story books.

Angela was watching over them all. She went pale on seeing Jack and Jill enter the room. She opened her mouth but clearly couldn't bring herself to utter the question on her lips.

'Nat's fine,' Jack said.

'Where is he?' Jade's halo was still on but her wings were crumpled as she lay on her side, close to Elise.

'He had to go to the hospital,' Jill told her. 'He needs special looking after, just for a day or two, and then he'll come back.'

'We saw the helicopter,' Mel said. ' Where's Jarred?'

'That's what we wanted to ask you.' Jill caught Jack's gaze but had to look away quickly. He cared as much as she did for the welfare of the oldest of these children. He was just as worried. 'You haven't seen him, then?'

'Not since Nat went away.'

They did a quick search of the rest of the hospital, including the kitchens. The ovens had been turned well down and Faith and Maisie sat at the table. Wally was topping up their brandy glasses.

'It's been a shock,' he was saying. 'Everyone will understand if dinner is a little later than usual.'

Maisie spotted Jill. 'There's been a phone call,' she said importantly.

'From Dunedin?' Jill caught her breath. 'Are they at the hospital already? Why didn't Mum call me on my mobile?'

Maisie flapped her hand at Jill. 'Don't interrupt, Jilly Metcalf. Where are your manners? No. The call was from that woman from Invercargill. Margaret somebody.'

'The social worker?'

'That's the one.' Maisie took another fortifying sip of brandy.

'What did she say?'

'She said to wish you all a Merry Christmas.'

'Oh…' It wasn't very merry, was it? So far, it was shaping up to be the most disastrous Christmas Day Jill had ever experienced.

'She also said they've got hold of the grandparents. In London they were, but they're rushing home to collect the children. Should be here in a day or two.'

'That's good.' But Jill couldn't help sounding dubious. They had to find Jarred. Had to reassure themselves that Nat was really on the way to a full recovery. These children needed reuniting and then settling before another major change was forced upon them.

'It's very good,' Faith said firmly. 'They need their family. It sounds as though these grandparents have been trying to help for a long time but their daughter refused to let them. Could be the best thing that could happen for them all.'

'Maybe he went to find Bella,' Jack suggested as they left the kitchen a short time later. 'He really loves that dog.'

They went to the gardener's shed but there was no sign of a boy or a dog.

They searched the gardens.

'Hey!' Jill stopped suddenly. 'What's your cellphone number, Jack?'

He told her. Jill pulled her own mobile from her pocket and began texting.

Jarred? Jill here. Where R U?

'He may not have it with him,' Jack warned.

'I saw the way he was looking at you when you gave it to him,' Jill responded. 'I don't think he'll be putting it down in a hurry.'

Sure enough, her phone beeped.

Lukin 4 Bela was the response.

Where? Jill sent back.

Hens came a succinct reply.

'I know where he is,' Jill said in relief. 'Come with me.'

She led Jack rapidly along the track beneath the old oak trees, through the squeaky gate and into the back garden of her childhood home.

And there, on the swing beneath the apple trees, was Jarred. His head down, his feet scuffing dusty earth. Spotted hens hovered nearby, keeping an eye on the newly disturbed dirt in case any edible treasure was uncovered.

'I can't find her,' Jarred said. 'She's gone.'

'She won't have gone far,' Jill said hopefully. 'We'll find her.'

Jarred wouldn't look up. 'Nat's dead, isn't he? Just like Mum.'

'No.' Jack squatted in front of the swing. 'He's not dead, Jarred.'

'I saw what you did.' Jarred sounded disgusted. 'You made him bleed.'

'I had to, mate. He couldn't breathe. I had to make a little hole and put a special tube into his neck so he could breathe. So he *wouldn't* die. He's OK, now, honest.'

'Why did they put him in the helicopter, then? And take him away?'

'Because they need to watch him for a while and then take the tube out and fix up the little hole. When they're sure it's safe to do that.'

Jarred finally looked up. A brief, hurt glance. 'I thought you were trying to kill him.'

Jill almost groaned aloud. It hadn't just been Jack's worst nightmare, had it?

'Oh, mate…' Jack's words were a soft groan. 'That is the last thing on earth I would ever try to do. You didn't *really* think that, did you?'

The eye contact was held longer this time. 'I guess not,' Jarred admitted. 'I…was scared.'

'Want to know a secret?' Jack asked.

'OK.'

'I was scared, too.'

'But you still did it.'

'Yeah. Sometimes you have to do things that scare you.' Jack rose to his feet again. 'Sometimes, if you're really lucky, you can find someone that helps you do the scary things and then they're not so scary.'

He was looking at Jill. Smiling.

She smiled back, loving the way he was looking at her. As though she was the most important person on earth. As though he didn't want to look anywhere else for as long as possible.

'So where's Bella, then?' Jarred asked. 'Why did she run away?'

'I don't know,' Jill said. 'But she's been sleeping on the

veranda. I put a nice woolly blanket there for her. Shall we go and see if she's having a nap or something?'

'OK.'

Jarred climbed wearily off the swing, the weight of the world resting on him again. Jack put a hand on his shoulder.

'How well do you know your grandparents, mate?'

'Nanna and Pop? We don't get to see them much. They live in the country up near Dunedin somewhere.'

'Are they nice?' Jill asked carefully.

'Yeah.'

'They're worried about you guys.' Jack also sounded a little wary. 'They're on their way home so they can come and look after you all.'

Jarred's shoulders hunched. 'I don't want them to look after us. I want to stay here.'

'You could always come and have holidays here,' Jill offered. She knew her mother would say the same thing if she had been here and seen how sad this little boy was.

Jarred looked up at Jill. 'Will you be here?'

'Um…I do have to go away.' Jill could feel Jack watching her. She couldn't look back. Couldn't let him see how hard it was going to be for her to leave. 'I'll be coming back for holidays, too, though.'

'Why do you have to go away?'

'Because I need to do my job. I need to be a doctor.'

'But isn't that what you're doing here?'

'Um…yes…' Jill's step slowed so that she was behind the others as they climbed the veranda steps.

It was exactly what she was doing here. Looking after inpatients like Betty and old Mrs Hinkley and the chickenpox children. Accidents like Nick and the cherry picker and Jack after his plane crash. House visits like the one to Sue and Emma.

She needed to go back there later today. To help with arrangements and offer support.

The kind of support that would be needed for a long time. The kind that built the bonds that could hold friends and even a whole community together.

Jarred turned to Jack at the top of the steps. 'You're a doctor, too, aren't you?'

'Yes, mate. I am.'

Jill caught her breath. He hadn't said he used to be a doctor but wasn't any more.

How could he say that after today? After caring for her father and saving Nat's life?

'So you have to go away, too?'

'Maybe.'

Maybe? Jill had to consciously release her breath. What did he mean, maybe? Was he thinking of *staying*?

In which case, what the hell was she thinking of going away for?

'I might stay for a while,' Jack continued calmly. 'Jill's dad needs some help around here and Jill's got a sore hand. That is…' he turned to catch Jill's astonished gaze '…if that would be OK?'

It would be a lot more than OK.

'That would be great,' Jill managed. 'Really great.'

'Hey!' Jarred ran to the end of the veranda and dropped to his knees. 'Bella *is* here! But what's *that*?'

It was a puppy. The first of four.

All three of them hunkered down beside the dog, watching

the miracle of the births. Jack had one arm around Jarred's shoulders. His other hand caught Jill's and held it.

'Wish I had my camera,' he muttered.

They stayed that way for a long time, until the last puppy had been born and cleaned up and then nudged towards the others, who were having their first drink of milk. Bella looked up at her audience and her tail thumped gently.

'You're a clever, clever girl,' Jill told her.

'Can I have a puppy?' Jarred begged. 'Please? A dog of my very own?'

'We'll have to talk to Nanna and Pop about that,' Jill said. 'But if they live in the country and they don't mind, it would be fine by me. It could be my Christmas present to you.'

They were all late for Christmas dinner but nobody seemed to mind. Jack carved the rather dry turkey but Jill couldn't eat a bite. Not until the call came to say that Jim had been taken to the catheter laboratory and had undergone angioplasty with all the lesions on his coronary arteries successfully stented with complete resolution of his symptoms.

Suddenly there a lot more than just Christmas to celebrate.

'He'll have to take things easy for a while,' Faith declared. 'It's high time that man retired.'

'Look who's talking,' Wally boomed. 'When are *you* going to retire, Faith?'

'I hope I can help,' Jack said. 'I'm going to apply for the locum position here.'

Faith gave her great-niece a look that Jill couldn't interpret. 'Excellent,' the old lady said.

Another call came, when the plum puddings and the not very strong brandy sauce arrived at the table, to let them know that Nat was doing very well and that a procedure to repair his airway was booked for the next day.

All going well, both Jim and Nat would be coming home the day after that.

Wally, Judith and the other staff and members of the Friends of the Hospital committee went to their own homes and families after the tables were cleared and the dishes done. Faith went to have a lie down and Maisie took something for her headache and put her feet up with the new romance novel Jill had given her for Christmas.

'Just what the doctor ordered,' Maisie said contentedly. 'You lot can all go away and leave me in peace for a while.'

Jarred went to spend the rest of the afternoon sitting beside Bella, watching her feed her puppies.

Jill paid a visit to the Wheelers.

Jack went to print off some photographs and keep himself available in case anyone needing medical care turned up at Ballochburn Hospital.

There were no emergencies.

Except one.

The urgency had been building all afternoon but it wasn't until much later that Jill finally found a moment to be alone with Jack.

After an evening meal nobody had really wanted and all the inpatients had been checked and settled for the night.

The lights still twinkled on the ward tree. Jill could see them reflecting on the windows when she went into the garden at dusk to find Jack sitting on the bench. *His* bench.

She sat down beside him. And took his hand in hers.

'Merry Christmas, Jack.'

He smiled. Then the smile faded and he looked very, very serious. But not sad. That haunted look Jill had seen that first day had gone from his face. From those gorgeous dark eyes. He bent his head and kissed her. Softly.

'It's been the most amazing Christmas I've ever had,' he said. 'Thanks to you. And this place.' He kissed her again, his lips settling for just a little longer. Moving over hers as though exploring a place he felt incredibly lucky to be. 'Magic,' he murmured, drawing away.

'Do you really think you might stay?'

'I'd like to.' Jack reached out and touched Jill's face. Tracing its outline as he smiled. 'I've always hated Christmas. Dreaded it.' His fingers reached the bottom of her cheek and ran along her jaw. 'It's a time for home and family and celebrating all the things I've never had. Never thought I could have. But here…' His finger brushed Jill's lip, butterfly soft, as he released his breath in a quiet sigh. 'I feel like it's *been* Christmas. Like I'm…home. Does that make any sense?'

'Perfect sense.' Jill nodded. 'I love you, Jack.' The words just came out all by themselves.

'You hardly know me.'

'I know everything I need to know,' Jill said with conviction. 'You have a heart that's so caring it got broken because you cared too much and nobody cared enough about you.' She put her arms around Jack. '*I* care,' she whispered. 'I'm sorry I don't have a Christmas gift for you. All I can offer is that caring. My love.'

Jack's voice sounded curiously rough. As though tears were getting in the way. He took Jill into his arms.

'That's the biggest gift anyone could ever give.'

Jill's heart thumped painfully as she pulled away far enough to be able to see Jack's eyes. Will you accept it?' She tried to smile but her lips wobbled. 'It won't take much unwrapping.'

'Only if you accept the gift I have for you.' His gaze was holding hers—as gently as a caress.

Jill felt the world stop turning for an instant. 'You have a gift for me? What is it, Jack?'

'The only thing I have to give.' Jack had to clear his throat. 'Myself. My heart.'

It was too much. Joy threatened to tip into tears. Tears that could wash away all the worry and sadness that had been mixed into this extraordinary Christmas Day. Jill struggled to believe what she was hearing. That this wasn't way too good to be true.

'Does…your gift have a ribbon?'

'I'm afraid not.' Jack kissed her again. A kiss that was going to lead to a whole lot more. But passion needed to be held at bay for just a few moments more. Until Jill could really believe.

'Does it come with an exchange card?'

Jack laughed. A sound that chased away any doubts in Jill's mind. It was the sound of happiness.

'Definitely not.'

'Oh….' Jill could smile now and it only trembled a little bit. 'In that case, I accept.'

The exchange of their gifts was sealed in the only appropriate way as they kissed each other again. And then Jack stood up, picked Jill up in his arms and carried her beneath the old oak trees, through the squeaky gate, past where Bella lay with a snuggle of puppies and into her home.

Their home.

EPILOGUE

BALLOCHBURN'S fundraising calendar went on sale in October, in time for the following Christmas.

It didn't matter that most of the images were nearly a year old because they were timeless. They captured the spirit of a country community and a celebration that would never change.

They were also the record of a love story.

'I'm glad you put Bruce in first.' Jill was sitting on the top of the veranda steps of her old family home, with Jack beside her and Bella lying on the step just below their feet.

She loved the picture of the farmer in his black singlet and khaki hat, a long stalk of grass clamped between his teeth as he surveyed a paddock dotted with peacefully grazing sheep.

'It's the same paddock, isn't it? The one you crashed in.'

'I didn't crash, Jillian. It was a perfectly well-controlled forced landing.'

'Hmm.' Jill grinned as she twisted to touch the almost invisible scar on Jack's temple. Jack caught her hand and kissed the palm. Then he pulled her closer. He would have kissed her lips for a lot longer than Jill was clearly prepared to allow.

'I want to see the rest,' she excused herself. 'They look different now. All glossy and professional.'

'Mmm.' Jack sounded suitably modest. 'It's not a bad hobby to have, is it? I might keep it up.'

'You'd better. Aunty Faith is going to love this one of her house. She'll want to frame it.'

'Do you think she's finding it a bit crowded now, having your mum and dad living with her?'

'She loves it. And she does need an eye kept on her, even if she won't admit it.' Jill turned a page. 'I'm going to frame this one of Jarred and Bella. It's precious.'

'He loves that pup even more than Bella now. They're doing well in that obedience class, aren't they?'

'They're all doing well. They've got a wonderful home for the first time in their lives. We'll have to go and visit them again soon. Oh…' Jill turned another page. 'Pets' day!'

She laughed aloud at the image of Aaron Baker's legs in the air as a large black lamb made its bid for freedom.

Then she smiled fondly at the picture of Enid Hinkley's toothless grin as she draped tinsel on the Christmas tree.

'Shame she won't be here for this Christmas.'

'Mmm.' The sound was one of agreement but Jack's fingers stole unconsciously to the back of his thigh to give it a thoughtful rub.

Jill's head rested on Jack's shoulder as they flipped through the rest of the calendar.

A picture of the camping ground with a limp but well-decorated pine-tree branch attached to a tent pole—a group of laughing men toasting the photographer with their beer cans and children playing in the river in the background.

One of the carol service with the glow of candlelight on the rich red of the choir's robes.

One of small children in pyjamas with expressions of total

wonder on their faces as they gazed at a Santa who had a huge walrus moustache.

And the last picture.

'Do you think anyone will mind that we put in a wedding picture?'

'It's Christmassy,' Jack pointed out. 'Look at all those cherries on the trees behind us. And Sue's holding your bouquet—all red and white.'

'She's due any day now. Getting pregnant like that was so unexpected.'

'She hated the idea, didn't she?'

'Yes. She thought people would think she was trying to replace Emma.'

'Some things that get lost can never be replaced,' Jack said quietly. 'But I think it was meant to happen. A way of starting again for them.'

'Like us. We were meant to happen, weren't we?'

'Just like us.'

'Shall we tell anyone yet?'

Jack laid a gentle hand on Jill's belly. He smiled and shook his head.

'We've only just found out ourselves. Let's save the news. We could surprise everyone at Christmas dinner.'

'Another one of those gifts that can't be wrapped.'

'The best sort.' Jack wrapped his arms around his wife and held her close. 'Don't you think?'

'Absolutely.' Jill raised her face for a kiss, no less precious because it was now so familiar. 'The very best.'

CHRISTMAS WISHES, MISTLETOE KISSES

BY
FIONA HARPER

As a child Fiona [illegible]
either lay [illegible]
world [illegible]
at least in [illegible]
imagination. [illegible]
worked as a [illegible]
trading [illegible]
When she became [illegible]
hours to spend [illegible]
littlest one [illegible]
moments [illegible]
writing.

From [illegible]
are the [illegible]
on a [illegible]
and any [illegible]
can't keep [illegible]
especially [illegible]
essays [illegible]
end [illegible]
are her [illegible]
her [illegible]

As a child, **Fiona Harper** was constantly teased for either having her nose in a book or living in a dream world. Things haven't changed much since then, but at least in writing she's found a use for her runaway imagination. After studying dance at university, Fiona worked as a dancer, teacher and choreographer, before trading in that career for video-editing and production. When she became a mother she cut back on her working hours to spend time with her children, and when her littlest one started pre-school she found a few spare moments to rediscover an old but not forgotten love—writing.

Fiona lives in London, but her other favourite places to be are the Highlands of Scotland and the Kent countryside on a summer's afternoon. She loves cooking good food and anything cinnamon-flavoured. Of course, she still can't keep away from a good book or a good movie—especially romances—but only if she's stocked up with tissues, because she knows she will need them by the end, be it happy or sad. Her favourite things in the world are her wonderful husband, who has learned to decipher her incoherent ramblings, and her two daughters.

For Mum, I love you

CHAPTER ONE

MOST women would have given at least one kidney to be in Louise's shoes—both literally and figuratively. The shoes in question were hot off the Paris catwalk, impossibly high heels held to her foot by delicately interwoven silver straps. The main attraction, however, was the man sitting across the dinner table from her. The very same hunk of gorgeousness who had topped a magazine poll of 'Hollywood's Hottest' only last Thursday.

Louise stared at her cutlery, intent on tracing a figure of eight pattern on her dessert spoon and eavesdropped on conversations in the busy restaurant. Other people's conversations. Other people's lives.

Her dinner companion shifted in his seat and the heel of his boot made jarring contact with the little toe of her right foot. She jerked away and leaned over to rub it.

'Thanks a bunch, Toby!' she said, glaring at him from half under the table.

Toby stopped grinning at a pair of bleached blonde socialites who were in the process of wafting past their table and turned to face her, eyebrows raised. 'What?'

'Never mind,' she muttered and sat up straight again, carefully crossing her ankles and tucking them under her chair. Her little toe was still warm and pulsing.

The waiter appeared with their exquisite-looking entrées and

Toby's eyebrows relaxed back into their normal 'sexily brooding' position as he started tearing into his guinea-fowl. Louise's knife and fork stayed on the tablecloth.

He hadn't even bothered with his normal comments about the carbs on her plate. She was supposed to be getting rid of that baby weight, remember? Never mind that Jack had just turned eight. His father was still living in a dream world if he thought she was going to be able to squeeze back into those size zero designer frocks hanging in the back of her wardrobe.

But then Toby had emotionally checked out of their marriage some time ago. She kept up the pretence for Jack's sake, posed and smiled for the press and celebrity magazines and fiercely denied any rumours of a rift. He hadn't ever said he'd stopped loving her, but it was evident in the things he *didn't* do, the things he *didn't* say. And then there was the latest rumour…

She picked up her cutlery and attacked her pasta.

'Slow down, Lulu! No one's timing you,' Toby said, eyes still on his plate.

Lulu. When they'd first met, she'd thought it had been cute that he'd picked up on, and used, her baby brother's attempts at her name. Lulu was exotic, exciting…and a heck of a lot more interesting than plain old Louise. She'd liked being Lulu back then.

Now she just wanted him to see *Louise* again. She stopped eating and looked at him, waiting for him to raise his head, give her a smile, his trademark cheeky wink—anything.

He waved for the waiter and asked for another bottle of wine. Then she saw him glance across and nod at the two blondes, now seated a few tables away, but not once in the next ten minutes did he look at her. Her seat might as well have been empty.

'Toby?'

'What?' Finally he glanced in her direction. But once, where she had been able to see her dreams coming to life, there was only a vacancy.

He rubbed his front tooth with his forefinger and it made a

horrible squeaking noise. 'Do I have spinach on my teeth, or something?'

She shook her head. What spinach would dare sully the picture of masculine perfection sitting opposite her? The thought was almost sacrilegious. She was tempted to laugh.

The words wouldn't come. How did you ask what she wanted to ask? And how did you stand the answer?

She tried to say it with her eyes instead. When she'd been modelling, photographers had always raved about the 'intensity' in her eyes. She tried to show it all—the emptiness inside her, the magnetic force that kept the pair of them revolving around each other, the small spark of hope that hadn't quite been extinguished yet. If he'd just do it once…really connect with her…

'Jeez, Lulu. Cheer up, will—'

A chime from the phone in his pocket interrupted him. He slid it out and held it shielded in his hand and slightly under the table. The only change in his features was a slight curve of his bottom lip. *Now* he looked at her properly. He searched her face for a reaction, and then returned the mobile to his jacket pocket and returned his gaze to his plate.

She waited.

He shrugged. 'Work stuff. You know…'

Unfortunately she had the feeling that she did know. And she kept knowing all the way through dinner as she shoved one forkful after another into her mouth, tasting nothing.

The rumour was true.

All afternoon, since she'd spoken to her friend on the phone, she'd hoped it was all silly speculation, someone putting two and two together and coming up with five. Six years ago, when the tabloids had been jumping with the stories of Toby's 'secret love trysts' with his leading lady, she'd refused to believe it, had given interview after interview denying there had been any truth in it. During the second 'incident' she'd done the same but, while her outward performance had been just as impassioned, inside she'd been counting all the things that hadn't added up: the hushed phone calls, the extra meetings with his agent. Never enough to pin him down, but just enough to make her die a little more each time she shook her head for the reporters and dismissed it as nonsense.

She blocked out the busy restaurant with her eyelids. No way could she go through that again. And no way could she put Jack through it. He'd been too young to understand before, but he was reading so well now. What if he saw something on the front of a newspaper? She squeezed her jaw together. What kind of message was she giving to her son by lying to the world and letting Toby use her as a doormat? What kind of man would he become if this was his example?

'Oh, my God! It's Tobias Thornton! Can I have your autograph?'

Louise's eyes snapped open and she stared at two women hovering—no, make that *drooling*—next to Toby's chair. Toby smiled and did the gracious but smouldering thing his fans loved him for as he put his ostentatious squiggle on the woman's napkin. Louise just tapped her foot.

Only when they'd finished gushing and jiggling on the spot did they glance at her. And a split second scowl was obviously all she was worth. They didn't even bother keeping their voices down as they walked away. Huddled over her new treasure, she clearly heard one say, 'He is *so* hot!'

Toby opened his mouth to speak but, once again, his phone got the first word in. He glanced at the display, stifled a smile, then gestured to Louise that he was going to have to take this one. 'My agent,' he mouthed as he walked off to stand near the bar.

My foot, thought Louise, as the waiter cleared her half-eaten pasta.

She watched him out of the corner of her eye as he talked. Her husband smiled and laughed and absent-mindedly preened himself in the mirror behind the bar. His agent was male, over fifty and as wide as he was tall. No, Louise could do the maths. And the number she kept coming up with was *four*.

Even as something withered inside her, she sat up straighter in her chair. She demanded eye contact from Toby as he finished his call and sauntered back towards her. Now she got her smile—warm, bright, his eyes telling her she was the most wonderful thing in the world.

As he sat down at the table, he reached for her hand and brushed her knuckle with the tip of his thumb. Louise leaned forward and smiled back at him, turning on the wattage as only a former model knew how to do. And when Toby leaned in, clearly hoping he was going to be able to have his cake and eat it too this evening, she let the grin slide from her face and spoke in a low, scratchy whisper.

'Toby…' She paused, mentally adding all the names she wasn't about to call him out loud. 'I want a divorce.'

A hefty gust of wind blew up the river and ruffled the tips of the waves. The small dinghy rocked as Ben tied it to an ancient blackened mooring ring on a stone jetty. He stared at the knot and did an extra half-hitch, just to be sure, then climbed out, walked up along the jetty and headed up a narrow, stony path that traversed the steep and wooded hill.

He whistled as he walked, stopping every now and then just to smell the clean, slightly salty air and listen to the nagging seagulls that swooped over the river. At first glance it seemed as if he was walking through traditional English countryside, but every now and then he would pass a reminder that this wasn't a wilderness, but a once-loved, slightly exotic garden. Bamboo hid among the oaks and palms stood shoulder to shoulder with willows and birches.

After only ten minutes the woods thinned and faded away until he was standing in a grassy clearing that was dominated by a majestic, if slightly crumbling, white Georgian mansion.

Each time he saw this beautiful building now, he felt a little sadder. Even if he hadn't known its history, hadn't known that the last owner had been dead for more than two years, he would have been able to tell that Whitehaven was empty. There was something eerily vacant about those tall windows that stared, unblinking, out over the treetops to the river below and the rolling countryside of the far bank.

He ambled up to the front porch and tugged at a trail of ivy that had wound itself up the base of one of the thick white pillars. It had been nearly a month since his last visit and the grounds were so huge there was no way he could single-handedly keep the advancing weeds at bay. Too many vines and brambles were sneaking up to the house, reclaiming the land as their own.

Laura would have hated to see her beloved garden's gradual surrender. He could imagine her reaction if she could have seen it now—the sharp shake of her snowy-white head, the determined glint in those cloudy eyes. Laura would have flexed her knobbly knuckles and reached for the secateurs in a shot. Not that her arthritic hands could have done much good.

At ninety-two, she'd been a feisty old bird, one worthy of such a demanding and magical place as Whitehaven. Perhaps that was why he came up here on the Sundays when it was his ex-wife's turn to have Jasmine for the weekend. Perhaps that was why he tended to the lilies and carnivorous plants in the greenhouses and mowed the top and bottom lawns. He stuffed his hands in his pockets and shook his head as he crunched across the gravel driveway and made his way round the house and past the old stable block. He was keeping it all in trust on Laura's behalf until the new owner came. Then he'd be able to spend his Sunday afternoons dozing in front of the rugby on TV and trying not to notice how still the house was without his whirlwind of a daughter.

He ducked through an arch and entered the walled garden. The whole grassy area was enclosed by a moss-covered red brick wall, and sloping greenhouses filled one side. It was the time of year that the insect-eating plants liked to hibernate and he needed to check on them, make sure the temperature in the old glass-houses was warm enough.

And so he pottered away for a good ten minutes, checking pots and inspecting leaves, until he heard a crash behind him. Instantly, he swung round, knocking a couple of tall pitcher plants off the bench.

The first thing he saw was the eyes—large, dark and stormy.

'Get out! Get off my property at once!'

She was standing, hands on hips and her legs apart, but he noticed that she kept her distance and worried the ends of her coat sleeves with her fingers. His hands shot up in surrender and he backed away slightly, just to show he wasn't a threat.

'Sorry! I didn't realise…I didn't know anybody had—'

'You're trespassing!'

He nodded. Technically, he was. Only up until a few seconds ago he hadn't known anybody cared—save a dead film star who'd loved this place as unconditionally as the children she'd never had.

'I made a promise to the previous owner, when she was ill, that I would look after the garden until the house was sold.'

She just stared at him. Now his heart rate was starting to return to normal, he had time to look a little more closely at her. She was dressed entirely in black: black boots, black trousers and a long black coat. She even had long, almost-black hair. And, beneath her heavy fringe, her face held a stark and defiant beauty.

'Well, the house has been sold. To me. So you can clear off now,' she said.

He pressed his lips together. There wasn't much he could say to that. But the thought of leaving Whitehaven and never coming back shadowed him like a black rain cloud. This new woman—striking as she was—didn't look like the sort to potter around a greenhouse or dead-head flower borders.

He picked up his coat from where it lay on the bench and turned to go. 'Sorry to disturb you. I won't come again.'

'Wait!'

He had almost reached the door at the end of the long, narrow greenhouse before she called out. He stopped, but didn't turn round straight away. Slowly, and with a spark of matching defiance in his eyes, he circled round to face her.

She took a few steps forward, then stopped, her hands clasped in front of her. 'The estate agent told me the place has been empty for years. Why do you still come?'

He shrugged. 'A promise is a promise.'

Her brows crinkled and she nodded. A long silence stretched between them, yet he didn't move because he had the oddest feeling she was on the verge of saying something. Finally, when she knotted her hands further and looked away, he took his signal to leave.

This time, he had his hand on the door knob before she spoke.

'Did you really know her? Laura Hastings?'

He let his hand drop to his side and looked over his shoulder. 'Yes.' A flash of irritation shot through him. For some unfathomable reason, he'd not expected this of her. He'd thought her better than one of those busybodies who craved gossip about celebrities.

'What was she like?' Her voice was quiet, not gushing and over-inquisitive, but her question still annoyed him.

He stared at her blankly. 'I really must be going. I meant what I said. I won't trespass here again.'

She ran after him as he swung the greenhouse door open and stepped out into the chilly October air. He could hear the heels of her boots clopping on the iron grating in the greenhouse floor. The noise echoed and magnified and he let the door swing shut to muffle it.

'Hey! You're going the wrong way!'

No, he wasn't. And he wasn't in the mood for chit-chat, either.

She didn't give up, though. Even though it must have been hell to stride after him in those high-heeled boots, she kept pace. Something to do with those long legs, probably. Either the changeable riverside weather had turned milder, or he could feel the hot anger radiating out from her as she closed the gap. He left the walled garden through a different gate from the one he'd entered by and chose a path that took him back down the hill towards his boat.

'I asked you to get off my land!'

He stopped and turned in one motion, and was surprised to find himself almost nose to nose with her. Not that she quite matched his six foot two, but she had the advantage of heels and a slight slope.

She stepped back but her eyes lost none of their ferocity.

He didn't have time for mood swings and tantrums. He had more than he could handle of those from Megan at the moment. That was why coming to Whitehaven was such a good distraction on a Sunday afternoon. It soothed him.

He looked Miss High-and-Mighty right back in the eyes. 'And I'm getting off your land as fast as I can.' Even though he had a strange sense that *she* was the trespasser. *She* was the one spoiling the peace and quiet of the one perfect spot in this world.

Her lips pressed together in a pout. One that might have been quite appealing if he weren't so angry with her for being here. 'The road is that way.' She jerked a thumb in the direction of the drive.

'I know.' He deliberately didn't elaborate for a few seconds. Just because he was feeling unusually awkward, although, in the back of his mind, he knew she was bearing the brunt of his frustration with someone else. But the woman in front of him was cut from the same cloth—exclusive designer cloth, by the look of it—and he just couldn't seem to stem his reaction. He took a deep breath. 'But my boat is tied up down by the boathouse.'

He blinked, waiting for more of her frosty words.

'I have a boathouse?' Once again, the tide had changed and she was suddenly back to being wistful and dreamy and far too beautiful to be real. That just got his goat even more. When she spoke again she was staring off into the bare treetops above his head. 'It's real? It wasn't just a film set?'

He shrugged and set off down the path and his features hardened as he heard her following him.

'Now what? I'm going, okay?' he called out, only half-turning to let the words drift over his shoulder.

'I want to see the boathouse.'

Ben normally loved the walk back down the hill on an autumn afternoon, but today it was totally ruined for him. He couldn't appreciate the beauty of the leaves, ranging from pale yellow to deep crimson. He didn't even stop to watch the trails of smoke snaking from the cottages of Lower Hadwell, just across the river. All he could hear were the footsteps behind him. All he could see—even though she was directly behind him and completely out of sight—was a pair of intense, dark eyes looking scornfully at him. It wasn't a moment too soon when he spotted the uneven stone steps that led down to the jetty.

As he reached the top step he heard a loud gasp behind him. Instinctively, he turned and put out a hand to steady her. But she hadn't stumbled. And she hadn't even registered his impulsive offer of help. She stood with her hands over her mouth and her eyes shining. Great. Now it was time for the waterworks. He was out of here.

As quickly as he could, he made his way to where his boat was tied and started untying the painter, busily ignoring her slow descent of the steps behind him. Just as he was about to step off the jetty and into the dinghy his mobile phone chimed in his back pocket. He would have ignored it, but it was Megan's ring tone. Something might have happened to their daughter.

And, since she was standing within reaching distance, not doing much but staring at the old stone boathouse, he slapped the end of the rope into the frosty woman's hands and dug around in his jeans pocket for his phone.

'Dad?' Not Megan, but Jasmine.

'What's up, Jellybean?'

There was a snort on the other end of the line. 'Do you have to keep calling me that? I'm almost twelve. It's hardly dignified.'

Ben's brows lowered over his eyes. Less than twenty-four

hours out of his custody and she was already starting to sound like her mother. 'What's up, Jas?'

'Mum says she can't drop me off this evening. She's got something on. Can you come and get me?'

Ben looked at his watch. Jasmine had been due back at five. It was past three now. 'What time?' Maybe it was just as well he'd had to leave Whitehaven early. It would take all of that time to cross the river, walk back to the cottage and drive the ten miles to Totnes.

He waited while his daughter had a muffled conference with her mother.

'Mum says she has to be out by four.'

Ben found himself striding along the jetty in front of the boathouse. 'I can't do it, Jas.' He kept walking while Jasmine relayed the information back to Megan. And when he reached the end of the jetty he turned and went back the way he'd come.

'Mum says she wants to talk to you.'

There was a clattering while the phone changed hands. Ben steeled himself.

'Ben? I can't believe you're being difficult about this! I know you've still got a soft spot for me, but it's time to let go, move on… This kind of behaviour is just childish.'

He opened his mouth to explain there was nothing *difficult* about not doing the physically impossible, but Megan didn't give him a chance.

'Everything always has to be on your terms, doesn't it? You'd do just about anything to sabotage my new life, wouldn't you?'

His voice was more of a growl than he'd intended when it emerged from his mouth. 'I do hope you are not letting our daughter overhear this. She doesn't need to witness any more arguments.'

Megan gave a heavy sigh. 'That's right. Change the subject, as always!' Still, he got the distinct impression she had moved into the hallway as her voice suddenly got more echoey.

'Megan, I'm at Whitehaven. This has nothing to do with

sabotage and everything to do with being too far away to get there by four o'clock.'

He waited. He could almost see the pout on his ex's face. And, as he found himself back by his boat, he noticed a similar expression on the woman standing there watching him. He abruptly turned again and carried on pacing. Not *exactly* the same expression. The lips were fuller, softer.

'Fine! Well, if you're too selfish to come and get her, I'll just have to take her with me. I'm having supper with…a friend. I'll drop her back at eight.'

And, with that, Megan ended the call. He was tempted to hurl his phone into the slate-grey waves. This was what that woman did to him—riled him until he couldn't think straight, until he was tempted to do foolish things. And he never did foolish things.

He jabbed at a button to lock the keypad, then stuffed his phone back in his pocket. Then he marched back to his boat.

'Thanks a lot for giving me some privacy,' he said dryly as he got within a few feet of the glowering woman on the jetty.

She gave him what his grandmother had used to call an 'old-fashioned look' and waved the rope she was holding from side to side. Incredible! How did the woman manage to make a *gesture* sarcastic?

'You didn't give me much choice, did you?' she said.

Ben ran his hands through his wind-tousled hair and made himself breathe out for a count of five. He had to remember that this wasn't the woman he was angry with, not really. 'Sorry.'

He'd expected the pout to make a reappearance, but instead her lips curved into the faintest of smiles. 'Divorced?'

He nodded.

'Me too,' she said quietly. 'That half of your conversation was giving me déjà vu. I bet I could fill in the blanks if I thought hard about it.'

Against his will, he gave half a smile back. 'You've got kids?'

'A boy,' she said, her voice husky. When she caught him

glancing up towards the house, eyebrows raised, she added, 'He's staying with his father while I move in down here.' She turned away quickly and stood perfectly still, staring at the woods on the hillside for a few long seconds.

When she turned back to him, a smile stretched her face. 'What do you know about the history of the boathouse?'

He played along. The same smile had been part of his wardrobe in the last two years. Thankfully, he was resorting to it less and less often. 'As far as I know, it was built long before the house. Some people say it's sixteenth century. And, of course, it featured prominently in the film *A Summer Affair*, but you know that already.'

The defiant stare vanished altogether and she now just looked a little sheepish as she stared at the glossy seaweed washed up on the rocks nearby. 'Busted,' she said, looking at him from beneath her long fringe. 'It was a favourite when I was younger and when I saw the details of the house, I knew I had to view it.' She turned to look back at the two-storey brick and wood structure. 'I didn't realise this place was real. I suppose I thought it was just fibreglass and papier mâché, or whatever they build that stuff out of…'

'It's real enough. I ought to…' Ben looked at the rope in his hand '…get going.'

She nodded. 'I'm going to explore.'

Ben stood for a few moments and watched her climb the steps up to a door on the upper level. It hadn't been used for years. Laura hadn't been steady enough on her feet to make the journey down the hill for quite some time before she'd died.

He climbed into the dinghy because it felt like a safe distance and carried on watching. The wooden floor could be beetle-infested, rotten. He'd just stay here a few moments to make sure the new owner didn't go through it.

His hand hovered above the outboard motor. Any moment now, he'd be on his way. He readied his shoulder muscles and brushed his fingertips against the rubber pull on the end of the cord. The loosened painter was gripped lightly in his other hand.

The boathouse was on two levels. The bottom storey, level with the jetty, had large arched, panelled doors and had been used for storing small boats. The upper level was a single room with a balcony that stretched the width of the building. He was waiting for her to walk out on to it, spread her hands wide on the railing and lean forward to inhale the glorious, salty, slightly seaweedy air. Her glossy dark hair would swing forward and the wind would muss it gently.

A minute passed and she didn't appear. He began to feel twitchy.

With a sigh, he climbed out of the boat and planted his boots on the solid concrete of the jetty. 'Are you okay back there?'

No response. Just as he was readying his lungs to call again, she appeared back on the jetty and shrugged. 'No key,' she yelled back, looking unduly crestfallen.

All his alarm bells rang, told him to get the hell back in the boat and keep his nose out of it. Whitehaven wasn't his responsibility any more. Only the message obviously hadn't travelled the length of his arm to his fingertips, because he suddenly found himself retying the boat and walking back up the jetty to the steep flight of steps that climbed up to the boathouse door.

As he reached the bottom step, she turned and looked down at him, one hand on the metal railing, one hand bracing herself against the wall. Her thick, dark hair fell forward as she leaned towards him.

'Do you know where the key is?'

With his fingernails, already dark-rimmed from the rich compost of the glasshouse plants, he scraped at a slightly protruding brick in the wall near the base of the stairs. At first, he thought he'd remembered it wrong, but after a couple of seconds the block of stone moved and came away in his hand. In the recess left behind, he could see the dull black glint of polished metal. Laura had told him about the secret nook—just in case.

He supposed he could have just told the woman about it,

yelled the vital information from the safety of the dinghy. He needn't get involved. Even now his lips remained closed and his mouth silent as he climbed the mossy stairs and pressed the key into the soft flesh of her palm.

There. Job done.

For a couple of seconds, they stayed like that. He pulled his hand away and rubbed it on the back of his jeans.

CHAPTER TWO

'THANK YOU,' she said, then shook her long fringe so it covered her eyes a little more.

She slid the key into the lock and turned it. He'd half-expected the door to fall open, but it swung in a graceful arc, opening wide and welcoming them in. Well, welcoming *her* in. But his curiosity got the better of him and he couldn't resist getting a glimpse.

'Wow.'

He'd expected shelves and oars and tins of varnish. Decades-old grime clung to the windows, and the filmy grey light revealed a very different scene. A cane sofa and chairs huddled round a small Victorian fireplace, decorated with white and blue tiles. A small desk and chair occupied a corner in front of one of the arched windows.

She walked over to the desk and touched it reverently, leaving four little smudges in the thick dust, then pulled her fingers back and gently blew the dust off them with a sigh.

'Did she come here often, do you know? Mrs Hastings?' she said, still staring at the desk.

Why exactly he was still here, keeping guard like some sentry, he wasn't sure. He should just go. He'd kept his promise to Laura. He wasn't required. And yet…he couldn't seem to make his feet move.

She turned to look at him and he shrugged. 'Not when I knew

her. She was too frail to manage the path down, but she talked of it fondly.'

She blinked and continued to stare at him, expressionless. He wasn't normally the sort who had the urge to babble on, but most women didn't leave huge gaping gaps in the conversation. He stuffed his hands in his pockets and kicked at the dust on the bare floorboards with the toe of his boot. Everything was too still.

'Not really the sort of place to interest a woman like you, is it?' he muttered, taking in the shabby furniture, the broken leg on the desk chair, held together with string. The place was nowhere near elegant enough to match her.

Her chin rose just a notch. 'What makes you think you know anything about what sort of woman I am?'

Just like that, the sadness that seemed to cloak her hardened into a shell. Now the room wasn't still any more. Every molecule in the air seemed to dance and shimmer and heat. She strode over to the large arched door in the centre of the opposite wall, unbolted it, threw the two door panels open and stepped out on to the wide balcony.

He was dismissed.

He took a step towards her and opened his mouth. Probably not a great idea, since during his last attempt at small talk he'd found a great muddy boot in it, but he couldn't leave things like this—taut with tension, unresolved. Messy.

Her hands were spread wide as she rested them on the low wall and looked out over the river, just as he'd imagined. The hair hung halfway down her back, shining, untouchable. The wind didn't dare tease even a strand out of place. He saw her back rise and fall as she let out a sigh.

'I thought I'd asked you to get off my property.' There was no anger in her tone now, just soul-deep weariness.

He turned and walked out of the boathouse and down the stairs to the jetty with even steps. She didn't need him. She'd made that abundantly clear. But, as he climbed back into the dinghy, he couldn't help feeling that part of his promise was still unfulfilled.

This time there were no interruptions as he untied the painter and started the motor. He turned the small boat round and set off in the direction of Lower Hadwell, a few minutes' journey upstream and across the river.

When he passed the Anchor Stone that rose, proud and unmoving, out of the murky green waters, he risked a look back. She was still standing there on the balcony, her hands wide and her chin tilted up, refusing to acknowledge his existence.

Louise had been staring so long at the field of sheep on the other side of the river that the little white dots had blurred and melted together. She refused to unlock her gaze until the dark smudge in her peripheral vision motored out of sight.

Eventually, when it didn't seem like defeat, she sighed and turned to rest her bottom on the railing of the balcony and stared back into the boathouse.

He couldn't have known who he'd looked like standing there below her on the steps as he'd offered her the long black key. It had been one of her favourite scenes in *A Summer Affair*—when Jonathan came to see Charity in her boathouse sanctuary, the place where she hid from the horrors of her life. Not that anything really *happened* between them. It was the undercurrents, the unspoken passion, that made it one of the most romantic scenes in any film she'd ever seen.

He had looked at her with his warm brown eyes and, somehow, had offered her more than a key as he'd stood there. For the first time in years, she'd blushed, then hurried to hide the evidence with her hair.

And then he'd had to go and spoil that delicious feeling—the feeling that, maybe, not all men were utter rats—by reminding her of who she was.

Louise stood up, brushed the dirt off her bottom and walked

back into the little sitting room. Of course, she wasn't interested in hooking up with anyone just now, so she didn't know why she'd got so upset with the gardener. Slowly, she closed and fastened the balcony doors, then exited the boathouse, locking the door and returning the key to its hiding place.

The light was starting to fade and she hurried back up the steep hill, careful to retrace her steps and not get lost, mulling things over as she went. No, it wasn't that she was developing a fancy for slightly scruffy men in waxed overcoats; it was just that, for a moment, she'd believed there was a possibility of something *more* in her future. Something she'd always yearned for, and now believed was only real between the covers of a novel or in the darkness of a cinema.

She shook her hair out of her face to shoo away the sense of disappointment. The gardener had done her a favour. He'd reminded her that her life wasn't a fairy tale—she snorted out loud at the very thought, scaring a small bird out of a bush. She was probably just feeling emotional because she wouldn't see Jack for two weeks. Toby had kicked up a stink, but had finally agreed that, once she was settled at Whitehaven, their son could live with her and go to the local school. She and Jack would be together again at last.

Toby had been difficult every step of the way about the divorce. Surprising that he would lavish so much time and energy on her, really. If he'd only thought to pay her that much attention in the last five years, they might not be in this mess at the moment.

She pulled her coat more tightly around her as she reached the clearing just in front of the house. The river seemed grey and troubled at the foot of the hill and dark woolly clouds were lying in ambush to the west. She ignored the dark speck travelling upstream, even though the noise of an outboard motor hummed on the fringes of her consciousness.

Not one stick of furniture occupied the pale, grand entrance hall to Whitehaven but, as Louise crossed the threshold, she smiled. Only two rooms on the ground floor, two bedrooms and one bathroom had been in a liveable state when she'd bought the house. All they needed was a lick of paint and a good scrub so she could move into them. The furniture would arrive on Wednesday but, until then, she had an inflatable mattress and a sleeping bag in the bedroom, a squashy, slightly threadbare floral sofa she'd found in a local junk shop for the living room, and a couple of suitcases to keep her going.

She'd let Toby keep all the furniture, disappointing him completely. He'd been itching for a fight about something, but she just wasn't going to give him the satisfaction. Let *him* be the one waiting for an emotional response of some kind for a change. She didn't want his furniture, anyway. Nothing that was a link to her old life. Nothing but Jack.

None of that ultra-modern, minimalist designer stuff would fit here, anyway. She smiled again. *She* fitted here. Whitehaven wasn't the first property she'd owned, but it was the first place she'd felt comfortable in since she'd left the shabby maisonette she'd shared with her father and siblings. She knew—just as surely as the first time she'd slid her foot into an exquisitely crafted designer shoe—that this was a perfect fit. She and this house understood each other.

The kitchen clock showed it was twenty past eight. Ben sat at the old oak table, a lukewarm cup of instant coffee between his palms, and attempted to concentrate on the sports section of the paper instead of the second hand of the clock.

Megan had never been like this when they'd been married. Yes, she'd been a little self-absorbed at times, but she'd never shown this flagrant disregard for other people's schedules, or boundaries, or…feelings. He wasn't sure he liked the version of Megan that she'd 'found'. Or this new boyfriend of hers that he wasn't supposed to know about.

Twenty minutes later, just as his fingers were really itching to pick up the phone and yell at someone, he heard a car door slam. Jas bounced in through the back door and, before he could ask if her mother was going to make an appearance—and an apology—tyres squealed in the lane and an engine revved then faded.

'Nice dinner?' he asked, flicking a page of the paper over and trying not to think about the gallon of beef casserole still sitting in the oven, slowly going cold. Eating a portion on his own hadn't had the comfort factor that a casserole, by rights, ought to have.

Jas shrugged her shoulders as he looked up.

'Just dinner, you know…' she said. And, since she was eleven-going-on-seventeen, he supposed that was as verbose as she was going to get.

'Have you done your homework?'

'Mostly.'

This was quality conversation, this was. But he was better off sticking to neutral subjects while he was feeling like this. In the last couple of years as a single dad, he'd learned that transitions—picking up and dropping off times—were difficult, and it was his job to smooth the ripples, create stability. Being steady, normal, was what was required.

'Define mostly,' he said, smoothing the paper closed and standing up.

Jas dropped the envelope of assorted junk she was clutching to her chest on to the table and threw her coat over the back of a chair. 'Two more maths questions—and before you say anything—'

Ben closed his mouth.

'—it doesn't have to be in until Thursday. Can I just do it tomorrow? Please, Dad?'

She stared at him with those big brown eyes and blinked, just once. She looked so cute with her wavy blonde hair not quite sitting right in its shoulder-length style. His memory rewound a handful of years and he could hear her begging for just one more push on the swing.

'Okay. Tomorrow it is.'

'Thanks, Dad.' Jas skirted the table and gave him a hug by just throwing her arms around him and squeezing, then she lifted a brightly coloured magazine out of the pile of junk on the table. 'Recreational reading,' she said, brandishing it and attempting to escape before he could inspect it more closely.

He wasn't so old that his reflexes had gone into retirement. The magazine was out of her fingers and in front of his face before she'd fully disentangled herself from the hug.

'What's this trash?'

Jas made a feeble attempt at snatching it back. 'It was Mum's. She'd finished it and she said I could have it.'

Ben frowned. *Buzz* magazine. He'd never read it himself, but he knew enough from the bright slogans on the cover that it was the lowest form of celebrity gossip rag. The lead story seemed to be 'Celebrity Cellulite'. Nice. What was Megan thinking of giving Jasmine a publication like this? Didn't his ex know how impressionable young girls were at Jas's age?

'I don't think this is appropriate.'

Jas rolled her eyes. 'It's interesting. All my friends read it.'

He raised his eyebrows. 'All of them?'

The nod that followed couldn't have convinced even Jas herself.

'That's what I thought,' he said. 'I mean, there's no substance in here. It's just rubbish…' He flicked through the pages, hoping his daughter would see what he saw. 'It's the worst kind of gossip. I—'

But then he stopped flicking idly through the pages, his whole frame frozen. His mouth worked while his brain searched for an appropriate sound. Getting a grip on himself, he carefully placed the magazine down on the table and stood, arms braced either side of it, as he stared again at the grainy photographs.

'Told you it was interesting,' Jas said with a smirk.

'But that's…'

Jas turned so she was side by side with him and leaned against his bunched-up arm muscles, looking down at the magazine too. 'Louise Thornton,' she informed him in an astoundingly matter-of-fact voice. 'Mum thinks she's a waste of space. Most people do.'

'Louise *who*?' he whispered hoarsely.

Jas punched him on the arm. 'Da-ad! You're stuck in the Stone Age! You know…She married Tobias Thornton—the actor.'

Who?

'We watched him in that action movie last weekend. The one with the bomb on the private jet?'

Oh. *Him.*

The picture was dull and not very clear—the product of a telephoto lens the size of a space shuttle, no doubt. But there was no doubting the fierce glare in those eyes as she squared up to the paparazzo, her son clutched protectively to her, his face hidden. He'd been on the receiving end of that very same look just a few hours ago and it still gave him the shivers thinking about it.

'And she's famous?' he asked Jas, trying to sound as uninvolved as he actually was, but less involved than he felt.

Jas nodded. 'Well, famous for being married to somebody famous. That's all.'

Married. He should shut the magazine right now and condemn it to the recycling bin. Only…she'd said she was divorced. And, in the few moments that she'd let her icy guard down, he'd known she was telling the truth. The gaudy headline splashed across the top of the feature seemed to confirm his gut instinct: 'Louise's private hell since split!'

He took one last look at her image and felt a twinge of sympathy. Going through a divorce was bad enough, but having every spat reported for the world to see? More like a public execution than a private hell. No wonder she'd freaked out when she'd found some strange man in her greenhouse.

He closed the magazine and looked at Jas. 'Sorry, Jas. I think these sorts of magazines are a gross invasion of privacy. I'd rather you didn't read it.'

She chewed her lip and her fingers twitched. He could tell she was torn between doing the right thing and insatiable curiosity. Thankfully, when she gave him a rueful smile and a one-shouldered shrug he knew he'd been doing an okay job of counteracting all the psycho-babble her mother had been subjecting her to since their separation.

He grinned. 'Good girl.'

Jas's smile grew and changed. 'Since I've earned a gold star, can I have fifteen pounds for a trip to the theatre with school?'

Ben looked heavenward. What was it with women and money? Any good deed seemed to need a reward—preferably in the form of shoes. Perhaps he should be glad that at least this was something educational. The shoes would come later. Oh, he had no doubt the shoes would come later. 'Give me a second while I find my wallet. What are you going to see, again?'

'The Taming of the Shrew.'

Ben nodded approvingly while he searched the kitchen worktops for his battered leather wallet. He hunted through the junk drawer. Where had he put the darn thing when he'd come in this evening? 'Jas, I'll come and give you the cash when I've found my wallet, okay?' he said, slamming the drawer in an effort to get it to close in spite of the disturbed odds and ends inside.

'Cool.'

'And Jas…?'

She turned at the doorway to the lounge.

'This Louise Thornton woman. Do *you* think she's a waste of space?'

She looked up at the corner of the ceiling and then back at him. 'Mum says any woman who puts up with that kind of…rubbish… and puts a man's happiness before her own is TSTL.'

TSTL.

'Too stupid to live,' Jas elaborated, knowing, as she always seemed to, when he needed a bit of help with her strange preteen speak.

The sounds of the television in the adjoining room accompanied his search for the wallet for the next ten minutes. He checked his coat, the car, the kitchen again… Just as he was racking his brain and replaying the day in his head, it struck him. He knew exactly where he'd left his wallet. He could see it so clearly in his mind's eye, he could almost reach out and touch it.

A rough wooden bench, long rays of the afternoon sun slanting through uneven Victorian glass. A black, soft leather square with cards and ancient till receipts poking out of it sitting next to a plant pot containing a rather spectacular nepenthes.

He sat back down on a chair and frowned. His wallet had been too bulky in the back pocket of his jeans and he'd taken it out and put it on one of the shelves in the greenhouse this afternoon. And then, with all the scowling and marching back down to the boat, he'd forgotten it.

He blew out a breath. If it had been just the cards and the few notes that were in there, he might have just left it. There was no way his face was going to be welcome back at Whitehaven any time this century. But the wallet contained one of his favourite photos of Jas and him together, taken in a time when she'd had ringlets and no front teeth and when he didn't seem to have permanent frown lines etched on his forehead.

There was nothing for it. He was going to have to go back.

Ben knocked on the door twice. Hard enough to be heard, but not so forcefully that he seemed impatient. And then he waited. The clear, pale skies of yesterday were gone and a foggy dampness dulled every colour on the riverbank. He turned his collar up as the mist rallied and became drizzle.

He raised his fist to knock again, but was distracted by a hint of movement in his peripheral vision. He turned quickly and stared at the study window, just to the right of the porch. Everything was still.

He grimaced and shoved his hands in his pockets. At least he and Louise Thornton were both singing from the same hymn sheet. Neither of them were pleased he was here.

Knowing she was probably hovering in the hallway, he knocked again, just loud enough to make a dull noise against the glossy wooden doors.

'Hello? I'm sorry for the intrusion—' He'd been going to say *Mrs Thornton*, but it seemed odd to use her name when she hadn't revealed it to him herself.

'I really didn't want to disturb you again,' he called out as he pressed his ear to the door, trying to detect a hint of movement inside, 'but I left something behind and I—'

There was a soft click as the door opened enough for him to see half of her face. She didn't have the heels on today—not that he ever noticed women's shoes—and, instead of being almost level with him, she was looking up at him, her face hard and unreadable.

'I left my wallet in the greenhouse,' he said with an attempt at a self-deprecating smile.

She just stared.

He should have looked away, ended the awkwardness, but she had the most amazing eyes. Well, eye—he could only see one at present. It wasn't the make-up, because this morning there was none of that black stuff. It wasn't even the hazel and olive-green of her irises, which reminded him of the changing colours of autumn leaves. No, it was the sense that, even though she seemed to be doing her best to shield herself, he recognised something in them. Not a familiarity or a similarity to anybody else. More like a reflection of something inside himself.

He shook his head and stared at his boots. This was not the time to descend into poetry. He had come here for one reason and one reason only.

'If you give me permission to retrieve it, I'll be out of your hair as soon as possible. I promise.'

She looked him up and down and then the door inched wider. 'Wait here and I'll get the key.'

A couple of minutes passed and Ben stepped out of the porch and on to the gravel drive, the crunch underneath his boots deafening in the still of the autumn morning. Louise Thornton reappeared just as he'd managed to find himself a spot where the pebbles didn't shift underneath him. Her long dark hair was scooped back into a ponytail, but the ever-present fringe left her face half-hidden. In her jeans and a pullover she *should* have looked like any other of the young mothers who stood outside the school gates.

He followed her up the hill, round the house to the top lawn. When she moved, her actions were small, precise, as if she didn't want to be accused of taking up too much space. Megan and all her friends had reached an age where their body language spoke of a certain confidence, a certain comfort in their own skin. This woman lacked that, despite her high-gloss lifestyle and multi-million-pound bank account.

Once again he felt an unwelcome twinge. He fought the urge to catch up with her, to tell her that it would get better one day, that there was life after divorce. But, since he wasn't exactly a glowing example of a man with an active social life, he thought it was better if he kept his mouth shut.

She unlocked the greenhouse door, then stood well back, giving him plenty of room to pass through. She didn't stay outside, though. He heard her footsteps on the tiled floor of the greenhouse behind him and, when he looked over his shoulder, she was watching him suspiciously.

The wallet was right where he'd remembered it was, tucked slightly out of sight next to a glossy carnivorous plant, groaning under the weight of its purple and green pitchers. He picked it up, jammed it into his jacket pocket, then stooped to pick up the saracenia that had been a casualty of yesterday's meeting. He'd forgotten all about it after Louise Thornton had appeared.

Carefully, he placed it back on the shelf and pressed the soggy compost down with his fingertips. Despite his ministrations, the slender pitchers pointed at an odd angle. He would have to bring a cane from home and…

No. There would be no canes from home. Not any more.

He stepped back and indicated the listing plant. 'This needs a cane. There might be one around here somewhere—' Down the other end was a likely place. He started to walk in that direction, checking behind pots and peering under the bench as he went.

'Why should you care?'

That kind of question didn't even warrant turning round to answer it. He carried on searching. 'It's a beautiful plant. It would be a shame to leave it to die.'

Once again he heard footsteps. Just a handful, enough for her to have stepped further into the greenhouse. He found what he was looking for—a small green cane—hidden between the windowsill and a row of pots. He picked it up, careful not to send anything else flying, and turned to find her fingering the delicate cream and purple foliage of the ailing saracenia.

'Then you really are a gardener?'

He moved past her, retrieved a roll of garden wire from a hook near the door and returned to the plant, unwinding a length as he walked. 'You think I like to play in the dirt for fun?'

She remained silent, watching him fashion a loop of wire wide enough to help the plant stand up without pinching it to the cane. When he'd finished, and the little plant was straining heavenwards once again, she took a few steps backwards.

'In my experience, most men are like big kids, anyway. So, yes, you may well be playing in the dirt for fun.' There was a dry humour behind her words that took the edge off them.

His lips didn't actually curve but there was a hint of a smile in his voice when he answered. 'It is fun. The earth feels good beneath my fingertips.' She raised an eyebrow, clearly unconvinced. He'd bet she'd never had dirt underneath her fingernails in her life. And he'd bet her life was poorer for it.

'Gardening gives you a sense of achievement.' He fiddled

with the stake and wire loop around the saracenia until it was just so. 'You can't control the plants. You just tend them, give them what they need until they become what they should.'

She broke eye contact and let her gaze wander over the plants nearest to her. 'These don't look like they're *becoming* much. Aren't you a very good gardener?'

He fought back the urge to laugh out loud. 'They're in their dormant phase. They'll perk up again, when the conditions are right.' He stood looking at her for a few seconds as she stared out into the gardens. 'Well, I've got what I came for. I'll be out of your hair now—as promised. I did say I was one not to break a promise, didn't I?'

He took a few long strides past her, breathed out and opened the greenhouse door. He was halfway across the lawn before she shouted after him.

'Then promise to come again.'

CHAPTER THREE

BEN didn't want to turn round. He'd told himself he wouldn't respond this time. After all, he'd had enough of high-maintenance women. But…

She stood on the lawn, watching him, her hair whipped across her face by another surly gust of wind. Once again, her eyes held him captive. Not for their dark perfection, but because something deep inside them seemed to be pleading with him. His friends had told him he was a sucker for a lady in distress, and he'd always denied it, but he had the awful feeling they might just be right.

She tugged a strand of chocolate-brown hair out of her mouth. 'The garden. It does need looking after. You're right. It would be a shame to…'

Once again, the eyes pleaded. He should have a sign made, reading 'sucker,' and just slap it on his forehead.

He'd do it. But not for her—for Laura. Just until he was sure this new owner was going to care for the place properly. And then he'd pass it on to one of his landscaping teams and charge her handsomely for the privilege. After all, he reminded himself, life was complicated enough already without looking after somebody else's garden.

Louise watched him go. She kept watching until long after his tall frame disappeared round the side of the house into a tangle of grass and shrubs and trees that were now, technically, her back garden. Not that she'd had the courage to explore it fully yet.

She forced herself to turn away and look back at the greenhouse. Was she mad? Quite possibly.

In all seriousness, she'd just given a man she knew nothing about permission to invade her territory on a regular basis. Yet…there'd been something so preposterously truthful about his story and so refreshingly straightforward about his manner that she'd swallowed it whole. Next time she'd have to frisk him for a long-lens camera and a dictaphone, just in case.

She'd left the greenhouse door open. Slowly, she closed the distance to the heavy Victorian glazed door, with its beautiful brass handle and peeling off-white paint. On a whim, she stepped inside before she closed the door and stood for a few moments in the warm dampness. It smelled good in here, of earth and still air, but very real. She liked real.

The assorted plants lining the shelves by the windows really were quite exquisite. She'd never seen anything like them. Venus fly-traps sat next to frilly, sticky-looking things in shades of pink and purple. Then there were ones with large waxy leaves and bulbous pitchers the colour of ripe bruises. She walked over to the little plant that the gardener—Ben?—was that his name?—had saved. A thin green flute rose vertically, widening at the top with a frilly bit on top that looked a bit like a lid.

She felt an affinity with this little plant, recently uprooted, thin, fragile. Now in a foreign climate, reaching hungrily heavenwards with an appetite that might never be satisfied. She reached out and touched the damp soil at its base. It did feel good. She pulled her hand away, but didn't wipe it on the back of her jeans.

Near the door were the stubby brown plants that had started to hibernate. Just like her. All those years with Toby now seemed like a time half-asleep. Her mind wandered to a photo of a famous actress that had graced the pages of all the gossip magazines a few years ago. She'd been caught whooping for joy when the papers finalising her divorce had arrived. Since then she'd lost twenty pounds, received two Oscars and had been seen with a string of hot-looking younger men.

Shouldn't this be the time when *she* blossomed, came into her own? But it wasn't happening. She still felt dead inside.

Abruptly, she exited the greenhouse, closed the door behind her and marched back down the path to her new home. Once the house was sorted, she'd feel better. Only a few more days until the furniture arrived. Until then she could visit Dartmouth, the bustling town just a bit further down the river, and visit some of the art galleries she'd seen advertised. And she could find out what Jack would need when he started at the local school after the half-term holiday.

Yes, she'd definitely feel better when Jack could come here permanently. That was why she was feeling all at sixes and sevens. And he couldn't live here with a bedroom full of dust and cobwebs. He'd be here on the twenty-seventh of October—less than two weeks away. She clapped her hands together and smiled as she took a detour round the back of the house and entered through the back door. She had work to do.

Almost a fortnight later, Louise was putting the finishing touches to Jack's room. She looked at her watch. It was almost one o'clock, but she couldn't even contemplate eating anything. Only five more hours and Jack would be here. Her eyes filled with tears as she fluffed the duvet and smoothed it out, making sure it was perfect—not bunched up in the corners or with an empty bit flapping at one end.

It looked so cosy when she had finished that she flumped down on top of the blue and white checked cover and buried her head in the pillow.

Three weeks had been too long to go without seeing her son. She sighed. It had been the longest they had ever been apart. Toby had used to moan that she didn't travel with him any more, and maybe that had been part of the reason their marriage had crumbled. Even strong relationships were put under pressure when the couple spent weeks at a time apart. But how could she leave Jack? He was everything. He always would be everything.

It wouldn't have been fair to uproot him and ask him to change schools before the half-term break. She snuggled even further into the pillow, wishing it smelled of more than just clean laundry.

Toby had agreed—thank goodness—to let Jack live with her, even though they had joint custody. Her ex was away filming so often that it wouldn't have been fair to Jack to leave him at her former home in Gloucestershire with just a nanny for company. Even Toby had seen the sense in that.

So Jack would be with his father on school holidays and alternate weekends. And, just to appease Toby and make sure that he didn't change his mind, she'd consented to let him take Jack to stay in their—make that *Toby's*—London flat for the half-term week.

But tonight Jack would be coming to Whitehaven. He'd be here.

She turned to lie on her back and stared at the ceiling. She wasn't sure whether to laugh or cry. Mostly she just ached.

Minutes, maybe even half an hour, drifted past as Louise hugged herself and watched the light on the freshly painted ceiling change as the October wind bullied the clouds across the sky. Eventually, she dragged herself off the bed and sloped towards the window.

Something shiny glinted in the bushes and instantly her back was pressed against the wall, every muscle tense. After five seconds, she made herself breathe out. Nosing very carefully round the architrave, so only half of an eye and the side of her face would be visible from outside, she searched for another flash of light.

No-good, money-grabbing photographers! And trust one to turn up on the day Jack was due here. If she caught the…amoeba, she'd slap a lawsuit on him so fast his digital camera would fry.

In her effort to remain hidden, she only had a partial view of the front lawn. She remained motionless for some time, until her left leg started to cramp and twitch and then, only when she was very sure nobody was in her line of sight, did she lean out a little further.

Another glint! There!

Once again, she found herself flattened against the wall. But this time she let out a groan and slapped herself on the forehead. It wasn't a telephoto lens but a big shiny spade that had reflected the light. Ben the gardener-guy's spade. It was Sunday afternoon and he was here. Just as he'd been for the previous two weeks. Only she'd forgotten he'd be here today in all her excitement about Jack coming.

Not that she ever really saw him arrive when he came. At some point in the afternoon, she'd become aware that he was around. She'd hear him whistling as he walked up to the top lawn, or hear the hum of a mower in the distance.

So why had she felt the need to slam herself against the wall and pretend she wasn't here? This was stupid.

She stopped leaning against the wall and drew herself upright. There. Then she walked primly across the room and out of the door. No one was hiding. She was just walking around inside her own house, as she was perfectly entitled to do. Okay, she'd chosen a path across the room that had meant she couldn't have been seen from the window, but that didn't mean anything. It had simply been the most direct route. Sort of.

She found herself in the kitchen. It was in serious need of updating, with pine cabinets that had darkened to an almost offensive orange, but it had a fantastic flagstone floor and always seemed warm—probably because, in the now defunct chimney breast, there was an Aga. It looked lovely and spoke of families gathered in the kitchen sharing overflowing Sunday lunches, but she had no idea how to work it.

Well, that wasn't strictly true. She knew how to boil the kettle. And, at this present moment, that seemed like a shockingly good idea. She filled the battered old thick-bottomed kettle with water, lifted the heavy lid on the Aga hotplate and left the kettle to boil.

She hoped Jack would love it here as much as she did. What was she going to do if he decided he didn't like living in the depths of the countryside, far away from the flash mansion she'd shared with Toby? It was the only place he'd ever known as home. Well, that and the London flat. And the villa in Beverly Hills. Whitehaven was charming, but it lacked the gloss of her former houses.

She'd been getting what she needed out of the cupboards while she'd been thinking, and now discovered that she'd placed two teabags in two mugs. Something she'd done regularly in the early days after her split with Toby, but hadn't done for months now.

Her first instinct was to put the teabag and mug back in the cupboard, but that urge was hijacked by another one.

She might as well make one for Ben. She gave a short hollow laugh. It would be the nearest thing to payment she'd given him for all his hard work. The lawns were looking fabulous and, little by little, the shrubs and borders close to the house were starting to lose their wild look.

It wasn't that she hadn't intended to pay him. Just that she'd been heartily avoiding the issue. She'd acted like such a diva that first week, and she didn't know how to undo that all-important first impression. As if summoned up by her thoughts, she heard the crunch of footsteps outside. A moment later Ben passed the kitchen window, probably on his way up to the greenhouses.

A cup of tea seemed like a poor effort at a truce, but it was all she had in her arsenal at the moment. Boiling water lifted and swirled the teabag in the cup. Louise hesitated. Sugar, or no sugar?

On an instinct, she put one level spoon in the cup and stirred. He looked like a man who liked a bit of sweetness.

Another laugh that was almost a snort broke the silence. Well, she'd better have a personality change on the way past the herbaceous border, then. Especially if she was truly on a peace mission. At the moment she was the dictionary definition for the absolute opposite of 'sweetness'. *Meet Louise Thornton, sour old prune.*

When Louise arrived at the greenhouse, she realised she had

a problem. Two hands and two cups of tea meant that she had no spare limbs to open the door, or even knock on it. But it had seemed stupid to leave her mug of tea in the kitchen. By the time she'd delivered Ben's, discussed payment with him and walked back to the house, it would have been stone cold.

She peered inside the greenhouse and tried to spot him. The structure was long and thin—almost thirty feet in length and tucked up against the north side of the walled garden to catch as much sun as possible. Down the centre was the tiled path with wrought iron grating for the underfloor heating system. The side nearest the wall of windows was lined with benches and shelves, all full of plants, but on the other side large palms and ferns were planted in the soil at floor level.

Halfway down the greenhouse a leg was sticking out amongst the dark glossy leaves. She banged the door with her foot. The leg, which had been wavering up and down in its function as a counterbalance, went still.

She held her breath and tried to decide what kind of face she should wear. Not the suspicious glare he'd received on their first meeting, that was for sure. But grinning inanely didn't seem fitting either. In the end, she didn't have a chance to decide between 'calm indifference' and 'professional friendliness' because the leg was suddenly joined by the rest of him as he jumped back on to the path, rubbing his hands together to rid them of loose dirt, and looked in her direction.

She held up his cup of tea and then, when his face had broken into a broad grin, she breathed out. He was obviously really thirsty because he practically ran to the door and swung it wide. She thrust the mug towards him, ignoring the plop of hot liquid that landed on her hand as she did so.

He took it from her, smiled again and took a big gulp. 'Fantastic. Just how I like it. Thanks.'

Louise took a little sip out of her own chunky white mug. 'No problem. It's the least I can do.'

Ben leaned back against one of the shelves and took another long slurp of tea. He seemed completely at ease here. She tried to copy his stance, making sure she was a good five feet away from him, but she couldn't work out what to do with her legs and stood up straight again.

'Um… about payment…'

Ben raised his eyebrows.

'I can't let you go on doing all this for nothing.'

He shrugged. 'It started as a labour of love. I'm just sorry I haven't been able to do more.'

He wasn't making this easy. All she wanted to do was to work out what the going rate was and write him a cheque. She didn't want him to be nice. Men who were nice normally had a hidden agenda.

She put her mug down on the only spare bit of space on the shelf nearest her and drew herself taller. Only he didn't make that easy either. Her five-foot-eight wasn't too far away from his six-foot-plus height, but however much she straightened her spine, drew her neck longer, she still felt small beside him. But this was no time for weakness. She was the boss. She was in charge.

'Well, if you could just let me know how much you'd routinely charge for this sort of job…'

He drained his mug and looked at her with a more serious light in his eyes. 'I can't say any of my 'routine' work resembles this in the slightest.'

Louise crossed one booted foot in front of the other and a corner of her mouth rose. Oh, this was his game. Make it seem like he nobly didn't want anything, but sting her with an exorbitant price when it came to the crunch. And, if he played this game well, she was probably supposed to be shaking his hand and thanking him profusely for being so generous when the moment came.

She folded her arms, but only had to unfold them as he handed her back the empty mug.

'There's no rush for money. I'll send you a bill if you're really desperate for one, though.' He smiled, and it had none of the sharkish tendencies she'd expected after a conversation like that. 'Thanks for the tea.' And then he turned his back on her and returned his attention to a large plant with floppy leaves.

If there was one thing Louise didn't like, it was being ignored. It had been Toby's favourite way of avoiding anything he didn't want to talk about. All she'd had to do was utter the words, 'You're late. Where have you been?' and the shutters had come down, the paper had been opened and the television switched on. Nobody liked to be rendered invisible. She coughed and Ben looked up.

'No rush?' She'd promised herself she wouldn't be pushed around by any man again—ever. Okay, in her mind she'd meant *significant others*, but suddenly it felt important to stand her ground, to have this conversation on her terms. 'I'd much prefer it if we could talk figures now.'

He straightened again. 'Fine. It's just that I know you've just moved in, Mrs Thornton—' The pause was just long enough to indicate that he hadn't meant to say that. For the first time in their conversation he broke eye contact. 'I thought you might like a little more time to get settled.'

Louise felt her features harden. 'Why are you being so nice to me?'

Ben looked for all the world as if he hadn't a clue what she was talking about. Boy, he was good. She'd almost fallen for that straight-talking, man of the earth and sky nonsense. He knew who she was, and he wanted something from her. Maybe not money, but something. People always did.

Eventually he scratched the side of his nose with a finger. 'I suppose I felt I needed to make up for being a little…awkward… the first time we met. I was angry with someone else and I took it out on you. It's not something I'm proud of.'

A man who apologised! Now she *knew* the act was too good to be true.

Still, she was prepared to play along for the moment. He'd show his cards eventually. 'Well, if you're not going to be businesslike about this, I may just have to look in the *Yellow Pages* and find a gardener who is.'

He didn't seem that worried about losing her business; he just went back to fussing with the floppy plant. After a few seconds he looked back at her. 'Suit yourself.'

Once again, Louise felt as if she'd been dismissed. How dared he? This was her garden, her greenhouse. Those were her plants he was messing around with. 'At least give me your card.' That was a pathetic attempt at gaining control, getting him to give up something, but it was all she could think of.

He patted his pockets. 'I don't think I have one…ah!' He pulled his wallet out of his back pocket and rummaged around inside. The card he pulled out was creased and the edges were soft. She took it from him and backed away.

Oliver Landscapes. Very grand for a one-man band outfit.

'Feel free to let me know if you don't want me to come any more, but if I don't hear any differently, I'll just assume I should just pop by again next Sunday.' This time he didn't turn away and continue working; he just looked at her. Not with barely concealed curiosity, or envy, or even out-of-proportion adoration. Those kinds of responses she was used to. No, this was something different. He looked at her as if she were transparent.

She didn't know what to do.

'Just come,' she said and fled, leaving her mug of lukewarm tea in the shade of a wilting ficus.

Louise couldn't help grinning as she climbed out of the car, even though the weather was disgusting and she was about to get on a tiny ferry and cross an angry-looking river. Just as well she could see their destination—the village of Lower Hadwell—only a few minutes away on the opposite shore.

The rear door opened and Jack climbed out, tugging at the collar of his new school uniform and looking a little uncomfortable. He was tall for his age and he had his father's good looks.

Half the class at his previous school—the female half—had cried for a week when he'd told them he was moving away.

Not that Jack cared. He had no idea that his golden blond shaggy hair was anything but a nuisance to comb in the mornings. He might have Toby's physical characteristics, but he lacked any of his father's swagger. And long may it stay that way. Louise knew from first-hand experience just how devastating a weapon all that beauty mixed with a little too much confidence could be.

'All ready to go?'

Jack nodded and clutched his book bag. Louise wanted to take his hand and hug him to her. He was being so brave. Starting a new school was difficult for any kid, but Jack was going to face an extra set of challenges. She'd had a meeting with the headmistress to discuss it and they'd both decided that, quietly, the word would go round that Jack was to be treated like every other child in the school. He wouldn't get any favours, but he shouldn't be subjected to endless questions about his dad or expected to buy the whole class shed-loads of sweets, just because his parents were rich.

She laid a reassuring hand on his shoulder. Jack was a normal boy in that he wouldn't allow public displays of 'soppiness'.

At this time in the morning there were regular ferries across the river and they walked to the edge of the high stone jetty and waited for the little wooden boat, painted white with a blue trim, to sputter up to a seaweedy flight of steps.

The ferryman paid them absolutely no attention other than to take coins off them and Louise breathed a sigh of relief. Lower Hadwell was a small community and news of her arrival in the area had to have spread. She just hoped they were all like this guy. Completely uninterested. And, with that blissful thought in her mind, she sat on the hard wooden bench that circled the stern of the boat and turned her face into the wind.

By the time they reached the jetty on the other side of the river, she was sure her hair had picked up a bucket-load of salt that was blowing up the river from the sea. Never mind. She'd deliberately dressed down in a tracksuit and baseball cap, hoping she'd blend in a bit more with the other mums at the school gate.

Jack declared the boat ride 'wicked' and jumped out of the ferry in one smooth motion. Louise followed, although her clamber on to dry land was nowhere near as graceful.

The school had to be at the top of the steepest hill in the whole of south Devon. Oh, my goodness! Louise's calves begged for mercy as they trudged past a pub, cottages in hues of cream and earthy pink and a handful of shops. Jack stopped and turned round to face the river.

She grabbed on to his coat and tried to inhale enough oxygen to talk. 'Jack!' The noise that came out of her mouth barely registered as a croak. 'Come on!'

Jack gave her his usual I'm-eight-and-I-understand-the-universe-much-better-than-you look. 'Try walking backwards. It doesn't hurt so much.'

Louise couldn't work out if that was the most sensible idea she'd heard in years or the most stupid. She stared at her son as he started ascending again, this time with his backpack pointing up the hill. Heck, she'd do anything to stop the fire in her calf muscles. She did a one-eighty and followed suit. Her legs fairly sang with relief.

This was much better! At least it was until she came unexpectedly into contact with something tall and warm. Something that went 'oof'. Louise squeezed her eyes shut, yelled an apology and turned and ran up the hill after Jack, who had made much better progress.

Coward, she thought, as she reached the level ground just outside the school gates. But it was only a minute before the bell was due to go and she didn't need someone recognising her and delaying her by asking for an autograph or something.

Jack stopped just short of the wrought iron fence around the quaint village school. Louise bent over and tried to suck in more air. She knew from the furnace in her cheeks that her face was probably pink and blotchy and sweat was making her back feel all sticky.

She laid an arm on Jack's shoulder—more to support herself than anything else. She went to the gym every now and then. So why had this finished her off?

The jangle of an old-fashioned brass school bell rose above the screams and shouts of the playground. She stood up, put a hand on each of Jack's shoulders and stared into his eyes. 'You ready?'

Jack pressed his lips together and nodded just once. She grinned at him and, as she spoke, she turned to walk through the gate. 'Then it's show t—'

A bright flash seared her retina. At first she couldn't work out what had happened, but the guy who jumped out from behind a parked car with a whacking great camera round his neck kind of gave it away. Instinctively, she pulled Jack to her and started to run. She really, really wanted to swear, but this was neither the time nor the place.

As they reached the safety of the school building, all grey stone and arched windows, she started to chastise herself. She'd been stupid not to have been prepared for this! Of course the tabloids would want a picture of Jack starting at his new school. They were desperate for any titbit about either her or Toby. And, while Toby had gushed at length about the new love in his life, she'd steadily maintained her silence.

Jack was in tears. And it took a lot to make her little man cry.

Louise marched up to the school reception and fought back tears herself while she waited for the receptionist to stop fiddling with the photocopier. Maybe she should just have given an interview to *Celebrity Life* or something. Her refusal to play their game had just made incidents like this inevitable.

Jack was hugging on to her, his face buried under her armpit. She stroked the top of his hair.

Now she was good and angry. She and Toby were fair game.

They'd chosen this life. But Jack had no choice. When she'd got her son settled in, she was going back outside and she would find that photographer and she would shove his camera so far down his throat that he'd be coughing up bits of his memory card for weeks.

CHAPTER FOUR

BEN was happily walking down the road, minding his own business. Well, almost. He'd just spotted a picture of the Wilkinsons' cottage in the estate agent's window and was actually paying more attention to that than the direction in which his feet were heading. He and Megan had dreamed about buying that cottage for years.

With his current income and the maintenance payments to Megan, could he afford it? Maybe.

But, before he could do the mental arithmetic, he was winded by some idiot charging up the hill backwards.

He didn't even have the chance to say *hey!* before the track suited figure garbled out an apology and ran off.

Hang on a minute! He *knew* that idiot!

He was so busy staring up the hill at the pink-clad bottom with the word *'Juicy'* emblazoned across it that he was almost knocked over a second time by a man in a large anorak and a wild look in his eyes. He had a huge camera in his hand.

Ben shrugged. Bit late in the season for bird-watching, but what the heck did he know? Global warming was having a weird effect on the wildlife in this area. Last year some strange-looking bird only seen in the isles of Scotland had been blown down to the south coast of England by a freak storm. The local 'twitchers' had gone bananas. That man had had the same crazed look in his eye. Marauding ornithologists aside, nothing was going to stop him from wandering down to the newsagent's and get his morning paper before his meeting today.

However, Mrs Green, owner of the shop for the last thirty-three years and purveyor of local gossip, was in a chatty mood. Ben valiantly attempted to tuck his paper under his arm and drop the money in her hand, but her arms stayed firmly folded across her ample chest and he was forced to hover, one hand reaching over the counter, as the inquisition began.

'I heard that another celebrity has bought Whitehaven, Mr Oliver. What do you think of that?' She narrowed her eyes and analysed his reaction. He was trying hard not to have one. Something might have given him away because she added, 'Of course, I expect you know all about that—having been so friendly with Laura Hastings and all.'

'I just helped out in the garden, really.' He waved the coins again, hoping the glint of something shiny might distract her.

'Yes, but you'd know if the place had been sold, wouldn't you?'

'Not necessarily.' He didn't know why he was protecting Louise Thornton. Just that, having been the source of local gossip himself a few years ago, he knew how unpleasant, how…invaded…it could make one feel.

'Well, whoever it is…' Mrs Green leaned back and looked down her nose at him; it made him feel like a slice of something on a glass slide under a microscope '…they'll be fine with the residents of Lower Hadwell. After all, we've been used to living with a bona fide Hollywood legend on our doorstep for the last twenty years, haven't we?'

He nodded and thrust the money at her again. This time he wasn't going to be put off. Just as she started to uncurl her hand to accept it, she paused and nodded in the direction of the magazine rack that was half-hidden by a tall shelf containing pet food and assorted stationery. 'That mag that your Jasmine was waiting for has come in. I expect you'll be wanting to pick that up as well.'

Ben's mouth straightened into a thin line. He stuffed the coins back in his coat pocket and retreated to the safety of the other side of the shop, pleased that he was hidden by the boxes of envelopes balanced on the top shelf.

Now was it *Pink!* or *Girl Chat* that Jasmine liked? One had a free lip gloss with it, and he wasn't sure about that, so he picked up the other one.

There was a sudden jangle of the shop door and a rush of cold air. A figure slammed the door closed and darted behind the shelving unit to join him.

'Louise?'

She pulled the baseball cap she was wearing further down over her eyes and crouched a little lower. 'Shh!' she whispered loudly, without looking at him. Then she froze and slowly turned her head to look over her shoulder. 'Ben?'

He didn't say anything back. It was obvious who he was.

'You're wearing a suit,' she said, forgetting to hunker down.

Just then the wild-looking ornithologist appeared, running down the street. Louise must have seen a hint of movement out of the corner of her eye, because she practically flattened herself against the shelves, sending a box of ballpoint pens flying. 'Did he see me?' she hissed at him, looking a little wild-eyed herself.

Ben tried to look nonchalant and peered out of the shop window, but it was difficult to see clearly with all the posters for local events and cards offering bicycles for sale and adverts for paperboys.

'I think he's gone.'

Louise edged closer to where he was standing and craned her neck. 'Are you sure?'

He nodded. 'He was going at some speed when he shot past here. On a hill this steep, it's pretty difficult to stop when you've built up that kind of momentum. Why are you worried about—'

Oh. If Jas had been in his shoes she would have slapped herself on the forehead and said *duh!* Paparazzi. Definitely not a species seen around Lower Hadwell before. It put a totally new spin on the whole 'invasion' issue.

'Couldn't you just let him have a picture and then he'd be on his way?' That seemed like a reasonable solution.

Louise looked at him as if he'd just suggested she do a nude photo-shoot on the jetty—in sub-zero temperatures.

'I'm so…flipping cross with him, I might not be responsible for my actions. He just scared the life out of Jack as we were on our way into school.'

Her son was here? Good. Perhaps then she'd lose that slightly haunted look from her eyes. The look that unwittingly begged him to rush in and be her knight in shining armour. His armour had gone into retirement when he'd signed his divorce papers, and he'd better remember that fact.

She sighed and straightened up a little. 'A photo of us looking shocked is bad enough, but a shot of me turning pink in the face and spitting obscenities at him would only stoke the fire. By Friday there'd be a whole pack of them camped out at the local inn waiting for us.' She rubbed her face with her hand. 'Thank goodness I'd calmed down enough to realise that when I spotted him following me again.'

She stopped talking and looked him up and down. 'You're wearing a suit. A very nice suit.'

'You already said that.'

'Won't it get dirty?'

'Nope.'

She glowered at him. 'Stop being obtuse.'

He was tempted to chuckle, but decided it wouldn't help her current mood. 'I know you think I'm only fit for weeding the flower beds, but actually I'm not a gardener by trade. Not exactly.'

Louise's mouth dropped open. A sensation of achievement swelled inside him. Although why he should feel so stupidly proud of the fact that *he* was bamboozling *her* for a change, he wasn't sure.

'I'm a landscape architect. I design outside spaces—town centres, open spaces, parks, private homes. This morning Lord Batterham, the owner of the large stately home near here, wants to chat to me about restoring a knot garden on his estate and building an environmentally friendly play area for visitors.'

She blinked. Twice. And closed her mouth. 'Oh.'

She seemed to have forgotten all about the photographer, which had to be good news, so he decided to keep her distracted. 'You look a little different yourself.' Gone were the elegant clothes in dark, muted tones, replaced by a baby-pink tracksuit and bright white running shoes. And what was the cap with the ponytail sprouting through the back all about?

'I look a mess,' she muttered.

He took in her appearance again, went beyond the surface impression. Her face was free of make-up and her cheeks rosy with fading anger. A slightly more dishevelled appearance suited her. It made her more approachable…touchable.

He took a step back.

'Every day for months I've not gone out without my best clothes or my make-up on. Trust some rat with a digital camera to turn up when I'm looking…well, less than perfect.' She shook her head. 'I swear they must have some kind of radar to target me on my off days.'

'You look fine.'

She tipped her head to one side and gave him a weary look. 'I think what you said was that I looked "different". Believe me, it spoke volumes.'

'I just meant…not your normal self.'

That's right, Ben. Just dig yourself in deeper.

He was bad at this kind of stuff, he knew. He didn't have the ability to dress words up and make them pretty. And what was so wrong with the plain, unvarnished truth, anyway?

'Not my normal self?' she said, staring hard at him.

He sighed inwardly. Megan hadn't appreciated his 'lack of

tact and incredible insensitivity' either. Some women were just too much hard work.

'Well, here's your explanation…' She pulled a magazine off the rack and thrust it in front of his face. It took him a few moments to realise that the blurry picture on the cover was Louise herself—playing catch on a beach with a little boy. But that wasn't all. The caption read 'Celebrity Bulges' and large red lines circled her tummy and thighs.

He snatched the magazine from her and slapped it back in the rack, upside down and with the cover facing inwards. She locked him with a steady gaze and, when she spoke, her voice was low and dry.

'Apparently, I've been letting myself go. I'm surprised you hadn't heard.'

Her ability to mock herself blind-sided him. Laughter rocked him from the inside and burst out of his mouth. And then, after a few seconds, she joined him. Her eyes widened, as if she was as surprised at her own response as he was.

It was kind of surreal to be huddling in a little country newsagent's, hiding from the press and chortling with Louise Thornton. The laughter subsided to a level where he could get a bit of control and he wiped his hand over his face.

Louise was no longer laughing, but she was still smiling. If the topic of conversation was transformations, here was one that beat them all. The remains of his laughter died away instantly.

She was truly beautiful when she smiled. Her eyes sparkled and her skin glowed. Why did she think she needed all that black stuff to make her look pretty? He almost wished the photographer was here right now to capture this moment.

Thinking of cameras and lenses, he walked to the shop window and looked up and down the street. 'No sign of him now. I think you're safe.'

Louise's brows changed shape as she frowned, then relaxed again. The smile vanished and the remote beauty returned. 'Of course.' She stood up properly and started picking up the pens scattered all over the floor. When she'd finished, she gave him another smile, but this time her eyes were unaffected. 'I'll see you on Sunday?'

He nodded.

'I promise I won't make you weed the flower beds, if you're really too grand for that.'

It was his cue to laugh again, but he couldn't bring himself to. 'I've been itching to sort that garden out properly for years. Just indulge me, okay?'

She nodded. And, although she was as collected and self-contained as always, he could see a hint of something in her eyes. As if she wanted to reach out but was too afraid.

'I promise I'll charge the earth and drink all your tea.'

That earned him a real smile. Small, but real.

'It's a deal, Mr Landscape Architect.' She looked at her watch. 'Speaking of which, didn't you say you were off to a meeting?'

Lord Batterham!

He hurried back to the counter to pay Mrs Green for his paper. She was standing there, holding a magazine in her hand—the same one Louise had flourished in front of his nose. She stared at it and then at Louise, and then back at the magazine cover, as if she were playing some kind of mental tennis match.

For the first time in thirty-three years she wasn't making a sound. He plopped the change in front of her on the counter, grabbed Louise by the hand and dashed out of the shop.

'Mum? Can we go outside? It's stopped raining.'

Louise stopped herself from putting the kettle on the Aga for a fifth time. She didn't really want another cup of tea. It was just that, at some point this afternoon, somebody might.

'Can we? Please?' Jack's voice was so high-pitched on that last word she was sure dogs would be bounding towards them from all over the district.

'Can we *what*?'

Her son ran to the back door and opened it, letting in a gust of damp November air. Louise walked over to where he stood and stuck her head out of the door. Moisture dripped from the leaves of an evergreen bush in the little courtyard directly outside the kitchen, but the clouds were now a pale, pearly grey and she even thought she saw a hint of blue before it was hurried away by the wind.

Fresh air would do her good. Fresh air would stop her waiting. Or wondering why he was late. Well, not late, because they'd never really set a time for him to come and go, but later than normal.

She shook her head and reached for the scarf and hat on a peg nearby. Ben Oliver had turned all her assumptions about him on their heads once this week already. Why shouldn't he do it again?

The grass on the sloping lawn in front of the house was still damp, but it didn't stop Jack deciding a game of football was the ideal way to burn off a bit of energy. They used a couple of the big stones lining the driveway to mark out the goals.

She'd never been good at games at school, always too tired from acting as surrogate mother to her four younger brothers and sisters and part-time carer to her invalid father. Jack was running rings around her but then he misjudged a kick and the ball went flying past her towards the edge of the woods. She ran after it and stopped it with the side of her boot. If all went according to plan, she would have at least one goal to Jack's seven by the time they gave up and headed back inside for hot chocolate.

She swung her leg in an almighty kick. A jarring pain hit her as her lower back met something flat and solid and, all of a sudden, she was staring at the sky. She could hear Jack laughing his head off some distance away.

'Just you wait!' she yelled, giggling slightly herself, but the mirth stopped when she attempted to move. 'Ouch!'

'Here.' The voice was as rich as dark chocolate and she recognised it instantly. She also recognised the broad, long-fingered hand that came into her field of vision—although exactly when she'd noticed the shape of Ben Oliver's hands, she wasn't sure.

Even through the wool of her gloves, his skin was warm and he gripped her hand in such a way that she knew she could give him all her weight and he wouldn't let her fall. She winced as he gently helped her to her feet. 'Ow.'

'Where does it hurt?'

She didn't want to draw even more attention to her slightly-larger-than-planned and somewhat muddy backside. 'Where d'you think?'

'Do you want me to take a look?'

'No!' She twisted out of his grip and brushed herself down, more for something to do than for cosmetic effect. 'Don't tell me you're an almost-doctor as well as an almost-gardener.'

He laughed and she looked up at him, her irritation dissolving. It was only then that she noticed the girl standing slightly behind him. She had shoulder-length, honey-coloured hair, nothing at all like Ben's dark mop, but her eyes were all her father's.

Ben grabbed his daughter's hand and pulled her forward a little. She blushed and looked at the ground. 'Louise, I'd like you to meet my daughter, Jasmine.'

'Nice to meet you, Jasmine. I'm Louise. Your dad's been helping me out with my garden.'

'I know.' The reply was barely a whisper, and Jasmine flushed an even deeper shade of red.

Her father may not have known who 'Louise Thornton' was the first time he'd met her, but Jasmine certainly did. This kind of reaction wasn't unusual. Heck, she'd been just the same when she'd started going out with Toby and he'd introduced her to the latest Oscar-winning Hollywood actress.

'Come and meet my son, Jack. He's football mad, I'm afraid, though.'

Jasmine shrugged and followed her across the lawn as Ben strolled along, bringing up the rear. Jack took one look at Jasmine and Louise knew he'd decided she was okay. As the child of a celebrity couple, he had an uncanny kind of radar for discerning between hangers-on and real friends. He made instinctive decisions in a second and he was rarely wrong. Now, how did she go about getting herself some of that?

Jack picked up his football and started walking in the direction of the back door. 'There's chocolate cake inside. Want some?'

Jasmine nodded furiously and broke into a trot to keep up with him as he raced off towards the kitchen.

Ben fell into step beside Louise as they followed their offspring. 'Sorry I had to bring Jas with me. I hope it's okay.'

'Of course it's okay. Who do you think I am? The wicked witch of the West?'

He was smirking when she looked up at him. 'You can be a tad fierce at times.'

Was she? Really? She fell into silence for a few seconds while she pondered his remark. What had happened to the shy, sweet Louise she'd once been? Where was the awkward girl with the too-long limbs and a school blazer that had been far too short?

Eventually, she said quietly, 'If you'd been really afraid, you wouldn't have come.'

Ben laughed again. She liked that sound. She wondered if she could make him do it some more. So far, it had only happened accidentally, when she hadn't actually been trying to be funny at all.

'True. I hadn't intended on bringing Jas at all. It's just that…' he ran his hand through his hair '…it's complicated.'

'Trust me. I know *complicated*. What's up?'

Ben stared off into the distance for a few seconds and she stopped walking, aware that it would be better if this conversation wasn't overheard from the kitchen. Ben halted beside her.

'My ex-wife, Megan…' He made a microscopic movement with his head, as if he wanted to shake it but was stopping himself. 'She's a good mother, really. It's just that lately her priorities have been a little skew-whiff.'

Louise nodded.

'She seems to think that, now Jas is almost in secondary school, she can fend for herself a bit more. And, probably, she could. It's just with the divorce still in the recent past, I think Jas feels a little neglected. Megan had last-minute plans and cancelled their Sunday afternoon together. I don't think she even realises how shut out Jas feels sometimes.'

'How long?'

'Since the divorce? Two years.'

'Two months for me. Although I kicked him out about a year ago.' Louise breathed in. 'Girls need a mother at that age.'

She had certainly ached for her mother, going through those awkward years, but Mum had died just as she'd been on the brink of puberty, and she'd had to muddle through on her own. At least, when her sisters had reached it, she'd been able to help them along.

Maybe if Mum had been around she wouldn't have been quite as dazzled by Toby. Not that Toby hadn't loved her at first. It was just that he wasn't a good long-term choice. A little motherly advice would have come in mighty handy.

After years of looking after everyone else in the family—paying the bills, cooking the meals, wiping noses and changing bedpans—it had been like a fairy tale. A rich, handsome young man had arrived on the scene to take her away from all that. What seventeen-year-old girl wouldn't have jumped at the chance?

'Well, Jas is very welcome here. I understand completely.'

For the first time since she'd met him, she felt as if she wasn't a complete mess compared to him. Ben gave a small smile and looked at the ground. 'Thanks. Anyway, there's not much light left. I'd better get started.'

Jack started yelling his question as he ran down the hallway, finishing it as he skidded into the kitchen in his socks. 'Jas says there's fireworks on tonight. Can we go?'

Fireworks? Oh, of course. Time had taken on a strange quality since she'd moved to Whitehaven. The date was… what? The second or third of November? It was only days away from Guy Fawkes night and there would be bonfires and firework displays all over the area this weekend. She'd thought the bangs she'd distantly heard last night must have been shotguns, but now it all made sense.

'I don't know, Jack. What time is it? And where?'

'I'll ask Jas!' He raced out of the kitchen before she could quietly explain that maybe it wasn't such a good idea to be out in public, that maybe the Olivers wouldn't want a couple of extras tagging along. She fiddled with her cup of tea while she waited for her son to return but, after a couple of minutes, she decided he must have found something else to get all hyper about and had lost interest.

They didn't need to go out to see fireworks. Whitehaven was perched high on a hill and there would be great views from the attic windows. They could watch at a safe distance.

Ben knocked softly on the back door. There was no reply. He stared at the chunky Victorian handle for a second, then gripped it, the brass chilly against his palm, and turned. The door swung open on surprisingly creak-free hinges.

'Hello?'

Louise was standing at the old butler's sink, staring out of the window. He could hear water sloshing and see bubbles splashing and a moment later she dumped an upturned cup on the draining rack. It fell over. She didn't even look at it, just grabbed the next bit of crockery off the pile and started washing again. He coughed.

All the sloshing and splashing stopped. She didn't alter the angle of her head, but somehow he could tell that her focus was no longer off in the distance. She was aware of him, he knew. And, somehow, that made him aware of her too.

Suddenly, she started washing the plate she was holding again. When it must have been scrubbed clean of every last speck of food, she placed it on the drying rack with exquisite care, then turned to face him, wiping the bubbles off her hands with a tea towel.

'All finished?'

He nodded.

A million snatches of small talk whizzed round his head, but meaningless words weren't his forte. And Louise didn't seem to require any. She gave him a look—not quite a smile, more an expression of openness, of welcome—and then filled the kettle. He breathed a sigh of relief.

When he'd been married to Megan, he'd got used to having an arsenal of such phrases for the moment when he'd walked through the door. She'd always needed him to say something, to pay her attention, to make her feel noticed. And he'd adapted, because she was his wife and it had been what she'd needed.

Louise motioned for him to sit at the chunky kitchen table and started rummaging in a cupboard. After what he'd seen the other day, he wouldn't have been surprised if *this* woman was thoroughly fed up with being noticed, so he did nothing to break the wonderful stillness that surrounded her. He just drank it in and slowly felt his muscles relax. She handed him a mug of tea, sweetened to perfection, then pottered round the kitchen.

Rampaging children, however, could not be counted on to be so restful. Jas and Jack stormed into the kitchen just as the last knot was about to ease from his shoulders.

'Mum, I'm hungry!'

Even when she smiled, wide and full, as she was doing now, she still had a sense of elegance and poise that he'd rarely seen. At first he'd thought it was standoffishness, although it was merely reserve, but he could understand how people who perceived her to be an attention-hungry bimbo could misinterpret it as snobbishness. Louise Thornton was indeed an intriguing mix of contradictions. He was curious to know more.

'You're always hungry,' she said, looking at her son.

'Can we have some cake? Pleeeease? After all, we've got guests.' Jack looked hopefully at Ben and Jasmine, and Ben chuckled. Having been a hollow-legged boy once himself, he was pretty sure Jack's request wasn't entirely altruistic. However, he wasn't about to talk himself out of a nice piece of cake, so he watched for Louise's reaction.

She rolled her eyes and pulled a large tin off the counter. It was the item she'd been rummaging for earlier. Clever woman. She'd been prepared.

When she opened the lid the most delicious waft of treacle and walnuts, reminding him of warm November evenings by the fire, hit him. He almost had to wipe the drool from his mouth with his sleeve by the time a large chunk was handed to him on a plate. He didn't waste any time doing it justice.

Now, he could make a decent casserole and a great roast dinner, but baking evaded him entirely. This must be a prize-winning, locally made example. As he bit into it, he was almost tempted to growl with pleasure.

Light, moist cake with dense, spicy flavours and the earthiness of walnuts teased his taste buds. Almost half the slice was gone already. Would it be rude to ask for another one? He looked over at Jack, who had cleaned his plate, but was wearing a significant amount of crumbs over his face and down his front. Now, there was a lad who could be counted on to ask for more. All Ben had to do was hop on the bandwagon when the opportunity came.

Jack opened his mouth and Ben swallowed his last mouthful, confident that his plate would not lie desolate for long.

'So, can we go to the fireworks, Mum? Please?'

Louise frowned and put the lid on the cake tin. Ben felt his shoulders sag.

'I don't know, Jack. I thought we could watch from upstairs. That way, we might get to see more than one display.'

Jack pursed his lips. 'Jas says there's going to be hot dogs on the village green. Can't we go and have hot dogs?'

She looked pained as she shook her head. 'I'm sorry, darling. After the way that photographer… Well, it's just better we stay here where no one will see us.'

Jack's face fell and Louise's was a mirror image of misery. Ben wished there was something he could do. It was criminal that a mother and son couldn't do something as simple as watch a firework display without being hounded. He remembered only too well how hard he'd had to work not to stay inside every evening and mope when his divorce had been fresh and raw. With the extra pressures on Louise, he could see her turning into a hermit.

Jack slumped forward on the kitchen table, his chin in his hands and his bottom lip sticking out. Ben stared at the wall straight in front of him, racking his brain for a solution. Slowly, the pegs containing hats and coats and scarves near the back door came sharply into focus. He stood up.

'I've got an idea.'

CHAPTER FIVE

THE other three stopped talking and looked at him. He grinned, walked over to the row of pegs and pulled off a fluffy knitted hat and matching scarf. 'Come with me,' he said as he walked back towards Louise, whose eyes were wide and round, then he linked the tips of his fingers with hers and pulled her up to stand.

Her mouth moved, but no sound emerged.

He tugged her in the direction of the hallway, to the large gilt mirror he'd seen hanging there on his very first visit after Louise had moved in. He stood behind her and, while she continued to stare at him in the mirror, he pulled the dusky purple hat over her head. It was one of those tight-fitting ones with no embellishment or bobbles, and the crocheted hem came down level with her eyebrows.

Better. But she still looked like *Louise Thornton*. He scowled at her reflection and her eyebrows raised so they disappeared under the hat. It was the hair. That long, glossy dark hair was her trademark—instantly recognisable, indefinably *her*.

He brushed the hair framing her face back behind her ears and twisted the strands into a loose plait. When his gaze flicked up to the mirror again, she was staring at their reflections, her mouth slightly apart, and then she shivered and shook his hands away from her shoulders. He broke eye contact and busied himself wrapping the scarf once, twice, around her neck, letting it stand up so it covered the lower half of her face. Somehow his hands had made their own way back on to her shoulders with the flimsy pretence of keeping the scarf in place.

Only the eyes gave her away now, but there wasn't much he could do to diminish their impact. She could hardly wear sunglasses on a chilly autumn evening. That would only draw more attention to her.

'There.'

She was motionless, the only movement her eyes as they flicked between her own reflection and his. 'I'm wearing a hat and scarf. Is that your stunning plan?'

'No one will be able to pick you out of a crowd in this. It's going to be almost pitch-dark, after all. Top it off with a big dark coat and you'll look just like the rest of us.'

'I *am* like the rest of you.'

He knew celebrities weren't a different breed of human being, so he could almost agree. But there was something about Louise Thornton that defied explanation, that made her unlike anyone he had ever met before. And he really hoped he didn't feel that way because she was famous. He didn't want to be that shallow.

They stared at each other in the mirror a good long time. Her shoulders rose and fell beneath his hands.

'Mum, look!'

The stillness was shattered and suddenly he was moving away and Jack and Jasmine were running into the hallway, bundled up in coats and hats and jumping up and down. Jack was tall for his age and Jasmine petite, making them almost the same height. It took a few seconds for him to realise that Jack's overexcited squeaking was coming from underneath Jasmine's hat and scarf. Louise looked from one child to the other and burst out laughing. She pulled the fluffy hat with earflaps up by its bobble until she could see her son's eyes.

'If you'd have kept quiet, I'd have had no idea that you two had switched coats!'

Jack jumped up and down. 'Can we go? Can we?'

Louise rolled her eyes again. 'Okay, we'll go.'

Their cheers echoed round the tall hallway and up the elegant sweep of the stairs. Pounding footsteps followed as they raced back into the kitchen. 'You can wear your own coats and hats, though,' Louise called after them.

When the silence returned, she looked at him. 'Do you really think it'll work?'

'Of course, everyone is going to be craning their necks and looking up at the sky. They won't even pay attention to who's standing next to them. And, let's face it, it has to be a better disguise than your last attempt!'

She pulled the hat off her head and spent a few seconds de-fluffing her hair. 'You don't beat around the bush much, do you?'

He shook his head. Why waste time using inefficient words when you could use a few that hit straight to the heart of the matter?

Louise unwound the scarf and held it, together with the hat. 'Was it really that bad?'

He nodded and tried very hard not to smile. 'You looked like a celebrity trying very hard to *not* look like a celebrity. I mean, a pink track suit with the word "*Juicy*" splashed all over the…um…back.'

She gave him a knowing look. 'Oh, you noticed that, did you?'

If Ben Oliver had been a man prone to blushing, he'd have been as pink as Louise's '*Juicy*' jogging bottoms at that moment. Thank goodness his body was far too sensible for such displays of emotion. He gave her the sort of look a headmaster would give a gum-chewing schoolgirl. 'It was hard not to.'

'When are the fireworks going to start?' Louise looked first to the left and then to the right and clung a little harder on to the rope strung between rusting metal poles in front of her. Lower Hadwell's village green bordered the river just upstream from the main jetty and the fireworks had been set up on the stony beach with a clear boundary marked out to stop excited children getting too close.

'Twenty minutes.' Ben's voice was calm and reassuring, but it did nothing to soothe her. 'Don't worry.' His hand rested lightly on her shoulder and she jumped.

Don't worry. That was easy enough to him to say. Every time he let his guard down, someone didn't jump in front of him and pop a flashbulb. In recent years, she'd stopped letting down the wall she put up between herself and the rest of the world. Life was just too dangerous to lay herself open in that way. Only now the tabloids labelled her 'stuck-up' and 'fake'.

She sighed and, as her warm breath flowed out of her mouth, cool night air laced with wood smoke and sulphur filled her nostrils. She smiled.

Her family—well, what had been left of her family once Mum had died—had always attended the little firework display in the local park each November. The fireworks themselves hadn't been all that spectacular, but her memories were of cosiness, laughter and a feeling of belonging.

Then she'd met Toby and all that had changed. Had her family life really been that bad? On paper…probably.

As the eldest of five, with an invalid father, she'd had to fill her mother's shoes. The role had been too big for her. Like a little girl playing dressing up in her mother's high heels, there'd been obstacles she just hadn't been able to negotiate. In her dramatic teenage way, she'd imagined herself as a modern-day Cinderella—albeit looking after a much-loved family. She'd become cook, cleaner, carer, sympathetic ear, referee…

But what their lives had been lacking in money and glamour, they'd made up for with love. And she hadn't realised all families weren't like that until there was a big gaping hole in her life.

'Mum? Can I have a hot dog?'

Louise blinked and then focused on Jack, who was tugging on one of her arms.

'Pardon, sweetheart?'

He tugged so hard she thought her shoulder would work loose from its socket. 'I'm really hungry. Can I have a hot dog?'

The smell of onions, caramelising as they cooked on the makeshift grill on the far corner of the green invaded her senses. Hot on its tail was the aroma of herbs and meat. Her nose told her that when Jack said 'hot dogs' he didn't mean skinny little frankfurters but bulging, meaty local sausages, bursting out of their skins and warming the soft, floury white bread that surrounded them. Her mouth filled with saliva.

'Jack, you're going to pull my arm off! Give me a second to think!'

She was safe here at the front of the crowd. No one could see her face, only half lit from the bonfire off to the left. But over there by the grill, a generator grumbled as it provided power for a couple of harsh floodlights, making it as bright as any runway she'd ever walked down when she'd been modelling.

'Um…'

Ben took hold of Jack's hand, his eyebrows raised in a question as he searched her face. 'Why don't we let your mum save our spot here and we can go and get the hot dogs? If that's okay with you…' he added a little more quietly.

Her face relaxed so much in relief that she couldn't help but smile. She nodded and almost breathed her response. 'Thank you.'

It was only when Ben and the two kids had disappeared through the crowd that she realised she should have asked him to get one for her too. She opened her mouth to yell, but stopped herself and pulled the hem of her hat down until it was touching the bridge of her nose. Too many faces.

There were always too many faces these days. Yes, back in the beginning, she'd loved that aspect of her golden life with Toby. Dad had needed a lot of help when she'd been finishing secondary school and, after being in class so infrequently that some of the kids in her year hadn't even known who she was, it had been nice to be recognised. She'd underestimated just how addictive being noticed could be.

Her first hit had been the adrenaline rush she'd had when that talent scout for a modelling agency had come up to her when she'd been working in the supermarket one Saturday afternoon. Within weeks she'd been flying round Europe for photo shoots, attending industry parties, meeting famous people…

Dad had been so proud of her. And she'd ignored the guilt she'd felt at letting Sarah, the next oldest, slip into her Cinderella role whilst her big sister had danced away in an imaginary world where the clock never seemed to strike midnight.

And then she'd met Prince Charming—Tobias Thornton, rising star and darling of the British film industry. After that, she'd smothered all those nagging feelings by reasoning that now, at least, her family had decent food on the table. That they'd moved into a proper house with a bedroom for all of them… except Louise. And the school uniforms were no longer hand-me-downs or scavenged from local charity shops. Best of all, Dad had a full-time nurse to look after him.

It had been the nurse who'd been sitting beside him when he'd died only six months after she and Toby had said 'I do' on a private island in the Caribbean.

Tears stung Louise's eyes and the bonfire became a big orange blur. She stared at the mass of colour until it started to sharpen and move again. Slowly, she became aware of people talking and being nudged, but she didn't seem able to move. It was only when she heard Jack laugh and splutter with a mouthful of hot dog that she realised the others had returned. She carelessly rested a hand on top of Jack's head but he shook it off.

'You looked hungry too.' There was a smile in Ben's voice and she turned to look at him, even though the world was still shimmering slightly. He was holding up a big, juicy sausage in a roll, dripping with fried onions and ketchup. 'Of course, I've heard models don't eat, so I'm prepared to make the sacrifice of eating two if you don't want it.'

'Ex-model,' she said, snatching it out of his hand and stuffing one end in her mouth before he could change his mind. Ben threw his head back and laughed. And, when she had finished chewing, she did the same.

'Mum? What's so funny?'

Louise gave a tiny shake of her head, her gaze locked with Ben's. 'I don't know, Jack. Just…' Ben was still grinning, but his eyes weren't just smiling at her now. Deep underneath, there was something intense, something that drew her and terrified her at the same time. '…something.'

She breathed out and returned her attention to her hot dog, which wasn't hard to do. She hoped these had been happy pigs because, boy, they made one heck of a good sausage. Their sacrifice had been entirely worth it.

But then, sacrifices often were.

If Mum hadn't died, if Dad hadn't been ill, if she hadn't been standing at that particular supermarket till that day—looking 'haunting' as the scout had told her—then she wouldn't have met Toby. Okay, she might not have any regrets about erasing Toby from her life at this particular moment, but without Toby there would have been no Jack. And Jack was worth any sacrifice.

She looked at him, hanging off the rope and trying to edge closer to where the fireworks were being set up. Before she could reach for him, a strong male hand gently grabbed his coat and hauled him back into place.

A bonfire sprang into life inside Louise. In a place that had been cold and dead for so long, flames licked and tickled.

No. Not now. Not here. Not with this man.

Not that Ben Oliver wasn't worthy of admiration. After all, he was good-looking, thoughtful and kind. A good father. All the things a girl should put at the top of her list when searching for a prospective Prince Charming. And he had a presence, a quiet charisma that made it impossible not to search him out in a crowd or feel that he was someone you could trust your life with.

But this wasn't the time to be noticing those things about someone. This was time for her and Jack to heal, to rebuild. And she'd felt this way before, had trusted Toby with her life, and he had made it glitter and shine for a while, but ultimately he'd decided it wasn't worth his enduring attention.

So this was her sacrifice: she wouldn't go there. She'd cut off the oxygen supply to whatever feelings were warming her core. Jack deserved all her attention and her love at the moment and he shouldn't have to share it with anyone. He wouldn't.

The fireworks started. Louise had thought herself immune to the pretty showers of colour. Last year they'd seen the New Year's fireworks in London from a balcony of an expensive riverside apartment a quarter of a mile away. It had been a dramatic display, with rockets shooting off the London Eye and barges on the Thames, but she'd felt removed from it all somehow.

There was no ignoring anything tonight. Not the way the crowd collectively held its breath waiting for a bang. Not the warmth of the bonfire on one side of her face. Especially not the breath of the man standing slightly behind her that made her right ear tingle.

In the inky blackness of a country night, the sprays of light—from pure white to red and green, and blue and gold—were reflected in a river that had stretched itself taut and flat. The effect was stunning. Magical. Soon she was saying 'ooh' and 'aah' with everyone else, and clapping and watching Jack's reaction—and finding herself catching the gaze of a warm brown pair of eyes, then quickly looking away again.

The last firework glittered and fizzed, shooting so high up into the sky that she would have sworn that, briefly, she caught a glimpse of her big white house on the opposite bank. And then it exploded and split into a thousand stars that gracefully fell to earth. She sighed and closed her eyes. Simple pleasures.

How odd. She'd always thought that money and fame would nake it easier to find pleasure, but all it had really done was make t more complicated. Pure happiness, joy with no strings attached vas an unknown commodity in her life. When had she become o poor? And how had she become so blind she hadn't even ealised what a sorry state she was in?

'Come on…' Ben's hand, resting once again on the shoulder f her thick wool coat, caused her to open her eyes, releasing the nagic moment and letting it flutter away like the sparks from the onfire. 'I'll give you a lift home.'

Jack, who should have been totally worn out by now, jumped p and down even harder. 'Are we going on the dingy again?'

Jas put on a very superior tone. 'It's not a dingy, Jack. You ay it *ding-gee*. Dinghy.'

Jack pulled himself up to his full height. 'I knew that.'

Ben shook his head. 'No. I'll drive you.'

Louise opened her mouth to protest. It would take more than alf an hour to drive down to Dartmouth, catch the 'higher ferry', s the locals called it, and double back to Whitehaven.

'I wouldn't take the kids out in the boat when it's this dark,' e explained.

Louise followed him as he headed for the quiet spot where e'd parked his car and looked carefully at the scenery. It had een verging on darkness when they'd made the trip over, or at east she'd thought it was. The trees had been dark grey shapes nd the sky had faded from bright cobalt at the horizon to indigo verhead but, compared to how it looked at the moment, that had nerely been twilight. Everything was black if it wasn't lit up by ither starlight or electricity.

'And you and Jack would have to scramble back through the voods in the pitch-dark.'

Okay, he'd convinced her. She got lost in her own back garden n daylight still. No way was she dragging her eight-year-old hrough those woods tonight.

As she strapped Jack into the back of Ben's car, Louise went still. Ben must have known all along that they wouldn't be able to return to Whitehaven the way they'd come. It explained why he'd disappeared when they'd first arrived to move his car—away from the main road and the village centre, where the crowds were now ambling—into a quiet side road.

She sat in the front passenger seat and fastened her seat belt without looking at him. Pretty soon they were whizzing through isolated country lanes in silence, the only hint they weren' alone inside a big black bubble were the golden twigs and branches picked out by the headlights in front of them. The patterns the light made on the road and hedgerows shifted and twisted as they sped past. Every now and then, for a split-second an odd tree stump or a gate would be illuminated and then i would be gone.

Louise breathed in the silence. After a few minutes she turned her head slightly to look at Ben. His hands gripped the whee lightly, but she had no doubt he was in full control. All his con centration was focused on the road in front of them. He looked at it the same way he'd looked at her in the mirror that afternoon

The air begun to pulse around her head and a familiar craving she'd thought she'd conquered started to clamour deep inside her—the heady rush of simply being *noticed*. Immediately, she twisted her head to look straight ahead and clamped her hands together in her lap. They were shaking.

Simple pleasures.

She had an idea that Ben Oliver was full of them.

It was taking every ounce of his will-power to keep his eyes on the road ahead. Having Louise Thornton in the front seat of hi car was proving a distraction. And not an oh-my-goodness there's-a-celebrity-in-my-car kind of distraction. Unfortunately He could have talked himself out of that one quite easily.

And it wasn't even because she was the most stunning woma

he'd ever laid eyes on. She was way out of his league, he knew that. The logic of this situation would catch up with him eventually.

At the start of the evening, she'd stood tall and still, and a casual onlooker would have thought her relaxed and confident. But, unfortunately, he'd discovered he could no longer regard Louise casually.

He'd noticed the way her gloved hands had hung on to the boundary rope as if it were a lifeline. He'd seen the panic in her eyes when she'd thought she'd have to face the crowd and might be recognised. He had the oddest feeling that the real Louise had shrunk small inside herself, hiding beneath the thick outer shell. How long had she been that way?

Then, as the evening had worn on, he'd seen her hands unclench from the rope and noticed the unconscious, affectionate gestures that flowed between mother and son. He'd heard her laugh when ketchup had dripped on to her chin from the hot dog, and listened to the soft intakes of breath with every bang and crackling shower of the fireworks.

And he didn't want to notice these things about her. He didn't want to know how warm and rich her laugh was, or how tender and gentle she was below the surface. He just wanted to see the surface alone—much in the same way he only saw the rippling surface of the river and never the rocks and currents beneath.

He would rather remember the bare facts—that her divorce was still raw and fresh, that the last thing he and Jas needed in their lives at the moment was another woman with too much baggage for him to shoulder.

He'd known that Megan had had 'issues' when he'd first met her, but they seemed inconsequential to the situations facing Louise. And she faced them with such dignity and poise…

There he went again, admiring her when he should be concentrating on other things.

A flash of movement across the road caused his foot to stamp instantly on the brake. All of the joke-telling and giggling from the back seat stopped.

'It's okay,' he said, his heart pounding. 'Only a rabbit—and he's away up the hill by now.'

Jas and Jack returned to their knock-knock jokes and he put the car into gear. He pulled away gently, aware of the slim fingers that had flown to the dashboard and were now curling back into her lap.

Getting freaked out by a rabbit? What was happening to him? They darted in front of the car all the time and he never usually reacted this way. He pressed his foot on the accelerator, the car picked up speed and soon they were flying down the country lane as if nothing had happened. Ben concentrated on the road and pretended he didn't know how to answer his own question.

The other occupants of the car fell into silence and it wasn't long before he was pulling into the long drive that led to Whitehaven. Louise shifted in her seat, as if she was preparing to dart out of the door as soon as the wheels had stopped turning. Good. If she didn't feel the need to linger in his presence, that was fine by him.

'Can I have cake when I get in, Mum?'

Ben stifled a smile as he slowed the car and brought it to a halt outside the front porch. And then his tummy rumbled. It had fond memories of that cake.

'Jack! It's past your bedtime! Of course you're not going to have—'

'Cakes!'

They all turned and looked at Jas, whose eyes were wide and a hand was clamped over her mouth. Then she started to cry. Instantly, he was out of the car and opening the rear passenger door. 'Jas? What is it?'

Jas's lip trembled. 'C-cakes. My class are doing a tea party for the old people in the village. Mum was going to help me make cakes this weekend, but she went away…'

Ben tried not to let the irritation show on his face. Megan

could waltz off to Timbuktu for all he cared, but when her flaky ways affected Jas it was a different matter entirely.

'I'm supposed to take them in on Tuesday morning or I won't get any house points!' Jas wailed. 'Can you help me, Dad?'

'Um…' There was nothing he'd like more, but he wasn't sure Jas would be getting any house points for anything he tried to bake—'tried' being the operative word.

'I can help.'

As one, he and Jas swivelled round to look at Louise and stared. Her face was expressionless. Had he really heard that right?

Ben turned back to Jas. 'Can't you do it on your own? I'll supervise.'

There was a loud snort from the passenger seat. He ignored it.

Jas had the end-of-the-world expression on her face that was common to all eleven-year-olds in a crisis. 'I don't know. I can never get the beginning bit right when you have to mix the eggs and flour together.'

'Eggs and sugar.' Louise spoke quietly. In his experience, that tone was deceptive. He just might be in big trouble.

'Yeah, eggs and sugar. That's what I meant,' Jas said absently.

Ben sighed. 'Can't we just buy some?'

Jas shook her head and started to cry again.

'I can help.' This time Louise's tone was more insistent.

'Home-made cakes?'

'What do you think you were eating earlier? Scotch mist?'

Reality dropped away and Ben felt as if he were standing on nothing. '*You* made that cake?' He could tell by the look on her face that he was probably sabotaging Jas's only chance—which was a pity. He hadn't meant his words to come out quite like that, but they'd escaped before his brain had had a chance to give them the once-over.

Louise glared at him. 'No, the cake fairies left it on the doorstep.'

Okay. He'd deserved that.

Jas, who was wiping her eyes with her coat sleeve, piped up.

'I thought that if Jack needed cakes for school you'd have jus
bought them at Harrods.'

It seemed his daughter had inherited his capacity for opening
his mouth only to change feet.

Louise clamped a hand across her mouth and, just as he was
expecting her to flounce out of the car, slamming the door, her
eyes sparkled and she let out a raucous laugh.

Ben was floored. This wasn't the shy giggle he'd seen earlier
it was a full-bellied chuckle. And it was pretty infectious. When
the surprise had worn off, his mouth turned up at the corners and
pretty soon, all four of them were crying with laughter. Louise
was clutching on to the door for support and Jack's titter was so
high-pitched it was starting to hurt his ears.

Still giggling, Louise managed a few words, even though she
was a little short of breath. 'Sometimes…sometimes…when
was really busy…I *did* get them at Harrods!' That just set them
all off again.

When they all managed to get back on the right side of sanity
he felt as exhausted as if he'd done a cross-country run. Man, i
hurt to breathe.

Louise let out a long happy sigh. Her face was soft and relaxed
and her cheeks were flushed. It was just as well there were two
children in the back of the car, because he had the stupidest urge
to kiss her.

That sobered him up pretty fast.

'Are you sure? I know you're really busy. We don't want to
put you out, do we, Jas?'

Jas didn't say anything, but pleaded at him with her eyes.

'Busy doing what?' Louise raised an eyebrow. 'The house i
practically finished. There's only so much interior decorating a
girl can do, you know.' And then she winked at him—actuall
winked at him. 'I'd be happy to help. You gave us a great nigh
out tonight.'

Ben stuttered. That was the problem. In his mind, tonight ha een about making a nice final gesture to ensure that Louise was ettled into the neighbourhood before he backed off. How was e going to do that if she was going to be in his kitchen tomorrow?

After she'd put Jack to bed that night, Louise couldn't sleep. Didn't even want to try. It must be the fresh air or something.

She found herself flopped on one of the big velvet-covered ofas in the drawing room, the remote control in her hand, licking through endless cable stations searching for something o watch. A fire glowed in the hearth and the lights were low. The ich, deep colours and luxurious textures of the fabrics in here ruly had made a large draughty room incredibly cosy.

Wait a minute…

She stopped jabbing the button on the remote and went back few channels. Just as she'd thought—there was old film footage f Laura Hastings, not from one of her movies, but of her getting n a plane. Louise dropped the remote and snuggled back into he over-sized cushions that lined the back of the sofa.

It was obviously a documentary and, although she'd missed he first twenty minutes, she settled down to watch. Laura had een so beautiful when she was young. Her ice-blonde hair, pale kin and blue eyes looked fabulous in gaudy nineteen-fifties Technicolor.

She'd had such an interesting life. Two failed marriages—a int of a scandal. Louise smiled to herself. It all might seem very ashing and glamorous when it was reported like that, but she new from experience that living through it was just as painful s it was for the rest of the human beings on the planet. Not only id she admire the former owner of Whitehaven, but she identi-ied with her. Had Laura Hastings been happy in the end?

As she kept watching, she didn't really get an answer. Laura ad lived life to the full, taken every chance offered her. And that vas where Louise saw the difference between them. Yes, she'd rabbed at the chance to become a model and marry the man of

her dreams—literally. But then, even when things had turne
sour, she'd hung on to the empty shell of all her hopes, too scare
to let go and trust that things would turn out right in the end.

Her gaze drifted from the television and she huffed gently an
shook her head. She'd been a coward. It had taken Toby carryin
on, practically under her nose, to push her into leaving hin
She'd been scared that, imperfect as it was, if she let go of he
life she'd go into freefall and there'd be no one there to catch he

She still felt as if she were falling sometimes.

A picture of Whitehaven appeared on the screen and Louis
sat up. Wow. The footage looked like old black and white cin
film. Laura, now middle-aged but still stunning, walking on th
lawn in front of the house, staring out across the river.

Much more of the house was visible. The trees were, of cours
shorter but it wasn't just that. Everything looked a little more.
cared for. The garden still had a wild and unusual beauty, but the
was a harmony that was missing from it in its present state.

The house and garden might have been looking lovely, but th
voiceover indicated that Laura Hastings's life had been disinte
grating at this point. She'd fallen in love with both the house an
her leading man while filming on location at Whitehaven som
ten years earlier.

There had been a torrid affair, but the actor already had a wi
and Laura had married someone else on the rebound. Years late
the illicit romance had blossomed into life again and Laura, su
that happiness was finally in her grasp, had divorced her husban
and waited for her lover to free himself from his marriage to
The waiting had turned into yearning and the yearning into hear
break. The love of her life had never followed through.

A tear trickled down Louise's cheek and she hugged a pillo
to her. Laura Hastings might have made some bad choices alon
the way, but she couldn't help admiring her courage.

The credits rolled. The next thing on was *A Summer Affai*
the very film set at Whitehaven. It was the story of the youn

serving girl who'd captured the heart of the wealthy owner's son. The chemistry on-screen between Laura and her man was sizzling-hot. But, now Louise knew it had ended in a doomed love affair, every touch, every kiss had a bittersweet quality to it.

She sighed and settled down to watch, a chenille cushion hugged to her chest.

There was a scene halfway through the film, just as the lovers were starting to act on their feelings for each other, that had been filmed on the balcony of the boathouse. A picnic was set out on a little table with a red and white checked cloth. The sun was shining and shy, heated glances were flying between hero and heroine.

Louise sighed. That was what love should be like, she mused as she covered her mouth with a hand to stifle a yawn—overly bright and colourful, the sun always shining. The zing of electricity in the air. And the way he looked at her—as if he could see right through her and into her soul. As if he wanted to drown in her. That was what love *should* be like.

What a pity it was only like that in corny old movies, she thought, as the hero pulled the heroine into the shadowy interior of the boathouse and wrapped her in his arms.

CHAPTER SIX

LOUISE'S eyes were closed. A gentle summer breeze warmed her skin and she could hear the waves half-heartedly lapping against the jetty below the balcony. She let out a long therapeutic sigh, stretched her legs and opened her eyelids.

The sky was the colour of cornflowers and the sun a glaring dot of white gold high above.

'Perfect timing.' The male voice was warm and lazy, and accompanied by the dull pop of a cork exiting a wine bottle. 'I thought you were going to sleep all afternoon.'

She shook her head and stood up. The chequered red and white cloth on the small table fluttered, lifted by the warm air curling in and out of the boathouse balcony. Self-consciously, she reached for the wineglass he offered her and dipped her head to hide behind the curtain of her hair.

'Don't do that. Not with me.'

She froze, anticipation and vulnerability sending both hot and cold bolts through her simultaneously. He stepped forward and brushed the hair away from her face. His thumb was warm and slightly rough on the skin of her cheek. The tips of his fingers threaded through the hair above her ear until he held her head in his hand. She couldn't help leaning in to it, letting him support her.

Slowly, he tipped her head until she was looking him in the eyes.

'You don't have to hide from me.'

Oh, she would have given anything to believe that was true. Tears sprang to her eyes and clung to her lashes. Even in the bright sunshine, she could see his pupils growing, become darker and darker. But it wasn't just desire she could see there. Deep in the blackness were the answers to all the questions she'd ever wanted to ask.

Yes, the eyes said. Yes, you are good enough. Yes, you deserve to be loved like this.

One tear escaped, pulled by gravity, and raced away down her cheek. She couldn't move, not even to swipe it away. It carried on running as he continued to stare at her, his expression full of texture and depth, until it trailed down her neck.

A question flickered across her face—she felt it as surely as the salty river air.

Do you?

He didn't move a muscle, except to stroke the skin of her temple with the edge of his thumb. The eyes held the answer once again. *Yes.*

Something inside her, something that had been clenched tight and hard for years, unfurled. And Ben Oliver stepped back into the cool darkness of the boathouse, pulling her with him and repeated his answer over and over again with his lips on hers.

Louise woke up with a gasp, her eyes wide. The fire was little more than burnished embers and a talk show host was skilfully plying a reluctant guest with questions on the television.

She pressed a hand to her pounding chest. Just a dream. It had only been a dream. Calm down, you daft woman. Is this how pathetic you've become? A man shows you just a little bit of concern and neighbourly decency and your subconscious decides he's the love of your life? Just how starved of affection have you been?

Well, her subconscious could just think again. Starving or not, this was one meal she was going to refuse. All her brain had done was jumble up the events and people of her day with the events and characters of the late-night film. A simple crossing of wires, that was all. In the morning, when she was coherent again, she'd make sure everything was rerouted back the right way.

She straightened the stiff arm she'd been lying on and was rewarded with a click. Serves you right for falling asleep in front of the telly, she told herself. Although love *should* be like falling in love in a cheesy old movie, it wasn't. And it never would be. The sooner the right side of her brain caught up with that fact, the better.

At three-thirty the following afternoon, Louise still wasn't sure if she'd won the battle with her subconscious. She pressed the doorbell on the Olivers' cottage door and tried to work out where all the butterflies in her stomach had migrated from. Wherever they had come from, it seemed they were making themselves at home.

There was a click and the door started to open. Louise stopped breathing.

The blonde-haired woman who answered frowned slightly. 'Yes?'

Louise swallowed. 'I'm…er…here to help Jasmine. Mr Oliver is expecting me.'

The woman nodded, opened the door wide and Louise stepped inside and followed her into a funky modern kitchen with glossy red cabinets and black granite work surfaces. Not exactly what she'd pictured Ben Oliver would have chosen but, then again, maybe he hadn't chosen it. Maybe Mrs Oliver had had something to do with it.

Right there was a good reason to stamp on all the butterflies waltzing inside her. Both she and Ben had too much history, too much baggage.

'Hey!' Jasmine was sitting on a cushioned stool next to a breakfast bar with a glass counter. She jumped off and walked towards Louise, her hands in her pockets. A blush stained her cheeks and she looked at the floor as she came closer.

Louise smiled. It didn't seem that long ago that she'd been all awkward gestures and blushes herself. 'Hey, yourself. Ready to bake?'

Jas nodded. 'Is Jack with you?'

Louise shook her head. 'He's gone to football and then to a friend's for tea.'

'More cake for me, then!' Jas giggled.

'Is…um…' Louise glanced at the anonymous woman, who was standing in the doorway, staring at her with undisguised curiosity. 'Is *everyone* joining in?'

'Oh, no.' Jas shook her head. 'Just you and me.' She scowled at the woman, who took the hint and sloped away. 'Don't mind Julie. First of all, her nose is out of joint that she can't stay and snoop on a famous person, but most of all she's probably worried she won't get as much child-minding money if you're looking after me.'

'Your dad's not here?'

'Nah. He doesn't finish work until five o'clock and probably won't be home until six. She looks after me until then most days.'

Louise wasn't sure whether to be relieved or disappointed. Relieved, she told herself quickly. It was much better to be relieved. Still, that didn't explain the black hole that had opened up inside her tummy that the butterflies were now being sucked into.

Even before Ben's key had turned in the lock the most amazing smells hit his nostrils: warm butter and cinnamon, sugar and vanilla. He'd been on a site visit most of the day and lunch had merely been a fleeting fantasy as he'd tried to explain to his client, in the most polite way possible, that his ideas for a visionary garden were actually going to be a blot on the landscape. His stomach rumbled, and he ordered it to get a grip.

He didn't want any cake. He didn't want to be hungry for anything at all.

He found Julie sulking in the sitting room reading a magazine. She really wasn't the greatest substitute for the regular childminder, but at least she'd been amenable to relocating to the cottage today so Jas could cook. With Louise.

His stomach gave up growling and did something more akin to a backflip.

Get a grip, Ben.

It meant nothing. It would always mean nothing. He'd just not been on a date for a while, that was all. He nodded to himself as he made his way to the kitchen. That was it, he was sure. Lack of female company had left him a little hypersensitive to having a woman around. Especially a woman as beautiful as Louise Thornton. It was just his testosterone talking.

But did it have to yell quite so loudly?

His hand was almost on the kitchen door, but he snatched it back and veered off in the direction of his study. He closed the door firmly behind him and let out a long breath. Work would distract him. And he needed to update his files on today's project and come up with something that fulfilled his client's brief to be 'ground-breaking' and 'organic' without being hideously ugly.

Instead of turning his computer on, he reached for a large sketch-pad and a soft pencil. All his best ideas came when he did the designing the old-fashioned way. Somehow, just holding a pencil and having a creamy sheet of cartridge paper beneath it made him want to fill it with shapes and shading and curves, to change the blankness of the bare paper into something that came alive.

He threw the pencil and pad down on his desk, took off his jacket and hung it over the back of his chair, then sat down and set to work, his empty tummy momentarily forgotten.

Half an hour later, he stood back and surveyed his handiwork.

Great, just great. Best ideas? What a laugh.

He squinted at the drawing and then turned the pad ninety degrees. A long, low groan escaped from his mouth and he ran his hands over his face. From this angle, the aerial view of the garden looked like a giant cupcake with a cherry on top. Why, when he'd been thinking of paths and borders, had he come up with this?

Best thing to do was admit defeat. He should just go into the kitchen, say hello and then leave again, proving to himself that he was just working himself up about nothing. And maybe this evening he would call his pal Luke and get him to set him up with one of his wife's friends. Gaby had been trying to matchmake for more than a year now. Perhaps he should just put her out of her misery?

Ben grinned, but it turned into a grimace. The truth was, he didn't really want to go out on a date with anyone. No one he'd met in the last couple of years had been anything more than pleasant company for an evening. No one had been the sort of woman he could envisage fitting into his and Jas's lives. Even Camilla.

Camilla had been stylish and intelligent and funny, but there'd just been no spark—even though he'd done his utmost to get something to ignite. For a while now, he'd just thought it would be better to wait until Jas was older. She deserved love and stability after all she'd been subjected to because of his and Megan's mistakes, not a string of unsuitable girlfriends being tramped through the house. Not that he'd actually brought any of them home, anyway.

Unsuitable. That was a good word.

Louise Thornton was totally unsuitable, no matter how mouth-watering her cakes might be. Okay, she wasn't the airhead the tabloids made her out to be, but her life was full of turmoil, and that was the last thing he and Jas needed at the moment. He'd do well to remember that.

He pushed open the kitchen door and found exactly what he'd feared—turmoil. He blinked at the two females giggling on the other side of the room as a puff of icing sugar billowed up from a glass bowl and settled on them like microscopic snow. 'Not that way…' Louise was saying. 'Gently!'

Jas was laughing so hard she inhaled some of the icing sugar and started to cough and sneeze at the same time. Louise, who was starting to cough herself, patted Jas on the back. Neither of them had any idea he was there.

He looked around the room. On every available space, there were cake tins and wire racks, assorted cake ingredients and almost-clean mixing bowls with finger marks in them. Megan would have had a fit if she'd seen her precious kitchen like this. It looked wonderful.

'Dad!' Jas spotted him, pulled away from Louise and ran over to him.

'Jasmine.' He tried very hard to keep a straight face. Someone had to bring some sanity into the proceedings.

'Come and see what we've made!'

Before he could argue, she slipped a sticky hand into his and pulled him across the kitchen to where a row of cooling racks stood, with various cakes, all in different stages of decoration. Louise was there, standing straight and tall. She'd been laughing a moment ago, but now her eyes were watchful and her mouth was clamped shut. He saw her gaze sweep around the kitchen.

'Sorry,' she mumbled. 'We kind of got carried away.'

He wanted to say something grown-up, sensible, but not one word that fitted the bill entered his head. He was too distracted by the smudge of icing sugar on Louise's nose.

'What?'

'You've got—'

Ben leaned forward, meaning to brush it away, but she stepped back and went cross-eyed trying to see what he was looking at. Then she rubbed at her nose with the heel of her hand, which only served to add a drop of jam to the proceedings.

He stayed where he was. She could sort herself out. It was better that way.

Louise was staring at him. Slowly, she walked over to the double oven and checked her reflection in the glass door. He handed her a piece of kitchen towel and she took it, without looking at him, and dabbed at her face. When she stood up again, she was blushing.

It was so unlike her normal armour-plated façade that he couldn't help but smile. 'Much better.'

She blushed harder and smiled back. 'Good,' she said quietly.

Only he wasn't sure if it was better. There was something rather appealing about an icing sugar covered, vanilla-smelling Louise Thornton in his kitchen. She seemed…real. Not unapproachably beautiful or spikily vulnerable. Just real.

'It's time we started clearing up, Jas.' Louise reached for a tin and headed for the dishwasher.

Ben waited for the whining to start, but Jas just nodded and started closing up bags of flour and putting egg cartons back into the fridge. He shook his head, then decided to put the kettle on—mainly to distract himself from the rows of cupcakes, sitting silently on the counter, just *waiting* for someone to notice them. Saliva started to collect in his mouth and he found himself swallowing three times in a row.

He turned round to offer Louise a cup of tea and found her standing right behind him, a plate full of cakes in her hand. He swallowed once again.

'Would you like one?'

Now, if it had been Jas doing the offering, he would have immediately responded with, *What do you want?* However, Jas was earning her halo washing up the wooden spoons. He looked at Louise and just nodded.

'Raspberry and lemon muffins, jam doughnut muffins or iced fairy cakes?'

His eye fell on something golden-yellow and covered in sugar.

She smiled. 'Jam doughnut muffin it is, then.' She looked down at the cakes for a few seconds, then up into his face. 'Actually, I'm trying to butter you up.'

She was? 'You are?'

Louise nodded. 'I saw something on the television last night…' her eyes glazed over and she seemed adrift for a few seconds before she caught herself and carried on '…about Laura Hastings and Whitehaven. The garden…well, it looked lovely and I wondered if you'd consider…um…taking on the job of restoring it for me.'

He was speechless. For years he'd wanted to have free rein at Whitehaven. Now was his chance. He should be whooping with joy and dancing round the kitchen hugging someone—hugging *Jas*, of course.

'You do that kind of thing, don't you?' She was looking at him strangely.

Twice his head dipped in a nod. He'd started off in landscape gardening and when that had been going well, he'd trained as a landscape architect. The resulting design practice, with specialist teams to do the ground work when required, was one of the things that made his firm so successful. However, he didn't seem to be able to articulate any of this to Louise.

'Good. Perhaps we can chat another day—during work hours. I don't expect you to give up your time to…' A tiny frown creased her forehead and she stared at him for a couple of seconds, then her gaze dropped to the plate in her hands. 'Still want one?'

The muffin was still warm when he picked it up and, when he bit into it, liquid raspberry jam burst out and added its acidity to the dense but moist texture of the muffin. Pure heaven. Louise just nodded. Oh, she knew she was good! She knew exactly how much her baking had reduced him to a salivating wreck. And she was enjoying it.

Ben stood up very straight and resisted the urge to lick the sugar off his fingertips. Suddenly, this wasn't just about cakes any more. Perhaps it had never been about cakes.

Yup, he was pretty sure he was in big trouble. Because, despite all his efforts at logic, he was starting to think that, far from being the wrong kind of woman, Louise Thornton might suit him just fine.

December, so far, had been incredibly mild, but a cold snap was coming. He could feel it in the slicing wind that raced every now and then up and down the river. Ben hunched his shoulders up to try and escape the draught snaking down the back of his neck as he steered the little dinghy through the sharp, steely waves.

Jas moved into the stern with him and he held up an arm for her to snuggle under. He smiled down at her and she buried her head further into his side. His lips were still curved when he returned his attention to the river. It didn't matter if the weather was cold enough to freeze the Dart solid, the fact that he'd managed to create a living thing so wonderful would always melt his heart.

This was one of those perfect snapshot moments that would live in his memory for ever. Everything on the river seemed to be in shades of grey and silver—the waves, the reflection of the pearly sky. And, directly in front of him, perched on the hill like a queen on her throne, was the bright white house he was heading towards. In their waterproof coats—his dark green and Jas's vibrant purple—they were the only blobs of colour on the river spoiling the effect.

'Do you think it's going to snow, Dad?'

He pursed his lips, thinking. 'I don't know. It would be nice, though, wouldn't it? The last time we had a white Christmas I was a boy.' He hugged Jas to him, then released her as they neared the jetty below Louise's boathouse. 'We'll have to wait and see.'

After tying up the dinghy, he stood for a moment and stared up the hill. The house was hidden by the curve of the land and by the trees, but he knew in which direction it was.

There were ugly gashes in the earth near the house which his team had created in the midst of doing the hard landscaping. It would look a mess when he approached the front lawn. But, in his experience, things often had to get a lot messier before they were transformed into something beautiful. In the spring, the digging and paving would be finished and they'd be able to plant. Come summer, Whitehaven's garden would be transformed. And, over the years, it would mature into something unique and stunning.

Unique and stunning…

How easy it was for his thoughts to turn to Louise.

Recently Jas had taken to showing him any photographs of

Louise which she found in the Sunday papers or magazines. Most of them weren't current, as she hadn't really been anywhere to be photographed recently. Photographers who turned up in the village these days were often sent on a wild goose chase by the locals, who had warmed to Louise as quickly as he had and were now very protective of the celebrity in their midst.

'Ready, Jas?'

Jas, who had been throwing stones into the water, nodded and ran off up the hill. Ben tucked his hands into his pockets and strolled after her. As he walked, an image from an article in one of the Sunday magazines filled his head. Tobias Thornton had given an extensive interview about his new life with a blonde actress whose name Ben was struggling to remember. Of course, there had been photos of Louise and Toby in their glory days.

He punched his hands deeper into his pockets. What did it mean if he admitted to himself that the photos had made him feel sick? He couldn't figure out why; they were fairly innocuous shots of the then Mr and Mrs Thornton on the red carpet somewhere. The body language had been convincing—he'd had an arm around her waist and she'd hooked a hand around his neck. They'd been smiling.

Ben kicked a stone on the path and watched it hit a tree trunk, then roll down the hill out of sight. And then he thought about her eyes. There had been a deadness there, just a hint. Most people, if they'd noticed it at all, would have just assumed it was because it had been the five-hundredth photo they'd posed for that evening. Not him.

That same soul-deep weariness had been in her eyes the day he'd first met her, and no one had been watching her then. He had a good mind to track her ex down and give him a piece of his mind for putting it there.

Ben stopped in his tracks. What he really wanted to do was punch Tobias Thornton's lights out. When had he suddenly got so primitive? He never wanted to hit people. It just wasn't him. Not even Megan's new man. Actually, he felt kind of sorry for that guy…

Slowly, he started walking again, then picked up speed because he realised that he couldn't see Jas any more. He called out and a few moments later saw a flash of purple in between the trees up ahead.

His heart rate doubled. Would Louise be up there on the lawn, strolling as Jack played? Or would she be waiting for him in the kitchen, the kettle blowing steam? He could easily have sent a guy to care for the carnivorous plants in the greenhouses, but he'd kept on coming on Sundays, hoping she wouldn't ask him why he still dealt with it personally.

Sunday was now officially his favourite day of the week. And he had a feeling that Louise knew the plants were just an excuse. Each week they spent more and more of his visit talking, walking round the grounds. He'd never drunk so much tea in his life. But if those giant mugs kept him leaning against the rustic kitchen counters while she hummed and pottered round the kitchen, stopping every now and then to smile at him, how could he complain?

At that moment the trees parted and he saw her. It felt as if every molecule of blood had drained from his body. She was chasing both Jack and Jasmine, who were running round in circles, and when she saw him she stopped, brushed the hair from her face and waved.

Normally, he didn't have any problem speaking his mind. He was never rude or insensitive, but he just called things as he saw them. So why, when all he could think about was asking her out to dinner, or see if they could spend some time alone—just the two of them—did the syllables never leave his lips?

He was now within shouting distance. Hands that had been cold and stiff were now clammy in his pockets and he took them out and did a half-wave with one hand. Louise smiled and his insides jumped up and down for joy. The warm laughter in her eyes erased any form of sensible greeting.

Just admit it, Ben. You've got it bad.

* * *

He was here.

She waved, just to seem friendly. And, of course, if she didn't smile it would look funny, so she did. Only she didn't seem to be able to control how wide, how sparkling it was.

He took long strides across the lawn, minding the gouges of red earth revealed by the landscaping team. Something to do with re-establishing the rose garden, she'd been told. The details were a little fuzzy at present. He gave a little wave, but his face remained serious.

She didn't care. She liked it when he looked serious. His jaw would tense sometimes when he was in this kind of mood and his eyes became dark. She allowed herself a little sigh before he got close enough to see the exaggerated rise and fall of her chest.

She was playing with fire, she knew. But there was nothing wrong with fire if you kept your distance, let it warm you but not scorch you. And that was what she intended to do. To keep her distance from Ben Oliver—romantically, at least. But it had been so long since she'd felt this alive.

What was the harm in a little crush? To feel her blood pumping and all those endorphins speeding round her system. It was good for her. And no harm ever came from a little bit of daydreaming.

That was all it would ever be. That was all she would allow herself.

It would be enough, because to indulge in more just wasn't a good idea for her—or Jack. She'd felt this way before—worse, even. She'd fallen so totally in love that she'd lost herself completely, had allowed herself to become completely overshadowed. It would happen again if she let it. She couldn't help herself. When she fell, she fell hard, completely.

She took a sideways look at Ben as he joined her and they silently started walking towards the kitchen. Jas and Jack had already disappeared inside and were probably trying to work out how they could raid the biscuit barrel without being rumbled.

He was walking with his head bowed, looking at the ground

in front of his feet, but he must have sensed her looking at him, because he mirrored her and the smallest of smiles crossed his lips. Without warning, another sigh sneaked up and overtook her.

Ben Oliver represented all she'd ever wanted in a man, she could see that now. He was strong and kind, thoughtful and funny—although sometimes without meaning to be, but that just made it all the more charming.

He was all wrong for her, of course.

Or maybe, more to the point, she was all wrong for him. She could picture a new wife for Ben quite clearly in her mind: someone who was capable and strong. A woman who had a quiet confidence, a gentle heart. And when evening came, and it was time to turn out the light, he would reach across and stroke her face with the palm of his hand, look deep into her eyes…

Tiny pinpricks behind her eyes took her by surprise and she was glad they'd reached the back door and she could busy herself removing her coat and hat and putting the kettle on before she had to face him again.

He hadn't said it out loud, but she knew he would do anything to keep his and Jas's life on an even keel. And so it should be. It was just such a pity that the only thing she could bring him were the ups and downs of a rollercoaster life—a life that was way out of control and she was powerless to stop. She didn't wish it on herself, so how could she wish it on him when he'd worked so hard to build a solid foundation for himself and his daughter?

Louise watched Ben as he sat down with the kids at the kitchen table and refereed as they argued about who had had the most cookies. Another sigh. And this one hurt right down to her toes. If only this could be real…

She shook herself and made the tea. There was no point wishing for things that couldn't be, but something about Ben made her feel whole, alive in a way she'd never known. So she was going to hang on to that feeling as long as she could and use this crush, this infatuation—whatever it was—to help her heal.

And, one day, when she was good as new, she wouldn't need to dream about him any more and she'd let the fantasies go and watch them swirl up into the air and blow away like the autumn leaves.

CHAPTER SEVEN

LOUISE had convinced Jack to help her make gingerbread decorations for the Christmas tree. However, she'd overestimated the attention span of an eight-year-old less than a week before Christmas. Once Jack had consumed vast amounts of biscuit dough—mainly while she'd been demonstrating how to use the different shaped cookie cutters—he'd run off. She'd had to tell him off for sliding down the banisters twice already.

Carefully, she removed another tray of golden-brown angels from the oven, replaced them with uncooked stars and shut the oven door. They'd have enough biscuits for ten Christmas trees once they'd finished.

Later this afternoon, once Jack calmed down a little, they'd decorate the tree in the drawing room. She couldn't wait to see his little face when they dimmed the house lights and hit the switch for the twinkling lights. Yes, late afternoon would be best, when the sun was behind the hills and everything was getting gloomy.

In the meantime, she had twelve minutes to kill until the next batch of biscuits was ready. As she scooped the slightly cooled angels off the baking sheet and on to a cooling rack she drifted into one of her top ten daydreams…

It was a balmy summer day. A large picnic blanket was stretched out in the walled garden. Somewhere in the distance children squealed. Her eyes were closed and her head lay on

Ben's lap as he twisted lengths of her hair around his finger, then released them again. Time had slowed, the seconds now hummed out by the bees in the lavender rather than the hands of a clock.

Louise sank into a chair and rested her elbows on the kitchen table. Supporting her chin in her hands, she shut out reality by lowering her lids.

In the daydream, she opened her eyes. He was looking down at her, pure admiration on his face, and she knew he saw into every part of her. It took her breath away. For so long, all she'd seen in men's eyes was a certain wolfish hunger. They admired the packaging, but very few were prepared to take the trouble to unwrap it. And those who did, like Toby, considered the gift inside disposable.

She shook her head. This was supposed to be the bit where Ben leaned in to kiss her, and she was not having it invaded by the likes of Toby. He had no place here in her summer garden.

Just as the imaginary Ben blocked out the sun by leaning forward, leaving her in a cool shadow, better able to see his darkening pupils… Just as she could feel his breath on her skin…

The phone rang. The real phone.

Damn!

Louise snapped her eyes open and she jumped up from the chair. She could let the answering machine get it, but whoever it was would only ring back and interrupt her later. Reluctantly, she grabbed the handset from its cradle on the kitchen counter.

'Hello?'

'Hello, Louise.'

The rich, deep voice was as familiar to her as her own. All thoughts of bees, lavender and sunshine washed from her head on a tidal wave of irritation. 'Toby.'

She wasn't going to ask him how he was; she was past caring, actually. And she certainly didn't need to hear about his cosy new life with twenty-three-year-old Miranda, thank you very much.

Toby said nothing, and she was tempted to put the phone down on him. He'd always done this—made her do the talking, ask the questions, prise information out of him. Well, she wasn't playing his games any more. He obviously had something to tell her or he wouldn't be phoning. He could just spit it out all on his own.

He coughed. Nope, she still wasn't biting. Not even to say, *What do you want?* This time *he* could do all the work, do all the giving instead of the taking.

'Louise?… I wanted to talk to you about Christmas.'

'Talk away.' She leaned against the counter and waited.

'Well, you see… I've been given a freebie, a holiday in Lapland. And I wondered if you'd mind if Jack came with me.'

Louise's stomach went cold. She'd been trying very hard not to think about the fact that Jack was spending Christmas Day and the following week with his father. It would be her first Christmas without him. But Lapland… Jack would be enthralled!

'That's fine with me, Toby. I'll pack warm clothes for him. Are you still coming down on the twenty-fourth to pick him up?'

There was an uncomfortable silence for a few seconds.

'Toby?'

'The flights are booked for the twenty-second.'

Monday? That was a whole three days early! Just like that, the bottom fell out of Louise's Christmas.

'Can't you change it?' she asked, forgetting to hide the panic in her voice.

'Sorry. It's now or never.'

'I… I…'

Toby let out an irritated breath. 'Come on, Louise. Lapland. Jack will love it—and I've missed seeing him for the last month because I've been on location. It will be just Jack and me. Father and son time. He needs it.'

Unfortunately, Toby was right. Jack did need it. He'd missed his dad terribly since he'd left Gloucestershire.

'Just you and Jack? What about…' she wanted to say *her*, but she managed to force her mouth into the right shape '…Miranda?'

There was a sigh on the other end of the line. 'Miranda is… Actually, Miranda's history.'

Her eyebrows rose. Really?

'I miss you, Lulu.' His voice had that soft, gravelly tone that used to turn her insides to mush.

'I'm sorry, but you'll just have to get over it, Toby.'

She shuddered. No way could she ever go back to that life. No matter how far the tabloids thought she'd fallen, or how many celebrity magazines had her at the brink of suicide. She knew in her heart that she was free, happier now than she'd been in more than twenty years.

'Don't be like that, hon. I'm just trying to be friendly.'

It all came sharply into focus. Poor little Miranda probably hadn't realised what hard work a movie star fifteen years her senior would be. And Toby was a movie star who'd grown used to having absolutely everything his own way for most of that time.

Guilt washed over her. That was partly her fault. She'd let him get away with murder, had fooled herself she'd been doing it out of love, when really she'd just been scared he'd see through her glamorous exterior and reject her if she wasn't everything he wanted.

Well, he had. And she'd survived.

No way was Mr Tobias Thornton talking her into being his doormat again! She pulled the phone away from her ear and stared at it, desperate to tell him to go to hell. However, she had to keep the relationship amicable for Jack's sake. It was hard enough for a kid to have to deal with his parents' divorce, let alone hearing the bullet points of every argument in the playground. This wasn't about her; it was about Jack.

'Okay. You can take Jack to Lapland, but I want extra time at Easter.'

Toby blew out a breath. 'Thanks. I'll need to pick him up tomorrow afternoon. We have to leave early Monday morning from Gatwick.'

Disappointment speared through her, harder and deeper than before. 'Fine. See you then.'

She hung up without waiting for any pleasantries and drew in a long steadying breath. Now all she had to do was tell Jack the good news without bursting into tears.

There was a strange car parked slap-bang in front of Whitehaven. Ben noticed it the moment he stepped out of the woods and on to the front lawn. Strange, because it was unknown to him and strange because no one in their right mind would drive such a low-slung sports car in countryside like this. If it rained hard, he'd give the owner five minutes before it stalled in a ford or got stuck in some mud.

He was just wondering if he should check whether Louise was okay when she emerged from the house with Jack in her arms. She was hugging him tight, oblivious to anyone else. A man followed her out of the house, dressed all in black and wearing sunglasses. Ben snorted to himself. They were only days away from the solstice, the shortest day, and there was no crisp afternoon sun, just relentless grey clouds.

The guy removed his glasses and shoved them in a pocket and Ben suddenly recognised him. Weren't most people in films supposed to be shorter and uglier than they looked on screen? Unfortunately, Tobias Thornton was neither. He looked every inch the action hero. He smiled at his ex-wife and kissed her on the cheek. Ben thought he lingered a little too long, but Louise smiled brightly up at him.

Right. There was no use standing here like a lemon. This was family stuff. Private stuff. He might as well go and check on the greenhouses, as he did first every Sunday afternoon.

On reflection, he thought he might have over-pruned the first plant that received his attention in the greenhouse. Seeing Louise and Toby standing there in front of the house had reminded him of all those photos Jas kept shoving under his nose.

It was as if, until that moment, he'd *known* that Louise was Louise Thornton, but the woman in the magazines and the single mother who liked baking had seemed like two very different people. And, suddenly, those two completely separate universes had collided. It had left him reeling. Get a grip, Ben. Time to wake up and smell the coffee.

He spent as long as he could watering and feeding the plants. Then he tidied up the greenhouses and swept the floors. All the while a snapshot of Louise smiling stayed in his head, her lips stretched wide, her teeth showing. He stopped sweeping and rested the broom against the wall.

Suddenly it hit him. That was as far as the smile had gone. Her eyes had had the same hollow look he'd seen in those magazine pictures. She'd been faking it. For Jack.

Ben smiled to himself. The sun was starting to dip low in the sky and he was definitely ready for one of Louise's bottomless cups of tea.

When he reached the kitchen door it was locked. There was no warm cloud of baking smells wafting through the cracks. No light, no noise—nothing. He tried the front of the house but it was the same story. There was no movement in the study or the library. The curved French windows round the side of the house revealed nothing but a darkened drawing room with a bare Christmas tree standing in the corner.

Where was Louise?

Had she gone off somewhere with *him*? Well, if she had, it was none of his business. And, since his work was done here, he might as well go home. Megan was due to drop Jas off in an hour and a half.

He hardly noticed the scenery as he tramped through the woods on the way down to the boathouse. He did, however, spot the loose brick in the boathouse wall as he passed it. Someone might guess the key's hiding place if it was left like that. Slowly, he slid it back into position until everything on the surface looked normal again.

It was only when he had jumped into the dinghy and was about to untie it that he noticed a glow in the arched windows of the boathouse. Someone was in there. And he had a pretty good idea who. What puzzled him was the *why*. Why was she hiding out in a dusty old boathouse when she had a twenty-five-roomed Georgian house standing on the top of the hill?

There was only one way to find out.

He clambered out of the boat again and ran round the back of the structure, up the stone staircase and rapped lightly on the door. 'Louise?'

The silence that followed was so long and so perfect that he started to think he must have got it wrong. Maybe a light had been left on a few days ago…but he hadn't noticed it when he'd arrived. His fingers made contact with the door handle.

A weary voice came from beyond the door. 'Go away.'

A grim smile pressed his lips together. No, his first instinct had been right. She was hiding out.

He pressed down on the handle and pushed the old door open. Everything was still inside. She didn't move, not even to look at him, and at first he was too distracted by the transformation of the once dingy little room to work out where she was sitting. The inside of the boathouse now looked like the inside of a New England cabin. When had all this happened?

The cracking varnish on the tongue and groove walls was gone, sanded back and covered in off-white paint. The fireplace was still there, along with the desk and cane furniture, but something had happened to them too—everything was clean and cosy-looking. Checked fabric in blue and white covered the chair cushions and a paraffin lantern stood on the desk, adding to the glow from the fire.

A movement caught his eye and he twisted his head to find Louise, sitting cross-legged on something that looked like a cross between an old iron bedstead and a sofa, staring into the fire. She turned to look at him, her face pale and heavy. She didn't need to speak. Every molecule of her body was repeating her earlier request.

Go away.

He wasn't normally the kind of guy to barge in where he wasn't invited but, instead of turning around and walking out of the door, he walked over to the opposite end of the sofa thing and sat down, hoping his trousers weren't going to leave mud on the patchwork quilt that covered it.

'What's up?'

Louise returned to staring into the orange flames writhing in the grate. 'Christmas is cancelled,' she said flatly.

He shifted so he was a little more comfortable, avoiding the multitude of different-sized cushions that were scattered everywhere. His gaze too was drawn to the fire. 'That explains the tree, then.'

Louise made a noise that could roughly be interpreted as a question, so he pressed on.

'The one in your drawing room—standing there naked as the day it was born.'

Another noise, one that sounded suspiciously as if she didn't want to find that funny. 'There didn't seem to be much point in decorating it now. Jack's gone to Lapland.'

'Lapland?'

She turned those burning eyes on him. 'Father Christmas? Reindeer? Who can compete with that?'

He shrugged. 'Think yourself lucky. At least Lapland is worth being deserted for. All I'm competing with is a few days in the Cotswolds with Mum and the suave new boyfriend.'

Okay, that got a proper snuffling sound that could almost be interpreted as a chuckle.

'You win, Ben. Your Christmas stinks more than mine. Pull up a chair and join the pity party.' She gave him a long look, taking in his relaxed position on the opposite end of the sofa-bed thingy. 'Not one to stand on ceremony, are you?'

He grinned at her. 'Nope. So…how does one throw a pity party at Christmas? Is it the same as an ordinary pity party or is there extra tinsel?'

A loud and unexpected laugh burst from Louise. Very soon there were tears in her eyes. She wiped them away with the side of one hand. 'You rat, Ben Oliver! You've just ruined the only social event on my calendar for the next two weeks. I'm going to have to reschedule… Will the twenty-fifth suit you?'

It was good to see her smile. He knew from experience just how lonely a childless Christmas could be—and the first one was always the killer.

'This place looks nice,' he said, standing up and walking around the room to inspect it further.

Louise nodded, pulling her knees into her chest and tucking the cream, red and blue quilt over her legs. 'It's not bad, is it? I've even had the windows draught-proofed.' She glanced around the room and then her eyes became glassy. 'I'm tempted just to camp out here for the rest of the festive season. The house is just so…it's too…you know.'

He nodded. The bare Christmas tree had said it all.

He took a deep breath and walked over to her, holding out a hand. She frowned at him and pulled the quilt more tightly around herself.

'Come on.' He wiggled his fingers. 'I've got a lamb casserole that will feed about twenty ready to heat up at home. Come for dinner.'

She didn't move. 'Won't Jas mind?'

'Mind? She'll have so many invitations to go to tea after a visit from you that I'll hardly see her until she's twelve. I'll even let you be miserable at my house, if you really want.'

Louise smiled and shook her head. 'No, you wouldn't.'

He stuffed the hand he'd been holding out in his jacket pocket. 'Don't you believe me?'

'To quote a man I know: "Nope". In my experience, people say they want you to be *real*, but only as long as it involves living up to their expectations of you at the same time.' She wrinkled her nose. 'I learned a long time ago that disappointing them costs.'

He held out his hand again. 'Well, I already know how grumpy you can be, so I wouldn't mind at all if you disappointed me on that front.'

Despite herself, she smiled at him, the firelight reflected in her eyes. 'You're not going to give up, are you?' She lifted her arm, placed her long, slim fingers in his and pushed the quilt aside.

They both smiled as they anticipated his response.

'Nope.'

His hand closed around hers, slender and warm, and he pulled her up to stand. Without her shoes, she seemed smaller and he stared down into her face. The fire crackled and the light of the paraffin lamp flickered and danced. He realised that neither of them had taken a breath since he'd taken hold of her hand.

Louise dropped her head, letting her hair fall over her face, and disentangled her fingers from his. 'I think you're my guardian angel, Ben Oliver.'

He liked it when she said his whole name like that. Somehow it made it seem more intimate rather than more formal. She walked over to a hat stand by the door and pulled her coat off it. While she did up her buttons, she risked another look at him. 'You always seem to be there when I need someone to make me think straight.'

He pretended not to be touched as he turned off the lamp and ushered her out of the door. And he tried very hard not to be stupidly pleased at being what Louise Thornton needed.

Louise locked the door and hid the key in its usual hole and they walked the short distance down to the jetty in silence. He was still mulling it over, standing in the boat with the rope in his hand, ready to cast off, when Louise stepped into the boat beside him and, as she brushed past him to sit down in the stern, she stopped. He felt her breath warm on his face as she leaned close, just for a second or so, and the soft skin of her lips met his cheek.

He whipped his head round to look at her, but she was already sitting on the low wooden bench looking up at him. 'Thank you, Ben.'

A realisation hit him with as much force as the cold waves buffeting the little boat. He *wanted* to be what she needed. And he wanted to *keep* being what she needed. The only thing was, he had no idea if it was a role he could ever play. She didn't need a man in her life right now. What she really needed was a friend. He fired up the motor and untied the boat before heading off across the choppy water.

A friend. Now, that was a role he could manage.

The house seemed empty without Jack in it. Maybe moving to the country had been a mistake. If she'd been staying in London, she could have lost herself in the last-minute Christmas Eve panic in Oxford Street. It might have even been fun to try and spot the most harried male shopper with a look of desperation in his eyes.

Louise stopped by a shallow pool surrounded by bamboo. A copper statue of a Chinese Buddha, covered in verdigris, stared back at her. He was the closest thing to a human being she'd seen since Sunday evening. The statue stared past her, looking serenely through the trees to the river below, and she decided he probably wasn't the life and soul of the party, anyway, and moved on.

She only entered the house to collect a few things and make a flask of tea. In the last few days she'd spent a lot of time at the boathouse, preferring the cosy little space to the multitude of echoes that seemed to have appeared around Whitehaven.

Tonight, she was going to sleep in the boathouse, tucked up under both the duvet and the quilt, with the fire and a good book for company. Hopefully, Santa wouldn't discover her hiding place, set between the beach and the woods, and he'd fly straight past.

She pottered around the house, wandering from the kitchen to her bedroom and back again, picking up the few things she'd need. All the while, she distracted herself with her favourite Christmas daydream. At least in her imagination she could keep the loneliness at bay.

The fire was glowing and coloured fairy lights twinkled on a huge blue spruce in the bay window of a cosy cottage sitting room. It was early in the morning, the sky a deep indigo, and Jas and Jack were fighting good-naturedly about who was going to hand out the presents. She and Ben were laughing and eventually they let the kids get on with it, just to keep them quiet.

Then, amidst the sounds of giggling children and wrapping paper being ripped, Ben drew her to one side and presented her with a silver box with a delicate ribbon of white velvet tied round it. She stopped and smiled at him, a look that said 'you shouldn't have' glowing in her eyes.

Then she gave in and tugged the wrappings free with as much abandon as the children had. Before she opened the box, she bit her lip and looked at him again. Then she prised open the lid to reveal…

This was the bit where she always got stuck. What could be in the box? She didn't want fancy jewellery and body lotion and stuff for the bath was just a bit too *blah*.

Louise stood from where she was, putting a change of warm clothes into a holdall, and stared in her bedroom mirror. You're losing it, girl. Seriously. Hasn't this fantasising about the gardener gone just a little bit too far?

It had. She knew it had. But it was warm and comforting—like hot chocolate for the soul—and heaven knew she needed a bit of comfort these days. She gave herself a cheeky smile in the mirror. *And it's one hundred per cent calorie-free too!*

Her reflection gave her a look that said, *Yeah, right.* She turned her back on it, zipped up the holdall and slung it over her shoulder. The clock on the mantelpiece showed it was three o'clock. She needed to get a move on. No way was she trudging along the rough paths coated with soggy leaves in the dark.

Louise took her time wandering back to the boathouse. There was something hauntingly beautiful about her wild garden in winter. However, when she was only minutes away from her destination, it began to rain—hard, stinging drops with a hint of ice—and she decided to hurry.

She ran up the stairs to the upper level of the boathouse, only pausing to retrieve the key from its hiding place, and burst into her cosy upper room, only to stop in her tracks, leaving the door wide open and a malicious draught rushing in behind her.

What…?

She couldn't quite believe her eyes. What had happened to her sanctuary while she'd been gone?

On almost every available surface there were candles—big, thick, tall ones, the sort you'd find in churches—some balanced on saucers from the old china picnic set she'd rescued from the damp. The fire was burning bright, crackling with delight at the fresh logs it was hungrily devouring. There was holly and ivy on the mantle and, in the corner, near one of the windows…

Louise laughed out loud. How could this be?

A Christmas tree? Not a huge one, but at least five feet high, bare except for a silver star on top. She walked over to it and spotted a box of decorations sitting on the floor, waiting to be hung. Red, purple and silver shiny baubles would look amazing in the candlelight. She picked one out of the box and fingered it gently.

How…? Who…?

An outboard motor sputtered to life outside and suddenly all her questions were answered. She ran out on to the balcony and leaned over. 'Ben!'

The little wooden dinghy was already moving away from the jetty and he looked up at her, a sheepish smile on his face. He waved and yelled something back, but his words were snatched away by the billowing wind.

Her natural response would have been to stand there and shake her head in disbelief, but the rain—which was rapidly solidifying into sleet—was bombarding her top to toe. She pushed her wet hair out of her face, ran back inside and closed all the doors.

Not knowing what else to do, she sat cross-legged in front of the fire, staring at the patterns on the blue and white tile inserts until they danced in front of her eyes. Was this guy for real? No one had ever gone out of their way to do something so special for her before. Her father would have if he'd been able to, but he'd always been so fragile, and it had been her job to look after the others, to cheer them up and keep them strong when things had got tough.

Toby had been good with show-stopping gifts—diamonds, cars, even a holiday villa in Majorca once—but none of those things measured up to this.

Louise stood up and placed a hand over her mouth.

Oh, this was dangerous. All at once, she saw the folly of her whole 'daydreaming is safe' plan. It was backfiring spectacularly. Her mind now revolved around Ben Oliver, her thoughts constantly drifting towards him at odd moments throughout the day. And now her brain was stuck in the habit, it was starting to clamour for more—more than just fantasies. Especially when he did things like this. She was aching for all the *moments* she'd rehearsed in her head to become real.

Heaven help her.

So much for standing on her own two feet and never letting a man overshadow her again. Ben Oliver was an addictive substance and she was hooked. And the last thing she wanted was to lose herself again, not when she'd come so far. In the last few months she'd started to feel less like Toby's wife and more like someone else. It would be so easy to fall into the role of the woman who adored Ben Oliver, and nothing else.

Dangerous.

She looked around the room. As a declaration of independence, she ought to just pack it all up and leave it outside the door, but she couldn't bring herself to do that. If she did, the boathouse would seem as stripped and hollow as the mansion sitting on the hill, and she'd come here to escape that.

The decorations piled in the cardboard box twinkled, begging her to let them fulfil their purpose, and she obliged them, hanging each one with care from the soft pine needles, hoping that the repetitive action would lull her into a trance.

When she'd finished, she pulled the patchwork quilt off the day-bed, draped it around her shoulders and sat on the floor in front of the fire, her back supported by one of the wicker chairs. In the silence, all she could hear was the sound of her own breathing and the happy licking of the flames. She hadn't been sitting there more than a few minutes when there was a knock at the door.

She stared at it.

Whoever it was—and let's face it, she'd win no prizes for guessing who—knocked again. Slowly, Louise rose to her feet, keeping the quilt wrapped tightly around her, and walked over to open it. Her heart jumped as if it were on a trampoline when she saw him standing there, his wet hair plastered to his face, a large brown paper bag in one hand and a rucksack in the other.

'Ben.'

Nice, she thought. Eloquent.

'Louise.'

At least they both seemed to be afflicted by the same disease.

He brandished the paper bag. 'Can I come in?'

She stepped back to let him pass and he handed her the paper bag, which was warm and smelled of exotic spices. He moved past her and placed the rucksack on the floor.

'I ought not to let you in, really. Seeing as you've already indulged in a spot of breaking and entering today.' She kept her voice deliberately flat and emotionless.

He stopped halfway through struggling off his green waxed coat. 'You don't like it? Oh, Louise! I'm so sorry. I was just trying to…'

How could she be cross with this wonderful, sweet man? She grabbed the back of his coat with one hand and tugged at it, smiling. 'You succeeded.'

The relief on his face was palpable. 'Thank goodness for that.

I have food in here and I didn't want to have to sail it back across the river and eat it cold.'

She peered in the top of the brown bag. 'Curry? That's not very traditional.'

Ben took the bag from her and began unpacking its contents on to the low coffee table in the centre of the room. 'Nonsense. I'm sure I read somewhere that Chicken Tikka Masala has now overtaken traditional Sunday roast as the nation's favourite dish.'

Louise reached for the old picnic set and pulled out a couple of plates and some cutlery, grateful she'd given it all a thorough wash yesterday. Pretty soon they were sitting in the wicker chairs, feasting on a selection of different curries, pilau rice and naan breads. She broke a crunchy onion bhaji apart with her fingers and dipped it in some mango chutney before popping it in her mouth.

While she ate her bhaji, she looked at Ben, who was absorbed in his meal. Finally, when he glanced in her direction, he froze. 'What?'

How did she say how much this all meant to her? There just weren't enough words, so she settled for simple and elegant. 'Thank you, Ben.'

The hesitation in his eyes turned to warmth.

'Why did you… I mean…why… all this?'

He put his plate down and looked at her long and hard. 'I reckoned you needed some cheering up. I remember how awful it was my first Christmas without Jas.' He gave a half-grin. 'Put it down to me being a single dad with too much time on his hands. Jas is away, my parents live in Spain now and my sister has gone to visit her in-laws. I can't even rely on work to be my saviour—no one wants any gardening done at this time of year.'

Oh, that just sounded too good to be true. Too nice.

'Yes, but you didn't have to do all *this*.' A horrible nagging thought whispered in the back of her mind: nobody does anything for entirely altruistic reasons. He must want *something*. 'I'm not sleeping with you,' she blurted out.

Oh, Lord! Had she really just said that? Her cheeks flamed and burned.

Ben's grin turned to stone and he stood up and practically threw his naan bread down on the table. 'If that's what you think, I'd better leave.'

Instantly, she was on her feet. 'No! I'm so sorry! I don't know what made me say that. After you've been so kind…' At that moment, she hated herself more than she'd ever done for wearing fake smiles in front of the paparazzi and pretending her life with Toby was a glorious dream.

Ben was pulling his coat on, his back to her. She laid a hand on the still-wet sleeve, tears blurring her vision. 'Please, Ben! It's just…' Oh, hell. Her throat closed up and she couldn't hide the emotion in her voice. 'Nobody ever does something for me without wanting something—without wanting *too much*—back. I'm just not used to this.'

He turned to face her, his expression softening slightly. 'Really? No one?'

She shook her head, too ashamed to speak any more. How did you tell a man like him that nobody had ever thought enough of you to make that kind of effort? She always had to earn people's love—by being the one who gave and gave and gave. Even Toby had only kept around as long as he had because it was good for his image, nothing more. And her younger brothers and sisters had grown up thinking she never needed anything, and they had their own lives now. It was their turn to shine. She couldn't burden them with all her problems.

She turned away from him and sank down into the nearest chair, hiding her face in her hands. 'Oh, God. I'm such a mess.'

Ben wasn't sure what to do. Louise had the ability to make his head swim, to prompt him into doing outrageous things that the sensible side of his brain knew he shouldn't be doing. He looked round at the holly, the candles, the stupid tree. It was all too much.

Then he did a double-take and looked at the tree again. It was dripping with baubles. He'd abandoned the box when he'd seen Louise emerge from the woods, deciding it was best not to be standing there like a prize banana when she walked in. But, while he'd been away getting the curry, she'd decorated the *stupid* tree. Hope flared within him.

Louise was sitting, all curled in on herself, staring at the floor. With startling clarity he realised she was one of those people who didn't know how to accept things. She gave of herself constantly—any fool could see that if they looked hard enough—but she'd forgotten that giving was only half of the equation. Or perhaps she'd never known.

He'd pieced enough together from their chats over the last couple of months to realise that she'd had it tough growing up. She'd always had to be the responsible one, the one who carried everyone else. No wonder she didn't know how to receive what had been freely given. And her life since her childhood hadn't helped. Every good deed came with a web of strings attached.

He pulled his coat off and hung it on the hat stand. Louise turned round and stared at him, her mouth gaping in shock.

She hadn't expected him to stay. Not even after her heartfelt apology. Why did she think so little of herself?

He refused to answer the questions written all over her face with words. Instead, he walked calmly over to the chair he'd just vacated, sat down and crossed one leg over the other, resting his ankle on the other knee. She arranged her features into a more neutral expression and relaxed back into her chair, but her hands stayed tightly clasped in her lap.

'I don't know about you,' he said, 'but I could do with some dessert.'

Louise's mouth formed a circle of surprise. 'Dessert?'

He smiled to himself and reached down into the rucksack he'd dropped by the chair earlier and pulled out a bottle of red wine. Nothing extravagant. Just a bottle of supermarket Cabernet.

In one smooth second, Louise unclenched. She smiled at him,

started to speak and then just shook her head. She rose, extracted a couple of teacups from Laura's picnic set and plonked them on the coffee table. Thankfully, the bottle had a screw cap, because he doubted the picnic set came complete with corkscrew. After pouring a generous amount of wine into each cup, he handed one to her.

'A toast—to Christmas,' he said as they cheerfully clinked teacups.

Louise just laughed. 'Something weird is happening here… To Christmas!'

Ben took a sip of the warm, rich wine and kept his thoughts to himself. He knew exactly why he'd phrased the toast that way. Christmas was about giving—and receiving. That weird feeling Louise didn't recognise? That was the joy of letting someone show you how much they cared. If there was one thing he could give as a present this Christmas, it would be to show her that not all gifts had hidden traps, and that receiving them could be a pleasure.

She needed a friend. A true friend. And that was the sort of gift a *friend* could give safely.

As they worked their way through the bottle of wine, a tiny teacup at a time, they retreated to the sofa thing that was piled high with cushions. Even though it was on the opposite wall to the fire, the boathouse's upper room was small enough for them to get all the benefits of its warmth. They talked about anything and everything before falling into a comfortable silence. The candles flickered, the sun set and the temperature outside began to drop.

He was just starting to think that it was about time to get going when Louise suddenly said, 'I don't think I know who I am any more.'

Uh-oh. Good deeds, practical gestures, he was good at. Touchy-feely, girl-type conversations were not his forte. Thankfully, Louise seemed happy for him just to listen.

'The curse of being an ex-WAG,' she said, turning to smile at him weakly.

What was a WAG, anyway? He'd never been exactly sure what the term meant.

'Short for "Wives And Girlfriends",' she added, obviously able to read the look of confusion on his face. 'Probably more accurately used to describe the other halves of famous sportsmen, but it seems to fit me too. WAGS hunt in packs, love shopping and having their photographs taken and—above all—they love *bling*.'

'You're not a WAG!' he said, rather too quickly, forgetting he didn't know what to say in situations like this.

'Well, not any more—having divorced Toby.'

Ben shook his head, frowning. He couldn't see how that definition could ever have applied to Louise. She hated having her photograph taken! He was about to say so, but she pre-empted him again.

'Oh, I was at the start,' she said. 'I embraced it wholeheartedly—the parties, the magazine covers, the *bling*.' She chuckled to herself.

Didn't she realise what a rare quality that was—to be able to laugh at oneself?

'But, eventually, it grew old. I was famous because of him, because I was Tobias Thornton's wife, not because of anything I had done.'

He shifted to face her a little more. 'I thought you were a model when you met him.'

She nodded and looked into her teacup of red wine. 'I was. And we made it work at first. But it was hard to keep a marriage going when we spent weeks at a time on different continents. And then Jack came along and it seemed only right to give him a home and some structure…'

Why was she punishing herself for that? That was Louise all over—she'd thought of her family first instead of selfishly pursuing what she wanted.

She was lost in a daydream, staring at the rain lashing against the windows. There was a wistful expression on her face, as if she was remembering something or wishing for something she couldn't have.

Maybe it was time Louise did something for herself, got something for herself. Not out of selfishness, but because she deserved it. He rubbed his chin with his thumb. Now all he had to do was to discover what she wanted.

Pulled out of her daydream by some unknown thought, she turned her head, and the look she gave him sent a shiver up his spine.

Surely not.

Her pupils were large and dark, and there was such a heat in her eyes. He'd received that kind of look before from women, but he'd never expected to receive it from her. Surely, she didn't want… him?

His heart rate tripled.

Uh-oh. That put Being What Louise Needed on a whole new level.

CHAPTER EIGHT

WHAT she really needed, Louise thought, was to stop looking at Ben as if he were a Christmas present she wanted to unwrap. It was easier said than done.

The different-sized baubles on the Christmas tree twinkled, reflecting the light from the candles placed all around the room. This wasn't her festive daydream, starring Ben, but it was close. There was the tree, the fire, the sense that someone had thought about her for a change…

Actually, reality was better. The meal, the wine, the companionship had been a much sweeter present than the anonymous gift in the silver box in her fantasies. But, whatever was missing, whatever had changed from her daydreams, one thing remained the same. Ben. It all revolved around him.

The other thing she needed to do was to stop babbling on about losing herself. But the babbling was helping keep a whole other set of urges at bay, so it would do nicely for now. She folded her hands in her lap and smiled at him. 'So…that's what I am. A WAG. A woman who defined herself by her husband and is now adrift with no direction in her life, no purpose.'

Ben began to disagree, but she was on a roll, so she just kept going. 'I've got plenty of money, so I don't need to work, but I do need to do more than just look after Jack and—' she waved a hand to indicate the freshly refurbished room '—decorate. But, apart from knowing how to pout for the camera, I have no qualifications. I didn't even finish school.'

There. That would scare him off. He'd have to believe she was a bimbo now. Only, when she dared to look at him, he didn't seem convinced. She would just have to try harder.

'Oh, I tried all sorts of jobs while I was married to Toby. He was always encouraging me to do some of the things his friends' wives were up to. I did the whole charity circuit, then I tried a bit of television presenting on a fashion show—and was supremely bad at it.' She let out an empty little laugh and Ben fidgeted on the other end of the day bed. 'They never asked me back. I even designed my own range of sunglasses.'

She looked at Ben and waited for a reaction. He shrugged, as if to say, *So what?*

Yeah, so what? That was what the buying public had thought too. It had been an utter flop.

She took a breath, searching for another stupid exploit to fill the silence with. Nothing came. What a waste. She was thirty-one years old and this was the sum total of what she'd achieved in her life. It was pathetic.

'Why didn't you finish school?'

She looked at Ben, expecting to see that same superior look that many people gave her when they found out that little bit of information. Everyone knew that models were thick, and wasn't she a glowing representative of the stereotype?

'Louise? What happened?'

He genuinely wanted to know. She frowned and looked away. He might just be the first person to ask why.

'Dad's illness got worse when I was about fifteen. Some days he needed me at home. Of course, there were home helps and health visitors, but the area where we lived was poor and the local services were overstretched. On his bad days, it wouldn't have done any good to go to school, because I wouldn't have been able to concentrate anyway.'

Ben reached over and simply took her hand. That one gesture was enough to roughen her voice and moisten her eyes again. She ought to stop, but she couldn't. She'd needed to say all of this for such a long time.

'In my last year of school, when I should have been taking my GCSEs, he deteriorated even further. I'd missed so much by then that I didn't even want to go in. And some of the girls were horrible…you know how girls can be. But Dad was in so much pain, he became angry and difficult sometimes and took his frustration out on me—not physically—just verbally. But I understood, really I did.'

Ben's thumb gently stroked the back of her hand and she felt something hard inside herself crumple. More tears flowed and she pulled her hand away to mop them up with a tissue. Things were getting far too maudlin. It was time to brighten the story up.

'Anyway, Cinderella got her happy ending,' she said brightly. 'Just before my seventeenth birthday I was spotted by a scout from a modelling agency and the rest, as they say, is history.'

He held a box of tissues out to her and she took another one. 'What happened to the rest of your family?'

The noise she made using the tissue was truly disgusting. 'Well, my wages helped buy a new house, pay for university fees and things like that. Sarah, the next eldest after me, is a lawyer now and she emigrated to Australia five years ago. The rest have all gone out to visit her this year, but I didn't want to be away from Jack for that long. Billy and Charlotte still live in London—he manages a restaurant, she's a hairdresser. And Charlie, the youngest, is just finishing university. He wants to be an actor.' She rolled her eyes. 'There's no telling some people.'

Somehow, her hand was back in Ben's and he was stroking it again.

'What about your dad?'

Drat! Why did this man have to be so good at reading between the lines?

'He died less than a year after I started modelling.' She looked into Ben's eyes, desperate in this moment for someone else to understand what she'd done. 'I let him down,' she whispered. 'I should have been there.'

And then she started crying, really crying. None of that sniffing nonsense she'd been doing up until now. Big, fat tears rolled down her cheeks. She tried to talk, but her vocal cords had gone on strike.

Gently, slowly, so she wasn't even sure how they'd got there, a pair of strong arms wrapped around her. Time seemed to slow as she sobbed against his chest, but it could only have been a few minutes.

'I've kind of blown your plan for a Merry Christmas right out of the water, haven't I?' she said, thinking she should pull away but doing nothing about it. 'But thank you for trying. I'm not sure there was ever much hope for a woman who doesn't know who to be any more.'

Ben shifted beneath her. His hands came up to cradle her face and he made her look at him.

No one had ever looked at her that way before, as if she were delicate, precious. Her heart, which had been shrivelled like one of the dates her Auntie June used to serve up on Boxing Day, swelled.

His voice was low and scratchy. 'Louise, you are… I…'

For a man who always knew what to say, he was a little short on words at the moment. That couldn't be a good thing. Ben's features clouded and she could tell he was struggling.

Say something, she shouted in her head. *Tell me! Tell me who you think I am! I need to know!*

He was no longer looking at her, but was staring at a piece of blank wall behind her, his mind whirring and, when he looked back at her, her heart stood still for a beat. In his eyes was a renewed sense of purpose and she knew he had something to say. She waited. And Ben just looked at her as if there weren't adequate words to communicate what he was thinking. Oh, how she wished he would try.

His gaze dropped to her lips and she felt them part slightly and her breath catch.

He was going to kiss her. The world started to somersault.

Slowly, he bent his head to meet hers, giving her ample time to move away if she wanted to. But, despite all her ground rules about keeping things 'safe', about keeping things locked away in her daydreams, Louise found she didn't want to move. She wanted him to come towards her. She wanted to taste him, an experience her daydreams had never been able to provide.

The touch of his mouth on hers was exquisitely tender, soft as a whisper. She closed her eyes and gave up all hope of keeping fantasy and reality separate.

Oh, this was better than she'd ever imagined. As Ben kissed her again, still with the same soul-wrenching gentleness, the nerve-endings in her lips burst into life. He moved his hands from her face, ran them through her hair and pulled her closer to him as he fell back against the pile of cushions.

Louise followed him gladly, relishing the fact that she was in total control. Now, instead of *being* kissed, *she* kissed. Ben liked it—she could tell from the low sound he made in the back of his throat.

They kissed each other sweetly, slowly, as if time had stopped for them and all that existed was this moment. After a while, the intensity of their kisses deepened. His lips sought her neck, her jaw line, her earlobe, and Louise began to tingle all over.

She wanted to lose herself in this feeling. Of being desired. Of being feminine. And of being powerful. It was as if she'd entered a realm where she was who she'd always wanted to be, and she wasn't prepared to relinquish that feeling easily.

Rolling over, she pulled him on top of her, giving her hands access to the strong, broad muscles of his back. Ben responded by running a hand down the side of her torso, skimming the curve of her waist. The air between them crackled and popped like the logs on the fire.

Hadn't she said something tonight along the lines of not

knowing what she wanted? Well, she had no problem pinpointing that now—it was all blazingly clear. She wanted Ben. All of him. Right here. Right now.

Taking a deep breath, she wiggled her hands between their bodies and fiddled with the top button of his shirt. A shiver of nerves ran through her.

There had been nobody else but Toby—and he'd grazed in other pastures. What if she wasn't any good? What if she disappointed him? What if this all didn't live up to the fairy tale in her head? For years, Toby had looked at her with a familiar apathy, and she couldn't bear the thought of seeing the same deadness in Ben's eyes in the morning. She was just going to have to pull out all the stops.

Ben, who had been trailing kisses from her collarbone to just below her ear, went still. Her heart began to pound. Ben looked as if he wanted to stop and say something but just couldn't control himself. He kissed her again—hot and sweet and deep enough to make her toes burn.

She trembled as she tried to find a second button on his shirt, her fingers clumsy in the haze of her desire. Ben dragged his lips from hers and his hand closed over her fingers, which were still fiddling fruitlessly with the button.

'We don't need to rush into this,' he whispered.

She knew what he was trying to do. He was trying to be the perfect gentleman, to give her an out. Her gaze locked with his. 'Perhaps we do.'

Once again, he held her face in his hands and, this time, he delivered the sweetest kiss yet. She wiggled her fingers under his and succeeded in popping the button out of its hole. He gripped her hands more tightly.

'Really, Louise. You don't need someone taking advantage of you when you're feeling vulnerable. Maybe this isn't the right time to make this kind of decision.'

He traced the line of her jaw with his thumb and, although his eyes dropped to look at her mouth once again, he didn't kiss her.

'Why can't I decide what I need?' Even in her own ears her voice didn't sound one hundred per cent convincing. But she didn't want to give up yet. Moments like this were like Christmas itself—fleeting, magical. The day after tomorrow the glitter and the wonder would be gone and life would return to being grey and cold and ever so slightly emptier than before.

A slow, gentle smile crept across Ben's face and she couldn't help but smile back as his eyes glittered with fierce intensity.

'Trust me,' he said. 'We don't need to rush. I'm not going anywhere.'

Louise let out a shaky breath. It was very hard to believe that any of this could survive the night and live beyond the dawn. Her eyes must have betrayed her, because he lowered his head and kissed her again.

Carefully, he shifted until he was lying behind her and she was spooned up against him, her head resting on his arm. He pulled the quilt over the pair of them and they lay in the silence, staring into the fire and drawing strength and warmth from where their bodies made contact.

Louise's eyelids flickered. Her head was filled with crackling fires, spiced wine and silver boxes wrapped with ribbons. She yawned and stretched one arm. That was the best night's sleep she'd had since…

She wasn't alone.

Foggily, she tried to decipher what her senses were telling her. There was a warm body wrapped around her, breathing rhythmically…a strange bed…and a *Christmas tree* in her room?

The Christmas tree!

Her eyelids pinged the rest of the way open and, suddenly, she was very much awake. That warm body tangled with hers belonged to Ben Oliver. She didn't dare move, just in case it was all just another delicious dream.

Slowly, she made herself relax back against him. He

mumbled something in his sleep—nonsense—and hugged her tighter. She smiled.

This was what contentment felt like. She'd forgotten its taste, its flavour.

Her eyes scanned the room once again, this time taking in the details. The fire was out, as were quite a few of the candles, but even with the flickering yellow glow from the few that were left, there was an odd silvery-blue light bathing the room.

Mind you, she'd never been in the boathouse this early in the morning before and she had no idea what time it was. Perhaps this was the colour of dawn down here so close to the river.

No, that wasn't it. Gut instinct told her to go and look out of the window. She dropped one leg over the edge of the day bed and started to move, but Ben grumbled again and pulled her back, nuzzling into the side of her neck.

Half-asleep, he was adorable, but whether he'd feel the same way when he was fully conscious was another matter. She'd humiliated herself last night and the atmosphere between them was bound to be awkward. Things often looked different in the cold light of day. And, thinking about cold light, her curiosity got the better of her and she wriggled out of his arms, wrapping the patchwork quilt around her and leaving him covered with the goose down duvet.

As she stood, and could see out of the window, she gasped. Even a tug at the trailing quilt couldn't stop her running to the door, flinging it wide and walking out on to the balcony.

Snow.

Fresh and white and everywhere. It weighed down the bare branches of the young trees and topped the large stones on the beach so they looked like giant cupcakes. It seemed as if the whole world was buried under a blanket of purity, the past forgotten, everything new.

She twirled around in amazement, taking it all in, then reached for the layer of snow, only an inch deep, that topped the balcony railing. The icy crystals crunched under the weight of her fingertips.

A floorboard creaked behind her and once again she was wrapped up in Ben Oliver. He'd brought the duvet with him and he folded it over them both. She held her breath. She'd thought that maybe he'd been giving her the brush-off last night, but the way he was holding her now, as if he wanted to seal their bodies together, laid those fears to rest. He rested his chin on her shoulder so his head was right next to hers and kissed her cheek near her ear.

'Merry Christmas, Louise.'

She twisted her head to look at him, her eyebrows raised. She'd been so caught up in the magic of last night, the beauty of this morning, that she'd completely forgotten that it was Christmas Day.

'Merry Christmas,' she whispered back, suddenly feeling very shy. But, as she went to shake her fringe in front of her eyes, he stopped her with a gentle hand.

'Don't do that,' he said, moving so they were now facing each other.

She wasn't foolish enough to say, *Do what?* After glancing away for a second, she tilted her chin up and met his gaze.

'That's better.'

He smiled and, just like that, any residual awkwardness she'd been feeling evaporated. There was such warmth and light in his eyes, so many possibilities, that she felt an answering smile spread over her own face. So they stood there like that for goodness knew how long, grinning stupidly at each other, saying nothing and everything.

Then his eyes sobered and began to communicate all sorts of other things. Louise didn't wait for him this time. There wasn't much of a difference in their heights, and she reached up behind his neck and pulled him closer, lifting her heels off the floor just slightly.

Kissing Ben Oliver on a snow-dusted balcony on Christmas morning had to be one of the most romantic things she'd ever done. Not only were the kisses perfect, but the crisp cold air on her cheeks and the chill in her toes only seemed to increase the heat spreading from her core. She felt as if she was glowing from the inside out, so much so that shivers rippled through her.

Ben pulled away, just enough to focus on each other without going cross-eyed, and tucked the quilt tighter around her.

'How do you feel about cold curry for breakfast?'

She grinned. 'My absolute favourite.'

And, as he playfully pulled her back inside the boathouse, she took one last look at the picture-perfect scene outside. The river reflected the colour of the iron sky perfectly and smoke puffed from the chimneys in the village across the river. As far as the eye could see, the rolling hills were bleached and frosted like the icing on a giant Christmas cake.

It didn't matter to Louise if winter had stolen all the shades and tones and left everything monochrome. To her, this morning, life was very much in Technicolor.

Ben ran up to his bedroom, slammed the door open and stripped all his clothes off in under a minute. The last sock still hadn't hit the floor when he'd run into his bathroom and jumped in the shower.

He felt like a man possessed. Like a man with too much adrenaline coursing through his system, who was about to spontaneously combust. Realising he had just started to wash himself with conditioner, he forced himself to stand still and take a few deep breaths.

No good. He still felt like whooping aloud, or running down the street and knocking on every door just to tell them he'd kissed the most astounding, marvellous, complicated woman in the world and, once he was clean and changed, he was going to go back and do it again.

He yelled as shampoo got in his eye.

Slow down!

This time he was more successful. He managed to rest one hand against the tiled shower wall and watch the rise and fall of his chest slow a little. Relax. You can do it.

He finished his shower in a speed that could be classified more as 'brisk efficiency' than 'mania', cleaned his teeth and wandered back into the bedroom, whistling, a towel slung round his hips.

What time was it? He checked the digital alarm clock on his bedside table. Ten.

That meant he'd been gone about forty-five minutes. And it would probably be another hour until he saw her again.

Without really paying attention to what he was rummaging for in his chest of drawers, he pulled out clean clothes and got dressed. One last look in the mirror. He ran his hand through his wet hair, then stilled. Was this what Louise saw? A thirty-six-year old with dark hair and brown eyes? That description could probably fit hundreds of thousands of men up and down the country. Apart from the insane grin he just couldn't wipe away completely, he was just an ordinary guy.

Okay, he wasn't desperately bad-looking, but he'd be kidding himself if he thought he could compete with the men in Louise's world. A world in which he clearly didn't belong.

But Louise isn't with one of them, a little voice whispered gleefully in his ear. *She's with you. She kissed you. Heck, she even wanted to make love with you.*

At that point he told his male pride to get a grip.

Even so, the unquenchable grin widened.

He grabbed his watch, fastened it on his wrist and jumped down the stairs only two at a time. But when he got downstairs he couldn't find his keys. He never lost his keys. He searched the pockets of his jacket, which he found on the floor rather than on its usual hook. Nothing. Rather than dropping it again, he pulled it on.

A panicky feeling started to breathe fire in his stomach. He had to get back! He'd be late!

For what? the sane side of himself said. There's no timetable. So what if you arrive there at five past eleven rather than on the dot?

Okay, now he was scaring himself. He sat down on one of the chairs in the kitchen and thought about where he could have possibly left his keys since he'd run through the front door. Best thing was to retrace his steps. He went to the cottage door, opened it and found his bunch of keys dangling in the lock.

What was happening to him? The sky was under his feet and the earth above his head. When exactly had the universe turned itself inside out so everything was back to front? An image popped into his mind: Louise, wrapped in a quilt, standing on the boathouse balcony, tipping her head up to meet his eyes and daring him to love her.

It was a challenge he hadn't refused, he realised.

He loved Louise.

Now he wasn't so sure he wanted to wake all his neighbours up and share the news. Was he crazy? Quite possibly. How could whatever was happening between them have a future? His head told him to back out now; his heart told him not to lose faith.

With one startling flash he understood that the tables had been turned. He'd set out to be what Louise needed and, in the end, he'd discovered he needed her so badly it hurt. Fear sliced through him at the thought that there might not be a happy ending to this story.

He pulled his keys out of the lock and returned them to his pocket, then closed the door. He'd loved Megan, he was sure of that, but she'd never shaken his foundations like Louise did. What did that mean? Was this romance doomed or did that promise great things?

He ought to stay away, he decided. He ought to make an excuse to back out and stay away. That was the sensible thing to do. He nodded to himself, took off his jacket and carefully placed it on its hook.

Five minutes later he was in his dinghy, motoring across the river in the direction of the boathouse jetty.

* * *

Christmas was its own little universe for Louise and Ben. They shared a festive dinner of lasagne, which Louise found in the freezer, then retreated to the boathouse for the evening, where they talked and laughed and kissed and wished—not out loud, of course. Some things were far too delicate to be spoken aloud.

But this little universe was finite and, as night fell on Boxing Day, ugly reality started to shred the perfect picture they'd created.

Louise was sitting in one of the wicker chairs close to the fire with a book in her lap and Ben was stretched out on the day bed, trying not to doze. Suddenly, he raised his head and looked at her.

'Louise?'

Her heart did a silly leap. Shouldn't she be able to control that by now? It had started on Christmas morning when he'd reappeared, slightly damp and smiling, at her back door with a Christmas pudding big enough for ten and a bottle of port. Now, *that* was the way to spend Christmas. Especially if it involved being spoonfed the pudding in front of the fire.

She couldn't remember a Christmas as perfect. Not even Jack's first Christmas. Toby had spoiled it by getting drunk and disappearing off to a nightclub with one of his useless so-called friends.

'What's up?' she said carefully.

Ben shifted himself on to one elbow. 'What are we doing?'

'Well, I'm supposed to be reading that biography about Laura I borrowed from you and you're trying to pretend you didn't finish off the last quarter of that plum pudding.'

Ben didn't laugh as she expected him to. He gave a half smile, then jumped off the day bed and drew the other chair over so he could sit opposite her. He took her hands in his. 'No, I mean you and me. What is this?'

She folded the book closed and placed it on the coffee table. Laura's carefree smile and laughing eyes in the cover picture mocked her. She bet Laura wouldn't have got all tied up in knots about something like this. Laura would probably have said something droll and had her lover swooning at her feet in this kind of situation. But Ben wasn't her lover, and it seemed that she was the one in most danger of swooning at present. This was all so new—this thing with Ben—that sometimes it felt raw, even though it was wonderful at the same time.

'Ben Oliver, are you asking me if I want to be your girlfriend?'

There. That was as droll as she could manage. But she didn't manage to pull off the knowing sophistication that was supposed to go with it when he leaned in close, gave her a soppy grin and said, 'Yeah, I suppose I am.'

She grabbed him by the shirt collar and pulled him in close for a long, slow kiss.

He rested his forehead against hers. 'It's just that…'

What? Her heart began to thump. It was too perfect. *Something* had to go wrong, didn't it?

'Jas is home tomorrow and…'

She nodded. This had been a time out of time. Tomorrow they had to go back to their real lives, which seemed to be on parallel tracks, running close, but maybe never destined to cross and merge again.

'I understand, Ben.'

He pulled away and looked intently at her face. 'No… No, Louise. I meant…what are we going to say to the kids? Are we going to keep this a secret or are we going to shout it from the rooftops? It's a delicate situation and we need to decide how to handle it.'

Relief flooded through her. Followed hastily by confusion. What *were* they going to tell the children? Jack was the worst blabber-mouth known to man. She frowned. 'Do we want to tell *anyone*?'

And, more to the point, what would they say if they did? Everything was so new between them. How should they define it? Of course, there would be far-reaching consequences as well.

'You do realise that we might get media attention if we go public?' she said.

Ben's face was a picture of surprise, as if he'd totally forgotten about that side of her life. That only made her want to kiss him again. Everybody else always saw the glitter first and nothing second.

For the first time in days, she felt as if she were on familiar territory. 'Believe me, you don't want photographers camped on your doorstep. Why do you think I chose to live in such a remote place as Whitehaven? In the village, you and Jas would be easy pickings.'

'Jas?' There was more than a hint of panic in his voice. 'You think they'd take pictures of Jas?'

Just great. This relationship was dead in the water before it had even begun, wasn't it? She knew Ben well enough to know that creating a 'normal' life for his daughter was paramount.

She stroked his arm. 'Who knows? The paparazzi are a law unto themselves. But I think we have to consider the possibility.'

They both stared at one another.

There were no easy answers to this one. The only way to really protect Ben and Jasmine was to call the whole thing off right now. She broke eye contact and stared at her feet. Just the thought of saying goodbye to Ben now made her hurt—physically hurt. Cold fear shot through her. Contemplating the possibility of losing him brought things sharply into focus: somewhere along the line, she'd fallen in love with Ben Oliver.

He gently brushed his fingers under her chin and tipped her face up to look at him. 'Hey.' The word was filled with such tender softness, she felt her eyes moisten. He smiled at her. 'I told you before—I'm not going anywhere, okay?'

She nodded and the cold, sharp feeling gradually withdrew.

'Here is my idea,' he said. 'We tell Jas and Jack—because they're going to work it out pretty soon anyway—but we don't tell anyone else yet. It will buy us some time, give us and the kids a chance to get used to things first.'

Sensible. He wanted to wait before letting the world know, just in case it didn't work out.

'I've got to wait at home for Megan to bring Jas back tomorrow, but I still want to see you.'

Good. She wanted to see him too. And she was greedily going to grab every chance to be with him.

'Jas is due back at noon and it's going to be quiet tomorrow—everyone recovering after Christmas. If you come for one o'clock and drive round, using the lanes rather than coming through the village, nobody will see you. Once you're there, we'll put your car in the garage.'

She smiled at him. Maybe this could be fun. Maybe she'd get to live her dream life for just a little bit longer before it all came crashing down around their ears.

CHAPTER NINE

THE roar of a distant car engine got louder. Ben knew not to hope that this would be Megan bringing Jas back. She'd rung twenty minutes ago saying she was 'running a little late'. And usually when Megan said 'late', she didn't mean ten minutes late. He'd be lucky if he saw Jas before teatime. Megan had probably only just left the country house hotel near Stow-on-the-Wold where they'd been staying—not that her breezy message had communicated anything of the sort. He just knew.

Abruptly, the engine cut out and he dashed outside to open the garage doors. This must be Louise. He checked his watch. Yup, five minutes early. From one extreme to the other.

Mind you, if Louise was an extreme, he was quite happy being stuck out there in left field. Yes, the ride was going to be a little bumpy, but he could really see things working out between them.

Louise grinned at him from her car as he guided her inside and closed the garage door behind her. He walked round to the driver's window and waited as she pressed a button to wind it down. Acting on impulse, he leaned in through the open window and surprised her with a hot, sweet kiss.

The rush of endorphins he got every time he just laid eyes on her was amazing, but a long-lasting relationship took more than just feel-good chemicals whizzing round his system. While Louise wasn't the high-maintenance woman he'd mistaken her for, she was still smarting from a recent divorce. Only a fool would rush in too quickly, and he had never been a fool.

A crick in his neck forced him to draw back and let her out of the car.

'Good morning, yourself,' she said, smiling sweetly at him. Then she looked around. 'Where's Jas? I would have thought you'd have wanted to talk to her first, rather than have her catching us like that.'

He grimaced. 'Megan is running late. So I have you to myself for the next couple of hours. Come on.' He tangled his fingers with hers and pulled her out of the side door of the garage and across the garden, where small patches of snow still lingered. Most of the village was now back to normal, a warm wind from the west having melted the snow in all but the shadiest of spots.

Once through the back door, they fell into each other's arms again. The endorphins started partying.

Louise was different this morning, calmer, more peaceful. Since Christmas Eve she'd been like a skittish horse, jumping at every little thing, sensing danger where there was none. But something had changed. He could tell it from the way she kissed and held him, from the sound of her voice, even the way she moved.

Still kissing her, he pulled her hat and scarf off and threw them in random directions. She laughed against his lips. 'Not fair,' she murmured. 'You've only got your indoor clothes on.'

She undid the top button of her coat, but left the others fastened as she kissed him again. Everything went blurry for a bit and all he was aware of was the sweet spiciness of her perfume, the shallowness of their breathing, the pull of her fingers as they hooked into the belt loops of his jeans and contracted into fists.

Then, after hesitating for a second, she ran her hands under his sweater. He flinched as her cold fingers met his warm flesh, but the sensation was anything but unpleasant. The contrast of temperatures only heightened the sensation. He pulled her closer and deepened the kiss. Louise responded eagerly, surprising him by sliding her hands up his back, taking the sweater with them. Cold air rushed around his torso. Hot blood pumped through his veins.

Finding it impossible to go any further without breaking lip contact, she pulled back from him and continued to tug his top upwards. Just before she pulled it over his head, she looked him in the eyes. They stayed there like that while the kitchen clock loudly announced the seconds.

Wordlessly, he lifted his arms over his head and she disappeared as his sweater blocked his vision. The jumper went the same way as her scarf and hat.

'Not fair,' he said, trying very hard not to let on he was shaking. And he didn't think it was because he was cold. 'You've still got your outdoor clothes on.'

He reached for her, first dealing with the remaining large buttons on the front of her coat and pushing it off her shoulders, before stroking her face with his fingertips. That perfect bone structure might have produced a proud beauty, but he knew that the woman inside was soft and tender, carrying the scars of the years. He wouldn't add to them. He promised himself that.

The teasing humour evaporated and suddenly everything felt very serious, momentous. Should he stop her now? Was she really ready for this? What Louise *wanted* and what Louise *needed* might be two very different things.

'Louise…'

She silenced him with a kiss. 'You have to trust me to make my own decisions, Ben. And I've decided…'

He kissed her fiercely, then drew back to look at her, hoping his eyes conveyed the storm surge of feeling that was crashing over him. 'You know I love you, don't you?' She had to have guessed. It was stamped in every look he gave her, in every touch.

Her lips quivered and she tried to smile. A fat tear rolled down one cheek. 'No, I didn't.' Her answering kiss was rich and soulful. 'But I do now.' Her hands traced the muscles of his chest and he felt them quiver in response. 'Show me, Ben. Show me how much...'

That snapping sound in the back of his head must be his self-control breaking because, right now, he couldn't think about anything but doing exactly what she said. He would. He would show her how much he loved her. He would make sure that she never doubted for a second, ever again, how rare and precious she was.

He kicked her fallen coat out of the way, picked her up and carried her straight out of the kitchen and into the hallway. His foot was on the bottom step when the doorbell rang.

'Cooo-eee!'

Both of them froze.

He knew that irritating little sound anywhere. Megan.

The word he wanted to say, he couldn't, just in case Jas was standing outside and she heard it through the door.

Louise jumped out of his arms and ran back into the kitchen. Megan's blonde head was detectable as she tried to peek through the little window in the centre of the door. Thank goodness the glass was rippled and bowed. The bell sounded again and he jumped.

'Ben? Is that you?'

Realising he couldn't very well answer the door in his present state, he charged back into the kitchen and started to fight with his sweater. Why, in situations like this, did the neck hole and the armholes seem to switch places? When he'd finally popped his head out of the right opening, he ran back to the front door, yelling, 'Just coming!'

Megan did not look impressed when he swung the door open. Jas jumped into his arms. 'Daddy!'

'About time too,' Megan said, pushing past him into the hall. Never mind that she didn't live here any more and, technically, she was supposed to wait to be asked. 'Come along, Jasmine.'

Jas gave him one last kiss and turned to grab the handle on her Sleeping Beauty trolley bag and followed her mother inside.

Ben, in a fit of adrenaline, managed to slam the door, charge past his ex-wife and daughter and make it to the kitchen door first.

Megan eyed him suspiciously. 'What are you up to, Ben?'

He ran a hand through his hair and leaned against the door jamb, blocking her way. 'Nothing.' The problem with priding himself on being a straight-talker was that he didn't get much practice at lying. Megan was looking at him strangely.

'Coffee?' he asked, although the words felt as if they came out sideways. In an effort to maintain harmony and stability, he always offered Megan a drink when she dropped Jas home. Most times his ex was far too busy being fabulous to stop and chew the fat, but today she was showing no inclination to rush off.

'Thanks,' she said dryly and pushed the kitchen door open.

Louise had her hat and scarf on and was just retrieving her coat from the floor and heading for the back door when she heard the door creak open. Quickly, she hung her coat on one of the overcrowded pegs. If she couldn't disappear altogether, she was going to have to make it look as if she'd just arrived. Her skin was still heated and her cheeks were probably flushed. Hopefully, she could blame it on having just come in out of the cold weather.

'Louise!' Jas shot into the room like a bullet and threw her arms around her middle.

'Hey, Jas!' she said softly.

Jasmine looked over her shoulder and shouted at the woman who had just entered with Ben. 'Mum! Look! Louise is here!'

'So she is.'

Ben's ex-wife was nothing like Louise had pictured her. She'd imagined a housewifey sort, but Megan was only what could be described as a 'yummy mummy'. Her long blonde hair fell past her shoulders and ended in a blunt, straight line, and she was wearing a designer coat, military style, pulled in tight at the waist. Her high-heeled boots made a fingernails-on-a-blackboard sort of noise as she crossed the tiled floor and offered her hand.

Louise's jeans, jumper and clumpy fur-lined suede boots suddenly seemed rather casual. She pulled the hem of her jumper down, rumpled as it had been from being whisked into Ben's arms. She'd never thought of Ben as being a man who 'whisked'—the revelation was still doing odd things to her insides.

'Hello.' Not exactly original, but it was polite and it didn't give too much away. Jas, still hyperactive after a longish car journey, abruptly let go of her and dashed towards the door. 'Dad! Wait till you see the really cool presents I got from Nanna and Pops! Can I get them from the boot, Mum?'

Megan nodded and threw Jasmine a bunch of car keys that she pulled out of her pocket. Her exit left the adults in an uncomfortable silence.

'As Jas has already pointed out, I'm Louise. Nice to meet you.'

'Megan.'

Something about this woman reminded Louise of a cat arching with all its fur frizzed up. She noticed that Megan didn't bother removing her gloves to shake hands. Somehow, that made the whole situation easier. Being Toby's wife had made her used to this kind of response from other women. She was always a threat, the enemy, never someone that they wanted to gossip over cappuccinos with.

'I'm doing Louise's garden for her.'

Both she and Megan turned to look sharply at Ben, who seemed to be pulling every mug he could find out of the cupboard.

Garden? Good one. She'd forgotten all about the garden.

'Yes,' she said, nodding a little too hard. 'Ben is sorting out my rebellious garden for me… We were going to have a look at the plans.'

Don't wince, she told herself. You *were* going to look at the plans today—just later. Much later.

'Today? It's still the Christmas holidays.' Megan's voice was flat as she looked at Ben, then at Louise, then back at Ben again. Nobody moved.

Okay, the only way to get round this was to play the rich-and-famous card, much as she hated it. 'Yes. I'm sure you understand, Megan. Life can be so hectic, you know, flying all over the place…' The silly little laugh she gave turned her own stomach. She hadn't meant to do it; it must be the nerves. 'Sometimes we just have to squeeze the project meetings in whenever we can.'

'I'm sure it'll be marvellous,' Megan said, and Ben did a double-take and looked in astonishment at his ex-wife. 'Ben really is very talented.'

Louise stifled a smile as Ben gave her a dry look, held up a large, over-sized teacup kind of a mug and shook his head. Megan's back was to him, thank goodness, so she didn't see him reach for the smallest mug of the collection and, after giving Louise a wicked smile, spooned instant coffee into it.

Megan sat down at the kitchen table, her mouth pursed a little too tightly for Louise's liking. 'I must say, you're all Jasmine has talked about while we were away.'

Louise shot a nervous look at Ben, who was now making a cup of coffee with record-breaking speed. 'Well…Ben has brought Jasmine up to Whitehaven a couple of times. My son, Jack, is only a few years younger than her and it made sense for the children to play together while Ben was looking after the garden.'

Megan nodded and twisted to look at Ben as he plonked the mug of coffee in front of her, then dropped into the seat opposite Louise, his expression guarded.

'Well, Louise, I'm sure you'll appreciate that you're not the only one who leads a busy life. Ben and I have some *family* stuff to discuss—' as she said 'family' she laid a hand on Ben's arm '—so, if you wouldn't mind…'

'Dad!' Jasmine burst back through the kitchen door, her arms full of presents. 'Look what I got!'

Much as Louise would have liked to walk over to Ben, slide her arms around his waist and stake her claim, this was neither the time nor the place.

Ben turned to look at Megan, an exasperated expression on his face. 'Meg, I arranged to meet Louise at one o'clock, she shouldn't have to leave.'

The words *especially as you were late* hung in the air.

Louise did an extra knot in her scarf. 'No, it's okay, Ben. Family stuff comes first. I'll call you when I have an opening in my schedule. Goodbye, Jasmine…Megan.'

She collected her coat from near the back door and Ben rose and escorted her out of the kitchen and into the hall. She looked a little puzzled, but followed his lead. As she reached for the door latch, he grabbed hold of her hand. 'Don't go.'

She bit her lip and shook her head.

He turned her hand over, pulled it to his lips and planted a kiss into her palm. 'Actually, you can't go yet—not without giving away that your car is parked in my garage, which will only make Megan more suspicious.'

Okay, that was true, but she could always use the ferry and come back for her car later.

'If you could just…I don't know…take a walk on the beach for half an hour, I'll see what she wants to get off her chest and then I'll call you when the coast's clear. You do have your phone with you, don't you?'

She nodded. This was getting sticky, complicated, just as she'd feared when Ben had only been a daydream. That was the problem with reality. It was so…messy. She ought to take the ferry and leave them alone. But she found herself scrawling her mobile number on a pad by the telephone in the hall.

Ben closed the door behind Louise and then pressed his face against the little window to watch her disjointed shape walk down the garden path. There were some days when he regretted not being able to make his marriage work, but today certainly was not one of them.

Whatever he did for Megan was never enough. It never had been.

When she'd left him, he'd felt empty. Not really because he'd missed her—by then he'd been too exhausted to feel anything but regret on Jas's behalf. No, the emptiness had been more a sense of being bled dry. He was a pretty decent bloke, he thought, and he'd put his heart and soul into his marriage but, in the end, he'd had to accept that his best was not good enough.

Megan had wanted more. She'd been so needy—he could see that now. Blindly, he'd thought he could help her grow, be the foundation that she could build on. But she was the sort of woman who needed constant attention, constant flattering, and he just hadn't been skilled at that.

He still wasn't. He scrubbed his face with his hands and headed back to the kitchen. It was going to take all his energy for the next half hour to be nice and hear what her latest gripe was without telling her to get over herself.

The young woman who had been broken in spirit had not blossomed into the strong and confident mother he'd thought she would. She was still full of all the same insecurities. And what little confidence she'd possessed hadn't grown into self-esteem, but had hardened into self-involvement. She was the world's axis, and heaven help anyone who didn't agree with her.

When he re-entered the kitchen, he was disappointed to discover that her coffee mug was still mostly full. He sat down beside her.

'So…Megan. What's so urgent?'

She gave him a withering look. 'Thank you, Ben. I had a lovely Christmas. How about you?'

'Dad? Look at this journal… It's got an electronic lock and a password. I can keep all my private stuff in here. Mum says it'll help me grow emotionally to keep a diary.'

Ben resisted the urge to growl. 'It's lovely, Jas.'

Placated, his daughter started to flick through the book, full of 'all about me' pages. He steadfastly ignored the page entitled: '*Boys I like…*'

Turning back to Megan, he raised his eyebrows. She glanced at Jasmine, then motioned for him to join her on the other side of the kitchen. Too cloak-and-dagger for him, but it was easier to play along than have a row in front of Jasmine. He hauled himself back out of the chair and followed her, hoping that filling in the diary would command one hundred per cent of Jas's attention.

Megan's idea of 'subtle' was talking in a stage whisper.

'I want Jasmine to come and live with me.'

He shook his head. Nah-hah. No way. They'd decided all of this when Megan had moved out. Jas needed to stay in Lower Hadwell for school, for continuity. It had been Megan's idea to up and move to South Devon's New Age hotspot to 'discover' herself. He didn't like the idea of Jas being influenced by all of that mumbo-jumbo at such a young age. And some of Megan's friends…

Megan's voice rose. 'She's going to be in senior school come September. I think a girl that age needs her mother close by.'

The rustling noises reaching them from the direction of the kitchen table stopped.

He grabbed his ex-wife by the arm and propelled her out of the kitchen. Megan forgot her stage whisper and protested loudly.

'Pity you didn't think she needed a mother when you upped and left us.'

She ran a hand through her long hair. 'I realise what a mistake that was now, and it's time to put it right.'

'Right for whom?'

Not for him, not even for Jasmine. This was all about what Megan wanted, about what was good for Megan.

'Dad?' A nervous shout came from inside the kitchen.

Still fixing Megan with his fiercest stare, he yelled back, 'I'll be right there, Jellybean.'

'Yes, that's right, Ben. Take the easy way out, run away from the main issue.'

Lord, he really wanted to grab this woman by the shoulders and shake her.

'Megan,' he said from between clenched teeth, 'wouldn't it have been more appropriate *not* to have discussed this in front of Jasmine?'

She made a gesture he could only describe as a flounce. 'It should be her decision, you know.'

Give him strength! 'We are not doing this now! Okay? You are going to collect your handbag, say goodbye to your daughter and leave. And I will phone you during the week so we can discuss this properly.'

Megan glared at him. 'Fine.' She stalked into the kitchen, followed his suggestions to the letter—which had to be a first—slamming the front door behind her. She was going to stew on this for days, he just knew it. Which was only going to make the coming negotiations worse, but how could he let Jas overhear? It would have to be handled carefully, properly.

As he headed back into the kitchen, prepared to dole out plenty of cuddles and one-to-one attention, he heard the screech of tyres in the lane.

Well, that ought to put any of her ridiculous ideas that he was still carrying a torch for her to rest. And about time too.

Louise put her phone away. The coast was clear. Although, from the sound of it, it would be better to leave father and daughter to some quality time this evening. Despite Ben's protests, she insisted she was merely returning to collect her car, then she'd be on her way.

She stepped over the low wooden fence that separated the lane from the stony beach and headed back towards Ben's cottage. Only a moment later, she had to flatten herself against the hedge as a flashy four-wheel drive hurtled towards her.

Megan was in the driving seat and she looked as if she'd just sucked a whole pound of lemons. The car slowed slightly as she spotted Louise. At first, Megan's face registered surprise, but when she got closer her face contorted further and she gunned the engine, leaving Louise coughing on exhaust fumes.

* * *

The following day was Sunday. Through a series of text messages, Louise and Ben had decided that he should come to Whitehaven as usual and, after testing the water, they would tell Jasmine they were together.

As Ben motored across the river in the dinghy, he couldn't wipe the smile from his face. Life had a funny way of throwing surprises at you. If someone had told him six months ago that he'd fall in love with one of the glitzy women from the magazine covers, he'd probably have hurt himself by laughing too hard. But, in his eyes, Louise wasn't one of *them*. She wasn't run-of-the-mill, either. She was a unique individual, braver and stronger than she gave herself credit for.

The hike up the hill towards the house seemed to last for ever. It didn't stop Jas complaining that he was going too fast and pulling on his jacket to slow him down. Finally, he caught a glimpse of white masonry between the trees. Jas started running—probably because she had cakes on the brain.

Two seconds later, he sprinted after her.

When he laid eyes on Louise, who had obviously been hovering in the empty kitchen waiting for him, he hadn't counted on how hard it would be to be only feet away but not able to pull her into his arms and kiss her senseless. Not yet, anyway.

It was torture, having to go out to the greenhouse and look at the plants while Louise and Jas made banana muffins together. They'd decided a little 'bonding' time might help before he broke the news. When he returned, he drank his cup of tea so fast he scalded his throat. Did he care?

'Come on, Jas. You and I are going for a bit of a walk.'

Jas rolled her eyes. 'Aw. Can't I have another muffin?'

'When we get back.' He walked over to the back door and handed her coat to her, then, over the top of Jas's head, he winked at Louise. She rewarded him with the sweetest of smiles.

As soon as the door closed behind them and they started

making their way along the path towards the old stable complex, his heart began to thump. 'Jas? You like Louise, don't you?'

Jas bent down to pick up a stick. 'Yeah. She's cool—and really pretty.'

No arguments from him there.

Suddenly his mouth went dry. 'How would you feel if she…if we…' heck, this was more nerve-racking than when he'd proposed to Megan '…if she was my girlfriend?' he finished in a rush.

Jas twiddled the stick in her fingers. 'Cool!' she said, suddenly smiling up at him. 'Can I have another muffin now?' And, without waiting for him, she ran off back to the house.

He shook his head as a grin spread on his face. How easy had that been? He'd been expecting tears, arguments about why couldn't he and Mummy live together again, but Jas had taken it totally in her stride. Maybe he wasn't doing such a bad job of bringing her up after all.

Then, realising he could now go back to the house and, at the very least, hug Louise in front of Jas, he started to jog. If only telling the rest of the world could be that simple and uneventful, but he didn't have to worry about that yet. For now, this was their little secret.

Ben should have suspected something was up as soon as he walked into the little newsagent's in the village to collect his morning paper. Instead of the buzz of gossip, the rustle of paper and the ding of the old-fashioned till, there was silence, only broken by the echo of the brass bell that had announced his arrival.

There were around six people in the shop and they all stopped what they were doing and looked at him.

He felt decidedly uncomfortable as he headed for the rack full of newspapers. Had he turned green overnight or grown an extra head? What was up with these people?

As he bent to pick up his usual broadsheet there was a collective gasp.

Okay, that was enough. He stood up and turned around to face them, his arms wide. 'What?'

Still, no one uttered a word but, one by one, they all looked at something behind him on the magazine and newspaper rack. Without turning round, he had a feeling that a trap door had opened underneath him and he was standing on thin air.

Slowly, he twisted round and scanned the display. The other villagers burst into motion and chatter, and more than one darted out of the shop without buying anything.

What the…?

He shut his eyes and opened them again, just to make sure he wasn't hallucinating. There was a woman he knew very well on the front of one of the tabloids, looking grim and angry with her arms crossed. Only, it wasn't Louise—it was Megan!

'LOUISE GOT HER CLAWS INTO MY MAN', the headline screamed in tall white letters on a black background. Below, were two smaller pictures, one a heart-shaped photo of him and Megan from the last summer holiday they'd shared together—graphically altered by putting a jagged rip between the two of them—and a headshot of Louise, taken from below, so it seemed as if she was looking down her nose at something.

He snatched the paper off the shelf. What the hell was Megan playing at?

What if Jasmine saw this? Or even her friends?

At first he was relieved that there only seemed to be three copies on display but, eventually, his brain kicked in and he realised that must be because the rest had been sold. He grabbed all three of them, marched up to the counter and threw a two pound coin down. He wasn't about to wait for change.

'You should be ashamed of yourself for selling such trash,' he told Mrs Green.

She gave him a stony look. 'Well, Mr Oliver, we all know Megan left a while ago, but you know what they say…'

Suddenly, he *really* didn't want to know what the mysterious 'they' had to say about anything. He turned and walked towards the door. Mrs Green raised her voice, just so he wouldn't miss her pearl of wisdom as he opened the door and exited the shop.

'There's no smoke without fire.'

CHAPTER TEN

WHAT a pity the old stable block had deteriorated so badly. Louise pushed gingerly at one of the doors. The building was huge—a double-height room with gigantic arched doors at one end, big enough to take a carriage or two. The low-ceilinged central section had enough stalls for one, two, three…ten horses.

There was a hatch in the ceiling above one of the abandoned stalls. What was upstairs? Those skylights in the steep slate-tiled roof had to be there for a reason. She was dying to find out. Or, at least, she was dying to think of something other than the email that had blithely pinged into her inbox earlier that morning, and pulling things apart and putting them back together again was a familiar displacement activity for her. Safe. Comforting. All-consuming.

In a corner she found a stepladder, obviously not authentic Georgian as it was made of aluminium. Still, it would do. She dragged it underneath the hatch and unfolded it, making sure the safety catches were in place.

She was up the steps in a shot and, when she pushed the hatch door, she was showered with dust and dirt and probably a hundred creepy-crawlies. Holding on to the ladder for support, she brushed her hair down with her free hand.

When she'd stopped coughing, she poked her head through the hole. Enough light was filtering through the streaky grey skylights for her to see a long loft, with fabulous supporting beams in the roof. She turned round to look in the other direction. Goodness, this must run the whole length of the stables. It was easily sixty feet long. Just think what a great space this would be if it was converted into a guest house.

Now she'd finished with the main house and the boathouse, she needed a new project.

Louise turned round and sat on the large, flat step on the top of the stepladder.

She already had a house full of rooms she didn't know what to do with. What on earth did she need a guest house for?

'Louise!'

That was Ben's voice. A second later, he appeared in the stable door, breathless and dishevelled.

'Up here,' she called, her skin cold and tingling as he peered into the dingy interior. He spotted her and ran to the bottom of the ladder. How was she going to tell him? How did she prepare him for the poisonous taste of her world? He was going to hate her for this.

'What are you doing…? Never mind.' He held a hand out and she used it to steady herself as she descended the ladder. He looked unusually pale and serious, his mouth a thin line. Her heart began to stammer.

'Ben? What is it? Is everything okay?'

'No! Everything is not bloody okay!' He pulled away from her, then marched to the door.

It was too late. He already knew. Just as she thought he was going to disappear out of the door, he turned and strode back towards her.

'Louise, I'm sorry. It's not you…I'm not angry with you, but I could happily throttle—'

'Ben!' He wasn't making sense, and that really wasn't like him. Cold horror dripped through her at the thought that something else—something far worse—might have happened. She swallowed. 'Start from the beginning! Is somebody hurt?'

He looked at her, a confused expression on his face, then

shook his head. 'No. But…' He pulled a folded newspaper from his back pocket and she was surprised to feel relief that her original assumption had been correct.

'It's Megan. She's outdone herself this time and I am so, so sorry…'

'Ben?'

'I just went into the newsagent's this morning and…well, there it was…and the whole village staring…'

She tried to make eye contact but he was talking to himself, reliving some memory more than he was talking to her. 'Ben!'

'And we were trying to keep it secret, for the kids…'

She grabbed him by the shoulder. 'Ben!'

He stopped mid-sentence and stared at her.

'I know.'

He blinked, then looked down at the paper in his hands.

'Toby's agent sent me an email. He has a press agency that deals with all his cuttings…' She shrugged and gave him what she hoped was an encouraging smile. 'Seems the cat is out of the bag.'

The frown lines on his forehead deepened. 'How can you be so blasé about it? Don't you know what she said about you…about me? Don't you know how she made it sound?'

Yes, she knew. She knew Megan had told the papers that she and Ben had been on the verge of a reconciliation when nasty old Louise had slunk up and stolen her man away. People would believe it. Even after it had come out that Toby had been unfaithful, the public had forgiven him and, somehow, there seemed to be an undercurrent that it had been her fault. She was too cold, too remote. Couldn't give him what he needed.

Well, they were right about that. What Toby really needed was a good kick in the pants, but she wasn't about to generate even more column inches for herself by being the one who provided it. She only cared about the smudged print on the paper if it affected how Ben felt about her, about starting something with her. Anything else was irrelevant.

'Forget it,' she said.

He stared at the paper again, then hurled it into the nearest stall. 'I can't!'

Louise thought back to her first really awful press story. It had hurt, cut deep. Nowadays she just ignored them. But Ben wasn't used to this. In one fell swoop, his ordered, stable little universe had been set on its head.

Silently, she walked over to him and put her arms round him. He was shaking with rage. She kissed him gently on the cheek, on the nose, on the lips, until he threw his arms round her and kissed her back.

It didn't matter what anyone else thought. He'd understand that eventually.

'Ben,' she whispered in his ear, 'the only thing that matters is that I love you.'

He pulled away and looked intently at her, as if he were trying to peel open the layers and look right inside her head. 'You do?'

She laughed. 'Of course I do!'

He began to smile. 'You never said so before.'

A blush crept up her cheeks. 'Well, I'm saying it now—' She took a deep breath and let out a shout that would have scared the horses, had there been any left. 'I love you, Ben Oliver.'

All of a sudden, her feet were off the ground and she was spinning round. Ben had grabbed her round the middle and was just twirling and twirling, all the time laughing in her ear. And then he kissed her, and it thrilled her to her very toes because this kiss was all about promises, about the future, about tomorrow.

When the euphoria wore off and her feet were finally on the ground again, his frown reappeared. 'What are we going to do?'

'Do? Nothing.'

'Nothing.' He repeated the word as if he didn't understand its meaning. 'What do you mean, "nothing"?

She shrugged. 'As far as the press is concerned, we just don't comment. Any response from us will just keep the story running.'

'But I don't want people to think those things about you. It's not the truth!'

She silenced him with a kiss. 'The reporters don't care about truth. They care about the story—what's juiciest, what's going to sell more papers. The people who read that trash might think I'm a man-eating witch, but I don't care. What we think matters—what *we* believe about ourselves.'

'I know that's true, but it doesn't seem fair.'

'But that's how it is and we've just got to deal with it.' She exhaled long and hard. 'You might want to take Jas away for a few days, just in case people turn up wanting an interview or a picture. You've seen for yourself what some can be like.'

He nodded. 'I could ring up my sister in Exeter. She's back home now and could certainly have us for a few days, but you'll be here…all on your own.'

She took him by the hand and they walked out into the bright December morning, the sun so low in the sky it hadn't risen above the tops of the bare trees. 'I can deal with this—I have done for more than a decade. It's Jas who matters at the moment.'

He nodded. 'She's with a friend in the village right now. I'd better go and tell her we're off on an impromptu visit to Aunty Tammy's.'

Much as he'd like to wring Megan's neck right this very second, there were some important issues they needed to discuss. He jabbed at the doorbell of her flat for a third time and left his thumb on the button so it rang loud and long.

Nothing. And any calls he made to her mobile were going straight through to voicemail.

Why? Why had she done this? Had she not thought what sort of effect this would have on Jasmine?

No, of course she hadn't. Megan always thought of herself first and everyone else second. It had been her decision to end their marriage, her decision to leave Jasmine with him—saying she needed to learn to be a whole person herself before she could be a truly devoted mother—and now that he'd finally picked himself up and was moving on with his life, she was trying to sabotage that too.

Perhaps it was just as well he hadn't caught up with her, he thought as he climbed into his car and slammed the door. Choosing to hurt Louise had been cowardly; she was an easy target.

He put the car into gear and made the thirty minute drive back to Lower Hadwell. By the time he got back to his cottage it was almost two o'clock and he was supposed to be packing, then picking Jasmine up at three. It wasn't until he'd parked his car and walked round to the front that he noticed the figure on his doorstep. Megan was sitting on the low step, her face buried in her knees, drawing in jerky breaths.

He realised he wasn't angry with her any longer. If anything, he felt pity. How messed up must she be to think that selling her story to the papers would cause anything but a headache?

She stopped sniffing when she heard him walking towards her and raised her head to look at him. Her eyes were pink and her face was blotchy and puffy. He might feel sorry for her, but that didn't mean he was going to let her off the hook completely.

'Why, Megan?'

Her face crumpled, then she sniffed loudly again and wiped her nose with a crushed tissue. 'I spent the last two years following my heart, trying to work out what will make me happy, what will fill the hole in here—' She jabbed a finger at her chest.

Ben put his hands in his pockets. 'Well, maybe you did the right thing in leaving me. You obviously weren't happy, living here with me and Jasmine.'

She shook her head and rearranged the almost disintegrated tissue so she could use it for one last blow. 'No, I was happy—sort of. But it wasn't enough. I wanted more.' She fixed him with her clear blue eyes. 'Only I don't seem to be able to work out what *more* is.'

Welcome to the human race, honey.

He nearly always had a small packet of tissues in his pocket—required kit with a child in tow. He fished a packet out of his jacket and offered them to Megan, but her eyes were glazed and she was staring off into the distance.

'And then I realised—oh, about a month ago—that not only was I no happier than I had been when we were together, but that I was *less* happy. The grass truly wasn't greener on the other side of the fence.' Spotting the tissues, she reached up but, instead of taking them from him, she clasped on to his hand. 'You're a good man, Ben. And I was too blind to see that.'

She looked at him with large blue eyes and her breath caught in her throat. Oh, no. He had a feeling he knew what was coming next and he willed her not to say it. He pulled his hand away and stuffed the packet of tissues into her fingers.

'Megan, we can't go back. You don't really love me that way any more, not really. And I don't want to be with you by default, because you can't find anything or anyone you like better. I deserve *more* too.'

She pressed her lips together and nodded and a fresh batch of tears ran down her face. She squeezed his hand. 'Yes, you do. And I'm sorry for what I did. I suppose I got into a real state because I was…' she struggled getting the next word out '…jealous.' She gave him a weak smile. 'It was pretty obvious, you know. The pair of you couldn't keep your eyes off each other. Just…don't let her hurt you, Ben. I see the same ache in her that I have inside me.'

No. Megan was wrong about that. Louise was stronger than she was. But he wasn't going to stand on his own doorstep and discuss that right now. He reached for Megan's hand and pulled her up to stand.

Sometimes his ex-wife could seem like a force of nature—a cyclone—twisting her way through other people's lives and leaving destruction in her wake but, right now, she looked more like a frightened child.

He put his arms around her and gave her a brotherly hug. 'We both deserve more, Meg. Don't you forget that.'

She nodded and kissed him softly on the cheek. 'Thanks, Ben. Jasmine is lucky to have a dad like you. And I think—' she paused to take a shuddering sniff '—she ought to stay with you for the time being. I reckon I have a few things to sort out first.'

Relief washed through him. That had to be the most mature and sensible decision Megan had made in a long time. Perhaps there was hope for her yet.

Louise found herself back in the stables after Ben had left. She could tell an idea was brewing about this place, but she just couldn't put her finger on it at present. There was no reason to redevelop this area, other than to keep herself from getting bored. But she sensed a need for a bit more logic in her plans. It was time to stop floating, to stop being pushed around like a sailing boat buffeted by the wind, and make some choices.

These stables had something to do with it, she could feel it. She shook her head and muttered to herself. New Year's Eve was the day after tomorrow—time to think about fresh starts and new beginnings. A shiver of happiness ran through her. Time to start a new relationship with a wonderful man who said he loved her.

She corrected herself quickly. That had sounded all wrong inside her head. They hadn't been just words. It wasn't just that he'd *said* it. Ben did love her. He did.

She walked round to the front of the house and took a few moments to look at the view down the river. This morning's clouds had evaporated and the river now twinkled and the cool sunshine made the windows in far-off Dartmouth glint and shimmer. Through the haze, she could even see the chain ferry endlessly crossing the river, touching first one bank and then the other.

Inside the house, the phone started to ring so she dashed in the front door and grabbed it before the answering machine kicked in.

'Hello, gorgeous.'

She had to prise the grin off her face to answer. 'Ben.'

'I just wanted to let you know that Jas and I have arrived at my sister's.'

'That's good. Did you see anyone, you know, hanging around your house?'

There was a pause. 'No photographers or anything like that.'

She breathed a sigh of relief.

'Anyway, I'm also calling to ask you out on a date.'

'A date?'

Ben laughed. 'Yes, a date. It's what men and women do when they like each other, and I've kind of taken a shine to you.'

'Like dinner and a movie kind of a date?'

'Not quite,' he said slowly. 'Perhaps it was fate that this all came out in the press. I'd wanted to ask you, but I didn't think we'd be going out in public for a while.' He paused. 'Lord Batterham is having a New Year's Ball at his home and I would like you to come with me.'

Oh. That was kind of scary. Talk about a baptism of fire.

'Louise? Are you still there?'

She glanced up at her reflection in the big hall mirror and immediately was reminded of the day of the fireworks display, of how he'd stood behind her and all of her senses had suddenly retuned themselves so they registered nothing but him.

'Yes, I'm still here,' she said quietly. 'And I would love to go to the ball with you.'

Somehow, she could hear him smiling on the other end of the line. 'Fantastic. I'll see you in two days. I can't wait.'

Once they'd said their goodbyes, Louise hugged the phone to her chest. A ball. Normally, she'd have found an excuse not to go, but she'd be there with Ben, and that would just make the whole evening seem magical.

Slowly, she replaced the phone in its cradle. When she looked in the mirror again, she was frowning. It would be magical. It would. She forced her reflection to soften.

Then why was a sense of foreboding hovering about her? Why did she feel that everything was so perfect that something absolutely, positively had to go wrong?

How Ben had volunteered to take Jas and her two younger cousins shopping he couldn't quite remember. His sister was subtle like that. Dangerous. Especially when the twin nephews in question were at that in-between age when they were too big for a pushchair but too young to behave themselves in crowded shops. He supposed it was his penance for foisting himself on Tammy like this.

One slippery little hand wriggled free from his and one small boy was suddenly running into the busy crowd in the shopping mall. He yelled for Jas to follow him, scooped the other boy up into his arms and gave chase.

Thankfully, Peter—the tearaway—was stopped in his tracks by a rather fed-up-looking man in a furry turkey costume. Confronted with over seven foot of slightly disgruntled bird, he began to cry.

Angus, who was fidgeting frantically in Ben's arms, saw that his brother was in distress and started to howl too. Great. The end to a perfect shopping trip. Tammy was going to wonder what sort of ordeal he'd put them through when he got back to her house.

He was now in grabbing distance of Peter and he hauled him up to join his brother. The turkey guy gave him a dismissive look.

'Ought to watch out where them kids are going,' he said, and waddled off.

Ben was tempted to yell something after him, but compromised by muttering, 'Aren't you past your sell-by date, mate? Christmas was almost a week ago.'

Jas giggled beside him.

'Remind me what else is on the list, Jas.'

She gave him a self-satisfied grin. 'A magazine for me and colouring books for the boys.'

Ben hefted the twins, who had obviously been overdosing on Christmas pudding, under his arms and set off back to the other end of the mall. One of the large chain of newsagents had a shop up that way and he could kill two birds with one stone.

As he walked into the magazine and newspaper section at the front of the shop, something very much like déjà vu made his skin pop into goosepimples. Although he was sure it was just tiredness, he took a quick look around the shop.

Jas was heading over to look at the magazines and, in one swift action, he grabbed her arm and steered her in the opposite direction. 'Why don't you go and look over there?' he said, pointing to the slightly older teenage magazines.

'Cool!' Jas didn't need to be told twice.

He was probably going to hate himself for buying her one of those later, but it was a far better option than letting her see the front page of one of the newspapers on the other display stand.

There, in full colour, was a picture of Megan kissing him on the cheek, accompanied by the heading: 'LOUISE FOILED IN LOVE AGAIN.' There wasn't much text, but he could make out another small picture of Louise. She seemed to be sneering.

Of course, the main photo looked much worse than the actual event—like an intimate moment between lovers.

Hell.

He couldn't let Jas see that. Surreptitiously, he wandered over to the display and pulled another paper across to hide the offending article. Then he accepted the magazine that Jas was waving at him, stopped by a pile of colouring books, grabbed a couple and headed for the till.

His blood was one degree off boiling temperature.

After paying, he grabbed a twin in each hand and bustled Jas out of the shop so fast she gave him one of her 'madam' looks.

Problem one dealt with.

Problem two? How was he going to explain this to Louise?

When another email popped in her inbox from Jason, Toby's agent, Louise just knew that her perfect little daydream had exploded. Nausea swirled her stomach and every part of her body went cold.

'Front page of today's *Daily News*,' the header read. The message was short and sweet: *Sorry, love. Jason xx.*

Her finger hovered above the mouse button. She waited a second, and then another. Finally, she squeezed her eyes shut and clicked. When she opened them again, she stopped breathing. Ben was looking awfully cosy with his ex-wife. Everything inside her seemed to melt and slide away. Blood rushed in her ears.

Think, Louise. Think. Don't just react.

She tipped her head to one side. A pointless gesture. It wasn't going to look any better from a different angle. But she forced herself to remember the hundreds of photos she'd seen of herself in the past, all seeming to tell a true story when a split second taken out of context could tell so many lies.

Ben had said he loved her.

And she'd seen the way he was with Megan. He tolerated her, nothing more.

She closed the file but a ghost of the photograph lingered, a trick of the light, so she got up and walked to the window. She'd thought those days were behind her—the dread each morning when she watched the news or walked past a paper stand. And she'd never thought she'd have to worry about that with Ben. But then, she'd wanted him, and having him meant dragging him into her world and dealing with the consequences. It was more pressure than a fledgling relationship should have to take.

Ninety-nine per cent of her knew there was nothing to worry about. But too many years of looking over her shoulder, of second-guessing everything the man in her life did, had left her wary. And that one per cent was like an itch she couldn't help scratching. What if…?

She pressed her forehead against the cold glass and let her breath steam the window. Wishes and dreams were all very well when they stayed inside your head but, once they crossed the threshold into the real world, they were fragile, vulnerable—like the paper-thin glass baubles on a Christmas tree.

What was wrong with her? Hadn't she wanted someone to look at her the way Ben looked at her? To see right inside her?

But there was her problem. Daydream Louise had been her better self, her angel. When Real Louise looked deep down to see what Ben saw, it wasn't comfortable at all. No sugar, no spice, no all things nice. Just fear and loneliness and broken parts of the person she'd once been that she didn't know how to fix. And if Ben couldn't see all that, maybe he wasn't *really* seeing her after all.

Abruptly, she pulled away from the window. Stop it! You'll make yourself crazy playing mind games like this.

The crunch of boots on the gravel outside had her spinning round and pressing herself against the window once again. For the second time that day, she couldn't quite believe what she was seeing.

Ben?

He was supposed to be in Exeter.

She flattened a palm against the window, wanting to reach out to him, but glad the barrier was in place. Her movement must have caught his eye because he suddenly spotted her there and walked straight towards her.

His eyes said it all. *Believe me.*

Pinned by his gaze, she stood motionless as he raised his hand and pressed it against the outside of the window, covering the outline of her hand completely. She studied it, then let her eyes meet his again.

Let me in, they said.

Wordlessly, she peeled her hand away and moved towards the study door. Ben mirrored her and when she opened the heavy panelled front door he was standing there, waiting. Now, with no transparent barrier between them, they both hesitated. It was Ben who broke the silence.

'I can explain.'

She almost didn't need the words. His face told her everything she needed to know. The pain etched there broke her heart and she wrapped her arms around his neck and pulled him to her. He gave no resistance and walked into her arms, burying his face in the hollow of her neck. 'I'm sorry,' he whispered against her skin. 'She came to apologise. I was careless.'

She nodded, her chin butting into his shoulder. 'Why are you here? Where's Jas?'

He took a step back and steadied himself—or was it her?—by placing a hand on each of her shoulders.

'She's with my sister. Believe me, I'm heavily in debt in the babysitting stakes. But I had to see you, to know you were okay.'

He smoothed the hair away from her face with such tenderness. Her eyes began to tingle and fill. 'I'm okay. We're okay. It just…shook me for a moment.'

Colour that she hadn't realised had been missing returned to his face and his whole body seemed to exhale. She tried a shaky smile and it seemed to work.

'Come on,' she said. 'Let's do something normal. How about a cup of tea?'

Ben began to laugh. 'Please, no. Anything but that! I finally think I've drunk my fill.'

'We'll have to switch to coffee, then. You go ahead and put the kettle on. There's something I've got to do.'

He looked over his shoulder twice as he disappeared down the hall to the kitchen, and she watched him until he disappeared. Then she nipped into the study, highlighted Jason's email and deleted it.

As she turned to leave, she spotted Ben's palm print on the window. She felt it must mean something, but she didn't know what, and that bothered her. Some vital piece of information was missing, something she needed to know but couldn't yet. And that just made the *one per cent* of doubt tickle all the harder.

CHAPTER ELEVEN

THE lanes wound so tightly as he neared Whitehaven that Ben had to slow the car to a crawl. In places only an ancient stone wall separated the road from a steep hill that fell away into the river. Tall pines and beeches towered overhead and, even if the moon had deigned to glimpse from behind a cloud, it wouldn't have illuminated much.

The road dipped halfway down the hill, signalling the descent that led to Whitehaven's main gate, and Ben's stomach dipped with it. The last week had been an emotional roller coaster ride, yet those seven short days now felt like a lifetime.

Cold swirled around him—not from the vents; they were blasting warm air. It was just the physical reaction he seemed to have every time he thought about how he might have lost Louise. He never wanted to feel that way again.

In the drive from Exeter to see her, he'd felt completely unhitched from any point in reality. She turned him inside out and upside down. And, a couple of months ago, he would have thought that a bad thing.

Perhaps he was going insane. That would certainly account for the small satin-covered box in his pocket. It would make sense of the square-cut diamond nestled within. Just like a magpie, he hadn't been able to resist it when he'd seen it in the jeweller's window. Not that he was going to do anything with it yet. It was far too soon. It was just with him for safe-keeping. For luck.

And, besides, he had another, less conventional gift for her. One that would leave her with no shadow of a doubt that she was the only one in his heart. It was a gamble, but he wasn't prepared to sit down in defeat as Louise had. He'd decided to fight—for them. For her.

Amidst the shifting shapes of the wind-blown branches, his headlights fell upon the thick vertical posts of Whitehaven's gates. The level drive traversed the hill with only a slight curve. He squeezed his foot on the accelerator. Not that he was late; just because he needed to.

He parked right outside the front door. The gravel drive was probably murder to negotiate in high heels. Feeling as nervous as a sixteen-year-old on his first proper date, he eased himself from the car and rang the bell. No one came. It was only as he reached for it a second time that he noticed the small note taped underneath it: '*Come inside. L x.*'

Now his heart really started to race. Stop it, he told himself. There's no need for this. You're not going to say anything…ask anything…tonight. It's too early.

He entered the marble-tiled hallway and paused. 'Louise?'

'Up here.' Her voice drifted down through the crystals in the hanging chandelier. 'I'll be one more minute.'

Now, the untrained observer would have expected a woman like Louise to keep him waiting, but it didn't surprise him in the least when, almost exactly sixty seconds later, he heard a door open upstairs and the swish of expensive fabric on the landing.

At first he couldn't see her properly. The glittering crystals in the chandelier distorted his view. But, as she reached the top of the stairs and started to descend, he got the whole picture.

He couldn't say anything. He couldn't smile. Heck, he couldn't even breathe.

The dress was long and the shade of midnight, in some heavy, shiny fabric that flared slightly as it fell to her ankles. And her hair…it was held in glossy waves and pinned up at the back, just like a nineteen-twenties movie star.

'You look stunning,' he managed to mutter as she reached the foot of the stairs and smiled at him. Just as well he got that out before she turned round and revealed the impossibly low back.

Unfortunately, he needed to go to this party to keep Lord Batterham sweet, otherwise he'd have been tempted to see if that satin was as soft as it looked, if it would fall off her shoulders easily and ripple as it slid to her feet.

She gave him a sweet, sexy smile as she wound a wrap around her shoulders. 'You don't look too bad yourself, either. I must say, for the gardener, you scrub up pretty good.'

Pretty good? He'd show her.

Before she could back away, he caught her in his arms and showed her just how *good* he could be.

That horrible scratchy feeling that had plagued her for the last day or so had finally disappeared. She hadn't noticed when it had subsided, all she knew was that standing here, in the grand ballroom of Batterham Hall, with Ben at her side, the magic was alive and spinning again.

As the minute hand on the ridiculously ornate clock crept towards midnight, she felt as if she'd emerged from under a huge cloud. Finally, the past was behind her and she could look forward again. And not just to tomorrow, but beyond and beyond and beyond.

She'd been quite relieved to discover that half of Lord Batterham's guests had no idea who she was. Apparently, *Buzz* magazine wasn't popular reading amongst the upper crust. And, although she'd thought she'd find some of these people stuffy and aloof, she'd warmed to many of the people she'd met.

And there was Ben. Always there. Always anticipating what she needed before she opened her mouth to express it. Not in the annoying, sycophantic way some people did, but just in his own unique matter-of-fact, *I knew you needed it, so I got it* kind of way. His impeccable manners were making him a huge hit—she half-suspected there were a couple of elderly duchesses who were plotting to steal him away.

The orchestra—not a string quartet or a band, but a full orchestra—finished their piece and paused while the master of ceremonies announced a waltz to take them up to midnight, now only five minutes away.

Ben, who had cleverly managed to be otherwise engaged for most of the dancing, now swung her into his arms and struck the appropriate pose.

'Ben, I know you're wonderful, but do mind this dress with those great feet of yours. It's vintage Chanel.'

'My feet will behave themselves impeccably,' he said without a trace of irony, even though he'd managed to stamp on her toes at least ten times already this evening. Gardening, yes. Dancing, no. But somehow that just made him all the more adorable.

'I've been practising this one,' he said proudly. 'I wanted to learn more but Gaby, Luke's wife, refused to teach me anything else. She said this was all I'd be able to handle.'

God bless Gaby, thought Louise, as they started to move around the floor.

But, as they continued to move, he surprised her. Okay, he wouldn't win any competitions, but she stopped being terrified for her dress and started to enjoy herself. Round and round they went, circling the vast ballroom. Was this what it felt like—to have all your dreams come true? Because, right at this moment, she was living in a fairy tale.

The music began to fade and it took her a couple of seconds to realise that the musicians were actually ending the waltz, not that everything but she and Ben was melting away into a dream world.

The first shout made her jump. 'Ten…'

She looked at Ben, who was grinning, obviously pretty pleased with himself.

'Nine…eight…' the chant around them continued.

'What?' she asked, starting to smile.

'Seven…six…five…'

He nodded upwards and bent his head back to look towards the ceiling. They were standing directly underneath a large display of greenery, dripping with bright white lights and, tied at the bottom with a sumptuous red bow, was a generous sprig of mistletoe.

She laughed, then quickly went silent as a very serious look appeared in Ben's eyes—one that made her knees tremble and her heart rate double.

'Four…three…two…'

'One,' he said, then delivered a kiss that shook her to the toes of her sparkly shoes. The cheering and clapping and congratulating carried on around them, but it was as if she and Ben were in their own separate bubble.

Were you allowed to make wishes at New Year, or was that only on birthdays and when stars fell? Because she wished that it could always be like this—total perfection, just like her dreams.

When Ben ended the kiss, she couldn't bear to open her eyes. Instead, she threw her arms around his neck and hugged him tight enough to make her arm muscles shake. Pressed right up against his chest, she could feel his heart beating, racing even faster than her own.

He kissed the tip of her earlobe and a shudder ran through her. Then he whispered in her ear.

'Marry me?'

She froze. All around her the dream began to splinter. And she had no idea why, because that question should have been the perfect prelude to a happy ever after. She only knew she was terrified out of her wits. This was *too* real, *too*…much.

'Louise?' There was a shake in his voice and she hated the fact that she'd put it there. She pulled away from him and smoothed down the antique satin of her dress. 'I think we should leave,' she said, unable to look at him. She was angry with herself for hurting him and, perhaps a little unreasonably, angry at him too.

Ben ran after her as she marched off to the cloakroom and retrieved her wrap. She could tell he was itching to talk to her, but there were too many people around. And, coward that she was, she was glad.

Within five minutes they were in the warm of his car, pulling out of the gates of Batterham Hall and weaving down the country lanes back towards home.

'It's too fast, isn't it?' Ben finally said grimly. 'I got carried away.'

'Are you saying you didn't mean it?'

'No! I mean…no,' he said in a quieter tone. 'I would never play with your feelings that way.'

Not intentionally. But men were apt to promise the world when they were swept up in the first flush of love. Toby had been the same. It didn't mean it was going to last a lifetime. Just at the hint of the possibility that it wouldn't, her stomach turned to ice. Oh, she really didn't understand what was going on inside her head this evening!

She did her best to explain it to Ben, staring at her lap mostly and only risking the odd glance across at him as he drove. 'It's all so new. How can we possibly tell what we are really feeling? We're riding the first wave of infatuation and we need to leave ourselves time to get past that.' There. That sounded much more reasonable.

He took his eyes off the road and turned his head sharply to look at her. 'You think I'm just infatuated with you?'

She'd made him angry. That hadn't been her intention at all. He glared at her for a hard second, then returned his attention to the road. An instant denial should have popped out of her mouth by now, shouldn't it?

'No,' she said slowly.

'I'm not just infatuated with you, Louise.'

Suddenly, he swung into a passing place on the narrow road and wrenched the handbrake on. He reached upwards and flicked a switch for a small light on the inside roof of the car. She swallowed. She'd always sensed that beneath the down-to-earth, practical exterior, Ben was a man who cared passionately and felt deeply. She just hadn't expected it all to burst to the surface tonight.

He turned to stare out of the windscreen. 'Maybe I am a little bit infatuated, if thinking that everything about you is amazing, if wanting to spend my whole future with you fits the definition. I thought I'd found the woman who was my other half…'

Unshed tears clogged her throat. They were wonderful words, but if she picked them apart just a little…

Everything about her definitely wasn't amazing, and that told her she was more right than she wanted to be. They *did* need more time. Why couldn't he see that?

He turned just his head to face her, and his eyes were burning. 'It's more than that, Louise.'

She shook her head. 'You can't know that for sure. Not yet.'

His mouth settled into a grim line. 'You're wrong. I know what I feel, what I want. I've never been more certain. It's *you* that doesn't know for sure.'

How could she know? Real life wasn't like daydreams or the movies when it all became obvious in a blinding split-second. She'd felt this way before and she'd been spectacularly wrong. Of course she wasn't sure!

'You don't have any faith in me,' he said grimly as he put the car into gear and drove away.

Louise was pushing him away as hard as she could and it was his own stupid fault. He'd been hasty—which really wasn't like him—even so, he was one hundred per cent certain that she was wrong about the infatuation thing. And he'd prove it to her somehow. First of all, he had to find out what was behind all of this. Something had triggered Louise's panic button. Somehow he'd touched on a really raw nerve.

When they arrived at her house, he insisted on accompanying her inside, sure that if he left it now, she would retreat inside her shell and he might not have the opportunity again. He had to talk to her now while it was all brimming at the surface.

She wasn't pleased about him being there, he could tell. An air of irritation hung about her as she led him into the drawing room and poured him a miserly brandy. He took a seat across the room from her as she perched on a dark purple velvet sofa.

'Why can't you believe, Louise? What's happened that makes it so difficult for you to trust your feelings?'

She took a deep breath and he saw her shutters rise. Damn For five long minutes she stared into the cold fireplace. Then, still keeping her gaze locked on it, she said, 'I'm scared to. I so want it to be real, Ben.'

Instantly, he was across the room and sitting beside her. There were wounds here that were too old, too deep to be healed in a moment. He'd been a fool. If he'd realised they were there, he would have trodden a lot more carefully. But she'd seemed so different recently, happier, freer…

She leaned against him, but still continued to stare into the empty fireplace. He placed an arm lightly round her shoulders and stroked the soft skin of her upper arm with his fingers. She didn't push him away. It was no longer about convincing her, getting her to see the truth. For now, the important thing was just that she get a chance to vent things that had been buried for too long.

He waited, knowing that pushing her with questions might easily make her re-erect the defences.

When she spoke, her voice was so soft he had to strain to hear it. 'Right from when I was very young, life was about putting other people first—which isn't a bad thing. Don't get me wrong But even when I didn't want to, I had no choice. So I used to daydream about the life I couldn't have while I was being mother to my younger brothers and sisters and taking care of my father.' She turned to look at him and his heart broke to see her eyes full of such pain. 'I suppose it was my survival mechanism.'

'We all have those,' he said tenderly.

She turned back and he guessed she found it easier not to look at him.

'Well, one day,' she continued, 'someone walked up to me and offered me all my dreams wrapped up in a sparkly box with a big bow—fame, success, recognition, enough money so I'd never have to worry about not having any clothes except my school uniform, enough money so I wouldn't see the little ones' eyes when I served up beans on toast for tea again…And love. I thought I'd found love.'

He sighed. Louise had had the kind of childhood he worked his hardest to protect Jasmine from. He thought of this brave woman, not much older than his daughter, running a household, studying, caring for a sick relative. Who would blame her for reaching for the dream?

'And so I was selfish. I chose something for myself.' She buried her face in her hands and the tears came thick and fast. Ben hugged her tight and kissed the top of her head. He knew exactly who would blame her for such a thing—she blamed herself. One by one the puzzle pieces clicked into place, fragments of things she'd told him that suddenly made sense—her relationship with Toby, her father, why she continued to punish herself.

'You can't blame yourself for your father's death, you know. From what you've told me, he was a very sick man.'

Okay, maybe he could have phrased that a little better, because Louise broke down completely. She was crying so hard she could hardly breathe, let alone speak. Years of guilt and pain, of grieving she had never allowed herself to do, came spilling out in one go. He hugged her fiercely, as if he could protect her from it by sheer strength.

Through the sobs she croaked, 'But I…shouldn't have… left him!'

People thought she'd stuck with Toby all those years because she wanted the glitz and glamour more than she wanted her self-respect. How wrong they were. It came to him with crystal clarity: Louise had stayed with Toby because she believed she deserved him. He was her penance.

Then a second thunderbolt hit. That wonderful New Year's surprise he'd had planned for Louise. It was the worst possible thing he could have done.

Louise opened one eye. Stark light sliced through the windows, bearing testimony to the fact that she'd been too exhausted to remember to draw the curtains when she'd crawled upstairs in the small hours of the morning.

Her eyes, her head, even her throat ached. Nerves tickled her tummy. She had that awful sick feeling in her stomach. Too many emotions, too many tears. She wanted to call it all back and pretend it hadn't happened. What must Ben think of her now?

At the thought of him, she raised herself on one elbow. Last time she'd seen him he was curling up on the sofa with a blanket—which was completely ridiculous as she had at least ten empty bedrooms—but he'd insisted.

She got out of bed and her foot met something slippery and incredibly smooth. Her Chanel dress lay in a heap where she'd let it drop before falling into bed. She picked it up and draped it over a low upholstered chair in the corner before wandering into her bathroom and having a shower.

There was no noise from downstairs when she emerged. Yesterday morning she'd have been rushing downstairs to meet him. Today she wasn't even sure she wanted to see Ben. He'd pushed her too far, made her feel things she wasn't ready to feel. And, while she knew he'd had the best intentions in the world, that didn't mean she wasn't cross with him.

In her mind, she played out the argument she wanted to have with him, telling him to back off and leave her alone. Who did he think he was, dragging all that stuff out of her? What gave him the right?

She walked to the dressing table and picked up a comb and untangled her hair with unforgiving strokes.

When she could delay it no longer she padded down the sweeping staircase, dressed in a grey track suit and large pink slippers. The echoing silence made it seem colder than it really was and she crossed her arms across her chest and hugged herself.

She found a note in the kitchen: *'Be back soon. Something I have to sort out. Ben.'*

She scrunched it into a little ball and threw it in the bin. Then, while the kettle boiled, she rehearsed the coming argument in her head again. Who had given him the job of deciding what she needed? *She* ought to be what she needed, and she certainly didn't need some man to step into the slot Toby had left and take over her life. Okay, Ben wasn't the same. He was full of concern rather than apathy, but that didn't make her feel any less over-ruled, overshadowed.

As she drained the last of her cup of tea, she heard a knock at the back door and turned to see Ben standing there, his face grim. Outside, she might have looked as if she didn't care if he was there or not. Inside, she was seething. She walked over, opened the door, then walked away again before he could touch her.

He stepped into the kitchen and rested against the counter without removing his coat. 'I have something to confess.'

She almost laughed. What now? He had another wife, a spare one, raving mad and locked in the attic? That would just about be her luck. She retreated to the opposite side of the kitchen, crossed her arms and raised her eyebrows.

'I had arranged a meeting with a journalist for this week. I was going to give an interview about…us.'

Louise felt her jaw drop.

He closed his eyes and shook his head, just once. 'I know, I know. At the time I thought I was doing the right thing.' He opened his eyes and looked at her. All the carefully rehearsed lines of her row trickled away. 'I wanted to fight for you, to tell the world what a wonderful person you are, that you're not what everybody thinks you are…I wanted them all to see what I see.'

It was very noble. It was also very stupid.

'I'm not going to do it now,' he said. 'I cancelled the meeting.'

'Well, thank you so much for telling me.' The level of sarcasm in her voice surprised even her.

'Don't be like that.'

'Why not, Ben? Why shouldn't I be angry that you decided all on your own what was best for me? You should have talked it through with me.' She placed her hands on her hips and shook her head slowly from side to side. 'This is becoming a pattern, you know—you jumping in and rescuing me from myself. Well, you know what? Perhaps I don't need rescuing!'

He stood up and walked towards her. 'It's not like that, Louise. I love you.'

She backed away, still shaking her head. 'I'm not one of your stupid plants, you know, something to be trained or cultivated. You can't fix me, Ben. I am who I am and you need to accept that—all of that—and if you can't, then perhaps I don't need you at all.'

Ben stopped walking and stared at her. How could he convince her? 'I know I messed up, Louise. And I know I jumped in too fast, but that's only because…I've never felt this way about anyone else—ever. It excites me, confuses me, scares the life out of me. I don't want to lose you.'

Her shutters fell again, and this time they were clamped down and double bolted. With an increasing sick feeling in his gut, he realised that this was the kickback from last night. She was too raw, and she was protecting herself the only way she knew how.

The Louise he knew would never hold a grudge about that stupid magazine interview. It was just easier for her to feel anger, to hate him for that, than to let herself feel any of the other things last night's conversation had brought up. And he wasn't going to get anywhere by pushing. He had made that spectacularly awful mistake already and it had triggered this whole mess.

But he was going to leave her in no doubt as to how he felt about her before he gave her the space she needed. She had to believe him about that. Knowing she would just retreat if he approached her, he stayed rooted to the spot and hoped the truth of his words could pierce her shield.

He wanted to say something beautiful, elegant, poetic—something to reflect just a tiny bit of what he felt for her—but his mind was blank. No flowery words seemed to measure up. So he spoke with his eyes, his body, his whole being and, finally, he simply said, 'I love you. I always will.'

The shield around her buckled just enough for him to see a deep yearning ache behind the fire in her eyes. She wanted to believe him, but she was too scared, and he tried to pinpoint why that was. What was the overriding factor here?

Guilt.

The word popped into his head as if someone had whispered it in his ear.

The irony of it all hit him like a blow in the solar plexus. Once again, he was offering all he had—his heart, his life, his love—to a woman, and it wasn't enough. While she nursed her guilt, anything he could give her, even if he wrapped the whole universe up and put it in a silver box, would never be enough.

Until she believed she deserved the happy ever after she yearned for so desperately, it would always be out of her reach. Until she understood she was worth being loved, she would always doubt him. Always. And that tiny speck of doubt, like a grain of sand would irritate and irritate until she couldn't stand it any more. Even if he could talk her round now, their relationship would die from a slow-acting poison.

He had to let her go. Just the thought of that made his nose burn and his eyes sting. He coughed the sensation away.

Louise was looking at him with a strange mix of irritation and confusion on her face. It took all his strength not to reach for her, not to taste her lips one last time. Heavy steps took him across the kitchen to the door. He opened it, stepped through, then turned to take one last look.

'Goodbye, Louise,' he said, then closed the door and walked away.

The daffodils were gone and blossom was on the trees when work on the old stable block was completed. The garden was looking fabulous too, although that always made her feel a little sad. Ben's men had done a grand job. She hadn't seen him again, really, since New Year's Day. She kept away from the village, preferring to shop in the nearby towns, although she fancied she'd seen him from a distance a few times. On each occasion she'd turned tail and scurried away.

How could she face him? After all those awful things she'd said to him? She'd had a chance and she'd blown it. More than that. She'd blasted it to smithereens with dynamite.

At least she'd found something to do to take her mind off it all.

She'd spent most of January unpacking her feelings about her childhood. In her teenage years she'd just soldiered on, doing the best she could. But now, looking back on her past with the eyes of a mother, she wondered why there hadn't been more help. Social Services had been very keen to let them know when things weren't up to scratch, but nobody had ever offered to step in and help.

A break—just a week away from it now and then—might have made all the difference. She'd have gone back refreshed, ready to carry on. And she'd have been less susceptible to impossible fairy tales and knights. Not a knight in shining armour, but in black leather—wolves' clothing. She sighed. Maybe that was being unfair to Toby. He wasn't the devil incarnate; he was just immature, weak, spoiled.

Louise picked up her bunch of keys and headed out towards

the stables. It was time for one last look around before her guests arrived.

In the small cobbled courtyard in front of the stables there was now a fountain and bright flowers in pots, benches to sun oneself on. Inside was even better. Four apartments, which she'd really enjoyed decorating, had all the mod cons, everything needed for a week of relaxation and pampering.

As winter had faded and the snowdrops had appeared on the hillside, she'd approached Relief, a charity that specialised in giving respite care for young people who had to act as carers for sick or disabled family members. They were desperate for more locations to send the kids, places they could rest, unwind and meet others in the same boat. On site would be a cook and general den-mother, so the guests didn't have to do chores and cooking as they did at home, and a child psychologist would be making regular visits.

She took one last look around the apartments, checking everything was perfect. Three girls and a boy were due to arrive from London in the next hour. She plumped a cushion on one of the settees in the communal sitting room, which led on to the dining room and kitchen. She was getting too emotional about this, she knew, but she just wanted these kids to have the best. They deserved it.

CHAPTER TWELVE

BY THE end of the week, the occupants of the new apartments had stopped staring every time they saw her and were much more ready to beg for cake or tease her. Jack was really enjoying having the company too. He'd been itching for Saturday when he'd be able to join in the fun. He and Kate, the den mother, had taken three of their 'guests'—James, Letitia and Rebecca—on a guided tour of the grounds. Not that they hadn't explored every square inch already. But, apparently, only Jack knew all the best trees for climbing.

Only Molly had remained behind. She was a quiet, mousy girl who had only hovered on the fringes of the group all week. Louise found her in the stable courtyard when she went to collect a cake tin she'd left in the kitchen.

'Hey, Molly! How's it going?'

Molly dipped her head and looked at Louise through her thick, dark blonde hair. 'Okay.'

'Have you been having a good time?'

Molly grimaced. 'Yes.' She fidgeted. 'Can I phone home?'

Louise sat down next to her. The spring air was sweet and fresh and the sun was beautifully warm on her skin in the sheltered courtyard. If she sat here for more than a few minutes, she'd have to take her cardigan off.

'Of course you can. But I thought you already called this morning.'

Molly nodded and looked away.

'They're okay, you know—your family. They'll do fine while you're here. Relief will have sent some excellent staff to do all your usual jobs while you're away.'

Molly looked unconvinced. 'They might not do things right. I need to check.'

Louise dearly wanted to put her arm round the girl, but she wasn't sure it would be welcomed. Only fourteen, and already she carried the responsibility for her two disabled parents. The psychologist had warned her that some of the children might be like this.

'How would you like something to do?'

At this, Molly brightened. Just as Louise had guessed, she would feel less uncomfortable…less guilty…if she had a job to do.

'You lot are eating cakes faster than I can bake them. I was planning to do a chocolate one today and I could do with an extra pair of hands.'

For the first time that week, Molly smiled. 'Sure. I can help.'

As they measured and mixed and washed up back in Whitehaven's kitchen, Molly began to relax a little. Louise took the opportunity to dispense a little wisdom.

'It's okay to enjoy yourself, you know.'

Molly frowned. 'I know that.'

Hoping that this would be the right time, she walked over to her and put an arm gently round her shoulders. 'You don't have to feel guilty for being here, for having a nice time. It's what the scheme is all about.'

Molly sniffed. 'I know that. It's just that I feel bad leaving Mum and Dad alone while I get to stay in a beautiful place like this…and with you. It's too nice.'

One-handed, Louise tore a piece of kitchen towel off the roll on the table and handed it to the girl. 'Molly…' Oh, blow, she was tearing up too. She grabbed a piece for herself as well. 'You work hard all year round. Much harder than other kids your age.

You deserve this, you really do. And your parents would want you to enjoy yourself while you're here, not spend the whole time worrying about them or feeling guilty.'

As she hugged Molly, she could suddenly picture her own father's face the day she'd run home from the supermarket and told him about the modelling scout. He'd been so proud of her! And never once had he said anything to make her feel as if she was abandoning him. He'd been such a special man.

And yet, for all these years, she'd held on to the same feeling that was eating Molly alive. The girl beside her started to tremble and Louise pulled her close for a proper hug. 'Is it really okay?' Molly whispered.

'Yes.' The kitchen distorted and became all blurry. Louise's lip began to wobble. 'Yes, it is.'

Ben walked into Mrs Green's shop on a crisp May morning to get his usual paper. She'd been as meek as a lamb with him since that incident at Christmas. Louise now had a most loyal supporter in her. And that was good. For Louise. The tide of opinion might turn one person at a time, but it was still turning in the right direction.

Thoughts of Louise led to thoughts of Whitehaven and its luscious gardens. He would have loved to have seen how the gardens had turned out, if they matched the vision in his head when he'd drawn up the plans. Best of all would be the places he hadn't touched, the woods full of foxgloves and bluebells. Sometimes you had to know when to stop meddling and let things be, to let them retain their natural beauty.

He reached the counter and Mrs Green just handed him a paper without asking which one. Then she handed him a glossy women's magazine, not one of the cheap, gossipy ones, but one of the high-fashion mags that also ran articles on serious subjects.

'A bit old for Jas, Mrs Green,' he said, without looking at it, and handed it back to her.

She shook her head. 'I thought you might be interested.'

Him? He started to chuckle, but a glimpse of a pair of dark and stormy eyes on the cover made him look a little closer. Louise. She'd done an interview. He moved out of the way of the counter so the person behind him could pay and scrabbled through the pages until he found the article he was looking for. It was a long one.

He read it as he walked down the hill back to the cottage. He was working from home today. More than once he stopped in the middle of the road and shook his head. Especially when he realised he'd forgotten to pay Mrs Green. She'd understand. Then he started to smile, even though the ache in his chest that he thought had dulled a little in the last few months began to quietly throb again.

Amazing. He'd always said so. And here she was believing it. Living it.

Not only had she done something amazing at Whitehaven, she was doing the interview to raise the profile of the charity she was now patron of. Relief were lobbying the Government for new funding for child carers, not just respite care but proper practical help on a day-to-day basis.

And Louise Thornton, the woman who would rather cut off her right arm than talk to a journalist, had not only given an interview—and let the photographers into the new apartments at Whitehaven—but had opened up about her own childhood, her own lack of education, in an effort to prevent more children from living through the same things. He felt his chest expand as he read that she was planning to study part-time for a degree in child psychology.

He reached his front door and misjudged putting the key in the lock because he just couldn't stop reading. He flicked the magazine closed so he could stare at the cover. Yes, the eyes were dark and intense, as always, but they were no longer empty.

This could be the stupidest thing he'd ever done. Apart from jumping the gun on New Year's Eve, that was. Ben tied his dinghy on to the iron ring outside Louise's boathouse and wondered whether he should just sail straight back across the river because, actually, he'd been right the first time. This *was* the stupidest thing he'd ever done.

It was just past noon and the most glorious summer day. He stood for a moment on the jetty and considered his next move. Where was Louise likely to be at this time of day?

It saddened him that he didn't know, that her life had changed so much since he'd last seen her. But at the same time he was immensely proud of her. He'd seen all that potential inside of her, but it took strength of character and guts to turn that into something real.

Something flashed up on the boathouse balcony and he immediately craned his neck to see what it was. The sun had bounced off the glass part of the door as it had opened and out stepped…Louise.

She was wearing a faint smile and her long chocolate-brown hair glowed chestnut in the sunshine. He couldn't move, suddenly didn't know what to say. If it was possible, he'd forgotten how beautiful she was—or maybe she had just got more beautiful, because there was something different about her.

She rested her hands on the edge of the balcony and leaned forward, breathing in the salty river air.

And then she saw him and stiffened in surprise. He couldn't hear her from where he was standing, but he was sure he saw her mouth his name. The lapping of the river, the constant shrieking of the seagulls all died away as they both stood frozen to the spot, staring at each other.

She smiled. And then he was running—up the jetty, up the steps to the boathouse's upper room. He made himself stop when he got to the door that led on to the narrow balcony, half worried she would disappear into thin air if he got too close.

She was leaning against the rail, her back to the river. Her long, frilly-edged skirt fidgeted in the breeze. 'Ben,' she repeated.

Her smile was soft and warm, with a hint of sadness. 'It's good to see you again.'

He nodded. Nothing sensible was going to come out of his mouth unless he got his act together. 'You too.'

His heart started to pound in his chest as he crossed the threshold on to the balcony. He was close enough to touch her now, but he wouldn't—not yet.

'I saw the article in the magazine.'

Okay. If this was as smooth as he was going to get, he might just as well jump back into his dinghy right now.

She nodded. 'I'm going to be in the spotlight whether I like it or not, so I might as well get to choose where it shines.' She looked at her feet, then back up at him. 'So, Ben Oliver, why are you trespassing on my land again after all this time?'

It was a joke and he was supposed to laugh, but he seemed to have lost the knack.

'I…um…forgot to give you something.'

She frowned and her eyebrows arched in the middle. 'When?'

'At Christmas.'

His heart slunk into his boots. On the way over here this had seemed clever, now it just seemed…lame.

'Christmas was a long time ago.'

He reached into his pocket and his fingers closed around the palm-sized box hidden there. 'I know. But some gifts have their own seasons. This one was a little early back then.'

She bit her lip. 'Am I going to like this gift?'

It was now or never. And he was shaking in his sensible boots. He looped the little ribbon holding the box closed round his finger and used it to pull the silver parcel out of his pocket. Then he dropped it in her hands.

'I'm not sure it's in season even now, but sometimes…you can just…wait too long…'

It didn't seem to matter that he wasn't making any sense, because she was staring so hard at the little package he sensed she wasn't taking it in anyway. With excruciating slowness, she tugged the velvet bow and let it fall to the floor. Then she pulled the lid off the box.

'Oh.'

Oh? Was that a good 'oh' or a bad 'oh'?

'Oh, Ben!'

A good 'oh'. Warmth began to spread upwards from his toes.

Her nose crinkled in confusion. 'Mistletoe? But it's almost summer!' Gently, she reached into the box and pulled the sprig out to look at it. A thin white ribbon looped round the top and was tied in an elaborate bow. 'It's not even plastic! It's…'

'…the real deal,' he finished for her.

She stepped close enough for him to smell her perfume. 'How did you…?'

He shrugged. 'I have my sources.'

She twiddled the mistletoe between finger and thumb and suddenly grew more serious. 'What does this mean, Ben?'

'Isn't it obvious?'

She bit her lip and looked away. 'You want to…kiss me?'

Always. For ever. But he'd promised himself he wouldn't until she'd given him the answer he wanted to hear. 'I love you, Louise. I always will.'

Louise shook her head. 'After all the things I said to you! I don't deserve it!'

He couldn't use his hands to make her look at him, so he concentrated on just pulling her gaze to his by the force of his willpower. 'Yes, you do.'

Six months ago, he would have seen the doubt in her eyes, but the woman standing before him looked deep into his eyes and he saw the light of recognition flicker on. Slowly, she raised her arm so the little green sprig dangled above her head and, taking a deep breath, she closed her eyes.

This was it. Now or never. He thought perhaps he was going to hyperventilate, but managed to pull himself together. Louise was still poised, ready for the kiss, her lips soft and slightly parted. When he didn't respond straight away, she lifted one eyelid, making the other scrunch up.

Her whisper of uncertainty only made his fingers shake all the more. 'Ben?'

He nodded up to the little green sprig with its cluster of white berries above their heads. 'Look a little closer.'

With his fingers as deft as a bunch of bananas, he tugged her hand downward so the mistletoe rested at eye level and she could see the diamond ring held fast by the white velvet bow.

'Marry me?'

Louise's eyes snapped all the way open and she dropped the sprig on the floor, then her hands flew to her chest and stayed there.

His heart tap-danced inside his ribcage. He bent down and gently rescued both mistletoe and ring before he trampled it with his boots. Louise looked as if she was in a trance. Taking a chance, because she wasn't slapping him in the face or running up the hill, he twirled the mistletoe above their heads once more.

'Please…?'

'Yes! Oh, Ben, yes!' She threw herself at him and almost sent him flying over the edge of the balcony. He guided her hands so she gently pulled at the ribbon to release the ring and it dropped into his waiting hand.

She looked up at him, laughing and shaking her head, her eyes shining. 'Are you for real, Ben Oliver?'

He nodded and lowered his head, then brushed his mouth across hers, savouring the moment, and slid the ring on to her left hand. 'Merry Christmas, Louise,' he whispered against her lips, before wrapping her in his arms and pulling her into the cool darkness of the boathouse.